Lady in Red

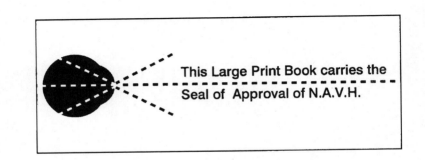

This Large Print Book carries the
Seal of Approval of N.A.V.H.

Lady in Red

Karen Hawkins

Thorndike Press • Waterville, Maine

This is a work of fiction. Names, characters, places, and incidents are products of the author's imagination or are used fictitiously and are not to be construed as real. Any resemblance to actual events, locales, organizations, or persons, living or dead, is entirely coincidental.

Published in 2005 by arrangement with Avon Books, an imprint of HarperCollins Publishers Inc.

Thorndike Press® Large Print Romance.

The tree indicium is a trademark of Thorndike Press.

The text of this Large Print edition is unabridged. Other aspects of the book may vary from the original edition.

Set in 16 pt. Plantin by Christina S. Huff.

Printed in the United States on permanent paper.

Library of Congress Cataloging-in-Publication Data

Hawkins, Karen.
    Lady in red / by Karen Hawkins.
        p. cm. — (Thorndike Press large print romance)
    ISBN 0-7862-7853-6 (lg. print : hc : alk. paper)
    1. Antique dealers — Fiction. 2. Nobility — Fiction.
3. Large type books. I. Title. II. Thorndike Press large print romance series
    PS3558.A8231647L33 2005
    813'.6—dc22   2005012400

Lady in Red

As the Founder/CEO of NAVH, the only national health agency solely devoted to those who, although not totally blind, have an eye disease which could lead to serious visual impairment, I am pleased to recognize Thorndike Press⋆ as one of the leading publishers in the large print field.

Founded in 1954 in San Francisco to prepare large print textbooks for partially seeing children, NAVH became the pioneer and standard setting agency in the preparation of large type.

Today, those publishers who meet our standards carry the prestigious "Seal of Approval" indicating high quality large print. We are delighted that Thorndike Press is one of the publishers whose titles meet these standards. We are also pleased to recognize the significant contribution Thorndike Press is making in this important and growing field.

Lorraine H. Marchi, L.H.D.
Founder/CEO
NAVH

⋆ Thorndike Press encompasses the following imprints: Thorndike, Wheeler, Walker and Large Print Press.

Chapter 1

My grandfather was an unpleasant old man. After he died, I frequently heard my grandmother say she missed him like a wooden leg. Though she'd grown used to his bark over the years, she didn't miss a single splinter and limped along just fine without him.

Mrs. Welterby to the Countess of Firth,
while waiting for the Prince
to make an appearance
in the drawing room of Carlton House

Devon St. John paced before the fireplace, his hands clasped behind his back, his brow furrowed. His abrupt footfalls, silenced by the thick rug that stretched the length of the huge chamber, were overshadowed by the crackle of burning logs.

Suddenly, he halted before a large wing-back chair turned toward the warming flames. "I know. *You* can tell him."

"*Me?*" His brother, Brandon, shook his head, the firelight casting blue shadows through his black hair. "The last time I delivered bad news to Marcus, he sent me to oversee the holdings in northern Scotland for a month. I nearly froze to death."

Chase glanced up from where he slouched on the settee opposite. "I was once sent to the wilds of Yorkshire in the middle of the season for an equally inane reason. And that was back during the time when our brother was tolerable."

"Which has not been of late," Brandon said.

Chase nodded morosely. "Lately, he has been nothing but a seething mass of ill temper. God knows where he'd order us now if he had a true reason to be upset."

Devon sighed heavily. "I must apologize to all of you; this is my fault."

The last and quietest member of the gathering finally stirred to life. Devon's half brother, Anthony Elliot, the Earl of Greyley, stretched his legs toward the fire from the depths of a huge red velvet chair. He surveyed Devon with a sleepy air. "Nonsense. The ring was lost by accident and nothing more."

"I should have made more of an effort to find it. But somehow, I thought it would be humorous to send Marcus chasing about for the blasted thing."

"It was amusing," Brandon said, "until Marcus could not find it. You sent Marcus the guest list for the ball where the ring disappeared, and we were all certain that ring would be in the hands of one of those guests."

Chase nodded. "Indeed, had the guests not brought guests of their own — that is where we caught cold. And now Marcus's humor wears more thin as the days pass and the ring is not found. He's like a great bear denied his food."

Anthony shrugged. "So let him growl. He is but a man."

"You know what Marcus is," Devon said. "Our brother is a gale wind in a world of gentle breezes."

Brandon sighed and slouched back in his chair. "He definitely has some very odd notions about marriage. I'm in poor case with him this very moment because Verena's father got into some trouble with the Italian authorities and I had to pay the scoundrel's way out of it. Marcus disapproved mightily."

Chase's brows lowered. "What else could you do? It's Verena's father."

"Marcus does not seem to understand that when you marry a woman, to some extent, you also marry her family."

"There's a lot about marriage Marcus doesn't understand," Anthony murmured, reclaiming his glass of port and taking another sip. "He seems to understand the concept of having a mistress far better."

"That he does. But a wife is a different matter altogether." Chase rose from the settee and stretched his arms over his head before crossing to the desk to pour himself a drink from a crystal decanter. "Lately he's been snappish. In fact, Harriet wanted to invite him to our new house for the holidays —"

"Excellent!" Brandon said, brightening immediately. "Bloody excellent!"

Everyone looked his way.

"Oh uhm, sorry." Brandon smiled uneasily. "Verena had the same idea, though I had no wish to have Marcus growling his way through our holidays. She and I finally agreed that we would invite him only if none of you did. But since Chase and Harriet are going to invite him —"

"You didn't give me time to finish my sentence," Chase said. "Harriet wanted to invite him, but then reconsidered. There's precious little to entertain Marcus out in the country, and since Harriet's not feeling well . . ." Chase grinned a little as he lifted his glass in a seeming toast. "Yet another reason I'm glad my lovely wife is increasing."

Brandon grimaced. "I wish Verena was increasing as well, especially if it would keep Marcus away from us during the holidays. He's become a grump. Only yesterday he said that Christmas was a waste of time and energy and he hated all the fuss."

Devon sighed. "He's impossible. He hasn't spoken a civil word to me since I lost the ring, and that was months ago. I must admit, I thought the blasted thing would be easier to recover than this." He rubbed his chin, a frown in his blue eyes. "It's almost as if the ring doesn't wish to be found."

Silence met this. Finally, Chase cleared his throat. "We have never really talked about it, but . . . are we all agreed about the ring?" He eyed his brothers carefully. "The legend is true?"

Anthony noted that his other brothers appeared uneasy with that bold question. The silence grew thick and then thicker. He supposed he couldn't fault them; after all, the ring had contributed in some way to each of their marriages. "I don't know about anyone else, but I believe it."

"And I," Brandon said, sending him a grateful look.

"So do I," Chase added with a relieved nod.

"I didn't want to, but now . . ." Devon managed a half smile before he shrugged. "If it hadn't been for the talisman ring, I don't believe I would have ever slowed down long enough to appreciate Kat for who and what she is. That would have been a tragedy indeed."

Anthony nodded. "For us all." He leaned his head back against the red velvet cushion. "Devon, there is no other way about it; you might as well just admit your failure to Marcus. He will be home in another hour."

"I know, I know. But I can't just blurt it out."

"The quicker you tell him, the quicker it will be over."

"The quicker what will be over?" came a deep voice from behind them.

Devon whirled toward the now open door. Chase, who had just taken a drink of port, began to cough, then choke. Brandon

12

straightened in his chair, unconsciously smoothing his coat.

Anthony, meanwhile, kept his expression carefully neutral, watching his half brother with interest.

"Don't answer all at once," Marcus drawled softly as he crossed the thick rug to his desk. He was built as were all the St. Johns, tall and lithe with broad shoulders and narrow hips. He paused by the desk, his dark blue gaze silently assessing them, his black hair matching his elegant black coat and breeches.

Though it was the rage to wear brighter colors in the day and reserve the darker colors for evening, Marcus dressed as he always did — to please himself. And over the last year, his clothing had gradually become more and more stark, mirroring his mood. Today he was dressed in unrelenting black from head to toe, the one exception being his snowy white cravat. Anthony wondered if it was the absence of color that made Marcus's blue eyes seem so deadly and piercing and so hard of late.

What had happened to the old Marcus? The one who had teased and laughed? Somehow, over the years, he'd faded from sight. Anthony felt a twinge of guilt. Had they allowed Marcus's duties to the family fortune and lands to become too burdensome?

Of course, Marcus rarely allowed anyone to assist him. And Anthony, head of his own household, could appreciate that. There were times when it was simply easier to do than to explain. But still . . . Marcus had changed, and it wasn't for the better.

Devon cleared his throat. "Good afternoon, Marcus. I — We — We thought you weren't due for another hour."

Marcus lifted his brows. "You thought wrong." His blue gaze, icy and relentless, flickered over Devon, then over each member of the small gathering. "All of you."

"Yes. Well." Brandon sent a warning glance at his brothers. "You startled us."

Marcus took this remark in silence, seating himself behind the desk and pulling the day's correspondence in front of him. He began to flip through the letters, then paused to cast a glance at Devon. "The talisman ring? I assume you have good news."

Anthony nodded at Devon, silently encouraging him to speak.

Devon clasped his hands behind his back, shifting from one foot to the other. "We . . . we were just talking about that. I attempted to interview Lady Talbot, who was the only person from the guest list who we hadn't yet

14

spoken to. She brought someone to the ball with her, a female guest. Unfortunately, Lady Talbot died a month ago and no one seems to know the guest's name."

Marcus's jaw tightened.

Devon hurried to add, "Lady Talbot had two servants. Neither could recall the name of the young lady their mistress took to the ball as her guest. They said the lady was a new acquaintance."

Marcus cursed, long and low.

Devon sighed. "I said the exact same thing, I assure you. The housekeeper remembered the young woman mentioning that she would be taking the mail coach through Southampton, so I went there and made some inquiries."

"And?" Marcus snapped.

Anthony winced. The word was more a bullet burst than a question, razor sharp and just as piercing.

Devon swallowed. "I could find nothing. I stayed two days and then . . ." He took a deep breath and said quickly, "And then I returned to Scotland because I'd promised Kat I'd be there for her new nephew's christening. It is her brother's first child, and the entire family is —"

"Blast!" Marcus threw his pen back onto the desk, his brows drawn. "That ring belonged to Mother. She left it in our care and you lost it."

"By accident," Anthony murmured, shooting a reproachful glance at Marcus. "As you well know."

Marcus's gaze flared, but Anthony refused to back down. After a moment, Marcus's mouth tightened and he managed a short shrug. "Accident or not, it is gone."

"It fell off Kat's hand," Devon said, his brow lowered. "You know I would never willingly lose Mother's ring. Besides, I have done what I could do to help find it. When I realized I couldn't stay in Southampton any longer because of my commitments, I sent Chase in my stead."

Chase took a quick gulp of his drink. "Yes. And because of the description Devon was able to get from Lady Talbot's housekeeper, I thought to at least get the name of the mystery woman, but I had no such luck."

"Description?" Marcus glanced at Devon.

"Lady Talbot's housekeeper remembered the woman well enough, though not her name. She was tallish and well-formed, with hazel eyes and dark brown hair. But the detail that I had hoped might allow us to find her was that she had a streak of white in her hair, at the temple."

Marcus leaned back in his chair. "A white streak. How . . . interesting. Did anyone in Southampton catch the woman's name?"

"I spoke to the innkeeper in Southampton," Chase answered. "He spoke to her briefly while she was waiting on the mail coach, but she never gave her name. All she said was that she was returning home, to London."

Anthony noted that Marcus did not appear surprised at that information. Was it possible . . . did Marcus know who this woman was?

"So the ring has come back to London," Marcus said softly. "Chase, were you able to find anything else?"

"No. Not really. Except . . . the innkeeper mentioned that she certainly knew a lot about the ancient sword he had on display in the front room. She told him some things about the execution of Italian sword hilts that he didn't know, though she was the most taken with an antique —"

"Snuffbox," Marcus finished with a final note, his jaw tightening. Bloody hell, of all the women in London, why did it have to be *her?* He could only hope he was wrong. But from the description . . . it had to be. There could be no other.

It was the last thing he needed right now. He was in the middle of acquiring the Melton estate after the bloody fool lost his fortune at the gaming table just last week. Marcus'd had his eye on the estate for years now, for it sat adjoining an especially rich piece of land he'd acquired years before at an auction. Now it was to be his, which was only fair, as he'd been patiently biding his time as ne'er-do-well Lord Melton ripped through his fortune one losing card at a time.

Twice before, Marcus had offered to purchase the lands outright, and twice before, Melton had haughtily sent him on his way. But now the dissolute younger man was desperate and willing to talk. Marcus was ready. A feeling of power surged through him; before the negotiations were through, Melton would wish with all his heart he'd settled before things had gotten so grim.

Marcus knew that was what he should have been focusing on — increasing his family's holdings and not this silly matter of Mother's missing ring. Blast it, he had important things to do, and the ring was becoming more and more of a distraction.

Anthony caught his gaze. "You know who it is."

Marcus gave a short nod. Of all his

brothers, Anthony was the one who most understood what it was like to be responsible for a name and a fortune . . . mainly because he was in charge of his own family, the ne'er-do-well Elliots. "There is only one woman who fits such a description and who would know about Italianate hilt work: Miss Honoria Baker-Sneed." The name lingered on Marcus's tongue long after it dissipated into the air. God, even the sound of it made his chest tighten unpleasantly.

Anthony pursed his lips. "I never heard of her before."

"Which is your good fortune," Marcus said grimly. "Miss Baker-Sneed is the bane of my existence." Marcus could tell from the interested stares that surrounded him that he was not going to get away with such a simple answer. "Her father travels far and wide and collects antiquities. To supplement their rather limited income, she often accompanies him to the sale on Monday morning at Neilson's Antiquities."

"Neilson's?" Brandon said. "Where you bought the tapestry in the front hall?"

Chase shuddered. "Horrid thing, that tapestry."

"It depicts one of the greatest battles of the Crusades," Marcus said.

"It has woven pictures of decapitated soldiers," Chase said, clearly unimpressed. "And it's not even very lifelike."

"It is very lifelike if you realize it was woven in the twelfth century."

"How do you know that?" Brandon's frown was heavy with suspicion.

"He doesn't," Chase said placidly. "That's just what they told him when they sold it to him."

Devon shrugged. "Daresay those antiquities places are all the same, willing to claim that any bit of rusted metal is a Viking helmet or some such nonsense."

A dull ache was beginning to form at the base of Marcus's skull. He had scores of things to do today, not the least of which was to meet with Melton's man of business to discuss the state of the man's holdings. "That tapestry is priceless."

"And ugly," Chase added.

Brandon nodded. "Wouldn't have it at my house, musty old thing."

Anthony gave a sleepy smile. "You're all fools. I've always coveted that tapestry. My only complaint is that I didn't find it first." He looked expectantly at Marcus. "Tell us about this Miss Baker-Sneed? Is she attractive?"

"Worse; she's intelligent. She knows as

much about antiquities as I. For that reason, she and I tend to end up on the opposite ends of the auction table, usually bidding against one another."

Anthony pursed his lips, his eyes alight with amusement. "Chase, this innkeeper . . . did he mention if Miss Baker-Sneed was a handsome woman?"

Chase blinked. "Actually, yes. He mentioned twice that she was deuced attractive. And he asked me if I thought she might be coming back."

Anthony nodded, amusement and satisfaction resting on his face. "I begin to see fate's hand at work. Or at least that of the ring. Be cautious, Marcus. It seems to me that Miss Baker-Sneed might well be your intended bride."

"Not while I'm alive," Marcus said, growing suddenly irritated with the whole lot of them. "And even if I were dead, not with *that* woman." With that final pronouncement, he stood and regarded his brothers with a dismissive stare. "Do you have any more information to impart?"

Looking annoyingly relieved, Brandon practically leapt to his feet. "Not that I can think of. Come, let us go and leave poor Marcus to his work."

"Wait." Devon sent a slanting glance at

Chase. "Don't you have something to ask Marcus?"

Chase blinked. "Me? What could I possibly have to ask M—" Realization dawned, followed quickly by a shake of his head. "Oh no you don't! I have nothing to ask Marcus. Nothing at all."

Marcus lifted his brows. "No?"

Chase's face heated and he glared at Devon before turning to his oldest brother. "It was nothing, really. Just . . . Harriet and I had thought to invite you to stay with us for Christmas, but since she's in the family way, I thought you might not wish to —"

"That is quite kind of you," Marcus said shortly. "But as you rightly noted, I have work to do."

"At Christmas?" Devon asked, pausing by the door. "Surely you will cease working for a few days and —"

"Unlike you, I have no desire to waste my time with frivolities. Chase, I thank you for the invitation, but no thank you."

Brandon brightened. "Well! I suppose that's all there is to be said about that. Verena also wished you to visit — but as you say, you have no time." He looked at his brothers. "I believe I shall repair to White's. Anyone wish to join me?"

Devon nodded briefly. "I'll accompany

you." He looked at his oldest brother and hesitated. "Marcus, surely you have plans of some sort for the holidays. I mean, you won't be alone, will you?"

Marcus pulled the ink well closer and dipped his pen into the ink, faintly amused at the concern he saw mirrored in his brothers' faces. "I'm in the midst of acquiring a new estate and I must retrieve the blasted talisman ring. I will be well occupied."

Brandon frowned. "That doesn't sound very much in the holiday way. Will . . . will you let us know if you need assistance?"

"If the ring is indeed in Miss Baker-Sneed's possession, you may rest assured it will be in mine by the end of the week." He drew his papers forward and began perusing the day's correspondence. "Thank you all for attending me. Enjoy White's."

There was a moment more of silence, and then one by one his brothers bade him a brief good-bye and left. All except Anthony.

He waited until all of them were gone before he stood and gave a leisurely stretch. "You are turning into a complete curmudgeon. A woman would soften that hard shell you're building."

"I don't need my shell softened, thank you. And I have a woman."

"A mistress who coos every time you sneeze does not count."

A flicker of irritation tightened Marcus's shoulders. "Lady Percival does not coo. She is discreet. Pleasant. And not given to giggles or chatter."

"She is also hinting that you will soon come to point. In fact, she seems quite confident that it is only a matter of time."

"Where did you hear that?"

"At breakfast this morning, at the meeting of the Four Horse Club. She apparently took Lord Chudrowe into her confidence. They used to be quite close before you arrived, you know."

A wave of irritation washed over Marcus. "I have never given Lady Percival any reason to hope our liaison is more than what it is — a flirtation."

"Perhaps she thinks it only natural. You have been seeing her for quite a while."

"A year, if that." Marcus lifted a letter from the stack on his desk and glanced through it. A sophisticated widow, he'd thought her a safe mistress . . . until now. "There are a dozen Lady Percivals; which is fortunate since I shall have to find a new one now."

Anthony sighed. "Marcus, I hope you will take a word of advice from a brother with your best interests at heart. Do not belittle the talisman ring. Fate does not spare those who mock her."

Marcus opened a letter from his Yorkshire solicitor. "I don't believe in fate."

"You will. And it just may be this mysterious Honoria Baker-Sneed who will prove it to you."

"Balderdash."

"Wait and see, Marcus. Just wait and see." With a quiet laugh, Anthony turned on his heel and quit the room, closing the door firmly behind him.

Marcus threw the letter back onto the desk. Anthony's levity was outside of enough. Had the man any knowledge of Honoria Baker-Sneed or her sharp tongue, he'd know that it would take a far more tolerant man than himself to bear such a harpy company. But that was Anthony of late; he suffered from the same illness as his other brothers. Since the lot of them had married, they were continually plaguing him with their high spirits. Plaguing him and probably everyone else they knew.

Marriage had changed every one of them, in various ways. Chase was more energetic and laughed aloud all the time. Devon, who had never suffered from ill spirits, was surrounded by smiling peacefulness. And

Brandon was more focused, more ambitious. But the biggest change was in Anthony. Anthony was gentler and far more willing to laugh at his fellow man.

Marcus wondered if perhaps his own spirits would rise if he were to find a woman who — "Bloody hell, what am I thinking?" he muttered. He flicked through the rest of the day's correspondence. He had far more important things to do than think of impossibilities. As soon as he met with his solicitor about the upcoming settlement on the Melton estate, he would schedule a very brief visit with Miss Baker-Sneed and retrieve the ring once and for all. Everyone knew the Baker-Sneeds were in desperate need of funds. All it would take was a little finesse and a strong dose of patience.

Despite Anthony's dire prediction, that would be that. Marcus was sure of it; there were few problems that money could not solve. Once he had the ring back in the hands of the family, he'd lock it away and spend his time doing more important things, like growing the family fortune.

Truly, it was a pity his brothers had allowed themselves to get so involved in the chaos of their own lives that they had forgotten the peace that came from a more orderly existence. But that was to be expected,

Marcus supposed. It certainly seemed that the cost of marriage was high indeed. One not only gave up one's peace, but one's faculties of reason as well.

Added to that — and in Marcus's estimation, this was the worse part — one was forced to accept another person's life and *their* relatives, mad or foolish or crazed as they might be. Why, just look at Brandon, who was now related to a family of complete shysters because of Verena. The last Marcus had heard, Verena's father was passing himself off as a Russian count and causing untold problems in Italy.

Devon, meanwhile, had just married Katherine Macdonald and had been forced to build a workshop for his lady in the back of his estate outside of London just for the seven huge, hulking Scotsmen who helped her do her glasswork. While Marcus admitted that Kat's talents were above the ordinary, he could not imagine the madness that was now Devon's life.

Then there was Chase, with his wife's herd of brothers and sisters; and Anthony, who had opened his home to a flock of noisome children as well as Anna's meddling grandfather . . . Bloody hell if Marcus would marry, ever! Not unless he could find a nice, quiet woman who could not speak and was orphaned in the bargain. Perhaps then he'd consider it.

And perhaps not. What would be the point, anyway? Marcus liked his life just the way it was. Or he had, until the ring went missing and he discovered that his discreet liaison wasn't quite so discreet any more.

Marcus sighed, drew forth a fresh paper and threw himself into his work. His pen flashed across the paper, and all thoughts of women and their disagreeable tendencies to change a man and make his life unpleasant faded away.

Chapter 2

Mr. Baker-Sneed possesses the purest blood in England, but he is more well known for running off with Baron Winchefield's youngest daughter, Mary. Winchefield was furious and the old fool blabbed to one and all that young Baker-Sneed had heartlessly seduced his "innocent" daughter, which is complete foolery. Anyone who'd ever met Mary must know that poor Baker-Sneed had no say in the matter — she saw him, she wanted him, and b'God, she got him. And so it is with the females who bear the hot, impetuous blood of the Winchefields; they are queens, not consorts.

The Countess of Firth
to Lady Jane Frotherton,
while strolling the grassy
banks of the Thames
awaiting the Regent's royal barge

"I hereby call this meeting of the Society for the Betterment of the Baker-Sneeds to order."

The whispers and giggles that had punctuated the small sitting room immediately silenced and all attention focused on the tall figure standing beside the pianoforte. Miss Honoria Baker-Sneed rapped her bare knuckles on the cherry-wood surface and smiled upon her sisters and youngest brother. "Please, everyone take a seat. We have much to do."

This request was met by a rustling of silk and muslin, and an occasional complaint as to who got the settee closest to the fire, as Honoria's siblings found their favorite seats amongst the scattered chairs and mismatched sofas that punctuated the faded red carpet of the sitting room.

As soon as everyone was seated, Honoria nodded to Olivia. "The treasurer's report, if you please."

Olivia flushed, pink with pleasure at being finally given a duty as worthwhile as the budget, her new job since Ned had left to join Father. Prior to this, Olivia's most important duty had been to assist in the planning of holiday celebrations, and while it was fun to string cranberries and place ivy about the house or prepare cake and surprises for each birthday, she was quite ready for something more substantial. After all, she was almost fifteen and nearly a woman grown.

Beaming, she made her way to the pianoforte to stand beside Honoria. Shorter than Honoria by several inches and not nearly as pretty as Cassandra or Juliet, Olivia tried to make up for her lack of presence with a convincing determination to eschew feminine frivolity. She instead aspired to a more exciting lifestyle, like the one their oldest brother possessed.

Olivia lifted an ink-stained scrap of paper and frowned at it with an important air, her dark head bent over the figures. "I've worked out our weekly expenses and figured in our income from both Father's jointure and the monies he and Ned have sent. Then I compiled a list of all of our expenses and —"

"Oh pother!" Portia flounced in her seat, her hazel eyes flashing annoyance. "We don't need to hear how you established our accounts. We just want to know how they stand."

Olivia frowned at this interruption. "And I plan on telling you as soon as I explain how I came about getting the figures."

"Portia, please allow Olivia do this her own way," Honoria said. "She has spent hours getting things organized."

Honoria nodded for Olivia to continue and hoped Portia's interruption didn't add too much to what was sure to be a long-winded report. Every time Ned wrote from India, where he was currently residing with Father in search of a way to recoup their recent losses, Olivia would soak in the letter, poring over each and every detail Ned let fall. Then she'd spend the next two weeks moping about because her life wasn't nearly as exciting as his.

Olivia would have given her eye teeth to be able to travel about the world, indulging in the adventures Ned portrayed in his infrequent letters. Honoria rather suspected that her brother, like Father, skimmed over the more unsavory details of their travels . . . like the sanitary aspects of some of the places they stayed and the indigestible food they were sometimes forced to eat. Neither were things that held any appeal to Honoria; she liked her clean sheets and well-roasted meat, thank-you-very-much. And she definitely didn't look forward to facing the great unknown. There was a good deal to be said about the comforts of a well-run home and surrounding yourself with the people you loved.

Portia settled back in her chair. "Yes, well, I liked it better when Ned was here to do the treasurer's report. He always went straight to the point."

Juliet looked up from her needlework, the light from the small fire dancing across her ripe golden curls. At sixteen, she was bidding fair to rival Cassandra in beauty, though Juliet possessed none of her elder sister's placid disposition. "Ned never went straight to the point. And he was forever salting his report with sea phrases, half of which I didn't understand."

Ned, who was the closest in age to Honoria, had at the tender age of sixteen served on a sailing vessel for two years under the auspices of their uncle, Captain Porterfield Baker-Sneed. Uncle Porterfield sailed under the flag of the Royal Navy and was a crusty, rough-spoken sailor who was supremely confident at sea and filled with lusty excitement at the thought of a battle, but was reduced to a mass of quivering bread pudding at the mere thought of spending a week on shore wearing a cravat and making polite talk to his nieces.

Juliet smiled her encouragement to Olivia. "I daresay you will be a better treasurer than Ned. He was forever making errors in his figures, and twice we overspent merely because he said there was extra in the accounts and there were not."

Olivia beamed. "I made no mistakes. Indeed, I checked the figures twice and even cross-referenced the —"

"Yes, I am sure you did," Honoria said smoothly. "And how *are* we doing this month?"

Olivia cleared her throat impressively. "As Ned would say, we're seaworthy, but taking on water fast."

Portia smacked her forehead, sending a wave of bounce through her dark brown hair. "Oh for the love of —"

"Portia, please!" Cassandra placed her embroidery hoop on her knees. As gentle as she was beautiful, she was forever attempting to keep the peace among her more active brothers and sisters. "Olivia, we understand that things are ill, but how ill?"

Olivia sighed heavily, and then said in a voice of long suffering, "We're floundering and will end in the deep blue if the wind doesn't change."

Seven-year-old George looked up from where he was trying to put his frog into the Dresden soup tureen that rested on the sideboard. "Damnation, Olivia! Can't you speak English?"

"Georgie!" Cassandra protested, her violet eyes wide. "Where did you hear that word?"

George looked at Honoria.

Honoria's cheeks heated. "*What?* I did no such thing!"

"Honoria," Cassandra said in a disappointed voice.

Olivia grinned. "And to think you banned poor Ned from saying 'bloody' when he was here."

Honoria ignored her. "George, when did I ever say such a horrid word?"

"Last week. When you hit your thumb with the hammer while hanging the picture in the front room. You said 'Damnation' and then you said —"

"I remember," she said hastily, catching the censure in Cassandra's gentle gaze. "George, do not say that word — either of them — again." Honoria quickly turned her attention back to Olivia. "Are you saying we have no money?"

"Exactly."

"But I thought that so long as we stayed in budget —"

"Which no one did. Our expenses this week included seven pounds over our expected expenses."

"Seven?" Honoria's chest ached, and for a moment she wished Ned hadn't had to join Father. It would be nice to have him here now, smiling reassuringly at her across the room. "But how did that happen? We figured every expense."

"No, we didn't," Olivia said bluntly. "For example, the price of coal rose and cost us two pounds six shillings more this month than last. Then George had a cold and we kept the sitting room a bit warmer for him."

Oh yes. George, for all his robust appearance, was prone to catching every case of ague that went about, some of which went into his ears and produced the most wretched pain and frightfully high fevers. What was worse, though, was that George never complained about the pain, even when it was at its worse. They had Ned to thank for that; unbeknownst to Honoria, before his departure Ned had taken George aside and gravely informed him that he was now the man of the house. Honoria was certain Ned only thought to get George to behave, but instead it had given the poor child an overburdened sense of responsibility, a weighty thing for a not-quite-eight-year-old.

Honoria sighed. "I had forgotten about George's ague."

"I'm not sick now," George said, his face fierce.

"Of course not," Honoria said. "You're healthy as a horse."

"And Honoria doesn't even like horses," Portia chimed in.

Which was sadly true. And all because Father's old mare had loved nothing more than to snap at anyone who wandered within sight. Honoria rubbed her arm where a scar lingered still. "That's neither here nor there. What other expenses were there?"

"The wheel on the carriage broke. That cost an additional pound and four shillings." Olivia consulted her paper. "Then Juliet took nine shillings on account."

Honoria tried to swallow her sigh.

Face slightly pink, Juliet shook out her sewing, and Honoria could see that the design was of a black stallion atop a hill, his mane blowing in the wind. Beneath it was transcribed the words *Run free and fast.* Juliet caught Honoria's glance and said in a defensive tone, "The money wasn't for me. It was for Hercules."

The Baker-Sneeds owned one horse, a broken-down old gelding. It was the one horse that didn't make Honoria jump every time it moved quickly, mainly because it had two speeds — slow and very slow. But to Juliet, Hercules was a priceless part of their family. She'd been mad for horses since she was old enough to walk to the stables by herself, and Father, horse mad himself, had never discouraged her. At one time they'd had no less than twenty-two horses in the stables. But that had been before the Crisis. Now they were down to just one — poor Hercules.

Honoria rubbed her temple where a faint ache was beginning to form. "What did Hercules need that cost so much?"

"He strained his right foreleg and Mr. Beckett said he needed a poultice, so I purchased one from the apothecary."

Mr. Beckett was their coachman, or had been when they'd had a coach. Now he was a combination of footman, errand boy, and handyman. "And the poultice cost nine entire shillings?"

"Well, no. I also bought Hercules a new

blanket." Seeing Honoria's expression, Juliet added, "I can repay it when Mrs. Bothton returns from Yorkshire. I promised to teach her niece how to ride sidesaddle. The poor girl is dreadfully frightened of horses, just as you are."

All eyes turned on Honoria. Her cheeks heated. "I am not frightened of horses. I just do not like them." At all. Even from a distance, but especially up close where they could bite. "Juliet, I know you will pay us back, but —"

"Next week," Juliet said serenely, tying off a thread. "You will see. I am an excellent teacher and it will take no time at all to get Miss Lydia riding as if she was born to it."

Honoria shook her head. "I don't doubt that. It's just that things are rather precarious with us now and —"

"Which is all Father's fault," Portia announced rather bitterly, looking at the papers in Olivia's hands. "None of us would be in this mess if Father hadn't —"

"Nonsense," Honoria said firmly. "Father cannot control the winds of fortune that made the ship get lost at sea any more than you can keep from loving pastries, especially cream-filled ones."

Portia had to smile at that, some of the bitterness fading. "I suppose you are right. I just wish Father hadn't invested *all* of our money in one ship."

Olivia nodded. "They say one should never put all of their eggs in one basket. I'd think that a good rule for investing in treasure ships as well."

Honoria agreed, but all she said was, "I'll be sure to add that little homily to the next letter we send him. He is working very hard to make up for the loss, you know. Staying with friends and acquaintances when he can, and eating far less than he should —"

"I know," Portia said, her cheeks flushed. "And I know he's working hard to repair our fortune and will do so, in time. It's just that . . ." She hesitated a moment, then blurted out, "I miss having things."

Cassandra reached over and placed her hand over Portia's. "We all do."

It was a sad thing to admit, but Honoria suspected that she missed their former luxuries worse than anyone else. She, more than any of her younger brothers and sisters, could remember the servants and gowns and fine food, the laughter and music and jeweled slippers — all of which disappeared after Mother's sudden death two days after George's birth. Father had never recovered from that blow, becoming lachrymose and lacking in energy. Naturally, his investments had suffered greatly and it had only been in the last two years that he'd attempted to recoup his losses.

Honoria glanced down at the toes of her morning slippers, which were faded and much darned. Ye gods, what she would give for a new hat like the ones she saw in the much admired copies of *La Belle Assemblée* that Cassandra received from Aunt Caroline every few months. It had been high brimmed and made of straw and decorated with the most delectable pink and green rosettes and matching ribbons. The entire effect had been fresh and springlike, something Honoria yearned for.

But now was not the time to be wishing for something as frivolous as a bonnet, not while her brother and sisters were looking at her as if expecting her to produce a sock filled with funds to solve their current difficulties. Gathering herself, Honoria smiled brightly at Olivia. "What else?"

Olivia consulted the much marked bits of foolscap. "Oh yes! There was one other expense." A martial light entered her eyes. "Portia bought some white silk for a new gown."

All eyes turned on Portia. She was twirling a lock of rich chestnut hair, much like Honoria's though without the horrid white lock that graced her right temple. Honoria touched her hair. Mother had called it her lucky stripe, which even now made Honoria smile. "Portia, did you take money from our accounts?"

"A little," Portia said proudly, not in the least remorseful. "It was more in the way of an investment though."

Olivia snorted. "Investment? In what? Your vanity?"

Portia's eyes flashed. "No! I plan on using that silk to earn money. We need money for our expenses while Father and Ned are working, don't we?" She glanced questioningly at Honoria. "Don't we?"

"Yes, but . . . I don't see how the silk will help."

"Neither do I," Olivia said.

"I," Portia said grandly, "am going to begin my own business. Within a year, I shall be extremely wealthy."

Honoria opened her mouth, then closed it.

Olivia snorted. "Portia, you would have to do something useful in order to make money. Or you could get funds the old-fashioned way."

Honoria frowned. "The old-fashioned way?"

Olivia nodded. "By inheriting it. Which is

not likely to happen since none of our relations are even sick." She eyed Portia up and down, her nose curled with disbelief. "Not that any of our relatives would wish to leave their hard earned fortunes to you, lazybones that you are."

Portia stiffened, her hazel eyes sparkling. "Aunt Caroline has promised me her pianoforte when she dies! That will be worth a lot."

Olivia snorted. "She's not a day over forty and healthier than you are, I daresay. You'll be blue before she sticks her spoon in the wall and leaves you so much as one piece of ivory."

"Oh! You — You — blockhead!"

"Barmybrain," Olivia replied without pause.

"Clodpolish!"

"Saphead!"

"Stop it," Honoria said sternly, though she was hard pressed not to grin herself.

Portia flounced in her chair. "Olivia started it."

"Yes she did. Olivia, Portia was asked a question and though we appreciate your insight on the matter, we find that the truth would be more useful." Honoria looked back at Portia. "Well?"

"I only borrowed a bit because the silk

was reduced in price and was so lovely. Have you seen it yet?" She leaned forward eagerly. "White silk with a lace motif and such sheen! I do believe it will be the prettiest gown yet."

"But we didn't have the money for silk."

"You wanted us to save, didn't you?"

"Yes, but —"

"Well, I saved you almost one whole pound! The silk was on sale, you know."

"How could you save us money by spending it?"

"Because I am going to make a gown with the silk, and then sell it," Portia said proudly. "Mrs. Vemeer said she'd buy it for fifteen pounds, if it was pretty enough. What's even better is that I should have enough silk left to turn Cassandra's gray gown and trim it. It should look almost new."

Cassandra beamed. "Oh Portia! How lovely of you! I have been wishing for a new gown." She caught Honoria's gaze and colored, then added hastily, "I don't really need it, of course, though it would be nice."

Honoria thought of a thousand things to say, but she hated to disappoint Cassandra. Still, she eyed Portia for a long moment. "I don't know what Father would say about you setting yourself up as a dressmaker.

That is a very difficult profession. Many go blind sewing over candles at night."

"Oh, I shall only use the best candles," Portia said with the confidence of the very young, waving aside her sister's very real objections.

Honoria stifled a sigh. It wouldn't do to start an argument with Portia. Not right this moment anyway. "Olivia, is that all?"

Olivia gave a smart nod and consulted her papers one more time. "Aye. The jibs are out of tune and we're sure to sink else we find a strong wind to carry us to shore."

Cassandra sighed. "I don't understand how things could be so wretched. Who put the jibs so out of tune?"

"We did," Honoria said promptly. "All of us together. With Portia's silk and Juliet getting Hercules a new horse blanket and the increasing cost of coal and my silly purchases for the shop . . . Olivia, exactly how much do we have left?"

"Less than sixty pounds."

A faint silence met this pronouncement. Honoria found she couldn't swallow. Surely Olivia was wrong. They should have had two hundred pounds left, enough to make it through the coming winter until Father could send them something from his new investment. It would not be much, but it would get them through a few more months after that and perhaps give Cassandra a little for her wardrobe. She was seventeen now and Honoria had hoped to see her sister presented this year.

She stole a glance at Cassandra, who was calmly setting small, perfect stitches on the hem of a delicate lace kerchief. Honoria's heart swelled. Tall, slender, with golden hair and a sparkling smile and rich violet eyes, her sister was as opposite Honoria as could be. But then Cassandra had inherited Mother's looks, while Honoria favored Father and the Baker-Sneeds.

But it wasn't just Cassandra's looks, blindingly beautiful as they were, that made her so special. It was a peculiar sweetness of expression, a gentleness of spirit. Cassandra was as pure in heart as she was in form. And Honoria was resolved to see to it that her sister had every opportunity to shine. If they could but find Cassandra a sponsor who would gain her entry into the right places, Honoria knew her sister could take the ton by storm. After all, she'd quite enraptured every man within a fifty mile radius of their home in Hampstead, where they'd lived before removing to London.

The thought made Honoria grimace, for of the many suitors who had come to call, none had possessed the gentle and refined spirit that would ultimately attract Cassandra. The experience had caused both Honoria and Ned a good bit of concern. They simply could not see gentle, loving Cassandra married to a coarse farmer. Thus they'd moved to London.

Of course, coming to London and becoming a part of society were two separate issues. They'd arrived without problem, but thanks to their aunt's refusal to honor her offer to sponsor Cassandra, they were now at a standstill. If only Honoria could find a way to get Cassandra into society . . . It would only be a matter of time before she attracted the attention she was due, a man of mature breeding and the sort of refined spirit that Cassandra herself possessed. And if he happened to be enormously wealthy as well, their problems would be solved. Surely Cassandra's new husband would agree to sponsor Portia and then Juliet and Olivia and perhaps even —

Honoria mentally shook herself. There was no sense in living in the future. What she had to do was take care of the now. They would have to economize. Part of the blame for their current condition could be laid at her feet, as well. Just last month she'd had to pay a little extra for Portia's music lessons.

And Honoria knew she had forgotten to include in their budget the pittance they gave the vicar every Tuesday for George's Latin and Greek lessons. But, worst of all, were her little purchases she sold at the antiquities shop. Though it turned a profit, this was the slow time of the year, and often she'd not been able to recoup her original investment for months.

She sighed and glanced down at the ring that rested on her finger. At least that had not cost anything. Small and silver, decorated with a dance of silver-etched runes, it had appealed to her from the first second she'd beheld it, resting on an iced cake at a ball, a party favor that had nonetheless appealed to her sense of beauty. She traced the ring with the tips of her fingers, wondering what it was worth.

When she first won the ring, she'd had the full intention of selling it, only . . . She closed her fingers over it, letting the warmed metal melt the icy uncertainty that encased her heart. For some reason she'd taken a fancy to the thing. "Olivia, are you certain about the amount?"

Olivia nodded, a grim line to her mouth. For an instant their eyes met and Honoria could see the concern in her younger sister's eyes. Honoria collected herself and managed a reassuring smile, though smiling was the last thing she felt like doing. "Well, now we know where we stand. Thank you for your efforts. You have done a smash-up job." As Olivia returned to her seat, Honoria faced her small audience. "We must economize."

There was a moment of silence and then everyone began to nod.

Cassandra clasped her hands together, her lovely violet eyes wide. "Lady Melrose wishes me to come and read to her each morning. She is only willing to pay a shilling a month, but it will help."

"But you hate Lady Melrose!" Portia exclaimed. At Cassandra's gentle look of reproof, Portia amended, "Well, I hate her. She's a nasty old woman, forever complaining."

"I rather think she has suffered some disappointments which have made her so difficult," Cassandra said softly. "Either way, I am certain it will be no hardship to merely read to her."

"That's an excellent idea," Honoria said. "I will see about selling some of my snuffboxes."

"Oh no!" Cassandra said. "You have been collecting those since you were young!"

Honoria didn't allow herself the luxury of

glancing at the glass cabinet that held her collection, some forty-two snuffboxes in all. In truth, the thought of selling them reduced her spirits to below the level of the rug beneath her feet.

Father had given her the first one when she'd been no older than George. As she'd grown older, it had been a passion she and Father had shared. She'd become an expert in the delicate French enamels that were so popular. And Father had delighted in her ability to spot a quality piece and to haggle the price even lower.

George piped up. "Honoria shouldn't have to sell her boxes. If you need more funds, I'd be willing to breed frogs."

Olivia made a rude noise. "Breed frogs? Lord love you, George, but you're a sail short this evening, aren't you?"

George pointedly ignored Olivia. "Father always said that if there wasn't a market for your goods, then you'd have to make one." He frowned at the fat frog that was even now hanging half out of the soup tureen. "Perhaps I can teach Achilles some tricks, for he is the smartest frog I've ever had. Then people would be anxious to buy his offspring."

"You don't need to do that," Portia said with a smug smile, eyeing the frog with a knowing gleam. "Just breed them as fat as Achilles there and all sorts of people will line up to toss them into their soup pots. The French love a good, fat frog, and there are few as plump as that one."

George turned wide eyes toward his sister. "The French *eat* frogs?"

"They don't call the Frenchies 'frogs' for nothing. They eat them all of the time."

George's bottom lip thrust forward. "I'm not selling Achilles to any Frenchmen! Just to Englishmen who will treat him well. Besides, Achilles is not your ordinary frog. He's smart and I daresay he tastes horrid."

"I daresay you are right," Honoria said, sending a quelling glance at the grinning Portia. "And George, while it is very nice of you to offer to help, I think you'd do better to keep Achilles in a safe place and let the rest of us work on our financial problems."

"But I want to help."

"You can. But we must think of something that doesn't involve Achilles."

"Well, *I* can help right now," Portia said. "By making that white silk into a gown. Honoria, it's close to Christmas and there are bound to be a few ladies wishful to have a new gown for the assembly balls. And you know I could do it in a trice."

That was true. Portia had nimble fingers

when it came to needlework. Honoria just had the feeling that things were changing far too fast. "I suppose making up one gown wouldn't hurt," she said, feeling a bit more hopeful. "But only one."

Cassandra, who had been staring rather fixedly at the embroidery hoop that rested on her lap, looked up at this and said in a quiet, resolute voice, "I will give up my season."

Portia gasped. "Cassandra! How can you suggest such a thing? Whatever else happens, you cannot give up that."

Olivia snorted. "You are only saying that because you want Cassandra to find a wealthy husband who will pay your season when your time comes, as you are next."

"That has nothing to do with it," Portia said, though she glanced at Cassandra with a faintly guilty expression.

Honoria sighed. "Even if Cassandra had a season, there is no guarantee that she'd find a wealthy husband. Besides, the purpose of Cassandra having a season is just so she can meet men with her own level of gentleness and breeding. Nothing more."

"Oh, Honoria. The whole idea is a wasted effort." Cassandra gave a wistful smile. "Aunt Caroline will not sponsor me. I had thought she would, for she certainly indicated in her letters that she might be willing to do so. But since her visit last spring, she has been very unreceptive to the idea."

"That is because she saw what a beauty you had become," Portia said bluntly. "While her own daughter is whey-faced and cursed with spots."

"Portia!" Honoria said, her brows lowered. "Cousin Jane cannot help having spots."

"No, but you'd think she could do something about her laugh. She sounds like a horse."

George grinned and made a loud whinnying sound that so closely approximated Cousin Jane's ungenteel laugh that the entire Baker-Sneed clan went into gales of laughter. Everyone but Honoria. She rapped the tabletop with her knuckles once again. "Enough, you ill-bred ruffians! Enough!" Slowly their laughter settled into snuffled giggles and chuckles. "We still have business to attend to. Portia, will you give the report on the improvements to the sitting room?"

Portia dutifully stood and began her report about the stenciling efforts of the female members of the Baker-Sneeds and how George had had the brilliant idea to dip Achilles's feet in red paint and let him hop across the paper for their best and most impressive design. Honoria listened with half an ear, her mind working through the problem with the Baker-Sneed finances.

Her gaze fell on her ring, and as usual the warmth of the metal against her bare finger made her smile. It was then that she knew, come what may, she would persevere.

Chapter 3

I once had a rather toothy spaniel named Fluffy. He snarled at my stepmama every time she came into the room, snapped at Clarissa Ethleridge when she laughed at my new coif, and chased Lord Geoffrey Fellington out of the house and into the pond when the fool came to propose. Without a doubt, darling Fluffy was the best dog I ever had.

Lady Jane Frotherton to Viscount Melton
in Hyde Park, while walking
Lady Jane's wheezy pug

". . . even though I searched everywhere." Honoria looked up from where she sat at the escritoire in the sitting room, lost in a sea of figures as she painstakingly reworked their failed budget. "I'm sorry, George. I didn't hear you. What is it you are searching for?"

Georgie shifted from one foot to the other, his coat awry, a smear of dust down one cheek. He favored Honoria with a flat stare. "I'm not searching for a 'what,' I am searching for a 'whom.' "

Honoria sighed and returned her quill to the ink stand. "I gather we are talking about the ever busy Achilles."

George nodded, his expression severe. "I put him to bed for a nap, and when I went to wake him, he was gone."

Honoria pursed her lips. "He seems to run away quite a bit, you know. Have you ever thought that perhaps Achilles does not like living in a hatbox under your bed?"

"He likes that hatbox. I can tell."

"How?"

George's brows lowered, his violet eyes sparkling with disdain. "I know he likes it because he sings when he's in that hatbox. I don't think he'd bother unless he enjoyed being there."

"Perhaps he is not singing, but yelling for help." She put her hands in the air and said in as froglike a voice as she could muster,

"Help! I'm being held prisoner in a horrid hatbox! Please save me!"

George eyed her morosely.

Honoria lowered her hands. "You didn't find that the least bit funny, did you?"

"No. I've heard Achilles yell. When he's in the hatbox, he just sings."

"When have you heard him yell?"

"When I was trying to teach him how to slide down the banister in the front hall."

"Thank heavens I'm not a frog! I believe I might yell, too." She rubbed her temples. "But I daresay you do know his yelling from his singing."

"I just wish I knew why he kept running away."

Honoria could hear the genuine distress in George's voice. "Perhaps he misses his old pond."

"You think he might?" Georgie's bottom lip jutted out, a stubborn gleam rising in his eyes. "Perhaps he does, but if he didn't live in the hatbox under my bed, he'd be very sorry indeed. He would miss me much worse than he could ever miss his old nasty pond."

"Yes well, if he keeps getting out you may have to put a lid on that hatbox. And a book on top of that."

"But that would make it dark! Achilles doesn't like dark places."

Honoria had an idea who didn't like dark places, and it wasn't Achilles. "Your frog used to live in a pond in the woods; it got very dark at night in those woods, too. I don't think he'd mind if you'd put a lid on his hatbox at all."

Georgie's chin firmed. "I won't do it. It would be the same as putting him in prison."

"It would be saving his life. There are many dangers to a frog in a house, you know."

George looked skeptical. "Like what?"

"He could be stepped on by an unsuspecting servant or accidentally knocked down the stairs by Portia while she was carrying some material for one of her sewing projects. He could be hopping through the kitchen and fall into a pan of soup. He could get his toe stuck in one of the floor gratings. There are an untold number of things that could happen to a hapless frog."

"No. If something bad happened to Achilles, I would know."

Honoria sighed and pulled George to her, giving him a gentle hug and resting her cheek against his hair. "I think putting a lid on Achilles's box could save his life. If nothing else, it might keep him from running away."

"He doesn't run away; he goes exploring, like Father."

Honoria pulled back and eyed her youngest brother a long moment. He was just as stubborn as . . . well, as stubborn as the rest of the family. And she supposed she could understand why he didn't wish to admit that perhaps he might be wrong. He was, after all, a part of Mother. And Mother had never been able to admit defeat. It was the one trait she'd given to each and every one of her children; to the last one, the Baker-Sneeds were thoroughly blessed with the famed Winchefield tenacity.

Honoria kissed her brother's forehead. "I suppose you need someone to help you find your adventuring frog."

"Would you mind? I asked Portia to help, but she was busy cutting the pattern for some gown or another." George looked properly disgusted. "Cassandra is with her and they are chattering like a pair of magpies. Ned would say they were creaking like ships in a dock and damned unpleasant it is, too."

"George!"

He peered up at her though his lashes. "What?"

"You know exactly what. I do not wish to hear that word from you again."

"I was just saying what Ned would say and —" George hesitated, then the tears spilled down his cheek. *"I miss Ned!"*

At the wail, Honoria gathered George close once again, holding him until his sobs quieted into soft hiccups. After a moment, he pushed away and dashed at his eyes with his shirtsleeve. "Sorry," he mumbled, glaring up at her as if daring her to say another word.

A lump rose in Honoria's throat and she longed to hold him close yet again. "George, Ned will be back in a trice, see if he isn't. Father just needed help with his new venture. Besides, he is having a wonderful time, exploring and such. You wouldn't take that away from him, would you?"

"I don't want Ned back. I just want Achilles." George sniffed again and wiped his nose on his sleeve.

Honoria reached into her pocket and pulled out a handkerchief and pressed it into his hand. "If you please."

He took it and gave his nose a belligerent swipe. "Girls. You always worry about silly things."

She took the handkerchief and tucked it into his pocket. "Be glad. Without us, there'd be no plum pudding at Christmas and no fresh, clean sheets like the ones you so love to snuggle between at nights."

"Yes well, I'm just glad I'm not a girl so I don't have to muss with gowns and ribbons and such."

"I'm glad for you, too, though there are times when such things can be pleasant." Honoria tucked away the papers she'd been working on and returned the pen to the ink pot. "Come. We'll find Achilles and you can take him back to his box under the bed."

George put his hand in hers and they started for the door. Honoria made a great adventure of their search — anything to keep George's mind off Ned. First they looked upstairs, peering into all of Achilles's usual hideaways, many of which were cobweb-strewn corners beneath large pieces of furniture. Then they moved downstairs, peeking beneath sofas and cabinets. They would have made faster time had George not been so hesitant about dark places, but so it was. And Honoria knew better than to act as if she noticed his reluctance. Instead, she nimbly crawled beneath the buffet in the dining room, the large draped side table in the sitting room and anywhere else that might hide a large frog.

George was poking in the sofa cushions and Honoria was just lying on the floor with her head beneath the sofa in the sitting room when the door opened.

A horrified feminine gasp filled the air. "Miss Baker-Sneed! Whatever are ye doing?"

"Hunting something," Honoria said, smiling up at Mrs. Kemble, the housekeeper. Honoria gracefully found her feet and dusted cobwebs from her shoulders. "Were you looking for me?"

The housekeeper's eyes were as wide as saucers, her hands clenched in the folds of her apron. "Miss! Ye won't believe it, but there's a marquis here to see ye! A real, live marquis!"

Honoria and George exchanged glances. "I suppose," Honoria said after a long moment, "that having a real, live marquis to visit is much better than having a dead one."

George giggled.

Mrs. Kemble plopped her hands on her hips. "Ye don't understand, miss. This isn't any marquis, but a very well-to-do one."

"How do you know?"

"He drove up in a coach and six, he did. The entire neighborhood must be agog to know who it is and why he's come to call."

"A coach and six?" George ran to the window and shoved back the edge of the curtain. Standing on his tiptoes, he pressed his face to the glass. "Bloody hell, that's a smack-up set of blood and bones."

"George!"

He had the grace to look slightly shame-faced. "I apologize. But come and look, Honoria. You'll say the same thing when you see them."

"I'll look at them when I return. We mustn't keep our guest waiting." She glanced at the housekeeper. "Where is this marquis?"

"In yer sittin' room, miss!" Mrs. Kemble fanned herself vigorously. "A real marquis! Who'd have thought?"

Honoria wondered which marquis it could be. She knew of five, all of them avid collectors. Perhaps it was the Marquis of Sheraton, recently returned from Italy. Ah yes, that must be it. No doubt he'd come to inquire about the Indian pearl desk his wife had so admired in the shop just two months before. "I will join the marquis shortly. I assume you offered him some re-freshment?"

"Indeed I hadn't. What with opening the door and finding a real live marquis on the step and wondering if I should put him in the front sitting room, there not being a proper fire and all —" Mrs. Kemble brightened. "Do ye think he'd like some of Mrs. Hibbert's apple tarts?"

"With some tea, if you please." Honoria glanced at George, who was still looking down at the horses. "George, I must go to our visitor, but I won't be a minute."

"Very well," he said, though from the sound of his voice, his mind was a million miles away. "If I had a coach and six, I'd have white horses and not gray."

Honoria smiled, glad to see him so distracted. She quietly left him to his dreams and made her way to the sitting room. In her haste, Mrs. Kemble had left the door open, so Honoria merely walked in, her feet making no sound on the thick rug.

The marquis was standing beside the fireplace, looking into the small flicker of flames that pretended to chase the chill from the room. Honoria took two steps into the room, then came to a sudden halt, her skirts swinging forward. It wasn't Sheraton at all, but the irascible, annoying and thoroughly irritating Marquis of Treymount.

Ye gods, what did the man want with her? She glowered at him silently, almost wishing she was wrong, but there was no mistaking those broad shoulders covered in a neatly cut morning coat of unfashionable black, that arrogant tilt to his head. The insufferable man carried himself with an annoying combination of blinding masculine arrogance and unnerving personal command. But why was the Marquis of Treymount *here?*

Honoria glanced around as if looking for clues, absently noting the weak blaze that barely cast forth heat. She wished she'd ordered a nice roaring fire, though she could hardly see the reason when the room was so rarely used. Still . . . it was one thing to keep the fires small to conserve what they could, and downright beastly to let a man like Treymount see evidence of what straits the Baker-Sneeds were facing.

Well, there was only one way to find out what the blasted man wanted. Chin up, heart steeled, she said as coolly as she dared, "Lord Treymount." She closed the door and came forward with what she hoped was a polite smile since she was fairly certain it was not pleasant. "What an unexpected surprise."

"Miss Baker-Sneed. How kind of you to receive me on such short notice." His voice rumbled pleasantly through her, jangling her nerves a bit more.

Really, it was unfair of God to make a man so incredibly handsome and then imbue him with the most pasteboard of personalities. Honoria swallowed a regretful sigh, noting that the sunlight from the window slanted across his face in a most intriguing way, marking the strong cheekbone, the firm jaw, the line of his mouth in a way that would have caused her pause had she not faced the man so many times before.

The sad truth was that she knew Treymount far too well to be put off by his masculine beauty. They'd found themselves on opposite ends of the auction table so often that just the sight of his carriage in front of an auction house made her shoulders tighten, her back stiffen, her eyes narrow. She was all but immune to his vivid blue eyes and the way one brow rose whenever he faced an unpleasant situation. Nor did she pay the slightest attention to the thick curl of his black hair or the way his mouth pursed in such a tantalizing manner when he was considering something.

No, Honoria had long since stopped seeing the devastatingly handsome marquis as anything other than a threat to her peace of mind and her purse. She glanced down and realized her hands were at her sides in tight fists.

Smiling a little at herself, Honoria forced her fingers to loosen and let a bit of air slip into her palms. "My lord, to what do I owe the pleasure? I cannot imagine this is a purely social visit."

A flash of irritation crossed his face, his chin lifting slightly in obvious disapprobation. "Yes, I do wish to ask you about something, although I had thought we'd at least engage in the minimum of civility first."

"How kind of you," she said, catching a glimpse of fire in his gaze. Perhaps she'd been a bit hasty in describing his character as pasteboard in consistency. To many people, the Marquis of Treymount seemed a cold, impersonal man, but to be perfectly honest, Honoria knew differently. Irritating and smugly sure of his own supremacy, he was far from cold. He was, in fact, a man of fierce desires and unremitting determination. Few members of the ton had faced the man when he was pursuing something he really wanted, be it an ancient tapestry or a priceless Chinese vase. When in genuine pursuit, his coldly controlled mask fell away and one was treated to the blaze of determination and cold acuity that was rather intriguing to behold.

Honoria searched his face for some glimmer of his purpose, but none came. Irritated, she dipped a slight curtsy. "My lord, welcome to my home. I daresay you've come on a matter of business . . ." She raised her brows and waited.

His deep blue eyes raked across her, lingering on her hair. Honoria had to swallow the urge to make a face at him. It was a peculiar tendency of his, to pause and measure one before engaging in conversation. She'd seen him depress the attentions of any number of toad-eating position worshippers. Under that hard stare, most people found themselves stuttering, anxious to please. Thank God she had her pride to hold her head upright, even before such an imperious gesture.

Still, she couldn't help but wish she'd worn her good morning dress, though she doubted it would make any difference other than to make her feel somewhat more confident; the man was used to the finest of the fine, and even her good morning dress could not be counted as such. She glanced at him and waited . . . but still he did not speak.

A flicker of uncertainty brushed across her. Was he silently taunting her? Or was it something else? Honoria's back stiffened. She did not like being put at such a disadvantage. Treymount's continued silence began to weight the air.

"Oh pother! Enough of this!" She crossed her arms over her chest, fighting the desire to merely order the cad out of her house. At least his rudeness freed her to speak her mind. "Treymount, what do you want?"

He bowed, an ironic smile touching his lips, his gaze still crossing over her face, to her hair and back. "I am sorry if I appeared rude but . . . did I interrupt you in something . . ." Again that flickering glance to her hair. ". . . important?"

Her face heated instantly. She was used to people staring at her hair whenever they first met — the streak of white at her right temple made a lot of people pause. Some stared. Some pointedly looked away. Some gawked as if she had two heads. But Honoria had faced Treymount more than once now. Surely he wasn't merely looking at her because of that silly streak.

She unconsciously touched her hair . . . Her fingers found something and her eyes widening. "Cobwebs!" She crossed to the mirror over the fireplace so she could see the damage, laughing when she caught sight of herself. Two frothy strands of cobwebs hung across her hair and draped dramatically to one shoulder. Worse, a faint smudge of dust lined one of her cheekbones. "Ye gods, I look as if I've been in a crypt! No wonder you were staring. I'm a complete fright."

His gaze met hers in the mirror, a surprising hint of amusement lightening the usual cool blue to something far warmer. "I was going to suggest you'd been counting linens from a dark, deep closet, but a crypt is a much more romantic location to gather cobwebs."

"Cobwebs are not romantic." Honoria whisked her hand over her head and cleaned away the sweep of misty white strands. "I am sorry to receive you while so mussed. I was assisting my little brother in locating something he's lost." That was what she got for even worrying about her appearance to begin with, she decided, shrugging at her own silliness.

The door opened and Mrs. Kemble entered, bearing a heavy tray. "Here we are, miss!" She set the tray on the small table by the sofa and then stood back, beaming. "There weren't no more apple tarts left, being as how Miss Portia visited the kitchen not ten minutes before I did and ate every last one. But Cook had some pasties a-cookin' and so I waited fer them to be ready."

"Thank you, Mrs. Kemble."

The housekeeper curtsied, though she managed to look the marquis up and down as she went. "Will ye be needing anything else?"

"No, thank you," Honoria said. "I believe this will suffice."

"Very well, miss." With one more curtsy and yet another lingering glance at the marquis, the housekeeper was gone, no doubt to regale the kitchen staff with her impressions of their lofty visitor.

Honoria went to the chair by the table and gestured to the nearby sofa. "Will you be seated, my lord?"

He hesitated, and she smoothly added, "I hope you are famished, for I am." She busied herself with the tray, adjusting the cups and putting a pastry on a plate, all the while her mind whirled.

Perhaps he'd come about an object he wished to purchase. It was unusual, but not unheard of. Certainly other members of the ton called occasionally when looking for something specific. Not often, of course. But still . . . Mentally, she reviewed the more recent acquisitions. None of them were of the quality that he normally pursued.

If there was something good to be said for the Marquis of Treymount — and she knew of only one thing — it was that he appreciated the finest of antiquities and bought only the best. She had to admire his taste, if nothing else.

He stirred, as if making a sudden decision.

"I suppose tea would not be amiss. I don't have long, but . . . why not?" He came to stand before the table, moving a loose pillow from the sofa and setting it out of the way.

To her chagrin, Honoria found herself at eye level with Treymount's thighs. It was strange, but in all of her dealings with the marquis, she had never noticed this particular part of his physique. Now that he was directly across from her, she couldn't help but admire the ripple of his muscles beneath his fitted breeches.

The man must ride often to keep such a fine figure —

He sat, his gaze catching hers. His brows rose as he caught her expression. "Yes?"

Her thoughts froze in place. Ye gods, did he know what she was thinking? Her neck prickled with heat, then her face. Hurriedly, she began pouring tea into a cup. "I — I —" She what? Admired his well-turned legs? What a horrid predicament! She could hardly admit —

His gaze dropped to the tray and he frowned. "Miss Baker-Sneed, I believe there is enough tea in that cup."

Honoria jerked back the teapot. She'd filled the cup over the brim and tea now sloshed into the saucer and tray below. "Oh dear! What was I thinking?" She reached for one of the linen napkins not soaked with tea. Just as her hand closed over it, Treymount reached over and clasped his hand about hers.

Honoria sat shock-still. His hand enveloped hers, large and masculine and surprisingly warm. His fingers were long and tapered, his nails perfectly pared and trimmed, and yet that did nothing to disguise the pure strength of the man.

Her heart hammered against her chest, the unexpected touch sending the strangest heat through her body. She was going mad. She'd faced the marquis time and again at numerous auctions and never had she felt this tug of attraction. But it was more than a tug. It was a powerful wave, pure and primal. It washed over her, crashing through her thoughts and leaving her confused and disoriented.

In her bemused state, she could only stare wide-eyed as the marquis pulled her hand to him, causing her to lean forward, over the small table. His hand slid to her arm, his warm fingers encircling her wrist.

"My lord," she gasped. "What are you —"

"That's my ring." His eyes blazed into hers, accusation and anger flickering brightly in their depths. "And I came to get it back."

Chapter 4

Life is about taking chances. Without them, our existence is just an airless, closed box of naught. I, for one, would prefer to die a horrid, painful death than pollute my lungs with the fetid fumes of nothingness.

Lord Melton to Lady Albermaryle,
while enjoying her ladyship's bed
(and her ladyship)
during Lord Albermaryle's annual visit
to his southern holdings in Yorkshire

"*Your* ring?" Honoria could only stare, first at the marquis, and then at the silver band about the third finger of her left hand.

"*Mine.*" The marquis's voice, deep and rich, snapped through his teeth, his grasp on her wrist tightening imperceptibly.

She winced and wriggled her fingers. "My lord, please! My fingers are numb."

His hold slackened, but he didn't let go. "I want my ring."

"And I want a new gown, a set of emeralds, and some jeweled slippers, but that is not going to happen, either." She sniffed. "Life is not so easy that we always get what we wish."

His brow lowered. "Miss Baker-Sneed, you don't seem to understand. This ring belongs to me, to my family."

"This ring *belonged* to your family. Now it is mine; I won it at a house party in S—"

"Scotland. Where you went as a guest to a certain Lady Talbot."

She blinked. "Why . . . yes! How did you know that?"

"I have been searching for this blasted ring ever since my brother's fiancée lost it at that very party."

His certainty touched her, and she gazed down at her hand, at the warm band of silver. "So this is your ring . . ." In the back of her mind a faint memory stirred. A rumor of the St. Johns and a ring and a curse of some sort. Or was it a blessing? She could not remember, try as she would. "So this is the St. John talisman ring," she murmured.

"Yes," he said shortly. "And now you know why you must return it to me."

Must was such a harsh word, especially coming from *him*. Honoria closed her fingers into a fist, remembering each and every time Treymount had outbid her at an auction, ignored her presence with a thoroughness that had even caused others to comment, and generally behaved in a way that could only be categorized as self-centered.

A strange tingle warmed her fingers, traveling across her palm, through the tender veins on her wrist right where Treymount's hand was clasped. The sensation was both bold and exotic, like the stroke of a warmed feather on her naked skin. She shivered, trying to pull her erratic thoughts together. "I've heard of the talisman ring. I always thought it would be bejeweled. This ring seems so simple."

"It is very, very old."

"I thought so from the first time I saw it." She leaned forward to peer at it more intently. "Well! If it's yours and you've been searching for it for such a long time, I daresay you'd pay dearly to have it back." She sent him a searching look through her lashes, her instincts coming to the fore. She could smell a good venture, feel it in her bones. And the fact that the money would come out of his coffers made the idea all the sweeter.

He stiffened, letting go of her wrist as if she'd just burned him. "I should not have to pay for my own ring."

"Ownership is such an interesting concept. You say it's yours, but I say it's mine. Who do you think a court of law would support?"

His face darkened. "I would never take this to a court of law and you know it. My name would be in every paper in England."

"And mine," she pointed out. "Therefore, possession is what will determine ownership."

Treymount watched her darkly. Finally, he said, "I will pay what the ring is worth, but no more."

Her wrist ached, not from his touch, but for the lack of it, which was strange indeed. She rubbed her skin absently, wondering at the odd bereft feeling that weighed in her heart. The sparkle of the ring caught her eye and she heard herself say, "There is a rumor about the ring . . . a legend." She frowned, searching her scattered memory yet again. What was it . . . something about the ring . . . and — "Ah yes! They say that whichever of the St. Johns holds the ring will find his one, true love."

He gave an impatient flick of his hand, irritation crossing his features. "That is foolish fancy and nothing more. The importance of the ring is in its historic value to our family. It is a part of our heritage."

"Which makes it even more valuable." She smiled just the tiniest bit. "I have to wonder what great sums you'd pay to have this ring back in your possession. Certainly if it has value as an heirloom, then it is nigh priceless."

His eyes narrowed suddenly, his nostrils flaring the slightest bit. "Do not tempt me into physically claiming what is rightfully mine."

Soft and threatening, the determination in his voice was palpable. Honoria lifted her brows. "Have you forgotten that antiquities are my business? When I find a customer who wants something dearly, that is usually the price I charge — dearly."

"That ring is important to no one but a St. John. You face a very limited market, my dear."

To Marcus's chagrin, the wench had the audacity to smile, to grin even, the straight line of her front teeth gleaming white between her perfectly formed lips. "It is fortunate for us all, then, that my one, lone customer is so very, very wealthy."

Marcus could not believe his ears. The little minx was going to make him pay — and a lot, by the sound of it. It was — inconceivable. It was outrageous. It was — bloody hell, who did she think she was?

As if in answer to his thoughts, his hostess calmly picked up the napkin she'd dropped and wiped up the spilled tea in the tray. "I wonder what I should charge for a ring of such personal importance?" She set down the napkin, retrieved the warmed pot and poured tea into a fresh cup. Smiling ever so slightly, she held out the cup and saucer. "Your tea, my lord."

What he wanted was brandy. Or perhaps port. Better yet, a good stiff bourbon that would douse the fire crackling in his stomach. But he supposed he was as stuck with tepid tea as he was stuck doing business with the one woman who thought an argument was a form of polite conversation.

What a horrid day. He'd been forced to attend to Lady Percival first thing this morning and break off their alliance. To his distaste, she'd allowed her feelings to become quite maudlin, so he handed her the sapphire and diamond bracelet he'd purchased as a parting gesture, and left post-haste. He'd always considered her the epitome of feminine beauty — cool, undisturbed by emotions, and yet welcoming when the time was right. Now he was beginning to realize that it had all been a hum — Violet had been playacting the whole time in an effort to get him to commit to something far more than a playful liaison.

Women, Marcus decided, were devious creatures. Though none so devious as the one who now sat across the table from him. Miss Baker-Sneed was not only a forward woman willing to brangle over a few guineas, but she had a rare talent for ascertaining value, and the wit to exploit that ability. He already regretted revealing the importance of the ring; that had been an error. But his case was not yet desperate and he was certainly unwilling to accept defeat.

Jaw set, he took the tea and affected an air of boredom. "I will give you a hundred pounds. That is more than fair."

She poured herself a cup and took a little sip, then pursed her lips as if considering his offer. "No." She picked up the tray with the fresh pasties and held them out. "Would you like a pastie?"

No, he did not want a blasted pastie. He wanted his damn ring. He swallowed a scowl, which would have no effect except give his enemy the felicity of seeing how much she'd manage to irk him. He forced himself to remember with painful clarity each and every time the heartless jade had outwitted him at various auction houses. Oh, she hadn't doused him every time — he wasn't a flat, after all — but often enough that the mere sight of her bedraggled carriage and broken-down nag at an auction site was enough to set his teeth on edge.

The damnable truth was that Miss Honoria Baker-Sneed was not a woman to be cowed by mere scowling, arguing, or any other emotional outbursts. Her outward appearance of civility and feminine softness hid a granite heart and a wily determination to drive a hard bargain. And that was the one thing he'd allowed himself to forget. But no more.

Marcus set down his cup, the china bottom clinking into the delicate saucer. "Two hundred pounds, then. But that is my final offer."

She clicked her tongue at him, as if distressed. "Such low numbers. We must rethink this." She tilted her head to one side, the sunlight from the window lighting her rich sable hair with warm golden red lights that made the white streak at her temple appear to almost glow.

Marcus's lips thinned. She was a beautiful woman, which was a fact he'd always known though never with such awareness as now. Of course, before this meeting, the occasional pleasure of beating her on the auction floor had been enough to distill any sort of temporary interest he might have had. She was his opponent, to be vanquished and thoroughly routed, not a sensually exciting woman to be trifled with until he'd tired of her. Although . . . his eyes were drawn to the gleam of the streak at her temple. It added an exotic tint to her features and made him wonder at her true nature. That she was a passionate woman could not be questioned — no one who'd ever seen her bidding on an object d'art could say otherwise. Which made him wonder what she would be like in bed?

Hmmm. That *was* an interesting idea. He wondered if she'd be as wild as that streak of hair that decried her rather pristine appearance. Would she throw herself into the act, just as she threw herself into acquiring antiquities? He had an instant vision of her, naked and writhing beneath him, head tossed back, her long sable hair streaming over his pillows —

By Zeus, what was he thinking? This was his enemy, the woman who held Mother's precious ring. Stirring impatiently, he snapped, "I don't have time for this sort of thing. Miss Baker-Sneed, just what *do* you think is a fair price?"

"Hm." She took another sip of tea, and his eyes were drawn to her lips where they touched the edge of the cup. The tea damped her lips, a dewiness resting on the pink slopes of her mouth.

A pang of pure lust ripped through him, settling in his nether regions with annoying predictability. Good God, it was senseless. He was reacting to her as if he was a boy of fifteen and not a man grown.

She replaced the cup on the saucer, her movements sure and graceful. "I believe I'd take . . ." She held out her hand and regarded the ring with a speculative gaze. "It *is* an heirloom and there *is* only one . . . Dear me, what a dilemma. Had I more time, I might be able to think of —"

"Just name your price and be done with it!"

She looked at him again through the shadow of those ridiculously long lashes. The little jade. She tapped a finger on her chin. "Hm. If I must give a price . . . shall we say seven?"

"Seven hundred pounds? You must be joking," he said stiffly.

"Oh no." Her voice sifted softly though the air, her thick lashes sweeping down as she blinked. "Not seven hundred. Seven *thousand* pounds."

"Bloody hell!" The words burst from his lips and rang through the room. He glared down at her, his hands fisted at his sides. He was standing, though he didn't remember getting up. "That is outrageous and you know it."

"No," she said almost regretfully. "I don't know that it is outrageous at all. Seven thousand pounds, my lord, or the ring stays mine."

"You are mad if you think I'll pay that much for a blasted ring."

"Then we have nothing more to say to one another." She smiled almost happily, then stood and held out her hand. "Thank you for visiting. I do hope you'll come again when you've more time."

The vixen! Marcus continued to glare down at her, ignoring her outstretched hand. Did she expect him to pay a bloody fortune for his own possession? Frustration welled through him, settling between his shoulder blades.

This was all some sort of fantastical mistake, a misunderstanding of some sort. Yes. That must be what it was. Gathering himself, he resumed his seat. "I am not leaving without that ring."

"And I am not giving it to you for anything less than seven thousand pounds." She returned to her seat as well, adjusting her skirt into graceful folds. "Since you aren't leaving just yet, would you like to try a pastie? They are quite good." She picked up the plate and held it out once again.

He didn't want a damn pastie. Still . . . he gathered his temper and forced himself to relax. It would not do to become emotional. Not now. He selected a pastie from the plate, though he didn't know if he could swallow it without choking.

It was an untenable position. Here he was, reduced to strategizing over something as paltry as a ring. He'd acquired estates — vast ones, in fact — with far less effort. Damn Devon for being so careless with Mother's ring to begin with.

"It's a very pretty pastie, isn't it?"

He realized he'd been staring at his plate an unconscionable time. "Indeed it is." He glanced up at Honoria to find her watching him with a gleam of humor in her hazel eyes. "Almost too pretty to eat."

"Yes, well, as pretty as it is, it tastes even

better." She took a small bite as if to demonstrate, a bit of crust flaking off on her bottom lip. She touched a napkin to her mouth. "Cook is excellent with desserts of all sorts."

"Taste is a matter of opinion."

"So is value, which is often bargained on and more often paid for. That is why your ring has such a large price attached to it — I can tell that you value it highly."

"I should never have admitted what it was," he said bitterly.

"That was indeed an error."

"I didn't realize you'd be so unscrupulous," he retorted. "I will not underestimate you again. I will recognize money-grubbing when I see it."

Any other woman would have been outraged. But Honoria Baker-Sneed merely waved a hand, amusement lurking in her hazel eyes. "Tsk tsk, my dear marquis. The exchange of the ring is a business deal. There is no place for emotion in a business deal." She held out her hand to the beam of sun that cut through the room, light glinting off the etched runes and dancing across her face. "It is quite a pretty piece. I am certain that seven thousand is not unrealistic."

Marcus stopped pretending he was going to eat the pastie. He set the dish back on the table and regarded his hostess with a baleful eye. Of all the people to end up with his ring, why did it have to be this woman? Anyone else would have been pleased, proud, even honored to be of assistance. He certainly wouldn't have minded tossing a favor or even a gold piece or two for their efforts. But the little minx wanted more than a guinea or two; she wanted a blasted fortune.

She tilted her head to one side, a fat sable curl resting at the curve of her neck where it joined her shoulder. "When you consider it, seven thousand pounds is not so very much for you. I've seen you drop that much on a mere tapestry."

He made himself smile, though he felt like doing anything but. "My mother purchased that ring from a gypsy at a fair. She paid two shillings."

"Then your mother was a much better bargainer than you, for I can assure you I will not let it go for so little."

"I will not pay that much for that ring."

She regarded him for a long moment, all amusement gone from her gaze. "You mean that."

He smiled, and he was certain it was not a nice one. "Indeed I do mean it. I will not pay that much for that ring. *However,* I am willing to pay *something,* and whatever it is will be far more than you will get from anyone else."

"I see." She looked down at the ring and then sighed. "That is sad news indeed." A frown curved her lips downward. After a long moment, she said in a slow voice, "Perhaps . . . instead of money . . . perhaps there is something else we can exchange."

"Like what?"

"Well . . ." She bit her lip, her mind obviously flying over the options.

Marcus waited, wondering what she thought he might trade for the ring. Perhaps she wished for one of the tapestries he'd won whilst bidding against her. He considered this for a moment. He really didn't wish to give up one jot of his hard won antiquities, but if it meant getting Mother's ring back —

"The St. Johns are quite well respected in the ton, aren't you?" Her eyes rested on his face in unwavering regard. "You are invited everywhere."

He frowned. What was this? "True. We have never been neglected for any event that I know of."

"You are quite high on all the best guest lists. I daresay you get more invitations than you can possibly accept." She tapped a finger on her chin, as if putting the pieces of a great mystery together.

"I am invited everywhere," he agreed impatiently. "Why?"

"Well, since you seem quite determined not to part with funds —"

"I am quite willing to part with funds; just not seven thousand pounds' worth."

"Hm. Since you will not spend the money, perhaps you'd be willing to spend some of your time." She met his gaze, her eyes a mysterious hazel, rich with speculation.

"Miss Baker-Sneed, just what do you have in mind?"

"Simple. I was thinking about . . . marriage."

For an instant, Marcus thought his ears were deceiving him. But Honoria merely waited, a half smile on her lips, a hard gleam in her eyes. "Marriage?" he asked slowly. "Are you suggesting that if I wish my ring back, I have to marry you?"

To Marcus's utter chagrin, Honoria burst into laughter. "Ye gods, no! That is not at all what I meant. I'm not mad, you know."

Marcus glowered. What the hell did she mean by that? "Explain yourself, woman."

Her brows rose, delicate arches over those damnably intriguing hazel eyes. They were really more green, he realized with great reluctance. Green flecked with gold and brown.

"My lord, I didn't mean for you and I to marry. We would kill each other within a fortnight."

"Or sooner," he said grimly.

"We are in complete accord on that matter, at least," she said, not seeming the least put out by his agreement. "We would not suit at all. Not unless . . ." She regarded him from beneath her lashes, then shrugged. "But that is neither here nor there. It is certainly the last thing I would ever wish to happen, so it would be useless to conjecture."

Marcus knew he should have been glad to hear such words of wisdom tumbling from Miss Baker-Sneed's lips. But somehow it was almost a slap in the face to be dismissed so quickly. "Miss Baker-Sneed —"

"More tea?" The teapot was poised over his already full cup, steam wafting from the arched stem.

"No, thank you. Miss Baker-Sneed, what did you mean by suggesting matrimony for a trade if you didn't mean you and I? Who did you mean?"

"My sister, Cassandra — although not for you. I wish my sister to have all of the advantages of a good marriage, but I find that I have far too few acquaintances in London to arrange such a thing."

Marcus leaned back on the settee. "Oh?"

"Yes. Originally my aunt Caroline was going to chaperone Cassandra and see to it that she was presented as she ought. But something happened . . ."

He waited, brows raised.

"Aunt Caroline's daughters are not — and Cassandra is very — Well, she would have quite overshadowed them as she is . . . shall we say 'taller'?"

"Your cousins are plain and your sister is not."

She gave an obviously relieved sigh. "Yes! I am so glad you are of a quick wit. I did not know how to say that without sounding — For my cousins are sweet natured, if nothing else. Not that it matters, for there are few women as beautiful as Cassandra."

She said it proudly, though he had to wonder. Everyone thought their sister worthy of notice, and while he did not doubt that Cassandra was an attractive female, he doubted she was anything above the ordinary. "I see," he said, and rather thought he did. But still it would not do. "I have neither the time nor the interest to launch your sister onto society, even to save seven thousand pounds."

"Of course, you must do as you see fit. I am not forcing you to do anything,"

Honoria said coolly, not even having the grace to look flustered. "But you should consider my request before you reject it. It is not as if you would have to do much."

"No?"

"How much effort was it to launch your sister, Sara? I believe most of the work went to your aunt."

"You know quite a bit about my family."

"I was presented the same year as your sister and I saw her frequently for a short period of time."

Marcus wondered if he had known that. "I don't seem to recall seeing you at any events —"

"My mother died less than a month into the season and I withdrew. Not that it mattered . . . there wasn't much to remember. I wasn't all that amused by the trappings of society. Cassandra, meanwhile, thrives on them." Honoria brightened. "Would you like to meet my sister? I can assure you that she is very prettily behaved and would be a credit to your name."

"No. I do not need to meet anyone, thank you. For I am not going to agree to such an asinine idea."

"No? It wouldn't be much work for you. I am not asking for a ball or any entertainments, at least not at first."

"Thank you so much," he said dryly.

She grinned. Not smiled, but *grinned,* her soft mouth widening impishly, her eyes crinkled with mirth. Marcus tried to remember when he'd last seen a woman smile so widely — something other than the meek, polite folding of lips most women permitted themselves.

He felt his own lips soften a bit in return. "You seem to find that very amusing."

"Well, I certainly don't expect you to put yourself out too much." Her grin faded and an earnest look entered her eyes. "I am, of course, perfectly willing to pay your aunt for whatever costs she —"

"Let me say this once more: I cannot and will not sponsor your sister, if for no other reason than it would give rise to rumors that would quite kill any hope you have of settling her respectably."

Honoria's cheeks pinkened. "Oh! I never thought — That is, surely people wouldn't think you and Cassandra —"

"They would indeed. So your offer is not very well thought out."

Honoria sighed. How sad, but the lout was right. "That is unfortunate. Now we are right back where we started. I have your ring and you do not agree to my price."

The marquis's expression tightened, his

93

eyes flashing bright blue. He leaned forward and the air instantly thickened. "Miss Baker-Sneed, do not make the mistake of underestimating me. I always get what I want."

The words hung for a moment, cold and cutting. Honoria set down her teacup. "Since you will not agree to my request, then I have no other option but to sell the ring. Perhaps to a man I know in France who collects such objects d'art. Or a countess I know who has a passion for unusual jewelry. Whatever I do with the ring, you will never find it."

"You are a vixen."

She ignored the vivid anger that flashed through his eyes and traced the taut line of his jaw. This was playing with fire and she knew it. But frankly, the fact that the marquis had shown up on their doorstep just as they faced the most horrid financial straits . . . it could only be fate.

Whatever Honoria did, she had to find a way to present Cassandra, and if she couldn't find a sponsor, then a large amount of funds was the next best thing. The thought of good, gentle Cassandra marrying someone far beneath her, someone crass and unworthy, was too horrid to contemplate. Honoria refused to allow that to happen.

With a renewed purpose, she met the marquis's furious gaze and shrugged. "I believe our meeting is at an end." She stood. "Now if you'll excuse me, I have matters to attend to that will wait no longer." With that, she etched a faint curtsy and turned to leave.

Marcus could only stare. She had refused him and now she was leaving — walking away as if his concerns were of no moment. Anger surged through him, bold and hot. He stepped forward, blocking her way. "I am not yet through talking to you."

"No?" she said.

"No," he snapped.

She turned and walked around the chair, out of his reach. "That's a pity, for I am through talking to you."

He would never remember stepping around the chair. Would have only the faintest recollection of catching her arm and pinioning her about to face him. But what he would remember in agonizing detail would be the way he scooped her against him and held her there, imprisoned against his chest. He'd just meant to hold her, keep her there and stop her from leaving. But as she settled against his chest and he felt the warmth of her body against his, something happened. Instead of just holding her, he kissed her.

His anger kept him from being gentle. It was meant to be a punishing kiss, one destined to teach a lesson in sorely needed comportment. And at first it was just that — punishing. But his anger, which had so quickly surged, melted almost instantly in an onslaught of heated lust.

Never before had he been aware of how closely related lust and anger were. They were both primitive, intense emotions that robbed one of coherent thought and often led to extreme sorts of actions, like deeply passionate, mindless kisses.

Marcus wasn't sure if it was because of the unadulterated lust, or because for one small second he had succeeded in silencing the divinely irritating Miss Baker-Sneed, but the kiss ignited a response that began in his toes and ended in more interesting places. To his surprise, the embrace seemed to have the same effect on his companion, for after a stiff moment, she moaned against his mouth and fell against him, her mouth opening beneath his, her body soft and pliant.

It was madness. Crazed madness. Yet he could not stop. He was primed and ready by the time she gathered herself enough to grab his arms and push herself free.

He immediately let her go, his mind and

body awhirl. To his bemusement, Miss High and Mighty Baker-Sneed actually staggered back a step, her face flushed, her lips swollen and pink. She had to clutch a small tea table for support. The small candy dish and the globe on the lamp rattled as her weight rocked the table.

Marcus would have been glad for some extra support himself. He felt as weak-kneed as an hour old colt. His heart pounded in his ears, his chest ached as if he'd been running, his entire body was as taut as a finely drawn bow.

"That — That was not necessary." She brushed her mouth with the back of her hand.

For some reason the childish gesture brought a smile to his lips and he realized that it had been a long, long while since he'd had such a reaction to a woman — to any woman, in fact. "I think it was very necessary. And pleasant, too. Damned pleasant."

"I didn't wish you to kiss me."

"And I didn't wish you to leave." He crossed his arms over his chest, feeling strangely pleased with himself. B'God, he'd shown her. Better yet, the instant reaction had intrigued him. There was something damned taking about the little Miss Baker-

Sneed. Something that begged for more investigation. "I'd say we were even."

"And I'd say you are an ass."

He lifted his brows. "What did you call me?"

"An ass. The braying, bullying kind." Her gaze raked him up and down. "Is this how you get your women? By force?"

Marcus shrugged. "I have never had to force a woman to do anything."

"Oh? You forced me to kiss you."

"Forced? You didn't make a single protest — not a one. Had you done so, I would have released you immediately. Furthermore, by the end, you were kissing me just as much as I was kissing you."

Her color bloomed brighter. "You surprised me. I didn't have time to register a complaint."

"Because you didn't have one to register. You liked that kiss. Admit it."

Her nose couldn't climb any higher. "I will admit no such thing. In fact, I will go so far as to say that I didn't like that kiss and hope it is never repeated."

His brows rose, a faint smile warming him. "Oh? Never?"

She shook her head. "Never."

"That sounds like a challenge. A delightful challenge, at that." He took a step toward her, and she scrambled away as if chased by flames. Marcus chuckled. "I didn't steal a kiss from you. I only borrowed one."

"I call it theft."

"Well then . . . if that's true, then I must make restitution."

She eyed him uncertainly, and it dawned on him that it nonplused her that he was suddenly in such a good mood. That made him grin the more. "If I stole a kiss from you, then I should give it back." He leaned forward, his gaze drawn to her lips. "Tell me, my dear, obstinate Miss Baker-Sneed, would you like to have your kiss returned to you now? Or shall we wait until a more auspiciously private time?"

Outrage heated her cheeks and sent a hot sparkle to her eyes. "You can't give a kiss back!"

He moved closer. "Are you certain?"

She bustled to the opposite side of the chair, all prim outrage and adorable flush. "You, my lord, are incorrigible."

"Only when someone denies me that which I want."

"I do not give kisses to everyone."

His lips twitched. "I was talking about my ring."

Her gaze fell to her hand. "Oh."

Was that a note of disappointment in her voice? Marcus decided not to find out. Not yet, anyway. The ring was why he was here and, tempting as it was, he didn't need to become distracted by something as silly as a kiss, even a hot and passionate one. If he wanted that blasted ring back, he would have to move very, very carefully. "I have made a decision."

"Oh?"

"I will consider your request for the seven thousand pounds."

Miss Baker-Sneed's amazing eyes brightened. "Yes?"

"In the meantime, I want your word that you will not sell that ring to anyone else."

Her gaze grew dark as she considered his proposal. "You will consider it? Seriously consider it?"

"Yes." Though it would take very little time to realize it was an impossible idea. He'd be damned if he'd pay so much for so little. "But while I am considering the idea, you will not sell the ring and will keep it safe."

Her lips pursed absently. "I suppose . . . Very well. But I will not wait forever. One week should do it."

He bowed, glad to have won that concession. "One week it is, then. Until then, good day, Miss Baker-Sneed. And thank you for the incredibly tasty . . ." His gaze lingered on her lips. ". . . pastie." With a bow, he turned on his heel and left, already working through a variety of plans that might give him back his ring as well as prolonging his contact with the thoroughly amusing Miss Baker-Sneed.

Perhaps this day hadn't been so wasted after all.

Chapter 5

What did I do while Albermaryle was out of town? I, ah, well, I — I moved the bed. Yes, I moved it from one end of the room to the other and oh, it looks much better now! You know, that's what I do every time he's out of town; I just move that bed all over the place.

Lady Albermaryle to her mother-in-law, the rather imposing Lady Southland, while waiting for Lord Albermaryle's return

White's Gentleman's Club was one of the more stolid bastions of male society. It was an amalgamation of dark paneling, large leather seats, excellent port, and all of the

other comforts necessary to men in general. To secure this masculine paradise, no daintily slippered females were allowed within its hallowed halls.

Anthony pushed back his plate and sighed. Roasted duck with mint jelly was usually his favorite, but somehow, without Anna and the children, his meal had seemed rather tasteless. The sad truth was that he missed his family. They had all gone north with Anna's grandfather for a tour of the lakes, and here he was, feeling like a pebble in a very empty box.

He took a drink of port and wondered if he could hurry his business in town and then join his family. They would be surprised and pleased, especially Anna. He pictured her face, her remarkable gray eyes and the rich shimmer of her red hair. A faint ache filled his heart. Somehow, over the course of the two years since they'd wed, he'd become rather addicted to seeing her face across his dinner table. How strange that happened.

A stir arose near the door, and Anthony watched as Marcus made his way toward the table. Everyone bowed or nodded, and Anthony reflected that it was strange how people just naturally seemed to defer to his oldest half brother. Marcus carried himself with an unconscious air of command . . . but it was more than that. It was a streak of unequivocal integrity. One knew just by looking at Marcus that not only was he strong and capable, but he was honest and forthright as well.

"The man's a bloody angel," Anthony murmured to himself. A dark angel, one given to a snappish temper, but an angel nonetheless.

Marcus reached the table. "I thought I'd find you here."

Anthony gestured toward an empty seat. "Have you eaten?"

"No, but I'm not hungry. However, I will have some of that port."

Anthony took an empty glass and splashed a small amount into the bottom from the flagon that rested by his elbow. "Here you are."

Marcus took a slow drink. "Excellent."

"So I thought, which is why I ordered more to be brought as soon as this was done." He eyed his brother, wondering what mood he might be in. Lately, one could never tell. "Well? Did you retrieve Mother's ring?"

A flicker of a smile crossed Marcus's face.

"Ah! You did!" Anthony sighed happily. "Finally we can put that —"

"You misunderstand. I found the ring but it is not in my possession." Marcus swirled the port in his glass, a thoughtful expression in his eyes. "Yet."

Anthony lowered his glass, wondering what to make of that. Marcus had been deadly set on getting that ring back. Yet now his brother sat across from him, seemingly unmoved by his lack of success. "You must explain . . . where did you find it?"

To Anthony's utter surprise, a slow smile lifted the corners of his brother's mouth. "Just as I predicted, Miss Baker-Sneed has Mother's ring."

"And?"

"And she won't return it."

"Bloody hell! Did you offer to purchase it?"

"Indeed I did. I offered two hundred pounds."

Anthony frowned. "That's a bit steep."

"Not according to Miss Baker-Sneed. I made the mistake of admitting that the ring was an heirloom and before I knew it, she'd demanded seven thousand pounds for it."

Anthony set his glass back on the table. "I beg your pardon . . . my ears must be closed. Did you say that she asked for seven *thousand* pounds for Mother's ring?"

Marcus chuckled. "Audacious wench, isn't she?"

"Bloody hell! What did you tell her?"

"Why, no, of course. Then she made another offer."

"What did she want this time? A coach and six? A castle on the Thames? A fleet of ships?"

"No," Marcus said slowly. "She wanted me to sponsor her sister for a season."

Anthony leaned forward, his chair creaking slightly at the shift of his weight. "You must be joking."

"No, I'm not." A glint of amusement lit Marcus's eyes. "But don't worry, I was not expected to host any large events, like a ball. Not at first, anyway."

"The audacity! What did you say?"

"No. Can you imagine what people would say if I agreed to such a thing?"

"That you had your eye on the sister and had most likely already sampled the goods."

"Exactly. I pointed that out to Miss Baker-Sneed — not in those words, of course — and she agreed that such a thing was an impossibility. Which left us back where we were, at the seven thousand pounds."

"An impasse."

"Exactly."

Anthony considered this, laughing a little as he did so. "To think of you, attending balls and soirees and musicales and all sorts of unpleasant events."

Marcus frowned. "I attend those now."

"Only when you must, which is rare enough. When Anna was last in town, she said she didn't see you more than twice in a fortnight. You've become a bit of a recluse, you know."

"I have not. It's just that I get no enjoyment out of such silliness. But I am hardly a hermit."

"Hm. Well. I can only say that Miss Baker-Sneed must not know you well to think you'd concede to such a troublesome request. Better to ask you to become a sheepherder as expect to see your unsmiling face at a number of society functions."

Anthony's slow smile irked Marcus for some reason. "I would go to more functions did they provide some sort of amusement. The last ten balls I have attended were noxiously similar, all offering indifferent refreshments, pallid musical entertainments, and vapid conversation. I was left with nothing to do but talk to some insipid females who could do nothing more than bleat 'Yes, my lord' and 'No, my lord.' It was enough to make one ill."

Anthony's smile widened. "Got caught by some marriage-minded misses, eh?"

"Indeed I did. Although how they thought that simpering in such an outrageous fashion and agreeing with every word I said would do anything but make me want to turn on my heels and leave, I do not know."

Anthony chuckled. "Poor man. I feel your agony. I quite remember how horrid it was before Anna saved me from all of those desperate mamas and giggling debutantes."

"What is worse is that they seem to believe that if I have one quiet moment to myself, I will disappear . . . which is probably quite true."

"There is only one way you can avoid such painful treatment. Get married."

Marcus didn't smile.

"It was just a suggestion." Anthony smiled his sleepy smile and leaned back in his chair, regarding Marcus over the rim of his glass. "Of course, if you had agreed to sponsor the younger Baker-Sneed chit, you could have gone to balls and sat amongst the other chaperones."

"Are you finished trying to be funny? This is a serious matter. The very troublesome Miss Baker-Sneed could very easily sell Mother's ring to someone else."

Anthony sat upright. "She wouldn't!"

"Indeed she would. She has more than

enough contacts to do so, some in other countries. We'd never find it then."

"Did she threaten to do that?"

"Yes. So I asked her to give me a week to think on her proposal."

"And in a week?"

Marcus stared at his glass. "I don't know, but I shall think of something."

"You sound sure."

"I am sure. I cannot afford for it to be otherwise." Silence surrounded them. After a moment, Marcus looked at his half brother. "Well? Don't you have something to say?"

"Me?" Anthony asked, his tone mild, though his brown eyes were lit with amusement. "What could I possibly add to that?"

"Blast it, Anthony! I know you have something to say."

"It seems to me as if fate is saying it for you."

"I knew you'd start back on that. It is not fate, but ill luck and I refuse to call it else."

Anthony shrugged. "Have it your way."

"Ass."

"I come from a long line of asses, my dearest brother."

"*Half* brother."

"I suppose that makes me half an ass." Anthony shrugged. "I can't argue with that."

Marcus sighed. "This is not funny."

"Of course," Anthony answered promptly. "It's not funny at all. I wasn't laughing at you. Oh no. I was merely laughing at, ah . . . what was that woman's name?"

"Honoria Baker-Sneed."

"Yes. That's who I was laughing at. She is in for quite a surprise. To find herself married to such a pompous, ill-tempered, overly ambitious man will be quite horrid for the poor woman. The worst joke in the world."

"If that's what you think of me, then why do I constantly find your large carcass draped over my favorite chair in my study?"

Anthony silently held up his glass of port. "As tolerable as this port is, it is nothing compared to that found in your cellar."

"Thank you," Marcus said caustically. "Thank you very much."

"Think nothing of it." Anthony sighed deeply. "What other exciting projects do you have going on?"

"Well . . . I need to gain an interview with Lord Melton and ascertain the extent of the east boundaries on his properties."

Anthony appeared surprised. "What? You are purchasing Melton's holdings?"

"His gaming debts have become too much." Marcus stretched his legs before him, smiling a little as he did so. "A week ago, I offered to purchase Melton's estates and he agreed."

Anthony regarded him a moment, a frown resting between his brows. "There is no need to take such pleasure in another man's misfortune."

Marcus shot his brother a disbelieving look. "I take no pleasure in the man's fall. I do, however, feel some satisfaction at adding such a gem to our own coffers. Surely there is nothing wrong with that. If he's been so foolish as to squander his fortune, why shouldn't I benefit?"

Anthony sighed. "I suppose. It's just that I've always liked Melton."

"So have I. But that does not excuse his irresponsible actions."

"No. I only thought —" Anthony sank into silence. After a moment he shrugged. "I suppose you are right. I hope he is not in desperate case."

"He did not like it, but he really has no choice, and I put out a goodly amount to settle his more pressing debts. All in all, it is a good bargain for us both."

"I daresay he is thankful, then."

"Hardly. Now he avoids me like the plague, which is damnably inconvenient."

"Then how will you get the information you need about the boundaries?"

"I will track him to his lair."

"His home?"

"Men like Melton cannot be found tucked snuggly into their bed. No, he resides more oft at the gaming table. I shall attend Lady Oxbridge's ball on Thursday. The Oxbridges always have a gaming room and the stakes are high, thanks to Lord Oxbridge. Melton will not be able to resist the temptation. Besides, I rarely attend such functions; he will think himself safe."

"Damn it, Marcus! You sound like —" Anthony shook his head, all of his previous lazy smiles gone.

"What?"

"There is a note in your voice — you enjoy this, taking from men like Melton."

"Perhaps. But so what? It's not as if I forced them to make idiots of themselves."

"There was a time when you were more compassionate that that."

Marcus eyed his brother for a long moment. "I wasn't aware that you thought so poorly of me."

"I don't," Anthony said. "It's just that lately . . ." He hesitated, sending a careful glance at Marcus.

It was the caution in that usually friendly gaze that gave Marcus pause. Bloody hell, surely he hadn't been *that* ill tempered of late? Or had he? "Spit it out. I can tell it's not pleasant, so just say it."

"No. I don't wish to —"

"Say it, damn it!"

Anthony's jaw tightened as he set his glass on the table, his eyes shadowed. "Very well. I fear that your success has tainted you in some way. You are filled with pride, Marcus. And not without reason, for you've managed to build a fortune few could ever hope to emulate. But it's taken its toll. You're . . . harder somehow, colder. And I am not the only one who has noticed."

Bloody hell, of all the things to say! Marcus found his hand had clenched so tightly about his glass that it was a wonder it hadn't broken. He forced himself to loosen his grip and set the glass on the table. "You make it sound as if you've been discussing me."

Anthony's face flushed. "We've been worried."

An icy coldness settled in Marcus's heart. "Are you finished?"

"No. There's something else."

"I can hardly wait."

"You've become damnably judgmental. I think it's time you stepped back and realized that no one is perfect. Not even you."

Marcus stood so suddenly that the table

skirted back an inch. "I don't have to listen to this."

"No," Anthony agreed, sagging back in his chair as if suddenly exhausted, a dashed expression on his face. "You don't have to listen to anything."

"Good day, Anthony." Marcus turned to leave, but Anthony's hand shot out and gripped his wrist.

Marcus looked down at his brother.

Anthony's eyes darkened. "I'm sorry. But it had to be said. We've all been — We're worried. That's all."

Marcus shook off Anthony's grip. "Do me a great favor, will you? Spare me any more of your worry. I don't like it and I don't need it."

With that, he turned and left, barely acknowledging those who bowed or called out greetings. Bloody hell, what was that all about? Disturbed more than he would admit, Marcus made his way to his carriage, wondering if the entire world had set out to thwart him today.

Two days later, Honoria sat in the sitting room with her sisters. It was a charming tableau, a fact she might have noticed had she not been so sunk in thought as to be oblivious to her surroundings. Cassandra, who was sitting beside Honoria on the sofa, had attempted to ask no less than three questions about the embroidery that sat unattended in Honoria's lap. Upon receiving no reply the final time, Cassandra had sighed and quietly given up.

But Portia, who was far less patient, had broken off pacing the room with a book balanced on her head in an effort to learn how to appear taller while walking, planted herself firmly before Honoria and then said in a very loud voice, "Are you asleep?"

Honoria had jumped, her embroidery hoop thudding to the rug at her feet. Heart pounding at such a rude recall, she'd pressed a hand to her thudding heart. "Ye gods, Portia! You gave me such a start!"

"Cassandra and I both have tried to get your attention and you've been staring off into the distance as if in a trance," Portia said, having to look down her nose at Honoria or else lose the book perched upon her head. "I was beginning to think you'd expired whilst sitting upright and just hadn't yet fallen over."

"Portia," Cassandra said, a faint note of reproof in her sweet voice. "How can you suggest such a thing?"

Olivia looked up from where she sat at the escritoire, ink stains on her fingers from penning a poem entitled "The Mighty Frigate of the Sea." "Cassandra, I don't know why that surprises you. You know how Portia is always looking at the dark side of life." Olivia gave Portia an approving look. "It's one of her best features."

"Thank you," Portia said, managing a curtsy that set the book rocking in a most precarious fashion.

"Dark side of life or no, it was unpleasant for Portia to say such a thing about Honoria," Cassandra said in a faintly disapproving tone. She glanced at Honoria. "I'm certain our sister has much weighing upon her mind."

Honoria did indeed have weighty issues on her mind. Issues like a heated, passionate and extremely inappropriate kiss. A kiss that she couldn't seem to stop thinking about.

Oh not constantly, of course. There were times when she almost forgot. Why yesterday, while helping Mrs. Kemble take inventory of the linens, Honoria hadn't thought of the kiss for a full twenty-two minutes. Then this morning, while searching for a larger hatbox for poor Achilles, she didn't think about the marquis or his blasted kiss for almost thirteen minutes and a half. Of course, none of those few moments of respite were much help when every other waking moment — and worse, every sleeping moment as well — were filled with a confusing array of memories and thoughts.

She supposed it was a good thing she'd received such a disturbing kiss now, while she was older and more in charge of her feelings. For certainly, had she experienced such a thing while younger — Cassandra's age or less — she might have thought herself attracted to the marquis. Which was a laughable thought indeed.

And had she been of an earlier age, such rubbishing thoughts could well have confused her into thinking that love, and possibly even marriage, were in her future; all thoughts she'd long ago put to rest.

Honoria absently turned the talisman ring on her finger, staring at the glittering runes. She didn't know what her destiny was, only that it was far more than mere marriage. While such a state seemed to have suited her mother when she'd been alive, and seemed to be Cassandra's only dream, Honoria wanted more. Over the years, she'd found her purpose in life beyond merely taking care of her family, and that was her true love of antiquities. For Honoria, they were more than mere objects. They were memories of history, of a time gone by, of people who'd lived and died and had left reminders of their passage.

By collecting antiquities, she was preserving a living reminder of those people and their talents. And that was far more important than merely being married and devoting oneself to making certain someone else's cravats had enough starch. Of course, with the marquis, there would be more to life than just cravats, if that kiss was anything to set store by.

The memory of the kiss tickled her lips and made her smile. No matter what one might wish to say about Treymount, he was certainly talented in —

"Honoria?" Juliet sat, feet curled beneath her in the largish chair by the fire, reading a book about horse care. But now her eyes were fastened on Honoria. "Do you feel well? It isn't like you to be so quiet."

Portia tilted her head and let her book slide into her hands. "It is especially not like you to stare at that ring in such a fashion. What *are* you thinking about so seriously?"

Honoria realized that her sisters were all staring at her, various shades of concern on their faces. She sighed. "I was just dozing with my eyes open."

Four flat, unimpressed stares met this blatant falsehood.

Honoria sighed irritably. "Oh very well! If you must know, I have been thinking about the marquis who came to call a few days ago."

Portia tossed the book onto a table and pulled a chair up so that she was facing Honoria. "I was so hoping you'd tell us what he wanted!"

"She did," Cassandra said. "He came inquiring about his ring."

"There has to be something more," Portia said, staring intently at Honoria. "Or she wouldn't be so distracted."

Honoria sighed. "I suppose I might as well tell you all. It's true that this ring is Treymount's. It's also true that I asked for a fortune and he would not agree. However, while bargaining with him, it dawned on me that there was something he possessed that would be of far more importance at this moment than funds."

"More important than money?" Olivia looked up from her foolscap and blinked. "Whatever could that be?"

"His standing in society. I thought that if he would but agree to sponsor Cassandra, all our troubles would be over. After all, once Ned and Father return with the new shipment and we can sell it through the shop, all will be well for the rest of us. But Cassandra must have her season now."

Color flooded Cassandra's face and she dipped her head, her golden hair gleaming softly. "Oh, Honoria! You didn't!"

Honoria's cheeks heated to match Cassandra's. "I did," she said a little defensively. "But don't worry; he refused. He pointed out quite correctly that it would not be at all the thing." She sighed heavily. "It seemed like the perfect plan."

"I daresay he receives twice the invitations as Aunt Caroline," Portia conceded.

Olivia lifted a silver etched sandbox and shook it gently over her new poem, the thirsty grains rapidly drinking up the extra ink and drying it. "Well, it is a perfectly excellent plan, though I must say I can see there are shoals along that route."

Honoria propped her elbow on her knee and rested her chin in her hand. "So we're back to the money, which can come in quite handy yet. But . . . I have not heard from the marquis for several days."

"Oh! Do you think he has lost interest in regaining his ring?"

"No," Honoria said, running her fingers over the warmed silver band that graced her hand. "I think he is playing with me . . .

hoping I'll get desperate for the funds and reduce my request."

Cassandra smiled. "He does not know you well."

"No, he does not. Perhaps it is time to up the stakes, as it were. I need to show his high-and-mighty lordship that a Baker-Sneed is not to be trifled with." She frowned. "All I need is to find one other person who might have an interest in the ring, and Treymount will be forced to accede."

The door opened and Mrs. Kemble bustled in, followed by a small, slight man with a wizened face. "Miss Honoria, Becket from the stables wishes to speak to you."

"Excellent!" Honoria said. And for the first time in two days, her heart lifted. She waited for Mrs. Kemble to leave before she said, "Yes, Mr. Becket?"

Their onetime coachman hurriedly pulled his hat from his head and began to wring it between his hands. He was a thin, smallish man with a permanently red face from being outside all of his life. He glanced uneasily about the room. "Miss Baker-Sneed, may I have a word with ye?"

"You may just tell me whatever you wish," Honoria said. "My sisters have an interest in your efforts."

"Very well, miss. I was watchin' his lordship the way ye asked me to —"

"Oh Honoria!" Portia cried, giving an excited hop. "You had Becket *watch* the marquis! How clever!"

"There's no culling to portside with Honoria," Olivia agreed. She smiled at Becket. "Pray continue!"

Beaming at the attention, he slipped his thumbs into his pockets and began his tale. "Well now, I been hidin' by his house, don't ye know. And fer two days all he's done is go to his house and then to his warehouse down by the docks and then to his solicitor's office and then to White's and then to —"

"Mr. Becket, did you discover what I asked you to?"

Becket flushed even darker, a smile curving his thin lips. "Indeed I did, miss! On arrivin' home from White's, I heard him tell his coachman that he'd be going back out. And this time to a ball. At the Ox—" Becket frowned. "What was that name again? Ox—" He bit his lip.

"Oxford's?" Portia looked at Honoria. "The Duke of Oxford, perhaps?"

Becket shook his head. "No. It weren't that. It was Ox— something with a B, I do believe."

"Ah!" Cassandra said, brightening. "The

Oxbridges! That is where Aunt Caroline is attending a ball this very evening. Cousin Jane told me so this morning when I saw her at the lending library."

Honoria stood, forgetting about her embroidery. This was it; the opportunity she'd been waiting for. It was time to remind her potential client that though she'd promised to give him a week to make up his mind about her offer, there were indeed other fish in the sea. Fish that might well be interested in possessing something near and dear to the hearts of the St. Johns. "Thank you, Becket. You have been a great help."

"Ah there, it weren't nothin' at all." Yet he looked pleased as he bowed and left.

As soon as the door shut behind him, Honoria turned to her sister. "Cassandra, could you braid my hair? Juliet, you are the best with the flat iron. I shall have need of your assistance. And Portia, may I borrow your pearl necklet?"

"What about me?" Olivia protested.

"You shall write a letter to Aunt Caroline and ask if I may go to the ball as her guest. She feels quite wretched about not assisting Cassandra, so I do not think she'll refuse us this one request."

Juliet leaned forward, her eyes wide. "What are you going to do?"

"Why, I am going to a ball. The very one his lordship is attending. Once there, I shall make certain the marquis does not forget that the Baker-Sneeds have something he dearly desires. Something that is only a few days from being sold right from beneath his very nose."

Smiling at her sisters, Honoria swept to the door, a satisfying rustle drifting through the air behind her as the room came to life. "Come, all! We've not a moment to lose!"

Chapter 6

Pray have a care with your pins, you wretch! It would be one thing to lose my head for political reasons — that would at least put a pretty epitaph upon my grave, which has been a life-long goal of mine. But I will be damned if I will die over something as uninteresting as a misplaced hair pin!

Lady Southland to her new French maid, while allowing that rather inept individual to arrange my lady's hair *à la Sappho*

The gown of blue watered silk opened over an undergown of white sarcenet embroidered with tiny pink and blue flowers. The small sleeves puffed at the shoulder, revealing Honoria's slender arms, while the rounded neckline emphasized her graceful neck. All in all, it was a well enough gown for her purpose.

"There. How do I look?" Honoria held her arms out to her sides and turned to her audience.

George looked up from where he sat on the floor by the dresser, ankles crossed before him, Achilles safely tucked in his coat pocket. "Must you wear such a silly gown? All those flowers and such." He made a face. "I like your regular gowns better."

"Oh hush, George!" Juliet said reprovingly. "Honoria looks beautiful and you know it."

Portia pursed her lips thoughtfully. "The tiara is a nice touch. Set amidst so many curls, no one would suspect it is made of paste."

"Considering it is on *my* head, everyone will *know* it is made of paste," Honoria said dryly. "The Baker-Sneeds may be related to half the ton, but only the less fortunate half."

Cassandra sighed. "It's true. If good breeding was all it took, we'd be wealthy."

"We don't need wealth," Honoria said. "Although I must admit I would not complain if such a thing came to pass."

"We will be just fine once Honoria gets the marquis to come about," Portia said stoutly. "And then Cassandra can land a wealthy, well-connected husband and sponsor the rest of us and we can *all* find wealthy husbands."

"Portia, I will not marry simply for money," Cassandra said in gentle reproof.

"Of course you won't," Honoria said. "But if you are to fall in love, it might be just as easy to love a wealthy man as a poor one."

"That is a very good way of looking at things," Olivia said thoughtfully. "All one really needs is the opportunity."

"Exactly," Honoria said. "Well? Am I ready? Aunt Caroline said she'd send the carriage for me at eight and it is a quarter 'til now."

"You look wonderful," Cassandra said in her gentle voice. "But . . . you wear brighter colors so much better than I do. You really should get a gown of red, although I daresay that would not be proper."

Honoria smiled. "One day, I shall wear red. See if I don't, and to Hades to all the nay-sayers!"

Olivia sighed enviously. "I wish I could wear a ball gown and go to a real ball."

"You are all mad," George said, shaking his head. "Nothing could be more insipid than standing around a room, trussed in gewgaws and finery."

Honoria smiled down at her brother. "You'll change your tune in a few years, my dear."

"I will not." George pulled Achilles out of his pocket and placed the frog on the tip of his knee. "Achilles and I have no need for such silliness."

"Yes well, I'm just glad Aunt Caroline was so accommodating," Cassandra said.

Honoria preferred not to think about how difficult it had been to wrestle the invitation from Aunt Caroline. They'd exchanged several volleys of notes before the old bat had agreed to allow Honoria to attend the ball. Her aunt was suspicious of Honoria's sudden interest in society and was positively determined to keep Cassandra from bursting upon the social scene and stealing the thunder from her own daughter.

Not that Cousin Jane would really suffer . . . Cassandra's rare beauty would draw earls and dukes and marquises, not a one of which would ever pay Aunt Caroline's poor daughter the slightest heed. Honoria had been forced to swear to her aunt that the invitation was for her only. To further throw her aunt off the scent, Honoria had concocted a story about Treymount admiring a certain object d'art and her hopes to gain his interest in it. Which was, now that she thought about it, not so very far from the truth.

"It's a wonder Aunt Caroline helped at all," Portia said, twisting her face into a moue of distaste.

Olivia sniffed. "Especially after she quite dashed poor Cassandra's hopes."

"She didn't dash my hopes at all," Cassandra said. "But I am glad she furnished Honoria with the invitation, although . . . Honoria, are you certain this is necessary?"

Honoria faced herself in the mirror, turning first this way and then that. "It is important to keep the ring in front of the not-so-merry marquis or he'll decide to merely wait us out. If I can whet his appetite, he might just go ahead and purchase the blasted ring outright. Then all we'd need is an invitation or two. It would not take much at all, for Cassandra is so very pretty."

Cassandra flushed. "I am no prettier than you. But I must question the wisdom of teasing the marquis so. Flashing the ring before him is certain to garner his ire. And Mrs. Kemble said he was quite a stern, unsmiling man."

"Oh pother! Let him be irked unto

death." Honoria adjusted her paste tiara so it twinkled a bit more from between the curls piled on her head. "Facing a worthy adversary will do him a world of good. And I intend on being very, very good at opposing him. At least until he agrees to do as I have asked."

Olivia chuckled. "If he thinks to outwit you, he'll be sadly mistaken. You never could back down from a challenge."

Juliet glanced up from where she sat curled on Honoria's bed with her book. "Much to her detriment. Remember the time I told her she couldn't swim across the lake and she —"

"Yes," Honoria said, "and we don't wish to hear that tired story again, thank you very much."

"I'd like to hear it again," Olivia said.

Honoria eyed her sourly. "You would."

Cassandra quickly intervened. "Fortunately for us all, Honoria has matured and can easily turn from a challenge now."

"Oh?" Juliet asked, her eyes twinkling with laughter. "What about last month when —"

"Oh enough!" Honoria said, throwing up her hands. "Pray do not bring up every time I have lost my temper and agreed to some foolhardy task! It is a failing of mine, I agree.

But I am much better than I used to be, and that is what matters."

Cassandra shook her head. "I certainly hope so. I just hope that this time, with the marquis, you are not going too far. Can you not just write the man a letter and ask for another interview?"

"And make him think I've been sitting here, waiting on him for the last two days? No. I cannot do that. It will make me look desperate, and I am most definitely not." Honoria gathered a shimmering wrap of silver that mirrored the silvered tips of her slippers, suddenly realizing that she'd not thought of the marquis's devastating kiss the entire time she'd been dressing. It was yet another sign that she was doing the right thing. "I believe I am ready," she said, drawing on her long gloves. "And while I appreciate all the concern you've been showing, please be aware that if there is one thing I understand, it is how to drive a bargain."

"That's true," Olivia said. "Ned always said that Honoria was up to every rig and row in town and that he'd rather be eaten by one of those horrid snakes in Africa than face her on the auction floor." She frowned. "I only wonder what he'd say about the marquis?"

Honoria fastened the small pearl button at the top of her gloves. "The problem with Treymount is that life has given him his way far too often and it has made him a little too certain of himself. Rather like an overfed lion, he thinks he has but to glare and we will all fall dead before him, ready to be eaten at his leisure."

Cassandra stood and adjusted a ribbon at Honoria's shoulder. "That sounds horrid, to be sure."

"Oh, not really. Once I arrive at the ball, I shall twinkle the ring beneath his nose. Not much, but enough that he sees it. And then . . ." Honoria rubbed the silver ring with one finger through the thin material of her gloves, smiling at the warmth that tingled through her hand and arm.

"And then?" Cassandra prompted.

"And then I shall dance with Lord Radmere."

"Who is that?" Portia asked.

"Merely the largest collector of antique jewelry in all of Britain. It will drive the marquis mad to see his family heirloom being admired by Radmere."

Cassandra sighed. "It sounds like a good plan, but I —"

"Oh dear, the time! I must be off!" Honoria gave her reflection one last glance and then she dropped a kiss on the cheeks of each of her sisters and gave George a quick hug. "Wish me luck, my dears. I go to war, you know. Not a ball."

"Pull anchor and heave the sails!" Olivia said, giving her sister a mock salute. "Canvas well!"

Portia grabbed up the poker by the fireplace and held it aloft like a sword. "For God and country!"

Georgie held a startled Achilles over his head. "Take no quarter!"

Olivia laughed. "Win, Honoria. And if there is some cake at the ball . . . perhaps you can wrap some up and put it in your reticule?" She rubbed her hands together, a beatific smile on her face. "I do so love cake."

"I shall do what I can. Now good night, my pretties. Don't wait up." With a flip of her hand and a smile, Honoria set out to make certain the annoying Marquis of Treymount did not forget that she possessed something he wanted very, very badly.

Marcus walked into the foyer of Treymount House, smoothing the sleeve of his evening coat. "Jeffries, has the carriage been brought around?"

Jeffries's usually stern countenance almost froze into a grimace. "Ah . . . no, my lord."

Marcus paused. "No?" he said softly. "Did I not request it?"

The butler glanced uncertainly at the door behind Marcus. "Yes, you did. However, I can explain, my lord."

Marcus raised his brows.

"Do not burn Jeffries with one of your fierce looks," came a laughing voice from behind Marcus.

He turned to find Brandon standing in the entryway. "Well, a visit from one of my esteemed brothers."

Brandon's amused expression faded, confusion evident on his face. "What —"

"Nothing." What was wrong with him that he was snapping at everyone? "Have you talked to Anthony?"

"Not since Thursday. Why? Should I —"

"No, no." Marcus managed a smile, leading the way to the library. "Never mind. I am just at odds this evening. So tell me, brother of mine, is it your fault my carriage is not yet ready?"

"Yes, it is. I came to ask for your assistance, but I can see you are on your way out —" Brandon's eyes widened and he came to a sudden halt. "You are dressed in formal attire. Did someone die?"

"No. I am on my way to a ball."

"I thought you gave up on social occasions years ago."

There it was, that hint that something was wrong with him. Marcus had to count to ten before he replied, "I do get invited out, you know. I have never been a hermit."

"Yes, but you so rarely accept any of the hundreds of invitations that come your way. I don't think I've seen you dressed in such a manner in months."

"Did you want something?" Marcus asked, beyond irritated. He glanced at his reflection in the wide mirror over the large fireplace that graced one end of the library and adjusted his cravat. First Anthony and now Brandon. It was annoying, but . . . Marcus sighed. Perhaps he *should* listen a bit more closely; they were his brothers, after all.

Jeffries held up the evening coat. "My lord?"

Marcus waved him away. "I shall not be leaving immediately. Brandon, stay have a seat."

Brandon waited until Jeffries had closed the door before facing Marcus. "I hate to do this but . . . I must ask a favor. Verena's father is in trouble."

"How unfortunate. I don't see how that

affects either of us, but Mr. Landsdowne has my sympathies."

Brandon frowned. "Marcus, it's not that simple. I must go and see what I can do to fix the situation. He apparently ran afoul of the local authorities and then took an illness. I must sort out the paperwork and then get him back to England."

"Why must you do such a thing?" Marcus poured two glasses of port and carried one to Brandon. "He's not your father, after all. I believe he has several other daughters, and a son, too, if I remember correctly."

Exasperation crossed Brandon's face. "It's Verena's father, which makes him my responsibility as well as hers. If you were married, you would understand —"

"If I was married —" Somewhere in the back of his memory, he could almost hear Anthony's voice accusing him of being judgmental. He took a sip of port and then made himself comfortable in a chair by the gentle crackle of the fire. "I'm sorry. I spoke out of turn. As you were saying?"

Brandon blinked as if surprised. After a moment, he shook his head and settled into the chair opposite Marcus's. "I don't think you understand. I know what my responsibilities are, even if you don't."

"Hm. Is Verena's father of age?"

"Of course he is."

"Is he incapacitated in any way?"

"He is ill, though not fatally so."

"So he can speak rationally?"

"Yes."

Marcus shrugged. "Then let him take care of his own situation."

Brandon flushed. "Damn it, Marcus! If you had someone — anyone — in your life, then you'd understand how it is."

Marcus cut a sharp glance at his brother. Bloody hell, did everyone think him a monster? "Brandon, I do have someone in my life. I have you and Chase and Devon and Anthony and all of your wives and your children. That is enough for me. But you must do what you think is necessary. I'm not sure what you need from me, but I will assist you in any way I can. You know that."

Some of the stiffness left Brandon's shoulders. "Thank you, Marcus. I didn't mean —"

"Forget it. What do you need?"

"Well, to begin with, I need to borrow your traveling chaise and the coach. I ordered one weeks ago, but it is not yet ready and the one we have now is not sufficient. The springs are weak and it sways far too much to carry an ill man."

"You need both the coach and the chaise?"

"Verena's sisters and mother will be coming, as well. Between all of them and their luggage —"

"Are you fetching the lot of them here?"

Brandon nodded. "Indeed. I hope to be gone only for a week or two, but . . ." He caught Marcus's expression and added tersely, "I'm certain it will not be for long."

Marcus raised his brows. "I didn't say anything."

"No, but you looked —" Brandon ran a hand over his face. "I'm sorry. I'm not myself."

Marcus shrugged. "Don't worry about it. Of course you can have my chaise and coach, and I'll just use yours until one of my others can be brought to town." In truth, he possessed far more carriages than that, but kept only four in town; a high perch phaeton, a light curricle for warm days, a traveling chaise, and the coach, which was a monstrous affair in buff and blue, the family coat of arms painted on the sides.

"Thank you, Marcus! That will be wondrous indeed. Now . . . there's one more thing I must ask . . ." Brandon paused as if to gather his thoughts.

Marcus's gaze narrowed. "Why do I feel as if you're about to deliver some bad news?"

A faint smile touched Brandon's mouth. "Because I am. Not only do I need to borrow your coach and chaise, but I will need the services of your two best coachmen as well."

"What?"

"I don't have time to locate capable individuals. I must get the coach and carriage and horses to Dover as quickly as possible. I don't have time to send back to my estates for one of the underlings."

"This just gets better and better."

Brandon grinned. "There is one more thing . . ."

Marcus waited.

"Herberts." Brandon took a drink of his port that was more a gulp than a sip. "He is yours to command."

"Your coachman? The one who steals?"

"He doesn't steal from us. He just steals from other people."

"Oh lovely. That will make me popular with the Prince."

"You don't like the Prince," Brandon pointed out. "And since you rarely venture out into society anymore —"

"Blast it all, I am not a hermit and I wish people would stop hinting that I am!"

"I never said you were any such thing, Marcus. Look, just forget the whole thing."

Marcus thought of Anthony's words at White's. *Had* he become closed off to his family? And to everyone else?

He looked at Brandon. "Very well. I will keep your ill-sprung coach and your sticky fingered coachman while you are in Italy. How long will you be gone?"

"Thank you! I think two weeks, perhaps more, depending on how things stand."

Well. Two weeks wasn't that bad. Not really. "I shall have to lock up all the silver in the house until you return."

"Oh come now. Herberts is not as bad as he once was, you'd have to admit that much, at least. He usually only steals from people he thinks have slighted him."

"Just two weeks ago when you came by while I was out of town, your coachman talked his way into the kitchen via a simpering maid and helped himself to two large hams. My chef almost had an apoplexy. He was threatening to quit and had worked himself into such a fit that by the time I returned, I was forced to offer him an exorbitant increase in wages just to get him to stay."

"Antoine is a bit high strung." Brandon sighed. "Look, I know I am asking a lot, but frankly, I am afraid to leave Herberts at home alone. He has such address that he is quite capable of talking the other servants into all sorts of ill conceived plans. And I cannot take him with me; Verena's father has already caused a ruckus with the local authorities. The last thing I need is Herberts filching the silver out of the pocket of someone important."

"But you said he only did that to people he thought had slighted him."

"And the French."

"Ah. He's not only loyal but patriotic. How fortunate for England." Marcus leaned his head back against his chair, noting the faint circles beneath Brandon's eyes. "Oh, don't look at me like that. I said you could leave him here and so you can. And I promise that he will still be here when you return."

"Thank you, Marcus! Herberts never misbehaves around you. Verena and I both have noticed that before."

Marcus looked into his glass of port, which was depressingly full. Really, it was outside of enough that Brandon wanted Marcus's carriages and both coachmen as well, but to foist his own ill-trained servant on Treymount House . . . Marcus paused. His brothers were getting rather annoying in their tendency to judge his more disciplined outlook on life of late. Perhaps if he took

Brandon's rambunctious coachman and, with solid discipline and stern oversight, turned him into a model of decorum, some of this dissatisfaction would dissipate. Perhaps then his brothers would realize the value of a life devoted to order.

It was an idea. A very fine idea, now that he contemplated it. Furthermore, it would answer Anthony's complaint that Marcus had grown hard-hearted and never put forth any effort on anyone's behalf. Why, doing this one favor for Brandon would quite disprove Anthony's overly harsh analysis.

Marcus drained his glass in one long pull and then set it on the table beside him. "Two weeks?"

"No more than two weeks, I promise."

Bloody hell, the things one did for one's relatives. But if it would muffle some of the outcry . . . well, it needed to be done. "Very well. But see to it that you return as soon as possible. *With* my carriages *and* my coachmen."

Brandon's grin spread from ear to ear. "Thank you, Marcus. You don't know how much this means."

"And you don't know what a pain this is."

"Nonsense," Brandon said, already up and heading for the door. "Herberts is a bit of a bother, but he has a heart of gold. I wish you well!"

"Herberts has a heart of gold and fingers made of sticky paste," Marcus retorted, but he wasted his breath because Brandon was already gone.

Marcus sighed. The clock on the mantel chimed and he stood. He wanted to see Lord Melton before the man had time to drink himself into a stupor. Since Melton's financial difficulties had begun, he was rarely seen without a glass in his hand and his cravat askew. It was sad how some people allowed their emotions to get the better of them. Thank goodness he was better than that.

Chapter 7

Mon dieu! First she tells me she wants her hair up. Then she tells me she wants it to the side. Then she tells me that she thinks I am an imbecile because I cannot seem to make up my mind! Next thing you know, it will be my fault she is fat!

Lady Southland's new French maid to Lord Southland's valet, while sitting at the upper stair servant dining table

The dangerously swaying coach racketed down the cobblestone drive of Oxbridge House, whisking past the line of waiting carriages, mud spraying each one from the large rear wheels. By the time they reached

their destination, the horses were lathered, the body of the carriage splattered with mud and road dirt, and the driver grinning from ear to ear.

The footman assigned to opening carriage doors immediately came forward to do his duty, but to his astonishment, the lanky, cadaverous-appearing coachman jumped down from the carriage seat and elbowed the man out of the way.

" 'Ere now, that marquis belongs to me, if ye don't mind!" Herberts said, glaring. "Keep yer mitts off'n 'im!"

The footman blinked. "B-But I was just going to open the door."

"And keep the vale fer yerself, oiye don't doubt. Well, this marquis *and* his vales are mine. And don't ye be forgettin' it, neither, ye greedy fool."

The footman cast a wide, wild look at the upper footman, who had been left in charge of the arrival of the guests. That stalwart individual, after a stunned moment, managed a confused shrug. Left with no more direction than this, the lower footman flushed a dull red and fisted his hands.

"Aye now, is that the way ye wants it?" Herberts wiped his nose with his thumb and then lifted his fists, his elbows cocked out to each side. "Come at me then, ye bovine spirited fool!"

The footman looked as if he was more than happy to oblige Herberts's request, but a sharp cough from the upper footman stilled that desire. Jaw set, the young footman glared at Herberts a second more, bowed and then moved aside.

"That's more like it," Herberts said, adjusting his new neck cloth and opening the door wide. "Out ye go, guv'nor!"

No movement came from within the coach.

Herberts leaned forward, peering into the darkness. " 'Ere now! Are ye there?"

Still no movement or sound appeared.

Herberts cupped a hand about his mouth and yelled, " *'M'lord!* Are ye asleepin'?"

A faint moan was heard, but nothing more.

"Of all the lazy gents!" Herberts stuck his head into the door and eyed Marcus for a long moment. "There now, guv'nor! Do oiye need to shake ye awake?"

Marcus forced himself to open his eyes, pressing a hand to his quavering stomach. He had to swallow twice to get the words past his clenched jaw. "Have we stopped moving?"

Herberts chuckled. "Indeed we have,

guv'nor!" The coachman stepped back and opened the door wider yet. "Out wid ye now!"

Marcus managed to climb out without stumbling too badly. His entire body protested the sudden move and he was certain his face had a nice greenish tint as he stepped down the final stair. "Bloody hell," he muttered, clutching the carriage door with both hands. The entire world seemed to be slowly moving, left to right and then, just as confusedly, right to left.

Herberts grabbed Marcus's arm and held him upright. "A drinker, are ye? Who'd have thought? Already shot in th' neck and we've just arrived."

"I am not drunk, dammit," Marcus managed to say through his teeth, though his stomach protested even that small expulsion of air. "There are no spirits in the carriage, though I wish there had been for I would have drunk them all." The heaving ground slowly sifted into a semblance of stillness. "You drive like a — a —"

"Pro-fes-sion-al?" Herberts asked in a hopeful tone.

"No," Marcus said, yanking his arm free. "More like a bloody loon."

Herberts puffed up his chest. "Oiye tol' ye that oiye'd get ye to the ball afore the strike o' midnight and here we are! O' course, oiye had to drive up on the walkway a bit when we came 'round that last corner, but there was no one but a flower girl there after all and oiye'm sure she'd a never sold those wilted violets anyhows." His brow lowered. "But 'tis a pity about that tilbury goin' into the ditch. Oiye didn't loike the way the driver screamed at us, but that's neither here nor there, is it, guv'nor? Ye wanted to arrive on time and so we have. And wif a good ten minutes to spare!"

Marcus took a deep breath, pulling the welcoming cool night air through his nose. "Surely you have not been driving my brother and his wife about town in such a reckless fashion."

"Not the missus. She has a bit of a stomach, if ye know whot oiye mean." Herberts shook his head. "Womens are a bit squeamish."

Marcus pressed his hand to his own midsection. "I can't say as I blame her."

"Yer brother, now. He's a roight one, he is. Why he once't offered me twenty quid if oiye could get him to Grosvernor Square from the old bridge in under seven minutes." Herberts beamed pleasantly. "Oiye got me twenty quid, oiye did."

Marcus didn't answer. He was slowly

coming to the realization that his own brother was an unfeeling bastard. The sad facts were clear and becoming even more clear by the moment. Brandon had to have known what a dangerously incompetent coachman Herberts was. Which now caused Marcus to wonder at the haste with which his brother had left the country.

Had Brandon been in a hurry because he had a ship to catch and a father-in-law to save? Or had that story been naught but a distraction? Perhaps Brandon had really been in such a rush because he feared Marcus would come to his senses and change his mind about accepting the swap in coaches and coachmen.

Marcus eyed Herberts for a morose moment. "Where *did* you learn to guide a coach?"

Herberts tucked his thumbs into his lapels and rocked back on his heels. " 'Tis a natural talent, rather loike breathin'. Oiye just does it and it does jus' fine."

"Natural, hm? Naturally incompetent."

"But roight fast, guv'nor." Herberts winked broadly and touched a finger beside his nose. "And thet's whot really counts."

"My brother should have left you as a butler."

"Oh, oiye was a fine butler, indeed. And

the vales oiye managed to snipe —"
Herberts caught Marcus's stern gaze and
colored. "Not that oiye'm one to borrow
things from the gentry as oiye was once't in
favor of doin'. Why oiye fancy oiye haven't
picked a pocket in, oh, several days, at
least."

"Days? Good God! Well, whatever you
did before, you will not thieve while in my
employ or it's to the gaol with you."

"Easy now, guv'nor! Oiye'll endeavor to
keep me nambers in me own pockets."

"See that you do."

Herberts smiled, revealing a myriad of
missing and broken teeth, his hooked nose
even more pronounced. "Oiye aim to
please, oiye do! Speakin' of keepin' me
nambers where they belong . . ." He held
out his hand, his none-too-clean fingers
cupped as if he expected largesse of no small
amount.

Marcus straightened his shoulders, a faint
hint of nausea still lingering. "There will be
no vales for such a wild ride."

Herberts blinked. He looked into his
cupped hand, incomprehension on his ca-
daverous face. "No . . . no vales." His
clawlike fingers closed over his empty palm
and he visibly collected himself, blinking his
eyes as if to ward off tears. "Pardon me,

guv'nor. But did ye say there would be no vales? As in . . . none a'tall?"

"When we go somewhere, I expect to arrive in one piece and not be tossed about like a salt shaker in a bin."

Herberts's hand dropped to his side and his shoulders slumped. "But oiye got ye here, and wif time to spare."

For a moment Marcus thought the man might cry. Really, it was unseemly. But if he wanted to reform Herberts so that he was a competent coachman, Marcus would have to speak to the coachman on his own level, one obviously paved in gold.

Fortunately, if there was one thing Marcus knew, it was gold. "Herberts, your job is not only to see to it that I arrive at my destination on time, but *also* that I get there in a seemly manner. Once you learn how to do both of those things at the same time, then there will be vales. A *lot* of vales, Herberts." Marcus leaned forward and added in a low, winning tone, "More vales than you can imagine."

Herberts's eyes widened, his downcast expression vanishing in an instant. "Oiye should warn ye, guv'nor! Oiye've a large imagination, oiye do."

Marcus adjusted his cravat. "I'm counting on it. There is another coach arriving, so you must move this one. Return in an hour. I shouldn't need any longer than that to find Lord Melton and conclude my business."

Herberts straightened, a renewed purpose in his rather watery gaze. "Aye, guv'nor! Oiye'll be here at one sharp, see if oiye'm not!"

"Good." Marcus turned toward the house, then paused, one foot on the steps. "And Herberts?"

The coachman cocked a brow his direction.

"It's not 'guv'nor' but 'my lord.'"

"Of course, guv— I mean, me lord." With that promising phrase, the coachman tipped his hat, winked broadly, and then clambered back on the coach.

Bloody hell, that man was a complete mess. Shaking his head, Marcus made his way up the rest of the stairs, the last vestiges of nausea leaving as he did so.

The mansion was ablaze with light and decorated in the latest fashion, if somewhat overdone. Marcus wasn't sure what it was — the colors were too bright or the furnishings too numerous or the use of gold foil trim painfully excessive — but the result was a flood of color and texture that made one wish to turn and run.

The Oxbridges were new money, having

acquired the title after gaining a respectable fortune in textiles only a mere thirty or so years ago. And like all new rich, they had eventually moved themselves to Mayfair. For all their vulgar propensities, they were welcomed almost everywhere. While a few, more traditional members of the ton would not allow that "new money" was necessary to refurbish old fortunes, most everyone else disagreed.

It was, after all, quite necessary to bring a touch of new money into the family fold every hundred years or so. And since the Oxbridges possessed not one, but two rather attractive daughters and no male heirs, their arrival on Regent Street was even more welcoming than they'd expected. Every younger son in search of a promising bride, and older son attempting to repair the family fortune, made it a point to be present everywhere the Oxbridges deigned to appear.

Thus it was that the Oxbridge ball was filled to overflowing. Marcus, sauntering to the receiving line, absently greeting acquaintances as he went, almost winced at the way Lady Oxbridge drew up on seeing him. She looked rather like an overstuffed sausage, her thick body encased in white feathers and blazing red silk. Marcus had a fondness for red silk, and it made him wince to see the expensive material so strained.

"The Marquis of Treymount!" Lady Oxbridge trilled, just loudly enough to be heard by every person in the grand hall. "What a pleasure to have you at our humble entertainment!"

Lord Oxbridge puffed up as well, blustering out a hello and bowing in a ridiculously fawning manner. "Devilish good to see you, Treymount! Didn't think you normally attended this sort of ruckus, but I'm glad you did."

Lady Oxbridge laughed in an affected manner, her eyes blazing a second. "Oxbridge, how you do go on! Lord Treymount is known to be very *particular* in which amusements he attends, but there is no reason to think he will find anything wanting at one of our little events!"

"Indeed," Marcus murmured, glancing past the florid lady and into the rooms beyond. Where was the card room? He'd wager a crown he'd find Lord Melton comfortably ensconced there, frittering away what tiny bit of income he still had left.

Lady Oxbridge took his interest in the other rooms in a different manner. She leaned over and said in a low voice, "I daresay you came to see Jane, haven't you?"

Marcus blinked. "I . . . ah, Jane. I don't believe I —"

Lady Oxbridge smacked his arm with her fan. "Don't play coy with me! I can see that you're pining away to join the young ones on the dance floor! Oxbridge, give the man a bow and let him be on his way." She leaned closer to Marcus and said in a loud whisper that he supposed she imagined to be an undertone, "My eldest, Jane, is in white and pink sarsonet beside the refreshment table. Tell her to give you her last dance before supper. I told her to save it in case the Prince should have shown." Lady Oxbridge shrugged. "It doesn't appear as if he will, so you may take his place."

Good God, it was more horrid than he'd ever imagined. Even Lord Oxbridge had the decency to look a bit shocked at this loud hint. "Judith! Really now, no sense in teasing the man!"

Lady Oxbridge took immediate exception to this public correction. Turning bright pink, she fluffed up like an outraged cat and snapped back an answer.

Marcus decided now was a good time to make his escape. Without interrupting the quarreling couple, he managed a short bow, turned on his heel and made his way into the ballroom. It was fairly easy to find the card room simply by following the trail of men making their way to two wide doors that were held open by attending footmen.

Marcus immediately spotted his prey; Lord Melton sat at a green-felt-covered table, his cravat perfectly tied, his face flushed from the contents of a half-empty glass at his elbow, a wild, desperate gleam to his eye. He was a young man, always fashionably dressed, and held by most to be both personable and quite handsome. But Marcus knew him for what he really was — a profligate gambler who had sold an ancient estate down the Thames on the flip of a single card.

Yet here he was, drinking and gambling yet again. Marcus moved to one side, offering a polite bow when Melton's gaze finally found him.

The younger man's smile — faint as it was — faded from his lips. He paled and grabbed impulsively at his glass and took a gulp, then set it back on the table, his hand visibly shaking. "Treymount."

The others at the table glanced curiously from the young lord to Marcus.

Marcus nodded coolly, keeping his gaze locked on Melton. "Good evening, Charles. I trust you are well."

Lord Pultney looked up from where he

was shuffling the cards, his extra chins quivering with the effort. "It's a good thing you aren't playing, Treymount. The devil's own luck is in it tonight. Neither Charles nor I have won a hand all night."

Marcus could feel his teeth almost grinding. Bloody hell, what was the fool thinking? Here he sat, his estates mortgaged to the hilt, his finances in a state of ruin, tossing hand after losing hand upon the green felt table. If there was one thing Marcus could not accept, it was irresponsible behavior. "Melton, I had hoped to see you this evening."

The young man was suddenly as red as he had been white. He started to lift the glass once more to his lips, but stopped when he realized it was empty. He set it back on the table and forced a broad smile to his colorless lips. "Well, here I am in all my glory!" He suddenly became quite animated, gesturing to a passing footman to refill his glass. "Come, Treymount, have a glass!"

"No, thank you."

Melton's eyes rested on Marcus, a strange glitter in their depths. "Too good to have a drink with me? Is that it?"

Pultney glanced from beneath his heavy gray brows at the young lord. "Heigh-ho, Melton. I daresay Treymount has just ar-

157

rived and, like a shrewd man, is simply pacing himself. Daresay he'd have a spot of the golden with you later."

"Perhaps," Marcus said, though he thought it highly unlikely. "Lord Melton, I was hoping that you would do me the honor of calling on me in the morning. We have unfinished business, we two. I'd like to conclude it as soon as possible."

Melton tossed his cards onto the table. "I believe I am busy in the morning."

"Oh? Then perhaps we should just discuss our business here. Now."

Melton cast a quick glance around, then colored an even deeper red. He shot Marcus a look of pure venom. "No. That won't be necessary."

"Good. Ten, then?"

"I won't be up at ten. Make it noon."

Marcus shrugged. "Noon. I really don't care, one way or the other. Just see to it that you are not late." He met the young man's gaze coolly. "Do we understand one another?"

Melton's jaw tightened, but he had no choice. He gave a jerky nod. "Noon it is."

"Excellent. Good day, gentlemen." With that, Marcus turned and left. Good lord, but Melton was a hothead of the worst sort — intemperate and filled with passion. No wonder the fool had lost his fortune. Be that as it may, the jackanapes would come in the morning and provide the necessary information and then sign the blasted papers or Marcus would track him down once again, only this time it wouldn't be as pleasant. Unless the fool was willing for the world to know the extent of his own foolery, he'd do as he was bid.

Marcus glanced at an ornate ormolu clock that graced the wide marble fireplace on one side of the salon. He still had almost fifty minutes to spare before Herberts returned, blast it. Perhaps this would be a good time to make himself seen and prove Anthony yet again wrong in his estimation of Marcus's character.

His gaze idly swept the room, lingering on a redhead here, a blonde there. He supposed he should at least take a walk about the room and see if any of his other acquaintances were present. Perhaps the Duke of Exeter was here; Marcus hoped to interest the man in a mining venture that could prove quite profitable for them both.

Clasping his hands behind his back, Marcus turned to stroll into the ballroom when his gaze fell upon a couple standing by the bottom of the grand stairwell. Because of the milling crowd, he couldn't quite make out the face of the man, but the woman was easily identifiable — it was none other than Miss Honoria Baker-Sneed.

Well! What had brought the gorgon out on such a night as this? Although . . . he had to admit that she didn't look anything like a gorgon this evening. In fact, she looked very attractive, beautiful even. Dressed in a pale blue gown that made her hair seem a deeper chestnut, that intriguing streak of white gleaming at her temple before sweeping up through her coif to disappear at a sparkling tiara, she was distinctive and easily outshone the rather mundane simpering misses he'd so far witnessed.

As he watched, she tilted up her face and laughed, the gentle sound lifting over the voices of those around them and floating through the hall. To his surprise, Marcus found himself smiling a little in return. She appeared younger and far more carefree in this setting. Almost . . . enchanting.

His gaze flickered to her eyes. They were lively and expressive, the line of her throat and shoulders graceful and elegant. Had it not been for her slightly aquiline nose and too firm chin, she would have been outstandingly beautiful. As it was, she was arresting. Entrancing. Even exotic, with that striking lock of white at her brow. As

Marcus watched, she shook her head at something her companion said, her laughter dying and a sudden wary look replacing her amusement.

Marcus frowned. What had happened? And who the hell was she speaking to? He took a step back, leaning to one side so he could see around the milling throng to where she stood. Her companion's face came into view — a man of medium height with a handsome if somewhat aging countenance.

Bloody hell, she was speaking to Lord Radmere! Marcus'd had plenty of dealing with the old reprobate. Radmere was a collector of no small means. He approached each auction, each purchase, as a battle. The fool seemed to take particular delight in snatching purchases from beneath Marcus's nose. Surely Miss Baker-Sneed wouldn't —

Honoria removed her glove and held her hand out to Radmere for his inspection, the silver sparkle of the talisman ring evident even from Marcus's vantage point. "Bloody hell!"

From Marcus's side, a lazy voice said, "Is that any way to greet a half brother?"

Marcus glanced over to find Anthony by his side, looking resplendent in a black evening coat, his cravat tied to perfection. "What are you doing here?"

"I was about to ask you the same thing. I don't believe I've seen you at a ball in over a year."

Marcus shrugged. "I believe we had this conversation this afternoon."

Anthony's smile faded, his brow lowered. "Are you still upset? I was only —"

"No. I'm not upset, I just . . . I suppose some of what you said came a little too close to the home fires." Marcus managed a smile. "I'm not sure I agree with your total estimation of my character, but parts of it were spot on."

Anthony flushed slightly. "Marcus, I didn't mean to suggest you weren't a good person or a good brother, it's just that —"

Marcus held up a hand. "Perhaps we can spend an evening together without discussing my character in quite as much depth as you seem to enjoy."

"Actually, I wasn't going to discuss anything but the lovely women who are decorating the room." Anthony's gaze flickered past Marcus to Honoria. "My. She's a lovely one. Who is she and what has you using such shocking language in public?"

"That is Miss Baker-Sneed." Marcus watched as Honoria smiled up at Radmere.

Marcus was certain Radmere was flattered at such a look of complete attention, but those familiar with Miss Baker-Sneed would recognize the smile for what it was — a tempting ploy and nothing else. She wanted something from the man and Marcus was certain he knew what it was. "Someone should throttle that woman."

"Or kiss her. Chase heard correctly; the mysterious Miss Baker-Sneed is indeed lovely. Far too lovely to throttle."

"Don't let her appearance fool you. She may look harmless, but in truth she is irritating, scheming, stubborn, irksome and obdurate."

"All the better. Demure women are a bore."

"Anthony, that woman is showing the talisman ring to Radmere. If he finds out that I am interested in it . . . it will not be good for any of us."

"There is enmity between you?"

"He and I often brangle on the auction floor. Last month I outbid him on an ancient Chinese vase. He has not yet forgiven me, which is why I do not like seeing Miss Baker-Sneed in his company."

"You worry that she might be charmed by him?"

"I don't give a damn about that," Marcus

snapped, not quite sure why such an innocent query made his chest tighten in such a way. "I worry that Miss Baker-Sneed might sell Mother's ring to that fool. There will be hell to pay if that happens; he will charge me a fortune to get it back from him, *if* he consents to sell it at all."

"She wouldn't do such a thing."

"You don't know Honoria Baker-Sneed. Or Radmere. He'd give his eye teeth to outdo me in some way or another."

Anthony regarded the couple from across the room. "Radmere is certainly taking his time examining Mother's ring. He hasn't let go of Miss Baker-Sneed's hand for a second. You know, Miss Baker-Sneed may think she's tempting Radmere with the ring, but I believe he has other things in mind."

Marcus's expression darkened. He wished he could see her face more clearly. Radmere was a reprobate and possessed the morals of a gutter rat, while Honoria . . . He frowned. Honoria was not a complete innocent; no, she'd been on her own far too long to be thought that. But still, her experiences weren't the sort to prepare her for a man like Radmere.

Marcus thought of his interview with her. Though she was brazen enough when it came to bargaining about the ring, it had been painfully obvious that her experience with men was limited at best. There had been a refreshing air of innocence about her, almost hidden by her poise and confidence, but there nonetheless. "Blast it! Perhaps I should see what is happening with Miss Baker-Sneed and that lout. Radmere is a dissolute fool and I would not put it past him to behave in an inappropriate manner."

Anthony's brows rose, surprise flickering through his brown eyes. "You are going to play knight-errant? That's a new role for you."

"Oh, be quiet. Wait here while I go and see what's to be done."

"Yes, march over there and make a cake of yourself. I will come and watch."

"No, you will not." It was certainly an odd coincidence that Honoria had presented herself here, tonight of all nights. There was really only one reason that Marcus could think of to lure her to the Oxbridge's . . . but how had she known he would be there? Surely he was mistaken and this was all a co-incidence.

But the troublesome thought would not let him be. For one thing, she'd admitted herself that she was in need of connections to garner enough invitations to sport her sister about. And for another, she and apparently every other person in London appeared to know that he didn't attend functions of this sort often at all. Yet there she was, presenting his ring to Radmere, of all people.

Each well-reasoned thought led him to the conclusion that she'd come for one reason and one reason only — to bedevil him. Fuming, Marcus made his way toward the stairwell, though his way was impeded with gushing greetings from a number of matchmaking mamas. Gad, but he hated social functions.

He was just about to break through a group of especially clinging mothers when a hand was placed on his elbow. He turned, excepting to see Honoria. "There you —"

It wasn't Honoria. Instead, a pair of familiar violet eyes blinked up into his.

Stifling his impatience, he said, "Lady Percival."

She looked as she always looked — blond and coolly elegant. Only a faint flush on her cheeks seemed different. "Marcus," she purred, her hand on his sleeve. "I have been thinking of you."

"Indeed?" Well, he hadn't been thinking about her. "It's nice seeing you. How have you been?" He looked over her head, trying to see through the crowd for Honoria and her escort. Blast it, where were they?

The hand on his arm tightened. "Marcus, I've missed you."

He leaned to one side, catching a glimpse of Honoria's distinctive hair. "Uhm-hm." Where was she now? He couldn't see a damn thing through all the turbans. Whoever had invented that particularly silly item deserved to be shot. Blast it, where was Honoria? Had Radmere convinced her to leave with him? Marcus's heart began to pound more fiercely.

"Marcus!"

He looked down and found that the melting violet gaze had hardened into a more icy one. "Yes?" he said, trying to hide his own irritation.

Violet turned her head, her gaze narrowing in the direction he'd been looking, her mouth thinned unpleasantly. "Who are you looking at?"

"No one." He shook his arm free, catching sight of Honoria's delectable profile in a sudden part in the crowd. "Lady Percival, it is delightful running into you. Perhaps another time —" Before she could collect herself enough to protest, he bowed and then slipped away, threading through the crowd, intent on catching his quarry.

He lost sight of Honoria and Radmere about halfway there, thanks in part to a very large woman wearing no less than three ostrich feathers. The silly widgeon looked like an overblown pin cushion.

Making his escape, he slipped through another throng of people, careful not to make eye contact. Good God, did everyone have to be at the same place at the same time? The ton was a herd of unruly sheep, the lot of them. It was no wonder he'd eschewed society whenever he could.

Finally, Marcus broke through the melee. He was now standing on the other side of the great hall, at the foot of the stairwell.

But he was too late. Honoria and Radmere had disappeared.

Chapter 8

I am certain Miss Heneford will find your new coat something to admire, especially if you stand near the Prince Regent. He always manages to appear overdressed and overfed, which is a boon to those beside him.

Lord Southland's valet to his lordship,
while brushing that young man's new coat
in preparation of attending
a party at Carlton House

"There!" Honoria said on reaching the other side of the ballroom. "Much better!"

Her companion blinked. He'd been quite astounded when she'd grabbed his arm and practically pulled him across the room. "Is it? I mean, of course it is. I wasn't sure what you were doing —"

"The smoke. From the card room. It was making me quite ill." Which was somewhat true. In reality, the sight of Treymount bearing down on them had sent her hotfoot across the ballroom, Radmere in tow. She didn't mind Treymount seeing her with Radmere — that had been part of the plan. But she hadn't had time yet to get Radmere's opinion of the ring, and that was something she dearly wanted.

She held out her hand. "About the ring?"

"Oh yes." He took her hand again and peered closely at the silver circlet. His gaze narrowed, his lips pursed. "It's certainly ancient. Possibly Romanian in design. Not of any great value, though I'm certain there are some people who might be willing to pay a decent penny for the thing. I'd say . . . one hundred pounds?"

Honoria looked at the silver band. The candlelight flickered off the surface, casting a shower of sparkles up at her. "I thought it might be worth something on its own and not just because of what it is."

"And what is it?"

"The St. John talisman ring."

Radmere's brows shot up. He snatched up

Honoria's hand once again and examined the ring even closer, a feverish expression on his round face. "I'll give you whatever you wish, just sell me that ring!"

Honoria smiled, curling her fingers over the band. "That's more in line with what I wished to hear."

"Then you *will* sell it?"

"Oh no. I have other plans for this ring."

"Hm." Radmere dropped Honoria's hand. "Do these plans involve Treymount?"

"Oh yes."

"Will he like these plans?"

"No. He will despise them."

"Then I sincerely hope you succeed." Radmere made a face. "Treymount has bested me once too often for me to wish him anything but ill."

"Then rest assured that when I finish my negotiations, I will have everything I want, and Treymount nothing. Except, of course, his ring."

"You hold the same low opinion of Treymount as I."

For some reason, Honoria didn't like the sound of that. She was frustrated with Treymount's refusal to acquiesce to her demands, to be certain, but she could hardly blame him for trying to negotiate lower terms. In fact, if he'd agreed to her first offer, or even her second, her opinion of him would have been decidedly lower. "You mistake me, Lord Radmere. Treymount has never behaved ill toward me. He's been callous, but not mean."

"Oh?"

She smiled, not saying anything more. Being with Lord Radmere was making her feel somewhat . . . uneasy. Almost as if she was betraying a trust of some sort. Which was, of course, ridiculous. How could she be betraying anyone just by having a simple conversation?

Radmere's smile deepened and he took her hand again, only this time he pressed his lips to the back of her fingers. "You look somewhat bemused. But on you, bemusement has a particular charm." He glanced at her through his lashes. "May I say that you are indeed a most intriguing woman?"

Honoria tried to wrest free her hand, but found her fingers locked in Radmere's rather beefy hand. "My lord . . . my fingers hurt."

"Oh dear! I apologize." He took her hand and tucked it into the crook of his arm, leaning closer. "Then let us go out on the terrace to discuss this ring some more. You look a little flushed and the cool air will do you good."

Honoria suddenly realized that Radmere's strange cologne was actually brandy. She studied him a moment more and saw that though he did not appear unsteady in any way, nor did his face show the usual ravage of too much drink, he was quite sotted. It showed in the hard glitter in his eyes, an expression she'd attributed to the smoky air.

Heavens, this would not do at all. If she wished Cassandra to be properly received in public, she herself simply could not become embroiled in a scandal of any sort. Especially not with an overstuffed peacock like Radmere. It was said that Radmere was the Prince's closest companion, a fact Honoria could readily believe at this point, especially when she observed her companion's florid style of dress. "Lord Radmere, if I am flushed, it is merely because I could use a bit of refreshment." She attempted to disengage her arm from his but failed. "Could you perhaps —"

"In a moment." He leaned closer, his noxious breath brushing across her face and making her turn away. "I've seen you at auctions, of course, but never looking quite as fetching as you do now."

She glanced about her at the swirling couples, trying to free her captured hand without resorting to an undignified tug-of-war. "My lord, unhand me."

He smiled and gestured to the curtains at their back. "If we took a step through this door, we might find ourselves without all this bothersome noise." He reached over and lifted the end of the ribbon that was tied in a bow at the bottom of her cap sleeves, his fingers brushing her bare arm. "We would be quite alone."

She swatted his hand from her ribbon. "Oh, do stop that! I only wanted to get away from the card room door, nothing more."

A hand came to rest on the small of her back. Actually, it rested slightly *lower* than the small of her back. Honoria stiffened, her eyes widening. "Goodness!" The hand began to slide lower still, and Honoria whisked herself out of reach, or as far as she could go while her hand was still being held tightly. "Lord Radmere! That is quite enough of that."

"No?" He smiled, obviously not believing her protest. To her further chagrin, he crowded closer, forcing her to step back, the heavy curtains brushing her back. She reached behind her for the wall, but . . .

nothing. Good Lord, it was a hidden alcove!

This called for action. She glanced about, but there was no assistance in sight — she knew practically no one, after all. Furthermore, if she did ask for assistance, the person could well turn out to be the ton's worst gossip, and news of this little exploit would be all over town within the hour, which would not do at all. What she needed was a way to warn him off.

So it was all up to her. Radmere pressed back a little, edging her into the curtains.

"No," she said firmly, planting her heels. "I am very, very ticklish. Even the slightest touch . . . off I go."

"Ticklish, are you?" His grin turned wolfish. "How utterly amusing."

What a fish. Thank goodness his back was to the crowd or she might be forced to do something extraordinary to protect her honor. "Lord Radmere, you don't seem to understand. I am very *very* ticklish. In fact . . ." She fanned herself with her hand. "My doctor says that convulsions are not likely to occur again providing no one attempts to tickle me in a continuous fashion —"

"Convulsions?" His smile froze in place. "Surely not —"

"Oh yes. I hate to say anything, but . . . I wouldn't want you to be the cause of my demise without knowing exactly what had occurred." She awarded him with a faint smile, hoping it seemed like embarrassment. "If it does happen, please tell whoever attends me to put a wooden spoon between my teeth. I could hate to break them."

"The spoon?"

"No, my teeth."

He shook his head, an uncertain question in his eyes. "You must be funning me. Surely you are not *that* ticklish."

"Oh yes."

"Everywhere?"

"Everywhere."

"Even . . . here?" His hand hovered over her shoulder.

She forced a high-pitched giggle and stepped away. "Oh yes."

"What about . . . here?" To her utter astonishment, the lout placed his hand on her hip.

Ye gods! This called for serious action. Honoria looked down at his hand — and promptly burst into laughter. She didn't just laugh, she chortled, long and loud, rising in volume and intensity until he was glancing wildly about as if hoping for a rescue.

"Miss Baker-Sneed!" he hissed. "Please!"

Honoria laughed a moment more — even more loudly this time, enough to make people stop and stare — and then ended with a loud snort, a touch she thought was exceptionally well done. She really should have been an actress. She could have outdone even Garrick.

Radmere backed off immediately, so quickly he bumped into a woman dressed in green silk. Muttering his apology, he glared at Honoria, his expression a blend of terror and embarrassment. He appeared so comical that it almost set Honoria off, only for real this time.

Honoria took advantage of Radmere's awkwardness. She stepped out of the thick fall of curtains and into the safety of the ballroom. As soon as she got home, she'd write Ned and thank him; he'd been the one to relay that little trick.

Radmere raked a hand through his hair. "Miss Baker-Sneed, I'm sorry that I — I did not realize what you meant by ticklish. Are you . . . are you well?"

She pressed a hand to her chest and said with another giggle and snort, "Oh yes! I'm quite all right now. So long as you don't touch me again."

"I won't," he said fervidly. "That . . . It must be horrid, being so sensitive."

"Oh, I daresay I will never marry. But that's quite fine by me —"

The couples on the dance floor parted and Treymount appeared, his burning blue gaze sweeping over them both. "Miss Baker-Sneed. What a surprise."

Honoria allowed her smile to melt. "Oh. It's you."

She was rather pleased with her languidly uninterested tone of voice, especially since her body had indeed reacted — Treymount had a very powerful effect on her. It must be acute dislike, she decided. What else could cause her heart to beat in triple time, her stomach to heat in such a thoroughly dissatisfied way? Anger was a very uncomfortable feeling, she decided with a grimace.

Treymount seemed to notice Radmere for the first time. "Oh. Radisson. How are you?"

Radmere's ears reddened. "It's Radmere. And I am fine." He reached over to place a possessive hand on Honoria's arm and then caught himself. His hand hovered over her arm. "I don't suppose I should —"

"No," she said smoothly. "I wouldn't, if I were you."

Treymount's blue eyes were alight with curiosity. Before he could comment, Honoria hurried to say, "So, what brings you here? I didn't think you liked social events."

Radmere's expression perked up at that. "Treymount doesn't like social events?"

"I never said any such thing," the marquis snapped, his gaze blazing down at Honoria.

She smiled. "Radmere, do not listen to a word he says. I daresay he had business to attend to else he would not be here now. The marquis is not very convivial, but he is willing to spread himself very thin indeed in the name of making money."

Treymount's gaze narrowed. "Miss Baker-Sneed, I see that though you have adorned yourself as a lady of fashion, the softness of your silks has not impaired the sharpness of your wit."

She immediately curtsied. "Thank you, my lord. From your august lips, that is a compliment indeed."

Radmere looked from Marcus to Honoria, then back again, a dawning expression on his chubby face. "I say, you two. Not on warm ground here, are we? I mean, have you quarreled over something?"

Marcus lifted his brows. "Me? Quarrel with Miss Baker-Sneed? Perish the thought. I came because Miss Baker-Sneed is promised to me for this dance."

Dance? She glanced past the marquis to the couples who were engaged in a lively quadrille. Ye gods, she couldn't remember the last time she'd even attempted this dance, but she was fairly sure the advent had not been blessed. "My lord, I don't believe you and I were engaged to dance at all. In fact —"

"You are wrong," he said, smiling as if for all the world he'd just paid her the prettiest of compliments. "I am quite certain this is the dance I spoke for. Shall we —"

Before Honoria knew what he was about, he'd grasped her elbow and escorted her past a rather astounded Radmere and onto the dance floor.

"But . . . Best watch out!" Radmere called. "She's deuced ticklish, you know!"

Everyone turned and looked at her then, and Honoria had to force herself to keep a pleasant smile pasted on her lips. What a fool, to yell such a thing across a dance floor. Really! What must Treymount think of her now?

She risked a look up at him through her lashes and found him returning her regard.

"Ticklish?" he asked, his brows rose.

Her cheeks heated slightly. "Only when certain people are attempting to maneuver me into a secluded corner."

His face immediately darkened. "Was Radmere importuning you —"

"Not after I succumbed to a laughing fit that caused quite a lot of attention." She smiled, more genuinely this time. "You should have seen his face."

But somehow, the humor of the situation was lost on the marquis. He glared over her head at the unfortunate Radmere, who was already foisting his attentions on another lady, this one almost half a head taller than he. "If I had known, I would have —" He snapped his mouth closed and glared down at her. "You are not to speak to him again."

She blinked. "Lord Treymount, are you forbidding me from doing something?"

"Forbi— No. I just think you should use better judgment is all."

The dance separated them at that moment, which was a good thing as Honoria was hard pressed to remember all of the movements. As soon as she was able, she watched the marquis from the corner of her eye.

What was it about him that set her so on edge? She simply was not used to dealing with such high-handedness, and it was becoming quite galling to discover that she was not quite as successful in dealing with

Treymount as she was with the other members of his sex.

The problem of the marquis was quite a challenge, one that would take all of her wits and resources. She went through the motions of the dance, glad to see they would soon meet again.

Just what *were* the man's weaknesses? She pursed her lips and considered everything she knew about him.

When they came together again, he sighed. "You really must stop that."

"Stop what?"

"Regarding me as if you'd like to dissect me like one of those medical students who are forever foraging for cadavers." He held her hand as they passed around the circle.

"I'm certain you would make a horrid example for such a study," she said, turning on her heel and presenting him with her other hand. They began to sashay in the opposite direction.

He slanted her a hard look. Finally he said, "I know I am going to regret this, but why would I make a horrid study?"

"Because you have no heart. Just a mind for business. In the place of your heart, I'm certain they will find naught but an empty cavern and perhaps a ledger page or two."

"I knew I wasn't going to like your answer.

Tell me, Miss Baker-Sneed, are you always so scathing in your compliments? Or is it just for me?"

"It's just for you," she replied with un-impaired cheerfulness. "I had no wish to dance, in the first place. Or to converse. You were the one who forced this issue."

"I didn't wish to dance, myself," he replied, smiling down at her, a disturbing glint to his eyes. "But you seemed in danger of being mauled by Radmere, so I rescued you."

The dance parted them at that moment, which was fortunate, for Honoria was beyond outraged. He thought to *rescue* her? Of all the arrogant, outlandish, stupid gestures! She turned to send him a hard glare but instead caught an envious glance from the woman on her right.

That was something of a shock. Honoria couldn't count on one hand the times she'd incited a look of envy from another woman. Lips pursed in thought, Honoria looked back at the marquis. Of all the men in the dance — indeed of all the men she'd ever met — none had his presence. His fine form — broad shoulders and narrow waist — and his legs . . . she had a weakness for a man with a well-formed pair of thighs. Added to that was a pair of striking blue eyes and that black hair falling over his brow. The man was disturbingly handsome. It was almost unfair.

She stifled a sigh. Radmere had been something of a leech. An easily cowed leech, but still . . . she supposed Treymount meant well by "rescuing" her. Honoria sniffed, glad when the dance put her back with the marquis. "While I appreciate your efforts, I didn't need your assistance with Radmere."

"No? Then why was that braggart holding your hand for so long?"

"Because he was looking at the talisman ring." She smiled down at the circlet that rested on her finger, her hand resting lightly on the black of his coat sleeve as they made their way through the set. "It is truly a magnificent piece."

To her surprise, the marquis grasped her hand and pulled her from the dance. They stood to the side of the floor, their place rapidly taken by another couple. The cool breeze from the terrace doors sent her skirts fluttering about her ankles.

Treymount's deep voice rumbled near her ear. "Did you tell Radmere the ring was mine?"

She glanced up at him through her lashes. "Should I have?"

His gaze flared in return. "No, damn you,

for if he knows that, he will want the blasted thing."

Honoria wasn't sure what was goading her to continue teasing Treymount. He was known for his stern temper. And the ring was something he prized highly. Even more, she knew that the marquis did not like to lose. She knew all that and more. Her purpose in coming tonight had not been to infuriate the marquis, but merely to make him aware of the fact that she, and she alone, owned the ring, and that his options were limited. He either paid the amount she requested or he lost the ring. It was that simple. In no way did she mean to make him furious.

And yet . . . and yet, despite knowing this course was madness, despite knowing that she might be hurting her own cause, she found herself flashing a determinedly wicked smile at the man. "Of course I told Radmere that this was the famed St. John talisman ring. You are right, he does want it. Badly. Which is a good thing because if you and I don't manage to reach an agreement . . ." She flickered her fingers before Treymount's narrowed eyes, the ring casting a glimmer over his face, reflecting the pure blue of his eyes. ". . . then perhaps I will indeed sell the ring to Radmere. I

185

suppose then it will become known as the Radmere talisman ring, won't it? That will seem odd for you indeed, seeing your mother's ring in the hands of another man."

The words hung between them a full moment as his face froze into a mask of pure fury. His eyes blazed, his lips thinned, twin white lines appeared at either side of his mouth. Honoria took an impulsive step back, but Treymount would have none of it. He caught her by the elbow and then, without a word, firmly led her toward the terrace doors, threading them between couples and back to the place where he'd found her with Radmere, to the side of the room where they could have a little privacy, though not much.

The orchestra changed to a lively waltz, and immediately there was a flurry of activity as partners changed, people took their places, and others fled from the floor.

"There really is no need for us to say anything else, is there?" Honoria said somewhat breathlessly, assailed by the need to leave and get some fresh air, air that wasn't quite so charged with awareness. "Thank you for the lovely dance, but enjoyable as it was, I am afraid I must leave."

"Not yet you don't," he said, fury evident

in every line of his body. "Though you may have the ring in your possession, in reality, you know that ring belongs to me."

"Not anymore." Her heart was thundering madly, her hands damp. "I know you don't like this situation any more than I. But if you do not agree to my terms, I will sell the ring to someone else. I will have no choice but to sell it."

"You promised me a week."

She shrugged, trying to manage a light laugh. "Let us not pretend. You have no intentions of accepting my offer and I know it. We are both wasting time by waiting a week. The season is soon to begin and I wish for my sister to be presented with all accompanying pomp and circumstance. That will take clothing, jewelry, shoes, and other purchases. It's truly a pity you wouldn't agree to sponsor her, as it would have been a far easier path for us both."

Marcus clenched his fists, vaguely aware of the music humming around them, the faded murmur of voices as people passed by. It was all a blur, for his attention was entirely focused on the world's most stubborn woman. She stood before him, her chin firmed, her eyes sparkling a challenge that he felt all the way to his soul. "You may not sell that ring."

Her eyes narrowed. "If I decide to sell this ring, or throw it into the Thames, you cannot stop me."

Marcus almost reached for her. It was only through sheer determination that he managed to keep his hands at his side. By God, he longed to grasp her arms and shake some sense into her.

Unaware of her close escape, the blasted woman smoothed her skirts and said, "Now if you will excuse me . . ." She turned on her heel to walk away.

But Marcus could not allow that. He grabbed her arm and spun her back to face him.

She gasped, colored, then looked around wildly.

Realizing they could be seen, Marcus released her arm. "Before you leave, I will have your word that you will not sell the ring until I have made my decision."

"I promised you a week and a week you shall have, but not a moment more." Her eyes glinted up at him, a pure and rich hazel, green mottled with brown and gray, surrounded by thick chestnut lashes that curled and tangled at the corners.

His gaze traveled past her eyes to her wide brow and on to the sweep of her hair. Thick and soft, it curled back from her forehead, the rich chestnut strands and the streak of white curving a line to the tiara. It was almost ludicrous, the large, ornamental, and obviously fake jewels that sparkled in her hair. "A bit much, that."

Her hand went to the tiara. "You think so? I wondered, but Portia said —"

"Portia?"

"One of my sisters. She is fifteen and hopelessly addicted to fashion. She seemed to think the tiara was quite the rage."

"I see them all of the time, only . . . not on you." Although somehow the sparkle of the jewels did suit her. He found himself imagining her with nothing but the tiara on . . . laying on his bed . . . her hair trailing over pillows . . . His body reacted, hardening, his breathing growing heavier. When had Honoria Baker-Sneed developed into such a sensual woman? And why hadn't he realized it before?

"No, I am not the type of woman who would normally wear a tiara," she said, her rich voice thrumming through him. "Although I did think it wouldn't hurt to wear one just for this evening. It . . . well, it gave me courage."

"Courage? For what?"

She didn't answer, and he suddenly knew the answer. He'd been right. She'd known he'd be here — she'd anticipated and even wished for this meeting.

That was an intriguing bit of information. If Marcus wished to regain the ring, he needed to know more about his enemy, the intrepid Honoria Baker-Sneed. More than the fact that she was an excellent bargainer, had a weakness for antique snuff boxes, and looked damnably fetching in a blue ball gown and a fake tiara. "Tell me, Miss Baker-Sneed. If you are not the sort of woman who would normally wear a tiara, what kind of woman are you?"

Her brows rose and she regarded him for a long moment. "Are you attempting to soften me up by pretending an interest in my life?"

"I don't think that's possible."

"You don't think what's possible? Pretending an interest in my life?"

"No, softening you up. I merely asked a question."

She looked utterly unconvinced. "I don't know that you need such personal information."

He shrugged and looked away, trying his damnedest to appear uninterested. He knew women. He'd bought more than his fair share of trinkets for the opposite sex, had played more than his fair share of feminine games to know that disinterest was a light to a fire.

And it worked. She was silent a moment, then she burst out, "If you must know, I am sadly addicted to bonnets. I have far more than I should, and every time I visit town, I find myself longing for another."

"There," he said, bowing a little. "That didn't hurt, did it?"

"No. I suppose not, though what your purpose is, I do not pretend to fathom."

"Perhaps I just wished to know a bit more about my adversary."

She pursed her lips, and he found himself looking at her tender mouth and wondering if it would taste as good today as it had two days ago. "I suppose that makes sense," she said. "Tell me, Treymount, what kind of man are *you?* What worthless items do you collect beyond the antiquities I've seen you cart off from various auctions?"

Marcus almost smiled. She was as direct as an arrow. "I suppose I own far more than my fair share of footwear. I cannot seem to have enough riding boots."

She looked surprised. And somewhat pleased. "What a delightful fault to have!"

"Not according to my valet. But then, he has to keep them all polished." Marcus decided that it would be lovely to show this prim miss his boots. The ones located in the dressing room off his bed chamber. Way, way in the back of his dressing room.

The thought of Miss Honoria Baker-Sneed walking through his room, her body draped with nothing but a sheet from his bed, made his body stir with more awareness.

Damn, there it was again — that surprising flash of heat that sparkled between them. Marcus crossed his arms over his chest. "It's a good thing I came to this ball."

She fastened those amazing hazel eyes on him. "Why?"

"Because if I had not been here, no one else would have saved you from that rakehell, Radmere." Marcus rocked back on his heels, complacent and ready. "You are too much an innocent to be with someone like that scoundrel."

"I am not an innocent. Besides, I had no problem dealing with Radmere."

"Men, all of them, are not to be trusted with a lady alone."

She eyed him for a disbelieving moment. "I take it you don't include yourself in that grouping?"

"Oh, but I do count myself." He leaned forward so his breath stirred the hair at her ear. "Miss Baker-Sneed . . . Honoria . . . you shouldn't trust me either."

She didn't flinch, didn't draw back. That rather pleased him. It pleased him even more that when she did speak, her voice brushed over him, warm and cinnamon scented with just the hint of a tremor. "I have an older brother, you know. And I know all manner of ways to defend myself."

"You may be able to hold off Radmere, but your wiles would not work on me."

"Do you think?" she replied with that damnably knowing smile that irked him to his boots.

That did it. It was in that moment that Marcus knew he was going to kiss the stern and stubborn Miss Honoria Baker-Sneed. Not here, of course, not in public. He had no wish to end up leg-shackled to the woman. But by damn, she was far too challenging to be ignored, an entrancing combination of bravado, pride, and self-sufficiency that just begged to be taught a thing or two, and he was just the man to do it. "You are a very warlike woman, Miss Baker-Sneed. Or perhaps . . . perhaps I should call you Diana, the huntress." He leaned back a bit and regarded her thoughtfully. "You look very much like a presentation of Diana I saw at the British Museum. One of the Elgin marbles, in fact."

"I am only warlike when necessary." She seemed so firm in her declaration, rather like a statue come to life.

Marcus found himself stepping closer. Now his legs brushed against her skirts. He bent slightly, his lips almost at her temple. "Miss Baker-Sneed, allow me to make a suggestion. If you would be more reasonable in what you desire for that ring, I would go away and you would not have to deal with me at all. But until you do that, I plan on being very nearby. Watching. Waiting. And I will not always be this polite."

She stiffened and flashed him a look of such intensity that for an instant he would have paid to have her alone. Bloody hell, but she was a woman of outstanding passion. Of verve and energy and something else that called to him. He was not used to a woman who possessed such strong opinions. The women he knew simpered and smiled and agreed with whatever he said.

But this woman was not accommodating and she was far from impressed with his title and possessions. Which had the strange effect of making him want to touch her all the more. To taste her. To sweep her into his bed and prove to her once and for all who was the master here. For it was not her.

So long as he had breath in his body, it would *never* be her.

Her eyes sparkled green fire. "My lord, I have but one thing to say to you. Never underestimate a woman intent on making a profit. I will have the money I desire for this ring. And I will not sell it to you unless you agree to my request — all of it. I will give you the rest of the week to think on it, and then . . ." She smiled, a pleased, none-too-nice smile, one he rarely saw on a female's lips. "And then it will be gone, lost to you forever."

With that, she turned on her heel and walked away, through the crowd and out the door, leaving Marcus standing at the side of the room. He should have been furious, but instead he found himself strangely pleased. So pleased that he even stayed through two more dances and did his duty to the daughter of the house by dancing with her, and even that painful experience didn't put a dent in his solidly good mood.

For if there was one thing Marcus enjoyed, it was a challenge. And Miss Honoria was proving to be all that and more.

Chapter 9

See that woman standing by the refreshment table not looking our
way? No, not the one in pink; the
one in green. Miss Heneford may
seem to be uninterested in me, and
indeed, that is what she wishes me
to think. A lesser man would fall for
such an obvious ploy. And a much
lesser man would charge ahead,
spurred by the challenge she threw
when she pretended she could not
recall my name upon meeting me
again on arriving this very evening.
Fortunately, I am not a lesser man. I
refuse to rise to such pitiful maneu-
vering. Instead of attempting to
gain her attention, I shall stand here
and wait. She will come, see if she
does not.

Lord Southland to his
friend and acquaintance,
Mr. Cabot-Hewes, while not looking at the
refreshment table at Carlton House

Honoria sat alone at the breakfast table.
She'd startled the servants by arising so
early that she almost beat the sun. Mrs.
Kemble had hurried to rouse the cook and
get breakfast set out on the wide buffet.
Honoria, her mind sunk in thought, had not
noticed. She'd accepted the pot of steaming
tea and Mrs. Kemble's assurances that
breakfast would be forthcoming. Then
she'd sat at the long table, staring at the talisman ring.

It sat snuggly on her finger, glimmering in
the morning light. Strange, but it had
seemed brighter at the ball, shimmering as if
set with diamonds. But here, in the breakfast room, it cast off just a faint shimmer, as
if it was as sleepy as she. For a moment
Honoria allowed herself to remember the
dance she'd shared with the marquis.
Though she was loath to admit it, he was an
excellent dancer. She wondered if he
thought her awkward. After all, she hadn't

had much practice, and the steps, though familiar, had been difficult and —

Oh for the love of — what was she thinking? Who cared what the marquis thought? She certainly didn't. She rubbed the ring absently, smiling a little when she noticed that it glowed a bit more brightly now.

Mrs. Kemble entered the room with a huge platter. Soon the buffet table was piled with silver trays. "There ye are, Miss Baker-Sneed! Shall I call the others?"

A thumping sound on the steps precluded Honoria from answering.

Mrs. Kemble chuckled. "Never mind. There they are now." She retired through the servant's door to fetch another jar of marmalade.

The wide paneled door to the breakfast room flew open. "Well?" Portia was still tying her sash, her hair hastily braided and pinned. Panting from her dash down the steps, she planted herself before Honoria. "Tell us everything!"

Olivia plopped into a seat at the far end, hiking the chair so it faced Honoria more squarely. "Cassandra would not allow us to stay up to meet you when you returned, and we must know what happened."

Juliet and Cassandra entered together.

Juliet frowned at Olivia. "You promised you wouldn't ask anything until Cassandra and I arrived."

Olivia blinked. "Did I say that?"

"Yes, not two minutes ago on the stairwell."

Olivia looked at Honoria and gave an awkward smile. "Oh."

Cassandra took the seat next to Honoria. "I thought you would be too tired to talk when you returned, so I sent them all to bed."

"You were right," Honoria said, taking a bracing sip of tea. "I was tired. And much too exhausted to talk." Which was a complete falsehood. Had she really been tired, then once she'd pulled on her night rail, tied her hair into a braid, and slipped between the covers, she would have immediately fallen into a deep sleep. But as it was, she'd lain awake, hour after hour, rethinking her conversation with the marquis.

George wandered in, rubbing his eyes and yawning. He sniffed the air, then grinned. "Mmmm! Brisket!" He was at the buffet before anyone could reply, pulling the cover off of a large silver salver.

Honoria pretended to be busy with the teapot. She could not shake the thought that she'd erred last night. Why had she allowed her wretched temper to get away from her? Blast it, she'd probably put the man into such a passion of disapproval that he would rather be tied to a wild bull than buy the ring from her for anything near a decent price.

Olivia leaned over to see what was on George's plate. "Did you leave any brisket for the rest of us?"

He grinned. "A little."

She cuffed him on the shoulder. "You are such a pig."

"Honoria?" Cassandra's gentle brow folded with worry. "You look fatigued. Was the evening difficult?"

Olivia mussed George's hair as she went by him to the sideboard. "Honoria can't be tired; she returned fairly early. The hall clock had barely chimed one."

"One?" Portia poured a dollop of crème into her tea. "Is that all?"

Juliet selected a piece of toasted bread and placed it in the center of her plate. "All Honoria wanted to do was speak with the marquis about the ring. That shouldn't have taken much time."

Portia sniffed. "If *I* had been at the ball, I wouldn't have left until the very last dance." She frowned at Juliet's plate. "Just one piece of toast?"

Juliet poked at it with her fork and wrinkled her nose. "I read about a new reducing diet in the *Morning Post*."

Cassandra frowned. "You only eat toast?"

"Oh no. I can have a boiled potato in vinegar for lunch and a little — a *very* little — lamb for dinner. But nothing more."

Portia rose from her chair. "I, for one, am not going to reduce. Whatever man I find will just have to take me the way I am, large or thin."

Olivia cut a piece of bacon. "All you need is a wealthy, titled man who will accept a slightly plump, poor woman as a potential bride."

Juliet giggled. "Now that's a lovely plan; I really don't see how it could fail."

Portia sniffed again. "Stranger things have happened."

"Not in real life," Juliet said, cutting her toast into tiny pieces and spreading it out so that it filled her plate.

"What do you know about real life?" Portia picked up a plate and began to fill it. "Notice that I didn't say the wealthy man had to be handsome. If I'm not, I don't expect him to be. That's only fair."

Olivia looked up at that. "Fair? You expect him to be wealthy and you're not. What's fair about that?"

"Yes, but I can have children. Therefore, I

bring my own value to the marriage. The least he can do is possess enough of an income for our family to live comfortably."

Olivia curled her nose. "You would sell yourself as a breeding machine?"

"Only for a very large sum of money," Portia said calmly. "And it's not as if I don't like children; I love them. I hope to have ten or eleven, at the least, wealthy husband or no."

Cassandra held up a hand. "Oh enough! We were talking about Honoria's evening." Cassandra turned to her oldest sister and smiled. "Well?"

"There's not a lot to tell, really," Honoria said. "I saw the marquis and . . . I made certain he saw me with Radmere." Cassandra looked at her, so much hope in her eyes that Honoria almost winced. Surely her stubborness hadn't challenged Treymount into some sort of rash action they would all regret. Not that he seemed like a rash man . . . but there was no doubting his pride. He wore that on his sleeve for one and all to see.

"Honoria?" Cassandra leaned forward. "Was the marquis . . . what did he say?"

Say? He'd said a lot of things. Honoria glanced around the table and found every eye upon her. "He said . . . he said . . . He didn't really say anything."

Portia blinked in amazement. "Surely he said *something*."

He had, of course. He'd pretty much said he'd be damned before he gave her one pence for the ring. Honoria bit her lip. She couldn't tell that to Cassandra. "I think I made some progress, though time will tell how much."

Cassandra appeared relieved. "Excellent! What exactly happened?"

"Oh . . ." Honoria waved her hand in the air. "We spoke. I let him know how things were to be with the ring. We danced —"

"Danced?" Cassandra exchanged a glance with Portia. "Well!"

"Everyone was dancing; it was nothing special. Anyway, after the dance, we talked some more and then I left." She shrugged. "We shall discover today if anything I said made an impression. He will either come to claim the ring or —" She bit her lip. "Or he will not show up and we will be forced to sell it elsewhere."

"To whom?" Juliet looked hungrily at Portia's overly full plate. "Who else might want the St. John talisman ring?"

"Everyone would want it," Portia said calmly. "It's magical."

George looked up from his plate, his eyes wide. "Magical?"

"Don't speak with your mouth full,"

Honoria said automatically. She turned her attention back to Portia. "That's nonsense. I informed Lord Radmere I was in possession of the St. John ring last night. I believe he would pay dearly to possess it."

"Dearly?" Cassandra asked, a question in her violet eyes.

"He has no love for the marquis. I could wrest a pretty penny from him, though nowhere near as much as Treymount could afford to pay."

"Then we had best hope that the marquis comes through," Cassandra said. "And if he doesn't, we'll use Lord Radmere as our emergency plan."

Honoria nodded, although . . . she really hated to think of giving the ring to anyone other than the marquis. It had been his mother's, after all. But if he was not willing to help her with the simplest of requests . . . what choice did she have?

"I suppose we will be staying home today, then," Portia said, sighing. "And waiting on the marquis. I had so hoped to visit the new silks warehouse Mrs. Tremble and her daughter mentioned." She sent a hurried glance at Honoria. "Not that I would buy anything! I just want to look."

Honoria shrugged. "There is no reason to wait here just in case the marquis decides to grace us with his presence. Besides, I want to view the Elgin marbles at the British Museum."

Juliet poked at her uneaten toast. "Again? You have been to see them a dozen times already."

Yes, but she'd never before paid much heed to the presentation Treymount had mentioned, the one of Diana. Was that the statue of a chubby woman, the one with thick thighs and heavy hips? Certainly there'd been some Greek statues that had portrayed women in just that manner. "It's been a week since I last went. Besides, I haven't visited the Elgin marble exhibit in over a month; I've paid far more attention to the new display from China. Portia, you might like that. It is chock full of silks of all kinds and some of the most glorious embroidery I've ever seen."

Everyone seemed to love the idea of going to the museum, except George, who declared that he'd rather be eaten alive by whales than visit a musty old building to look at stones and cloth. Honoria smiled absently and let her family talk and tease all around her. The sounds rose and fell like waves against a sea wall, but she didn't notice. She was too busy trying to think of what she'd do if the marquis didn't come to make her a new offer for the ring.

Honoria came to stand beside Cassandra where she was admiring a marble frieze, a large piece of the Elgin marbles. "They are so lovely." Lord Elgin was once ambassador to Greece. While there, he procured a large number of marble pieces from the Parthenon, which was being dismantled and sold to the highest bidder. When Elgin ran into ill fortune, he'd offered the marbles to the British government.

"I believe this is Hera," Cassandra said, her eyes shining with admiration. "If I could be a Greek goddess, I'd like to be her."

"Really?" Honoria looked at the next frieze, bending forward and squinting. It showed a rather athletic woman wearing a scandalously low drapery and leaning back against a divan. "If I had to wear so little clothing, I should take an ague." Honoria shivered. "It's always so chilled in here. Between that and the poor lighting it is no wonder this place is nearly empty today."

Cassandra pulled the collar of her pelisse a bit closer. "I do wish the displays were more plainly marked, too. I have no idea who your Greek goddess is. Honoria, you did a much better job at the display you made of Father's objects in the shop."

"So I've often thought." Honoria stepped back so she could eye the statue a bit better. "Whoever this is, I wish to be her. She looks very fine wearing her sheet and sandals, not a goose bump in evidence."

Cassandra giggled. "You do well enough with sandals. But the sheet? It just doesn't seem the sort of thing one could wear with a tiara."

Honoria smiled.

"There! I knew I could get you to smile today."

"I haven't been very jolly, have I? I'm sorry."

Cassandra took Honoria's hand and squeezed it. "We've all had a lot on our minds lately."

"I am fine. I'm just . . . mulling." Mainly about the mistakes she'd made in dealing with the marquis. Why was it that the very sight of the man set her defenses roaring to the fore?

"Honoria, things will turn out fine, wait and see. I wouldn't be surprised if —"

"Cassandra! Honoria!" Portia and Olivia came into the room, the leather soles of their slippers clicking on the hard floor. "You must come and see! We found the most amusing thing."

Cassandra sighed. "Oh, not another

naked statue. They can't glue fig leaves over them all, you know."

Portia stifled a laugh behind her gloved hand. "No, no! Something better."

"It is a man, though. But a real one and not a statue," Olivia said, angling up her chin. "He has shirt points up to his ears so he must stand like this at all times. It is the most amusing thing!"

Cassandra smiled. "And large buttons, too, I daresay."

"Shiny brass," Portia said, holding her hands in a large circle. "Like tea dishes!"

"I wonder if it is Sir Frothersby," Cassandra said. "I read in a scandal rag that he is the undisputed King of the Dandies."

"It must be he, for there can be no one worse. Oh Cassandra, you *must* see him!" Portia whirled and started for the door, Olivia scurrying behind her.

Cassandra started after her sisters, then paused. "Are you coming?"

"No. I've seen Sir Frothersby; he is indeed a sight, even without a fig leaf. But I'd rather stay here a moment." She gestured toward the frieze. "I fear that if I do not remember who this is, I will not be able to sleep a wink tonight."

"I do the same thing when I cannot recall something. Very well, stay here. We will re-

turn as soon as we find Sir Frothersby."
With that, Cassandra left.

Honoria bent closer to the frieze, hunching her shoulders against the chill. Except for her hand where the talisman ring rested, she felt far colder than she should. She pulled her mind off the troublesome ring and examined the marble before her. It was a large portion of frieze that, according to the small placard resting before it, came from the top rim of the Parthenon. Unfortunately, there was little else on the placard and Honoria was left to her sketchy knowledge of Greek mythology to try and discover the mysterious woman's name.

She tilted her head to one side, her brow low. What goddesses did she knew? There was Aphrodite and Hera and —

"She looks like you, doesn't she?"

The rich, deep voice washed over her, and she caught her breath, closing her eyes against the sudden surge of awareness. What was *he* doing here? Perhaps . . . she opened her eyes, hope fluttering through her. Perhaps she hadn't ruined anything after all! Perhaps — just perhaps —

She calmed her thundering heart. Whatever had brought Treymount here, she wouldn't know if she continued to stand with her back to him.

Gathering her wits, she turned to face her adversary. "Lord Treymount. What a surprise."

He glinted a smile down at her, looking devastatingly handsome, his black hair rather mussed over his forehead, his startlingly blue eyes seeming to shimmer in challenge. "Miss Baker-Sneed, how are you today? Your housekeeper told me where you might be found."

"Oh?" So he'd sought her out a-purpose. She clutched her reticule a bit tighter, hoping her eagerness didn't show. "You wished to speak with me?"

He crossed his arms over his chest, that amazingly sensual smile still touching his firm lips. He was dressed in morning finery, though his clothing was far more somber than the average man's. It was odd, but he seemed to be particularly partial to wearing black. She wondered why that was.

"Miss Baker-Sneed, we need to talk, only this time I am not going to allow you to walk away. And as I have an appointment at noon, we must be swift."

She watched him from beneath her lashes. He didn't seem as angry as he had been last night. If anything, he seemed reluctantly amused. She smoothed the sleeve of her pelisse, trying to stem the nervous quaverings of her stomach. "Lord Treymount, I don't believe we have anything to say. Unless, of course, you are going to reconsider —"

"Seven thousand pounds is still too much for one ring."

A sudden pang of disappointment caught her. "Then why are you here?"

He allowed his gaze to brush over her, lingering on her lips and then hair. "I spent a good deal of time last night considering our conversation. I have decided that if we wish to resolve this little matter, then we must *both* compromise."

The ring on her finger seemed to heat the slightest bit at his words. She frowned down at her gloved hand before straightening her shoulders and saying bluntly, "I don't need to compromise. I am perfectly willing to sell the ring elsewhere."

"Ah," he said, leaning a little closer, the deep scent of his cologne tantalizing her. Sandalwood and . . . something rich and earthy. She lifted her nose a bit and leaned toward him, trying to catch a deeper sample.

Suddenly, she realized what she was doing. She caught his gaze, and to her chagrin, a faint, lopsided smile touched his lips. His gaze roamed over her face, then flickered down to her bosom.

Though she was encased in a very respectable morning gown, and then covered to the neck in a red wool pelisse, she still could not help but feel naked. Face heated, she pulled away, clutching her reticule before her like a shield. Ye gods, did the man do that on purpose? With the flick of a glance he made her feel undressed.

His gaze passed by her and rested back on the frieze. "The huntress, Diana."

"Ah!" She turned to look at the marble, grasping the change of topic with relief. "I could not figure out who it was."

He stepped forward, his chest against her left shoulder as he pointed toward the bottom of the frieze. "See the bow and arrow at her feet?" His breath brushed over Honoria's cheek, sending a shiver through her.

"I — I — Of course. I missed that somehow."

"It's partially broken away. You remind me of the huntress very much." His low voice was casting a spell over her, trickling through her defenses.

Honoria moved away, though her shoulder was still warmed from where it had rested against his chest. "My lord, this is — we are wasting time. What compromises do you propose?"

"First, I want another reassurance that I will have the rest of my week. You left in quite a bustle last night, and I want to be assured that anger has not upset reason."

She stiffened. "I am a woman of my word. And if you hadn't made me so angry last night, I would never have threatened to take it back."

"We were both a little on edge last night."

Oh pother. Did he have to be so reasonable? It took all of the wind out of her sails. She sighed and flicked an impatient glance his way. "Treymount, may I ask you something?"

His brows lifted, but he bowed. "Anything."

His answer surprised her. She could ask him anything? Anything at all? That certainly was an interesting thought. She could ask him his favorite color. Or whether he liked brunette women over blondes. Or what he thought of a woman with chestnut hair with a white streak.

Honoria gathered her wayward thoughts. "Yes, well, I was wondering . . ."

"Yes?" Marcus watched his quarry bite her lip. By Zeus, she had a lovely mouth. Full and juicy as a ripened strawberry, it made his own mouth water with the need to taste it.

"Lord Treymount, seven thousand pounds is not that much to you."

"No. But I have never in my life paid more for something than I thought it was worth. I fear I would be less than true to my own sense of value if I agreed to such an outlandish price for the ring."

"If you have already decided that, then why should I bother even waiting the week?"

"Because I intend on finding a way to make you change your mind."

Her hazel eyes blazed, her lips thinned, and her shoulders sprung back as if readying her for an attack of some sort. "You can't." And with that terse sentence, she turned back to the frieze and studied it as if her life depended upon it.

Marcus watched her, admiring the line of her profile, the delicate curve of her full bosom beneath her pelisse, the graceful arch of her neck and shoulders. It was odd, but the more contact he had with the prickly Miss Baker-Sneed, the more he found her presence tolerable. Pleasant, even. He was also becoming more and more convinced of her beauty, a fact that surprised him a good bit. It was not a conventional sort of beauty — but rather a quiet, elegant line of cheek and chin and throat. Her eyes were her most remarkable feature, brought to even more prominence by the streak of white that flashed from her temple.

He glanced about them, noting that they were alone in this room of the museum, which was to be expected at this time of the day. Most of his acquaintances were either deep in slumber or were just waking. Of course, had they been awake, he rather doubted they would be at the museum. "I am surprised to find you here."

"Why? You know my penchant for antiquities. I believe it matches your own." She sent him a sidelong glance. "Have you never been here?"

"Yes, I have. Many times." Marcus wondered what she would say if he told her that he had been instrumental in convincing the House of Lords to purchase the marbles to begin with. He doubted she'd believe him, true as it was.

He stifled a sigh. Honoria thought the worst things of his character, and he supposed, in some abstract way, he couldn't blame her. What had he done to make her think otherwise other than try to bully her into selling him back his ring? Though his intentions were good, he was afraid he'd been overly severe in his actions. That was the thought that had sent him to her house as soon as it was reasonable to visit.

He wasn't going to apologize; after all, he'd done nothing truly reprehensible. But he had planned on explaining himself. Trying to make her understand why the blasted ring was so important. His gaze rested on her hands where they were clutched about her reticule. Through the thin leather of her glove he could see the distinct outline of the ring. "Why do you wear it?"

Her brows rose, her gaze dropping to her own hand. "I don't know. I suppose . . . it just feels right." Her brow lowered. "It fits perfectly, which surprised me because it looked far too large. But once I slipped it on —" She bit her lips.

"Yes?"

Color flooded her cheeks. "Nothing. I just —" She managed a wan smile. "I daresay the rumors about the ring affected me somehow."

"But you didn't know that was the St. John talisman ring until I told you."

Her brows lowered. "That's true; I didn't. I wonder why . . ." Her voice faded off and she stared at her hand, perplexed and mulling.

He smiled a little, and leaned forward to say in a low, intimate voice, "Perhaps you felt something because the magic was already touching you, holding you in its clutches, beguiling you with the possibilities that perhaps . . . just perhaps, you and I —"

"Lord Treymount, please!" Her eyes flashed fire, now more green than anything else, her cheeks bright red. "I am not a naive girl to fall for a romantic legend, especially one that has to do with *you!*"

He'd made her angry, so he knew he shouldn't have taken offense when she tried to put him in his place. But her words raced over him like a heated needle, flashing his temper to the fore. In his entire life, no woman had looked at him with such a mixture of disregard and ill-concealed contempt.

Marcus's reaction was instantaneous. It was madness. Pure madness. But he didn't care. As soon as this woman was within touching distance, some force inevitably began to resonate between them. First as anger tinged with reluctant respect, and then as something else . . .

The thought of the last time he'd allowed impulse to rule him came flashing to the fore. He'd ended up kissing the delectable Miss Baker-Sneed, a feat he'd only just begun to appreciate. Now, it seemed it might be time again.

Perhaps if he kissed her just once more,

only this time very well and thoroughly, all of the tightness locked in his stomach and lower would release, and he would realize that she was nothing more than a woman. He would be freed from the curious fascination he seemed to be developing toward her.

Without further thought, he stepped forward and slid an arm about her waist.

"Lord Treymount!" She gasped, but didn't move away.

"You are wearing the ring. Perhaps I can't help myself."

She didn't move, but he could see her breath was now coming harder, her breasts rising and falling rapidly. "Unhand me or I shall be forced to protect myself."

"Then do so." Somehow, he knew better than to move too quickly. He bent slowly and placed a kiss on her temple, her skin silky smooth below his lips.

She shivered, her lashes dropping to the crests of her cheeks. "Stop that now."

"Make me." His lips traveled down her cheek to her chin, where he placed a gentle kiss before nipping at the corner of her mouth. She gasped, shivered, and put a hand on his chest.

But she did not push him away. Marcus noted it vaguely, his body and mind completely engaged on the woman before him.

He nipped at her bottom lip, catching it between his and then gently moving into a sweet, sensual kiss.

It seemed to last forever, that first meeting of their bodies. A surge of pure power flowed through him. He had yet to place a hand on her. Only his mouth. Yet his lips were wreaking their own havoc. "Honoria . . ." His kiss slid from the corner of her mouth to the tender spot at the corner of her jaw. "You aren't making me quit."

Honoria didn't want to. God help her, but what she wanted to do was pull him closer. She wanted to wrap her arms about him and pull his mouth to hers, to lose herself in the feel of his warmth about her.

Somehow, the thought became action. Suddenly, she *was* pulling him closer, wrapping her arms about him and folding beneath his kiss. It was madness and magic, sweetness and sin. It was everything a kiss should be but so rarely is.

Somewhere in the back of her mind she knew she had planned to thwart him. But she could not seem to remember her reason. After all, one kiss was not going to move the ring off her finger. All one kiss would do was make her very, very aware of the man who tortured her with such an exquisite glimpse of passion that her entire body swayed toward him.

He caught her firmly and melded her to him, the kiss deepening, lengthening. Each moment sent her senses tumbling further away from logic, further away from thought, further into the hot, wet depths of passion.

Just as she thought she would explode into flames, he lifted his head, yanking it up as if he'd had to force himself to do so. Blessedly cool air began to cleanse her muddled senses. Heaven help her, but her entire body trembled, her hands clutched about his lapels. At sometime during their embrace he had lifted her, and her feet now dangled off the ground. "Y-You may put me down."

His gaze traveled over her face, lingering on her lips. "And if I don't wish to?"

She took a steadying breath, her heart still thudding against her collarbone. He was smiling down at her, though it wasn't a gentle sort of smile. Rather, it was a superior, Treymountlike smile. "Please." The word was wrested from her, more because she couldn't think enough to make an entire sentence. Not without first putting some space between them.

He paused. Then, with a reluctance that was not lost on her, he slid her down, allowing her feet to rest back on the ground, though he did not loosen his hold. "I thought you said you could deal with bounders and cads." He lifted a hand to trace a lazy path from her cheek to the corner of her mouth. "Despite your fierce exterior, you are an innocent, and any man with a modicum of sense can sense that. That was my point to you last night about Radmere, though you would not listen."

Her back stiffened. "I — I may have suffered a lapse just now, but I assure you that is not a normal reaction for me."

He lifted his brows, amusement clearly etched on his handsome face. "Consider this a lesson then, in dealing with a real man."

"I do not need your 'lessons,' my lord. I can take care of myself."

"You seem to think your only danger is in rebuffing unwanted advances. At least admit that you are in no way prepared for someone who knows the way of seduction."

"Like you?"

"Like any man who might see you and thus desire you," Marcus said. He shouldn't have kissed her and he knew it. But he could not seem to resist the woman. She was an oddly wrapped package, all prim lace and proper clothing over a seductively enticing body and a nature as passionate as the most brazen courtesan. He knew this about her, knew it as if he'd known her for years. The contradiction made her intriguing, to say the least. He managed a faint smile. "Oh stop drawing those dagger glances at me. I should not have kissed you, but you must admit that you enjoyed it."

"I don't have to admit anything."

He caught her to him once again, holding her tight against his chest, her feet dangling inches above the ground. "Deny you enjoyed our kiss. I dare you."

She met his gaze, her cheeks flushed with fury, her eyes sparkling in outrage . . . but she didn't say a thing.

After a moment, he grinned and released her once again. "This battle is mine."

"What battle? We were just talking, not engaging in a battle."

"Nonsense. It was a battle and you know it."

She plopped her hands on her hips and leaned forward until her nose almost touched his. "Not one . . . more . . . word."

Had she stopped there, he might have been tempted to crow a bit more about his conquest of her defenses. But to his chagrin, the faintest quiver touched her full lips, then fled. A laugh, quickly suppressed.

He'd been the object of flirtation from

many women, and he'd faced countless pointed overtures that encompassed everything from fluttered eyelashes to come-hither glances to roaming hands and more. He'd rebuffed them all. It was his job to pursue, not the other way 'round. But somehow, all of his innate defenses went awry with this one woman and her tendency to chuckle, or worse, to make him chuckle, at the most importune times.

She turned away, saying in a muffled voice, "You shouldn't have. And neither should I."

"I couldn't help myself. There is something about you —" He blinked. Good God, what made him say that aloud?

She turned to face him, her eyes wide. "You . . . you couldn't help yourself?"

Wonderful. The cat was definitely out of the bag. Oh well, what the hell. He might was well admit all now. "There is something about you that makes me want to taste you."

"Oh," she said, rather breathlessly. She seemed to consider this a moment, for she swallowed, then said, "Well, it *was* a rather good kiss."

"Sweetheart, of all the kisses I've ever had, it was one of the best."

She stiffened. "*One* of the best?" Apparently outraged, she turned her back on him, scowling at the frieze before her.

Marcus laughed softly. She was a strange mixture of pride and purpose, a conundrum of sexuality and innocence. And he was beginning to relish every delicious inch of her. He regarded her for a moment more, admiring the curve of her cheek in the moonlight, the way her gown curved over her breasts and hips. The shimmer of light in her hair and the glisten of that fascinating streak of white.

Damn it, after all that, he wanted *another* kiss. He crossed his arms and leaned against the wall, turning so that her profile was outlined against the gray expanse of exhibits. "Of course, good as it was, that wasn't a *real* kiss."

She sliced a glance at him, then looked away.

He could tell she didn't want to respond, and yet she wanted to. He waited.

After a long moment she threw him a reproachful glance. "What *is* a real kiss?"

"I'm not certain you're ready to find out."

"Oh?"

There was a lot of question in that "Oh." Marcus hid a smile. "I stopped our little embrace before it could have become a real kiss. I wasn't completely . . . immersed in it.

I was trying to gauge your reaction and that spoiled it for me."

"I see. Yes. Well. Aside from that —" She waved a hand, her color high. "What we should be discussing is your ring and not a silly kiss."

He reached out and lifted one of her sable curls, twining it about his finger. "If you are so determined to discuss business, then we shall. Miss Baker-Sneed, what compromises can you offer in this matter?"

"None."

He let the thick curl sift through his fingers. "Come. Would you go down in price at all?"

Her jaw tightened but she didn't answer him. Finally, she said, "Six thousand, but not a pence less."

"That is still too high."

"Fine. If Radmere comes with an offer, I shall be forced to consider it."

Blast Radmere. "The ring was my mother's."

"I know. I will not seek out Radmere; but that is all I will promise you."

Marcus raised his brows.

She sighed, pressing her fingertips to her temple. "You do not understand my situation. You see, my father put all of his investments into a ship that was lost at sea."

"That was a poor choice."

Her eyes flashed green fire. "My father is a fine investor. Perhaps he should have been more circumspect and not placed so much upon one venture, but he will fix things. No one is better at finding antiquities than he. Anyway, we were counting on his funds to launch Cassandra and now they are gone."

Marcus eyed her curiously. "That is why you are so determined to get such a sum for the ring."

"It will be a year at least before Father can rebuild to a level of self-sufficiency. And then another year before he is in a position to afford something as expensive as a society launch."

"And your sister is ready to be launched now."

"She is almost nineteen now. In two years . . ." Honoria frowned. "It is unfair, but she will be thought quite on the shelf by then."

"Like you."

To his surprise, she nodded, not looking the least upset. She was very unaffected, his warlike Diana. "Why are you so determined to present your sister?"

"Because it has always been her wish. Besides, where we lived before, there were not many suitable men about and I feared she'd end up married to a farmer or worse. She's too fine for that."

"And you?"

"Oh, marriage has no place in my life," she answered, a faint quirk to her full lips. "I am much too fond of my own opinion for it to be otherwise."

Marcus found that he could appreciate that. He, himself, felt the same. Over the years, he'd grown used to having his own way. He wasn't sure he could live otherwise.

"I was presented, you know. But then, a few weeks into the season, my mother got ill. I was relieved to leave town, for I was awkward and bored and not at all accepted. But Cassandra likes that sort of thing and she is so beautiful that she will do well."

"So, rather than stand in a stuffy drawing room, you'd rather find yourself in the heat of an auction, pursuing an antiquity."

Her eyes sparkled. "Indeed! I cannot think of a better way to spend a day."

Neither could he. "I begin to see why you are so adamant about wanting your sister sponsored."

"And I understand why you want the ring returned." She sighed. "My lord, let me be frank. I engage in professional auctions and I understand emotional value.

Which is why seven thousand pounds is not that high of a price."

"You said six."

"That was before I realized that when you said we should both compromise, you meant that only *I* should compromise."

He laughed. "I feel as if you have already won."

"I have." She gave a self-satisfied smile. "You just don't wish to admit it."

Damn but when she looked like that, it made him want her all the more. "Miss Baker-Sneed, do not make me force this issue."

"And how would you do that? With another kiss?"

Marcus wanted to yank her to him again, but he knew, if he did, that he would not be able to let her go.

"Treymount?"

The deep, slightly slurred masculine voice came from behind him. "I believe someone is calling for you," Honoria said.

"Treymount?" the voice came again, upraised and echoing slightly. The man had yet to enter the room, but was calling from outside, tromping noisily through the hall.

Marcus glinted down at his prey. "Rescued by a drunk. The fates are watching out for you, my dear."

"Bloody hell, Treymount, I know you're here!" The man yelled louder still, the sound echoing off the high ceilings. "I saw your carriage and talked to that fool you call a coachman!"

Marcus finally recognized the voice. "It's Melton. He was to meet me at my house at noon. What the hell does he think he's doing, following me here and then yelling as if he's in a tavern?"

Honoria listened a moment. "He sounds angry."

"He has no love for me and would do anything to see me ruined."

Silence met this sentence. Marcus suddenly realized that if Honoria had raised her voice a moment ago, she could have drawn Lord Melton into the room. If someone found the two of them alone and engaged in a passionate embrace, she would be ruined and he would be responsible.

She seemed to read his expression, for she said coolly, "I have no love of scandal either." She stepped away from him and turned toward the doors. "We must leave. Lord Melton will be in here in a few moments and I, for one, have no wish to explain how we came to be alone."

He went with her into the next room. It was empty as well, but the wide archway into the adjacent room made it acceptable. Small groups of people could be seen walking from exhibit to exhibit.

"There are my sisters."

Marcus glanced in the direction she nodded. He could see a small group of women, three of them obviously school age, while one was older, and quite beautiful, at that. They were talking excitedly, their voices muted by the distance.

Lord Melton's voice sounded again, but farther off. Honoria looked around. "It sounds as if he has taken a wrong turn."

"It is but one of many," Marcus murmured.

"Yes, well, I should rejoin my sisters. I am sorry we were unable to reach an agreement. Fortunately, you still have several more days to mull things through."

She was a composed one, he had to give her that. Sighing a little, he nodded. "I shall think of something."

"I hope you shall. Good day, Lord Treymount." With a regal nod of her head, she turned and walked away, going to join the knot of women by a statue.

Marcus wanted to stay and watch her, see if some sign of their embrace lingered on her cheeks and in her eyes. But the thought of standing here, watching a woman like a lovesick pup — it was too much. Good God, what was wrong with him?

Frowning, he pushed himself from the column he'd been leaning against and left, making his way to his waiting carriage. Let Lord Melton come to his house, as he'd promised. Marcus could not leave the museum quick enough.

Chapter 10

No, really. I am certain Miss Heneford will look this way any time now . . . She is simply flirting by not paying me any attention . . . I'm certain of it . . . I think.

Lord Southland to his
friend and acquaintance,
Mr. Cabot-Hewes, while still not
looking at the woman standing by the
refreshment table at Carlton House

Marcus glanced at Anthony. "Must you do that?"

Anthony looked up from where he sat in a large chair by the fire in the library. "Do what?"

"Hum. It is most annoying."

Anthony raised his brows, his habitually sleepy look disappearing for a moment. "I was not humming."

Mr. Donaldson, Marcus's man of business, softly cleared his throat. "I beg your pardon, my lord, but you were indeed humming."

"Oh. I was, was I? What tune was it?"

A thoughtful expression crossed Mr. Donaldson's round face. "I believe it was a Hayden concerto, though I could not be certain."

Marcus scrawled his name across the papers before him. "No one could be certain of the exact tune as you were horribly off key."

Anthony looked inquiringly at Mr. Donaldson, who became suspiciously busy opening his leather satchel. Anthony sighed. "I am never appreciated."

Marcus slanted him a glance. "It is Anna's job to bolster your flagging sense of self-worth, not mine."

"Thank God for that. She is much better at ignoring my faults than you." Anthony stretched his legs before him. He dwarfed the chair he occupied, as usual. Marcus made a note on a piece of foolscap to order a larger chair for his brother. Comical as it was to see Anthony crammed into the seat, it had to be uncomfortable. Marcus handed the note to Donaldson, who read it, glanced at Anthony, then nodded and tucked it away.

The order for the larger chair would be placed before the day was out. Donaldson was worth his weight in gold, which was fortunate since that was almost what Marcus paid him.

Anthony yawned. "I am famished. Have you concluded your business?"

Mr. Donaldson adjusted his round spectacles and then placed a paper before Marcus. "Only one more issue. That of Lord Melton."

Marcus scanned the page, then glanced at the clock over the mantel and frowned. "We'll have to wait another twenty minutes at least, *if* that jackanapes even shows." He glanced at Anthony. "He is to sign over his lands today."

"All of them?" Anthony asked.

"I left him his house and some little land. He owes over thirty thousand pounds."

Anthony whistled silently. "How did that come about?"

"Gaming, mainly."

"I see." Anthony considered this a moment. "How old is Melton?"

"Twenty-three or -four, I believe. Old

enough to know better than to throw good money after bad on a gaming table."

"Do you think —"

"Anthony, how old were you when you took over the Elliot fortune?"

"Seventeen."

"Then I think a man of twenty-three might be expected to refrain from throwing away his entire fortune on the turn of a card."

Anthony sighed and stood, stretching as he did so. "You are right, of course. The man has been foolish, especially if he is that far into debt. However, I cannot help but think that you and I are different from most. My stepfather saw to it that we knew more than men of means even at the young age of seventeen. Not everyone has had our advantages."

"No. That is true." Marcus flexed his shoulders where they were tight. "It's an ugly business, any way you look at it. But do not think I am totally heartless."

"I don't. I just want to be certain you're really looking at this man, listening to him, and not just judging him."

Marcus frowned. What did Anthony mean by that? But before Marcus could ask, Anthony shrugged. "I'll leave before Melton arrives. It doesn't sound like a meeting I'd like to witness."

"As you wish." Marcus glanced at Mr. Donaldson. "Are you ready?"

"Yes sir. Quite ready. I have all the papers here. Now all we need is Lord Melton and it shall be done."

A discreet knock sounded on the door. "Yes?" Marcus called.

The door opened and Jeffries stood in the entry, impeccably dressed as ever.

"My lord, Lord Melton to see you."

"I'm off!" Anthony said. He winked at Marcus. "Go gently on the lad." And with that, he walked past Jeffries and left.

Normally, at this stage of the game — the moment of capitulation — Marcus felt a certain flush of victory. However, after Anthony's quiet appeal, nothing remained but a rather uncertain hollow feel, as if Marcus had been robbed of some opportunity.

Mr. Donaldson set aside the heavy account book and reached for his leather case once again. "Finally we can settle that little matter."

Marcus nodded at Jeffries. "Send him in."

"Yes, my lord." With a quiet bow, the butler left the room.

"Such a pity," Donaldson said, pulling out a thick sheath of papers. "I don't know how Lord Melton could be so irresponsible. You'd imagine that at some point in time he had to be aware that he was sinking into debt and that it was against all sense to continue gambling, especially at such a rate."

"Youth has never been good at visualizing the future," Marcus said. Or so Father always said. Of course, as Anthony had pointed out, Melton hadn't had the benefit of Father's wisdom.

Jeffries admitted Lord Melton. The young lord was pale and there was a slight swagger to his step that suggested a strong dose of spirits, though fortunately he didn't seem nearly as inebriated as he'd sounded at the museum.

Marcus watched the young man approach, noting that his dark blue coat and morning clothing were perfectly pressed. Except for the garish blue and gold striped waistcoat, he was almost somberly attired.

Marcus stood, raising his brows at the sight of the waistcoat. "Four Horse Club?" The club was very exclusive, and only a whip of the highest order was allowed in.

Melton's face reddened slightly, a bitter smile on his lips. "One of my few accomplishments."

Marcus gestured toward a chair near the desk. "Thank you for attending me this morning, Lord Melton."

"I looked for you earlier, at the museum." There was a faint hint of accusation in his voice.

"Did you?" Marcus said blandly, waiting for the younger man to take his seat first. "May I offer you something? Some tea perhaps?"

Melton perched near the edge of his seat, as if ready to spring up and run at a moment's notice. "No, thank you. I just wish to sign the papers and get this over with."

"I understand." Marcus nodded to his man of business. "This is Mr. Donaldson. He has handled many such transactions."

Donaldson presented the neat stack of papers to Lord Melton. "Here you are, my lord. You need to sign the top of each section where I have indicated."

Melton took the papers, his hand trembling noticeably. He stared down at the papers. "There are so many."

"It is quite a complicated process," Donaldson said calmly.

Melton nodded, though there was a decidedly disbelieving look in his brown eyes. Marcus doubted the viscount was capable of actually reading in his current state of mind, but politeness forbade him from saying so aloud.

Time passed. Melton turned one page.

Then another. Each with more rapid succession, until he was almost flipping through them. When he reached the last page, he gave a bitter laugh. "Good God, what a lot of words there are here. I — I —" He stood as if sprung from the chair by force. "I will have to take these with me so that I can read them more carefully."

Donaldson frowned. "I assure you the papers are in order."

Melton's face flushed. "I am sure they are. But I need more time to be able to read through them and make certain — I want to be sure everything has been done correctly and that —"

Marcus frowned. "As we agreed when we first embarked upon this endeavor, I left you Melton House in Knightsbridge and the surrounding lands. All you've forfeited are the farmlands in Kent, which is rather generous of me at that, considering the number of your markers that are in my possession."

"Generous?" Lord Melton's voice cracked on the word. "How can you stand there and say that you've been generous?"

Marcus's temper flared. "*You* were the one who gambled your family lands."

"Damn it, I know that!" There was a desperate keen to the young man's voice. "I was a fool, I admit it. But I was young. I didn't realize — that is to say, the people I was with, they went out of their way to conceal the danger I was in."

Marcus looked at the stack of papers in Melton's hand. For some reason, he found himself remembering Honoria this morning, of her indignant reaction when he'd suggested that perhaps her father had been a poor investor. Her eyes had flashed with the same fire he saw now, in Lord Melton's rather desperate face.

Was it possible that the young man had been tricked into foolish behavior at a younger age? Certainly many of the notes Marcus had found that belonged to Melton had been signed several years ago, though he wasn't sure of the exact amount. In truth, he hadn't paid it a lot of attention.

Marcus rubbed his chin thoughtfully. "If you lost so much then, why did you continue to gamble? Some of the notes I hold are recent."

"Because I didn't know how else to recoup my losses!" Melton gave a bitter laugh. "I don't have your ability to make money out of nothing. I was desperate and I thought —" He closed his eyes, his lips clamped together. After a moment, he took a slow breath and said, "I thought wrong, I know that now. But it just seemed that there was no other way. I kept thinking that perhaps . . . if I got lucky, I could win enough to fix things."

There was no doubting the man's sincerity. Still, there was the matter of the notes, all of which Marcus had purchased with painstaking care. "I am glad you realize the error of your ways."

"My lord — Lord Treymount — could we not find another way to work this out between us? If I could have two more months, I could find some funds — not all, but enough perhaps to satisfy some of my more pressing debts."

"How? By gambling yet more?"

Melton flushed. "I am no longer gambling."

"Oh? Then why were you in the card room at the Oxbridges' ball?"

"At the — Oh that! We were just playing whist!"

"Ah, but you were wagering, were you not?" Marcus lifted a brow, noting Melton's tight expression. "How do I know that if I give you a reprieve, you won't just throw yet more of your lands and money onto a felt table somewhere?"

Melton's shoulders stiffened. "I am sorry I asked for your consideration. They say the

Marquis of Treymount has no heart, and now I believe it."

"I have a heart. But I also have a head for business. If I gave you a reprieve, what guarantee can you offer to prove that you won't squander it away?"

Mr. Donaldson blinked at Marcus, plainly shocked at the suggestion of reprieve, but Marcus ignored the man. "Well, Melton?"

Lord Melton stood, his chin high, a fierce light in his eyes. "I shall never again wager so much as a groat. You have my word on it."

Marcus looked at the sheath of papers now sitting on the corner of his desk. His own property in Kent would double in value with this addition. And yet . . . for some reason, he kept thinking about Honoria's father, and about Honoria herself. About how at times effort and skill could not make up for ill luck. Marcus nodded toward the papers. "I'll accept your word. For now. Take those papers with you and think about your situation. Perhaps, if you can find a more legitimate method of regaining your fortune, I *might* accept your proposal."

"You — I —" The young lord snatched up the papers, gripping them so tightly his fingers left indentions. "You will not regret this."

"We don't have an agreement yet. I'll give

you two weeks to find a solution. After that, we are back where we started, and then you *will* sign those papers. Am I understood?"

"Yes, my lord. I will return in two weeks and you'll see —"

"I'm certain we shall." Marcus picked up his pen and pulled the rest of the day's correspondence toward him. "Thank you for coming to visit, Lord Melton."

Melton reached across the desk and, heedless of the damage he was inflicting to the papers between them, he grabbed Marcus's hand and shook it. "You will not be sorry, my lord! Not for a moment!" And with that impulsive gesture, Lord Melton left, a spring in his step, his head held high.

As his tread faded down the hallway, Marcus threw down his pen and sighed. "I hope I have no cause to regret that."

Donaldson wiped his glasses and then blew his nose in a most suspicious manner. "From the look on Lord Melton's face, I don't think you will. That was — It was quite good of you, my lord."

"Nonsense," Marcus said, though he had to admit that his heart felt oddly lighter. "It was just good business, that's all. Now the lad will work his heart out, and be the better for it, too."

Donaldson replaced the papers in his

satchel. "Of course, my lord. I look forward to seeing what type of endeavor the young man will undertake. Will there be anything else today?"

"No. But tomorrow we will go over the annual rents and —"

A soft knock sounded, and then Jeffries once again stood at the door. "Pardon me, my lord. A Mr. McTabish wishes a word with you."

Marcus nodded to Jeffries. "Send him in."

Jeffries bowed, then withdrew.

"Now we shall see which foot is in the fire," Marcus said with some satisfaction.

Donaldson raised his brows in inquiry.

"A former Bow Street runner," Marcus said. "I had the man watching something that belongs to me."

The door opened to admit Jeffries. He introduced Mr. McTabish and then withdrew.

Marcus waited for the door to close before he looked at the rough-looking individual before him. "Well? What have you to report?"

McTabish straightened his shoulders. He was a squat, square man with blunt features and sharp, black eyes. Greatly flushed, his face red and perspiring, his neck cloth damp and askew, as if he'd run a great distance, he appeared a little distressed. He tugged his forelock at Marcus, never sparing as much as a glance for Donaldson. "I apologize fer comin' in like this, me lord, but ye said to tell ye quick if'n anyone from that household were to so much as look at a jeweler's."

Marcus tensed. "Jeweler? Which one?"

"Rundell's, sir. The lady went there not two minutes ago."

"Which lady?"

"The tall one, my lord. The one ye said I was to watch particularly."

Marcus stood so suddenly a stack of papers caught on his sleeve and scattered to the floor. "Tell me all."

"Aye. She tooked that ring to a jeweler. I waited 'til she went in then I peeked inside a window and saw her takin' it off and handin' it to the gent inside the store. She's there now, tryin' to sell it."

"Ten pounds."

"Ten pounds? That is not even enough to justify my trip here."

Mr. Rundell straightened his stooped shoulders in an apologetic shrug. "I am sorry I cannot go higher, Miss Baker-Sneed. But I have a surfeit of these items and —"

"Not like this one! It is an exquisitely made snuffbox. Look at the painting on the inside. And the silverwork is perfection."

The jeweler lifted his glass and peered at the snuffbox once more. He lowered the glass and regarded Honoria from beneath his lashes. She knew he was assessing her worth — the more funding she might have, the more likely it was that, after she left her current embarrassments behind, she might return as a customer. It was for that reason Honoria had dressed in her best gown of green silk with a scattering of pink rosettes and her favorite bonnet with Russian trim.

She looked well and she knew it. In fact, catching a glimpse of herself as she'd left her home, she'd been somewhat saddened to think that Treymount would not see her in such a fetching bonnet.

Not that she cared. She didn't. Especially after he'd been so presumptuous as to kiss her, and in the middle of the British Museum, too. Ye gods, if they'd been caught —

The jeweler finally laid down his glass. "It is a lovely piece. I suppose . . . fifteen pounds, but that is as high as I will go."

"Fifteen? But —" She clamped her lips closed. She could tell by Mr. Rundell's expression that this was his final price. Feeling slightly misused, she sighed, then nodded. Fifteen pounds was still a goodly sum, though nowhere near what the box was worth. Muttering to herself, she took the money and left the shop. She'd taken a hackney here, wanting to arrive just as the store opened, and the shilling it had cost her had been worth it. But now she was faced with a long, rather windy walk home.

Oh well. She'd just put her head down and go her way. She grasped her reticule and was about to put the pound notes in it when a band of steel snapped about her wrist. She blinked at her fingers, surprised to see that the band of steel was made of a human hand. A rather strong, masculine human hand at that. She allowed her gaze to travel from the hand to a muscular wrist enclosed in a snowy white cuff and then on up a strong arm to a wide shoulder. From there her startled gaze slipped to the marquis's face.

Honoria's heart sank a bit. His lips were thinned, his face almost white as he glared down at her gloved hand. He forced her hand into the air, his fingers tightening cruelly.

Honoria clamped her lips around a cry, but she could not but gasp when the money fluttered to the ground.

He stared down at it, anger darkening his gaze.

Honoria took advantage of his distraction to wrench herself free and scoop up the dropped money. The crumpled notes in hand, she flicked a furious glance on her captor. "What is the meaning of this?"

His eyes flashed with fury. "Fifteen pounds? Is that all you thought it was worth?"

Honoria blinked at him, her previous sense of outrage returning. "It's too little, isn't it? I thought so, too, but that blasted jeweler would give no more." She glanced back at the shop front with a baleful glare. "If I'd had the time, I'd have sold it at the auction being held two weeks hence, but —" She suddenly realized she was giving away far more information than she should. "Never mind. This isn't your concern."

"Like hell it isn't."

Honoria stiffened. "I beg your pardon!"

"Just because I did not accept your ridiculous offer for the ring, you think to pawn it off on whomever just to punish me."

"Punish? Why . . ." Her gaze went to the notes, comprehension dawning. "Oh! You think I sold your ring."

A moment's silence met this, his blue eyes never wavering. "Didn't you?"

"No." She tucked the notes into her reticule and then peeled off her left glove. There, shimmering gently, was the St. John talisman ring.

Relief flickered over his face. "Thank God! I thought you had gotten upset with me and disposed of it."

"Not yet."

She was gratified by his instant reaction. His brows twitched lower, his eyes narrowed in irritation. Really, the man was devilishly attractive on a normal day, but for some reason, when angered, he appeared positively devastating.

His eyes flashed blue. "If you didn't sell the ring, what *did* you sell?"

She pulled her glove back on and turned on her heel. "That, my lord, is none of your concern."

She made it two steps before his hand grasped her elbow and he inexorably led her toward his waiting carriage.

Honoria planted her heels and drew them both to a halt. "What do you think you are doing?"

"Taking you home." He pulled her another step.

She forced him to a halt. "Do you ever *ask* for things?"

"You cannot think that walking some twenty blocks is preferable to riding there in my coach?"

He had her there. And she had not been looking forward to the walk at all. Not to mention that the wind was picking up and would have tossed her skirts and bent her poor bonnet to bits. "I didn't say I didn't wish to ride in your carriage. I just said it would be nice if you would ask instead of demand."

He grimaced. "It is in your best interest to —"

"It is *my* job to decide what is in my best interest and what isn't. Not yours."

"Damn it!" He took a deep breath and rolled his shoulders as if shrugging off an unpleasant thought. "Very well. Have it your way." He made a curt bow and said in a voice of exaggerated civility, "Miss Baker-Sneed, will you do me the honor of riding with me to whatever location you wish?"

"That is much better," she said approvingly. "Now say it again, only unclench your teeth."

"Unclen—" He snapped his lips together. "I was not clenching my teeth."

"Yes, you were. You were also playacting in a very poor manner, rather like a participant in a family theatrical." She arched a brow at him. "Did you ever have those? A family play?"

"No."

"Not even when you were young?"

"No."

"I find that hard to believe. I mean . . . all those brothers. What did you do for entertainment?"

The arch to his brows was plainly supercilious. "When we weren't playing practical jokes on one another, we fought. Fisticuffs were our main form of amusement."

"I see. What a pity you never acted, for I'm certain you could at least pretend to be polite if you'd had some acting lessons of some sort. My sisters and I do plays all of the time. In fact, we are doing *Romeo and Juliet* during the holidays for the amusement of our aunts and uncles. You might wish to attend and get some instruction on how to perform more credibly."

"No, thank you," he said, plainly unamused.

"Pity. Believe it or not, my sister Portia is quite the thespian. She might have some suggestions on how to rid yourself of that unpleasant wooden manner."

An astonished silence met this generous offer. Honoria smiled kindly. "Now, if you will excuse me, I have several errands to run before I return home." That wasn't true, but it made it sound as if her life was somewhat more important. She turned on her heel once more, only to be stopped yet again.

She sighed, looking down at his hand on her wrist. "Must you do that?"

"Miss Baker-Sneed, I will have a private word with you. Now."

Honoria sighed and cast a careful glance at his carriage. Plush and well sprung, it would be much more comfortable. And it would be wonderfully snug and much warmer than trudging home on foot. Still . . . she had promised herself to never again be alone with the marquis.

A gust of cold wind skittered across the road and teased the edges of her skirts. She shivered, then said, "I suppose it won't hurt. I can conclude my errands later."

"Excellent."

"But . . . you must promise not to stop anywhere along the way."

He nodded and went to open the door of the carriage, but a tall, cadaverous-looking gentleman got there first. His clothing proclaimed him the coachman, though he met Honoria's gaze with an impudent grin that showed most of his missing teeth. " 'Ello there, miss! Allow me to open the door fer ye!"

Honoria smiled uncertainly and went to climb in, but was halted by the sight of his lordship's groom's hand thrust before her, cupped as if for a vale. Good heavens, she hoped she still had some pennies left. She started to open her reticule, but Treymount interceded.

"Herberts, put that blasted hand away. If I see it again, I shall make you drive with it tied up behind you."

"Ye wouldn't!" the man said, plainly horrified.

"I would." Treymount placed a hand on Honoria's elbow and almost lifted her into the seat.

He requested her address for the coachman and then, just as Marcus climbed into the seat, he added, "And Herberts, through the park if you please." With that, he shut the door firmly and then pulled the curtains.

Honoria frowned. "You promised —"

"I promised to take you home and not stop anywhere, but I did not promise to use the most direct route."

"That's — Oh! Why are you closing the curtains?"

"Because I don't wish your reputation to be in jeopardy. Therefore, we will leave the curtains closed, at least partway. No one should be able to see through them without pulling up directly beside us, and the way Herberts drives, that would be nearly impossible."

As if in answer to this, the carriage lurched forward and they were underway, the jolting motion rocking Honoria back in her seat. Marcus watched her through his lashes. Somehow he could not help but be pleased. She hadn't tried to sell his ring after all. But the scare had made him determined to end this standoff. Somehow, some way, he had to get that ring.

He supposed he was being rather high-handed in his dealings with his delectable Diana, but he couldn't seem to help himself. She challenged him just by the way she sat, shoulders back, chin tilted up, her eyes snapping fire and disapprobation.

Marcus stretched out his legs before him, as much as the carriage would allow, and settled comfortably into his corner. It wasn't as plush or as well-adorned a carriage as his own, but it was enough to keep Honoria from trudging through the dirty streets on her way to whatever errands she possessed. In a way, he felt rather . . . chivalrous. Whether she knew it or not, it was better to ride in the carriage. And far better than leaving herself open to the gawking gazes of the rakes and fribbles who abounded Bond Street.

In fact, now that Marcus thought about it, he had not only saved her from the dirt and a heavy wind, but he had also possibly kept her from being importuned.

Yet still she sat across from him now, stiff as a board, her feet firmly planted on the carriage floor, her mouth folded in disapproval, completely unaware of the good deed he'd just performed on her behalf.

He eyed her mouth a moment. "You are much prettier when you smile."

She slanted him a glance filled with fiery irritation. She had such unusual eyes . . . such a clear hazel. The fact that her lashes were the same rich sable of her hair only made them appear brighter. "My lord, with you, there is regrettably little to smile about."

"Oh? What about this?" And without any more thought, he leaned forward and kissed her. Not a harsh kiss, or even a very passionate one. They were, after all, in a carriage still navigating the bumpy trespasses of Bond Street. But a quick hard kiss, one that set her in her place and marked her as his.

Marked her as his. The thought froze him back in his seat. Good God, where had that come from? He had no more wish to make Miss Priss his than he desired to become a coal scuttler. Less, even. At least a coal scuttler had some hope for a better future.

Pushing the unwanted thoughts aside, he

straightened. His companion, meanwhile, simply glared. After an uncomfortable moment, he finally said, "I apologize for that. I just wanted to make a point."

"Oh you made a point. If before I thought you a bothersome man, now I'm certain you're that and more. You're rude, irksome, asinine, overbearing, arrogant, insufferable —"

"But talented at kissing."

Her mouth dropped open.

Marcus grinned. "Come, Miss Baker-Sneed. You seem like a woman to prize honesty above all else. Be honest about this: you have never been better kissed than in my company."

Honoria closed her mouth and snapped open her reticule in a vain attempt to appear as if she was looking for a handkerchief. In reality, she needed a moment to gather her thoughts. The lout was right — she *did* prize honesty above all other things.

The problem was, admitting to Marcus St. John that he'd given her not just a good kiss, but the best — and only real — kisses she'd ever known . . . well, that was an admission of no small price. He'd gloat; she was certain of it. And each and every gloat would turn her stomach bitter and cause her soul to cringe.

She found her handkerchief, deliberately wiped her mouth, and then returned the handkerchief to her reticule, snapping it closed for emphasis. "Whether you are talented at kissing or not, it was still inappropriate."

"That's the problem with kissing: there are so few appropriate times. And so, one must be creative. Still, I thank you for the compliment of believing me the best kisser of your acquaintance."

"I never said that."

"No, but you didn't deny it either, which is just as significant."

"That's nothing to brag about because my experience is sorely limi—" She suddenly realized she was not ready to admit the barren truth of her life — that she *had* no experience. Not in the area of kissing. At least not any that she could recall with clarity. There had been a rector in Kensington, but that had been years ago. And then there was the cousin of one of her father's business investors . . . he'd had very wet lips, as she recalled. That kiss had been rather unpleasant and . . . dampish.

Of course, the real difference between the cloudy kisses of her past and the painfully clear ones she'd experienced with the marquis wasn't just that he had fine, firm lips, the kind that made you want to trace your fingers over and feel the warmth of his breath.

No, the real difference had been that she'd actually kissed him back. Her previous encounters had been sneak attacks, unexpected clutches by men of awkward nature and lackluster character. But the kisses the marquis had pressed on her had been warm, naturally sensual, delivered by a person of passion and wit, and they had all sent her body into an instant flutter.

"Well?" he said, his deep voice laced with amusement. "What of your experience?"

She bit her bottom lip for a moment, wondering what she could say. Certainly not the truth — her pride wouldn't allow it. And she had no intentions of lying. That left her with one option. She clutched her reticule with both hands and sent her companion a glare of no small magnitude. "I refuse to answer that question. It is unmannerly and rude."

"I only repeated what you —"

"If you intend on attempting a seduction in the hopes of garnering the ring, it won't work."

His brow lowered. "Wait a moment, I wasn't —"

"Furthermore, it is far beneath you to press your unwanted attentions on someone who has clearly said she does not wish them."

"I think that is quite enough," he said grimly, all of his earlier humor gone.

The sight sent Honoria's heart plummeting, but she really had no choice. She either made the mortifying admission that she had no real experience in kissing, or she attacked the marquis's character to the point that he no longer wished to know about her past. Or her present, for that matter.

She swallowed, the words sticking uncomfortably to the roof of her mouth. "My lord, I believe you should stop the carriage and let me out."

He regarded her for a long moment. "No, I don't believe I will."

"It would be better for all concerned if —"

One moment she was sitting in her corner of the carriage, feeling miserable and alone, and the next she was lifted and unceremoniously placed in the marquis's lap.

"Well," he drawled, his deep voice deliciously rich against her ear. "Since I have no redeeming traits, I might as well toss all pretenses at decorum to the winds."

She glanced at him, astonished at the fiery brightness of his eyes. Her heart pounded a warning against her throat. "Wh-What are you going to do?"

"It seems we cannot talk without arguing," he said grimly. "However, our communication in other areas is extraordinary. Therefore, I am going to kiss you. Again."

"Again?" Surely that wasn't her voice, breathless and rather . . . excited?

"Indeed. I shall kiss you until you cannot talk. Cannot argue. Cannot even speak a coherent word. And that, my lady, is exactly what I am going to do, the ring and your scruples be damned."

Chapter 11

There we were, watching Miss Heneford the entire evening while she smiled and danced and talked to everyone but us. Poor Southland got more and more despondent, but he would not budge an inch and so we stayed not ten yards from the refreshment table for hours and hours, looking like the greatest gudgeons on earth. 'Twas deuced ridiculous. You won't catch me, sitting around and waiting on a woman, not if I live to be a hundred and twenty. That's for damn certain!

Mr. Cabot-Hewes to his sister,
Lady Marianne McDabney
at Fountainhead, their family home,
as they joined their parents for dinner

Up until this moment in his controlled and settled life, Marcus had never felt the least urge to cross the lines of propriety. But somehow, during the onslaught caused by the heady warmth of Honoria's lush body against his own, he found himself in the most extraordinary circumstances — he didn't really give a damn about society, about propriety, about anything but continuing to hold Honoria. As a gentleman, he should have instantly released her. And normally, he would not hesitate to describe himself as a gentleman.

But today . . . in this moment, something was different. And instead of rigidly maintaining his decorum, he found himself treading all over the boundaries of good behavior, trampling mercilessly through the maze of polite society, and ruthlessly tossing to the winds every lesson his oh-so-correct tutor and ever-so-polite mama had taught him about comportment. To make it all the more confusing, he felt not the least remorse. If anything, he felt rather . . . pleased. Very pleased, in fact.

And all because of a very kissable, very warm armful of woman.

Marcus was amazed at this welter of emotion and feeling. He looked down at her now. Held against his chest, she glared up at him, her bonnet askance, her skirts rumpled and tucked under her, her face a study in feminine outrage. Not quite sure why, he found himself grinning, a deep satisfaction rising in him at the feeling of her curvaceous form pressed against him.

"Let me go!" She struggled, once, briefly, her bonnet slipping the rest of the way off and hanging suspended about her throat by the ribbons.

Marcus almost chuckled. She looked so outraged — rather like a kitten that had no wish to be picked up but had been. Honoria suddenly stopped her struggles, obviously fighting an inner battle between the desire to win her freedom and a very feminine need to preserve her dignity. "I will not allow this," she announced frostily.

The carriage swayed wildly as they turned a corner. Marcus tightened his hold, grinning even wider. "I'm not sure you have a choice."

"My bonnet ribbons are choking me."

He doubted that the scrap of starched lace and straw that made up her bonnet could weigh much. Still, it was not something he really wanted her thinking about. What he really wanted, he decided, was for Honoria Baker-Sneed to think about *him* for a moment. Him and no one and nothing else.

That decided it. "Let me help you." He tucked one arm tightly about her shoulders and freed one of his hands so he could remove her offending bonnet. It came off without fuss, her rich chestnut hair gleaming in the sunlight that flickered from beneath the curtain. "There." He tossed the bonnet to the empty seat. "That is much better." He smoothed the hair from her forehead. Silky soft, the long strands glided beneath his fingers.

She shook her head impatiently, dislodging his fingers. "Oh, stop that!" she snapped. "That was my new bonnet!"

"It still is. I merely put it on the opposite seat."

"You *threw* it on the opposite seat."

He glanced at it. It had landed on one side and did look rather bent. He shrugged. "I'll get you another." Now there was a rather enjoyable thought, going bonnet shopping with the irrepressible Honoria Baker-Sneed. He imagined seeing her trying on an assortment of bonnets, each more frivolous than the last as they revealed and then concealed that intriguing streak of white.

He touched her hair again, running his

fingers through her thick curls, loosening the pins and scattering them to the carriage floor. It was intoxicating, being this close to her. She had a strange effect on him, imbuing him with vigor and lassitude at the same time. He wanted to seduce her, but not quickly. Rather, he wanted to slowly undress her, slowly stir her awake and bring her to the brink of passion, and then let the fires rage unchecked, devouring them both.

"Lord Treymount, I don't wish to — How can you — We shouldn't — Oh blast it all!"

He dropped his gaze from her hair to her eyes. Her face was thoroughly flushed, her eyes sparkling. "Yes, my love?"

"This is very improper. I am surprised at you."

There was a sulky tone to her voice that, instead of recalling him to his senses, merely made him want to kiss her red lips. "Yes," he heard himself agreeing. "It is very improper. And I am rather surprised at myself." He smoothed a particularly fat curl from her cheek. The silky texture sent a wave of heat through him. "This streak of white at your brow . . . where —"

"I was born with it." Her mouth turned down at the corners. "Treymount, what are you doing? If you think to embarrass me into giving you the ring, it will not work."

"Embarrass? Is this embarrassing you?"

Her cheeks were bright with color, her eyes sparkling mutinously. "No."

"Then why should I release you?" He placed a finger beneath her chin and tilted her face to his. "Do you really wish me to let you go?"

A flicker of something flashed through her eyes before her lashes dropped to her cheeks. Then softly, ever so softly, she said, "Please."

She just said the one word, low and soft. But in an instant Marcus knew he was bested. Damn, damn, damn. He'd really enjoyed holding her. Sighing a little, he lifted her to the seat opposite, beside her bonnet. "Very well, but you owe me."

"Owe you? You, sir, owe *me*." She smoothed her skirts, her hands moving jerkily over her knees, then she picked up her bonnet and returned it to her head with such force that he almost winced to think of the damage she was inflicting to her hapless curls.

He regarded her for a moment. She was flustered, and flushed, and not nearly as in possession of herself as she had been at the museum. It was, he decided, a very good thing. Since she would not allow him to kiss her again, perhaps now was the time to talk about the ring. A flustered Diana might not be able to maintain her rigid dignity as well as the frosty Diana. "Miss Baker-Sneed, shall we discuss the ring?"

She sniffed and scooted into the farthest corner. He supposed she thought the move would make her safer, but all it did was inflame him with the desire to chase her, to capture her once again, only the next time . . . the next time there wouldn't be such an easy release.

But now was not the time. Once they had settled the matter of the ring . . . time would tell.

He crossed his arms and leaned into his own corner. "Shall we put an end to this cat and mouse game we've been playing?"

She sniffed. "I haven't been playing a game. You want the ring and I have named my price. That is all there is to it."

"I will not pay that price."

"Ye gods, how can you be so stub—" She stopped, closed her eyes, and took a deep breath through her nose. Her color soothed a bit and she said, "I understand that you do not like the price, but there it is."

He pursed his lips, regarding her narrowly. "Seven thousand pounds is a ludicrous amount and you know it. It goes against every judgment I've ever made." He paused a moment, his mind working through a myriad of ideas. "Perhaps . . . Is there something — anything — that you might accept in lieu of such an amount? I have houses here and there that I do not use but for their rents, perhaps —"

She sighed, and he noted the sound was a bit weary. That was a good sign, the first one he'd had all day.

"Look, Treymount, there is nothing I — or rather, we — want or need other than the money so that we can launch Cassandra. In fact, other than helping to sponsor my sister, which you rightly pointed out you could not do because —" She stopped, her mouth half opened, her eyes fastened on him as if seeing him for the first time.

He lifted his brows. "Yes?"

Her mouth closed, her eyes narrowed, and he could almost see the thoughts burning through her quick mind. What was she thinking? "There is one thing," she said suddenly, her voice abrupt.

"Tell me." He crossed his arms and leaned into his corner of the coach as they swayed around another corner.

She clutched the edge of the seat and regarded him through her lashes. "There is one thing I do want, but it is a rather large request." The coach settled into a smoother path, and she adjusted the bow that graced her bonnet at one temple, her long fingers lingering over the ruffled edge. "It would take some time, too, which you seem quite loath to give."

Damn. Perhaps this *wasn't* a good sign, after all. "Miss Baker-Sneed, just say what it is. What will you take in exchange for the ring?"

"One thousand pounds . . ."

He almost smiled. "Well. That's not so bad. What else?"

"Well . . . I —" The carriage jerked and bumped, and for a disconcerting moment it felt that they were flying through the air a foot or two, before hitting the road again and bouncing.

Marcus, leaning against the corner, wasn't even displaced, but Honoria flew into the air and landed onto the seat with a solid jolt. She grabbed the door handle and held on a moment. "Ye gods, what an energetic coachman! Does the man know what he is doing?"

"They say so. And I have to admit, he's never so much as scraped a bit of paint from the coach." Not to mention that the man could get from one end of London to the other in quicker time than most high perch phaetons, which were known for their light weight and quicker maneuver.

Honoria cleared her throat. "Before we get to my other requirement, what say you to the thousand pounds?"

"Easily done."

"Excellent. So it will be a thousand pounds *and* your help in establishing my sister in society."

"What? I thought we'd agreed it wouldn't be wise for me to —"

Honoria waved a hand. "I don't mean you to sponsor her officially; that would be very improper. But . . . and this is not an impossible request. You must admit that Cassandra is more than ordinarily pretty and it will take very little to successfully launch her. I have everything planned. All I need is your presence at some of the events she attends."

"Presence? I have no wish to engage in such mishmash."

"I know. Which has made you an even more valuable commodity."

"Commodity?" He almost choked out the word.

"I saw how the Oxbridges were thrown into a positive tizzy at your mere presence at their ball. That's what gave me the idea." The coach swayed, and she grasped the seat edge with both hands, though her gaze never left his. "Before you reject me, hear me through. All I'm asking is if you would pretend to court Cassandra."

Marcus frowned. "No."

"Hear me out! If you will but come to a few events and make an effort to be seen talking to Cassandra, maybe even dance with her once or twice, it will make her instantly desirable." Honoria smiled at him, a flicker of a dimple in her left cheek momentarily catching him off guard. "Surely that is not such an impossible request."

Bloody hell, did Honoria think he had nothing to do but dance attendance upon a chit barely out of the nursery? People would talk — oh how they would talk. The St. Johns were fodder for every rumor mill in town, and if he, who hadn't been the most sociable man of late due to his pressing business demands, suddenly appeared at a number of events and paid attention to just one woman . . . He almost shuddered to think of the comments such a thing would raise. "No. I couldn't do such a ridiculous thing."

"Then we are back to seven thousand pounds." She shook her head. "Think about it, Treymount. Seven thousand pounds for what? A few dances? A conversation here and there? Perhaps an hour or two at your box at the theatre? It is a very reasonable offer and you know it."

Marcus scowled. Didn't the woman know how many things he had to oversee? There wasn't enough time in the day as it was. Of course . . . He caught Honoria's hopeful expression, her wide hazel eyes shining with excitement. To his chagrin, the word no, which had spring fully formed to his lips, froze on the tip of his tongue and lodged between his teeth.

"Look Treymount, let me explain how things are. I told you before about our misfortune. My father invested most of our holdings in a ship, *The Black Pearl*."

Marcus lifted his brows. "The one that disappeared. Supposedly with a cargo worth a fortune."

"We think pirates took her. All we know is that she didn't make it to Spain for her final stores."

"So your fortune was damaged."

"We scraped together what little we had left and gave it all to Father to reinvest. He and my brother, Ned, are already hard at work recouping our losses. However, that will take a while, perhaps even a year or two. In the meantime . . ."

"Cassandra will be too old."

A rich flush touched Honoria's cheeks. "A stupid way to do things, for twenty is hardly ancient —"

"Twenty is hardly old enough to engage in a civil conversation, as far as I am concerned," Marcus said dryly. "I try not to converse with anyone younger than my favorite pocket watch. That rule has made my life much more enjoyable."

Her lips quivered at that, but she didn't quite manage a smile. "How old is your favorite pocket watch?"

"Five and twenty." He looked her up and down. "I daresay I shouldn't be speaking to you, right now."

"You are safe with me, my lord. I am seven and twenty."

"Thank God, then. I'd hate to have to toss you from the coach."

Her smile did make it that time, bursting forth with a rich chuckle that made him want to repeat the effort.

"I wish I could adopt your pocket watch rule. Unfortunately, I have younger brothers and sisters and I must speak to them."

"That," he said with a touch of truthfulness, "is a great pity."

"Not to me. They are a joy." She smiled at him now. "Well, Treymount? What do you say to my offer? One thousand pounds and a few dances with my sister. It isn't that much to ask."

Marcus looked down at his boots where they rested against the seat before him, attempting to stabilize the sway of the coach. His cool and composed Diana had a point — her offer wouldn't take much effort. For one thing, he already knew that her sister was stunningly beautiful — he'd gotten a good look at the woman at the museum, although . . . It was odd, but he could tell in a glance that as beautiful as Cassandra was, she had none of her older sister's vivacity. None of Honoria's even-handed courage and collected maturity, although he had to admit that he'd noticed a certain sweetness of expression. He was fairly certain Cassandra was harmless enough.

Still, he did not relish the thought of spending time with such a simple creature. Had he been asked to pretend to court Honoria . . . now that would be a task worth undertaking.

His Diana seemed to think his silence warranted a bit of encouragement. "It would take your presence at a very few events to get the rumor started. And if you were to take Cassandra riding in the park as well, that would be even better."

The gossipmongers would love that, wouldn't they? As would Anthony — good God, his brothers. If they thought him courting a chit out of the schoolroom, they would never let him forget it. "I am afraid your idea — good as it seems — would engender a lot more talk than you seem to think. What if people think my pursuit in honest and then suddenly I leave? The whole world would think me a philanderer."

"I'll make certain no one thinks ill of you. Besides, we needn't say anything at all, just that you both decided you didn't suit. And if Cassandra already has another beau — which she will, for you know how men flock toward that which they think is unattainable — then you can be certain no one will think ill of you at all."

"Wonderful. I will instead become an object of pity, yet another of my great goals in life," he said, his voice tinged with sarcasm.

She puffed out a sigh. "Oh for the love of — must you always be so negative?"

"Where you are concerned, yes," he said ruthlessly, swaying as the coach wheeled about a corner. Good God, where the hell was Herberts taking them? The old thief couldn't be driving this fast through Hyde Park.

"Look, Treymount, all I'm asking is for

you to —" The coach hit a large bump and sent Honoria flying into the air, only this time her hands came loose from the seat edge and she was tossed upward. Marcus instinctively reached across the coach to catch her, but she grabbed the door handle and saved herself at the last possible second. "Goodness," she said with a gasp, her eyes wide, her hair now completely tumbled about her shoulders. "Where is your man taking us?"

Marcus lifted the curtain flap and peered out. "Around Hyde Park," he said grimly. He closed his eyes and let the curtain fall. "Very, very quickly."

"I should say." The carriage settled into a more usual motion, and she released the door handle and smoothed her dress. "Oh pother! My hair is ruined." She took the length and began twisting it up.

"Leave it," Marcus said. "You've no more pins."

Her eyes flashed. "Through no fault of my own."

"Oh, I take full responsibility." And he did — with amazing pleasure. It was *his* fault she sat across from him, sensually mussed and fuming. He smiled.

Her gaze narrowed. "Oh stop it. We were speaking about my sister. This is the perfect answer — you get your ring, and Cassandra gets her launch. There is no cost for you beyond the thousand pounds, unless . . ." Her eyes brightened. "What if you held a ball to introduce her?"

"Bloody hell, next you'll also want me to finagle her an appearance at court as well. And vouchers to Almack's, too."

His adversary clasped her hands, looking far too pleased with herself. "Oh — !"

"No," he said crushingly. "I will not do it. I won't take the time and I won't ask for favors for a woman I don't even know. No, no, and no."

Her lips clamped into a straight line. "That's all you will say? Just no? Even after I've gone out of my way to be helpful in trying to solve our difference of opinion?"

Normally, when a person glared at Marcus, he was assailed with a desire to glare back, which he usually did, and much more effectively than any of his opponents. But this time all he could think about was the heated sparkle in her eyes. He wanted that heated sparkle, but in a different context. What he really wanted, he decided, was to pull her back into his lap and kiss that ridiculous frown off of her face.

She sniffed and almost flounced in her seat. "You, sir, are a cheapsides."

Marcus blinked. "*What* did you say?"

She hunched her shoulder at him, sunlight from the edges of the curtain dappling her hair with gold and limning the white streak. "You heard me. You are a cheapsides *and* a cruel example of humanity."

"I am no such thing."

"No? Well I, for one, find it appalling that you would wager a higher sum on a horse race than you're willing to expend on my sister's future happiness."

"You don't know what I wager on horses."

She lifted her brows. "You wagered two thousand pounds on a horse just three weeks ago. I know because my aunt was there and she told me about it."

"I don't know what you're talking about," he said stiffly.

Her lips curled in amusement, not the warm friendly kind, but the cold, supercilious kind. "Admit it, Treymount — you would wager more on a horse you did not know than you would pay to regain your mother's ring and assist a poor girl that you have met. You, sir, are uncaring."

For an instant something in her words seemed to echo Anthony's equally harsh estimation from not a week ago. Marcus clenched his jaw, his earlier humor fleeing.

Bloody hell, the woman had a damnable way of twisting his words. "I am not uncaring. I do care, but for my own family. It is not my business to care about anyone else's."

She appeared astounded. "You cannot believe that."

"Of course I do. What is wrong with taking care of one's own?"

"Nothing, if there was no one else in the world but you and your family. But you are not alone. There are people out there; real live, breathing people, too. People who need help. People much less able to take care of themselves than the members of your family."

He almost ground his teeth. "Miss Baker-Sneed, I do not object to pretending to court your sister on grounds of the expense. I object to it on the grounds of making a cake of myself in public. I would be a laughingstock."

"Nonsense," she said, her voice low and reassuring. "You'd come, you'd court, and then you'd wander off as many men are wont to do. No one has asked you to make a cake of yourself in any way. With just a little effort, Cassandra would be set and your services no longer needed."

Her voice tumbled over Marcus like honey over the bowl of a spoon, rounded and lush. He steeled himself against her. "I still don't like it. Besides, think of the time such a thing will take. I cannot and will not spare that much effort for something so unimportant to me."

She raised her brows, the delicate arches making her hazel eyes appear even larger. "Time? What do you possibly have to do that takes up so much time that you cannot attend a ball or two?"

"It would be more than a ball or two."

"Not necessarily. If you'd agree to sponsor just one ball in her name, I'm certain we could excuse you from most of the other entertainments." She pursed her lips, her eyes unfocused as she considered this. "Except, of course, a foray to the theatre or some such thing. We really could not use your box without you present at least once."

Marcus raked a hand through his hair. Was he speaking French or Italian, that she did not understand him when he said no? Good God, but the chit was determined. He eyed her for a long moment, a reluctant admiration pushing to the fore.

She folded her hands in her lap and leaned forward, her expression earnest. "Tell me, Treymount . . . do you think it is frivolous to speak to your friends? Your peers?"

"I don't have any —" He snapped his

mouth closed. The woman had him so wrapped up, he'd almost said that he didn't have any friends. Which was ludicrous, of course. He did have friends. Why, when he'd been down at Eton, he'd made numerous friends and acquaintances and had been considered quite a jolly fellow.

Of course, that was years ago and he rarely saw any of his old compatriots. But that was to be expected. They'd all grown up, gotten married, and had families, just like his own brothers. Which meant they were less accessible, especially since his own schedule was less flexible than theirs.

Not that he missed them, though. He was perfectly fine without such frumpy companions. That, and he was far too busy with his own life, his business and pursuits to maintain empty, trivial relationships. "I have all the friends I wish."

"Name ten."

Bloody hell! He scowled at her, wondering how he'd been tricked into even having this conversation. "I vow, but you are a cheeky wench."

A wide smile spread over her face, her hazel eyes twinkling almost merrily. "So I have been told. Come, Treymount, name your friends. Surely you have a few."

"I have many, thank you. Let's see . . ." He

raked a hand through his hair, pondering the many people he knew, wondering why he found so few of them worth the effort of getting to know. "The Duke of Rutledge and I meet once a month at White's and discuss foreign markets and the state of our shipping company and —"

"Do you and Rutledge do anything other than discuss business?"

He shrugged. "Why should we?"

"Because if all you do is discuss business, then he is not a friend but a business acquaintance. A friend is someone you share your life with. The things you think about. The dreams you have."

"Oh for the love of — Rutledge and I discuss business ventures. Surely that is a component of a friendship."

"Do you discuss anything of a more personal nature? Your household? How your brothers are doing? How you feel about your current mistress?"

"My current mistress is none of your concern."

"Of course not. But then I am not one of your friends, if you have any."

He made an impatient gesture. "I wouldn't discuss my mistress with a friend, either. I don't discuss those types of things with anyone."

"Because you don't have any friends," she immediately said with a complacent air that set his teeth on edge.

"Because I don't wish to have friends. There is a difference." Really, she made it sound as if his life was dry and barren, which was far from the truth. He had his family, his brothers and sister and their spouses, and now their children. He had a busy and thriving household, money to invest and grow, and he had his antiquities. His collection was growing to be quite valuable. What more could a man want? "I don't appreciate you putting a low value on my life."

"I wasn't. I was merely trying to point out that, no matter who you are, you can always do a little better, enrich yourself and your life a trifle more. None of us have the perfect life. For example, you would be much better off if you'd pay more attention to those around you and not keep all of your efforts for yourself."

"If I don't take care of the St. Johns, who will?"

"There are six of you, counting your sister. Surely some of your brothers would be happy to have the opportunity to assist in some matters."

"They might. If I thought them ready."

"Aren't most of them in their thirties? You must be at least forty, so I'd think —"

"I am thirty-nine, thank you," he snapped.

Her lips quivered, that entrancing dimple appearing and then just as quickly disappearing on one cheek. She had a lovely mouth, wide and softly pink, the bottom lip a bit too full, which made him want to taste it. Really, if he was going to have to listen to such irritating drivel, he might as well enjoy the view. And from where he sat in the carriage, the view was very delectable indeed. He tilted his head to one side and let his gaze slide from her damnably attractive mouth to the smooth line of her high cheekbones, and on to her thickly lashed eyes.

All told, Honoria was a fine looking female. She was a bit taller than the average woman, but with a proud figure that made his body hunger. He let his gaze linger on her curves a moment more . . . She had magnificent shoulders and full breasts that would fill a man's hands and then some. Beneath that, her slender frame curved deliciously at the hips, the length of her skirts hinting at a nice long stretch of leg beneath. He remembered the feel of her hip against the curve of his lap, and his body stirred, firmed, and hardened. Honoria Baker-

Sneed had a lovely body, no matter how ill tuned her mind seemed to be.

"Oh!" She crossed her arms over her chest, her cheeks appealingly red. "Stop that!"

Marcus grinned. "Stop what?"

"Stop looking at me like that."

He shook his head. "You are going to have to make up your mind. First you berate me for not taking the time to pay attention to those around me, then when I do pay attention, you tell me to stop."

"Paying attention is one thing, leering is something else altogether."

"I was not leering."

She arched a brow. "No?"

He let his gaze wander back over her form. "Not yet, anyway. But . . . I must admit, you are worth leering over."

"I vow, but you are the most monstrously irritating man I have ever met. You're cold and impersonal, until I wonder if you have a heart, and then, just as I'm ready to give up trying to find that spark of life, you turn into an overly warm rakehell."

"An overly warm rakehell?" He had to laugh. "What a title! And you hand it to me just for looking at you."

Her lips quivered, and for a moment he thought he was going to be treated to one of her chortles of laughter. But instead her gaze fastened on him for a long moment, her smile fading as a different, more frightening expression took hold. She'd had an idea, he could read it in her face. "You are thinking about something," he said. "Something I will not like."

She looked at him through her lashes. "Why do you say that?"

"Because just now you looked as if you were measuring me. You always do that before you make one of your devastating observations."

She leaned forward, her eyes almost pure green in the light. "But I was thinking . . . since you wager on horses, would you be willing to wager on something else?"

"Are you suggesting the ring for a thousand pounds and pretending to woo your sister?"

Honoria had to admit that he was quick, his mind lightning across the sparkle of a still lake. "Exactly. We seem to be at an impasse. This way, we might settle it once and for all." She tugged at her glove and removed it, then held up her hand so the ring would sparkle in the light. "What do you say, Treymount? Do we have a wager?"

His gaze locked on the ring, his blue eyes flaring at the sight. She could tell he was tempted. Her heart thudded an extra beat. Perhaps *this* was indeed the way to solve everything. If only she could get him to agree, then he would be committed.

She scooted down the seat, holding the ring before him. The sun streaming in from the space between the window and the leather curtain caught the silver band and reflected a flash of light across the marquis. The light flickered over his jaw, slanted over his strong face, and then caught the blue of his eyes.

For an instant the light seemed to illuminate those eyes, making them brighter, so bright that Honoria's heart leapt as if in answer, her body melting slightly. At just that moment, the carriage careened around a corner and Honoria went flying through the air — only to land firmly in the marquis's lap. His arms closed about her instinctively and she was tossed about no more.

She sat there, stunned. It felt almost as if someone had plucked her up and dropped her right here, in this man's lap. She blinked up at him, too astounded to move.

He appeared to be as astonished as she. But then the faintest glimmer of amusement warmed his face. "Welllll," he drawled, his breath soft across her face, sending an instant shiver up her spine. "Wasn't that exciting?"

Exciting was exactly what it was. Her body tingled, her chest ached, her stomach was a solid knot of heat. She had to get away from him. Honoria placed her hands against his chest and pushed, but he didn't release her.

She should ask him. She knew from past experiences that he would release her if she did so. But somehow, instead of asking him to let her go, she said instead, "This wager is the only way we'll settle our differences."

"You think so?" he murmured, his hands warm on her back and hip.

"I am certain of it." It was obvious that he wasn't completely adverse to the idea, for he had yet to offer a single objection. "Well?"

His gaze dropped from her eyes to her mouth, and then to where his hand rested on the curve of her hip. Honoria became aware of the heat of his hand through the thin muslin of her skirts. "I — I believe I am losing feeling in my legs."

A faint grin flickered across his mouth, settling in his blue eyes. "Nonsense. There is no more pressure against your legs while sitting in my lap than when you were sitting on the seat." As if to prove his point, he moved his hand down her hip to her leg and began sliding his thumb over the curve of her thigh. His voice lowered a notch. "Can you feel that?"

Could she feel it? How could she not feel it? She started to say so when a thought caught her. If she agreed she could feel the pressure of his thumb rubbing her thigh, he would have his admission that her legs were not going numb. And if she said she could not feel the decadent gesture, he would continue with the motion, driving her absolutely mad in the bargain.

And she was definitely going mad. An onslaught of heated shivers trembled through her. Ye gods, but the man knew the art of seduction. That really shouldn't have been surprising, for heaven knew he was as handsome as they came, with black hair and blue, blue eyes, a firm chin and a wonderfully sensual mouth. Added to that was a set of remarkably wide shoulders and powerful thighs that even now pressed against the back of her legs —

She bit off the thought before it devoured her whole. Her heart was beating a mighty tune, her skin flushed, a strange heat building in the pit of her stomach. "I — I think you should let me go."

His gaze flickered over her face. "Oh?"

Honoria wondered if he could tell how his

caress was affecting her. If he knew that she had to fight the temptation to lean toward him, to move her leg restlessly beneath his touch. If he realized that her entire body was growing almost achingly aware of him. Of how close he was — her bottom pressed against his lap, her knees folded over his. The faint scent of sandalwood rose from him and filled her senses with the tantalizing idea of reaching out, pulling him to her, tasting him, holding him, being with him without reserve.

Memories of their previous kisses flooded back and made her even more wrackingly aware of him.

His voice sounded at her ear, low and melodic. "What exactly would we wager on? A horse? A game of skill?" The pressure of his thumb increased ever so slightly. "Perhaps I should challenge you to a ride. We could plan several hurdles and whoever clears them the fastest and with the most grace, wins."

"Anything but horses," she blurted, then wished she hadn't.

"No horses?" His brows lifted. "You don't like them?"

"No." Honoria knew it was ridiculous, but she never went near a horse unless forced. Even good old Hercules, their ancient gelding, made her nervous. "I — I don't think horses would be a good wager. But how about . . . archery?" Yes, that might do. She used to be good at archery . . . when she was fifteen. It had been years since she'd twanged a bow, but surely just a little practice would see her skill revived.

"Archery, hm? I am quite good, you know."

"So am I," she said in as frosty a voice as circumstances allowed.

There was a moment of silence, a narrowing of his eyes, and then his hold on her tightened. "Very well, my little warrior. Archery it is. Two shots?"

"Closest to the center ring."

"Done." He settled her a bit more firmly on his lap and pulled her toward him. "Shall we seal our bargain with a kiss?"

To her ultimate relief — and somewhat startling disappointment — the carriage drew to a stop. Outside, she could glimpse her house through the window. The carriage rocked as the coachman climbed down.

"Damn," the marquis said. He sighed, then set her back on the seat opposite his and handed her the mashed bonnet. "About the details —"

The door opened, sunlight streaming into

the darkened coach bringing reason as well as light.

Honoria didn't even wait for the steps to be let down. She plopped her bonnet on her head and hopped to the ground, ignoring the coachman's startled exclamation. "Just write and let me know what time would be good for you, my lord," she called over her shoulder, and then in a rustle of skirts all but raced up the walkway to the safety of her own home.

Chapter 12

I don't play cards to win. I play cards to see how people react to losing. That is where I get my true enjoyment.

The scintillating
Lady Marianne McDabney,
after winning a handsome sum
from the rather hapless Edmond Valmont

Honoria took a deep breath, focusing every fathom of determination she possessed on the target that stood in the back of their garden. Of course, "garden" was a generous word, as the strip of land behind the house was a rather long, narrow affair lined with small trees and box rows and little else.

She supposed the marquis had a real garden behind his palatial house. For a faint moment she wondered what Treymount House looked like inside. She'd only driven by it in a carriage, and at the time had thought it the haughtiest house in Mayfair, which was quite a feat. Once she had the opportunity to meet the mighty marquis himself, the house had seemed even larger and even more inhospitable.

Of course, she knew a bit more about the marquis now. Strangely, that had changed her perception of the house as well. She absently flicked the ends of the feather shafts through her fingers, remembering the grand Italianate facade, the sweeping marble portico, and the ornate decorative window trims. Now she rather thought the house was simply commanding. Thus Treymount House wasn't as unapproachable as it seemed. For that matter, neither was the marquis.

She sighed, lifted the arrow and sighted down the shaft. Understanding the marquis would do her no good if she lost the contest. She took a steadying breath, then brought up the bow and notched the arrow. She eyed the target, pulled the bow string back . . . back . . . back —

"Oh pother!" Olivia said, exasperation in

her voice. She sat to one side of the garden, comfortably ensconced in a large padded chair as she critically watched Honoria practice. "You're taking forever. Just let it fly."

"Yes," Portia agreed. She was seated in a matching chair to the other side, her legs tucked beneath her skirts, her entire attention focused on her oldest sister. "If you wish to win, you have to be more forceful in your actions. More authoritative."

Honoria lowered the bow, carefully letting the string rest back in place. "That is the silliest thing I've ever heard."

Portia stood, her skirts rustling about her. "Here. I'll show you what I mean." She pretended to hold a bow and arrow, lifting her chin a ridiculous amount and saying in a loud, theatrical voice, "Marquis, I defy you to win! Truth is my armor, integrity my soul." With a grand sweep of her arm, Portia closed her eyes . . . and let fly her pretend arrow.

Olivia obligingly said, *"Thunk!"*

Portia took a noble breath, a blinding expression of hope on her face as she opened her eyes. "Did I — Oh yes! I did!" Still in character, she threw back her head and laughed, long and melodiously, before tossing her arms in the air. "Goodness and beauty has triumphed over all! Never again shall I question the hands of fate!"

Olivia clapped. "Oh Portia! You are marvelous!"

"Brava!" Juliet cried, chiming in from where she'd come to stand on the terrace. "Isn't that the scene from *The Lost Earl?* The one where the innocent Cleo wins over the horrid villain by using his own mother's secret potion against him?"

Portia fell back into her chair, panting as if she'd just run a mile. "Yes it is! Honoria should —"

"No." Honoria said, the arrow still unshot, her hand clenched over the bow. "I will not say such vile stuff. And Portia, you look silly shooting with your eyes closed. If you did that, you'd miss the target completely."

"Oh. Have *you* ever shot a bow and arrow with your eyes closed?"

"No."

"Try it, then. See if you don't shoot better."

Olivia nodded thoughtfully. "I think Portia's right. Honoria, if you would just aim, and then close your eyes before you let the arrow go, perhaps you wouldn't pull up just as you let the arrow fly."

"I do not pull up," Honoria said with some exasperation.

"Yes, you do," Portia said calmly. "Your last arrow went right over the top of the target and hit the yew tree."

"I can see it from here," Olivia said. "It's a good foot higher than it should be."

"Come, Honoria. Try shooting one arrow with your eyes closed," Juliet suggested. "See if it doesn't help."

Honoria had to quell a sudden wave of irritation. They were only trying to be of assistance and she knew it. It was just that she needed to win this wager so badly . . . She flexed her shoulders, managing a faint smile for her waiting sisters. "I daresay next you'll wish me to shoot blindfolded."

Portia appeared much struck by this thought. "Honoria! Would you —"

"No, I would not." She notched the arrow and lifted the bow. "But I will stop this muddled nonsense about closing my eyes once and for all." She drew the string and sighted down the shaft of the arrow. Then, taking a steadying breath, she closed her eyes and let the arrow fly.

It seemed to her as if there was a long moment of silence, well after the time the arrow should have hit the target. Impatient, Honoria opened her eyes . . . The arrow stood quivering not an inch from the center of the target. "Ye gods," she said hollowly.

But no one heard her. Olivia and Portia let out identical screeches at that exact same time, and Juliet was not far in joining in, laughing and clapping.

Honoria looked down at the bow in her hand. Why had that worked? It made no sense, none at all. Her chest suddenly felt leadened. What she'd give to be able to reset her wager with something other than archery. She'd been put on the spot by her own ingenious idea and she hadn't thought the wager through at all.

Though she wasn't sure how or why, she was certain this was all Treymount's fault. Had he not made her so muddled with his kisses and touches, she'd have been able to think much, much clearer and she wouldn't now be standing on the terrace holding a bow and wondering where her senses had gone.

"Well?" Portia said, sighing with happiness. "What do you have to say now?"

A lot. Only none of it was fit for her sisters' tender ears. Honoria managed to say tightly, "While closing my eyes may have worked once, there is no guarantee that it will work when the time comes to fulfill the wager."

"But you hit the target," Olivia said.

"It was blind luck."

Portia shook her head. "I vow, Honoria! If

you would just close your eyes as you loose the arrow —"

"Along with that pretty speech Portia made about goodness and beauty," Juliet added helpfully. "That would really impress the marquis, I know it would."

Portia turned a pleased pink. "That *is* a pretty speech, isn't it? *The Lost Earl* is a wonderful play. I changed a few words here and there and I thought for certain none of you'd remember it."

"Well, *I* don't remember any of it," Honoria said, a bit annoyed. "Now if you will all be quiet, I will show you that hitting the target with my eyes closed was nothing more than chance." She raised her arms back into position. Carefully took aim. And —

"Wait," Juliet said in a musing voice. "That's wrong."

Honoria clenched her teeth. Good God, what now? She turned to her sister. "What's wrong?"

"That scene wasn't from *The Lost Earl* at all, but from *Two Sisters.*"

Portia frowned. "Was it?"

Olivia gave a startled exclamation. "Juliet's right! That *is* where that scene is from. Honoria, you should watch Portia and learn some of her lines."

Portia nodded. "It would make the whole

effort of wagering with the marquis much more . . ." She searched for words, groping blindly in the air as if to retrieve them from there.

"Dramatic?" Olivia offered.

"Foolish?" Honoria said, her exasperation rising.

"Dramatic is exactly the word!" Juliet said, nodding her approval at Olivia.

Honoria sighed and set down the bow and arrow.

Portia frowned. "Where are you going?"

"Inside."

"But . . . aren't you going to practice? You've barely shot a dozen arrows and only one hit the target."

"No. I believe I am finished for a while."

Disapproval colored Olivia's face, too. "I say, Honoria, you aren't taking this wager very seriously. You should practice for another hour at least."

"Or more," Juliet added. "You aren't any better than when you began. Except for knowing to close your eyes."

"Perhaps later," Honoria said, marching toward the doors leading to the sitting room, her frustration so high she didn't dare say anything else.

"But — you will fail tomorrow if you do not practice!" Olivia called after her.

"And no amount of playacting will help you then," Juliet added loudly. "Don't you want Cassandra to have a seas—"

Honoria shut the door on them all.

From where she sat at a chair by the fire working on some stitchery, Cassandra looked up and smiled. "There you are! How did —" She caught Honoria's expression and bit her lip. "Oh dear. Not well, I presume."

"Actually, I don't know how the practice is going, as I cannot seem to get a moment's peace in order to try." Honoria fell back against the sofa, letting her skirts billow out before her as she stretched her legs straight in front of her. It was hardly a ladylike way to sit, but it immediately released some of the tension in her shoulders.

"Portia?" Cassandra asked in a sympathetic voice.

"And Olivia and Juliet. Everyone but you and George." Honoria picked up a small pillow and crossed her arms over it, resting her cheek on the edge. "Where is George, by the way?"

"In the kitchen. Apparently Achilles has taken up residence underneath a large stone pot, and George is considering making it the frog's new home rather than the hatbox."

"Good for George and Achilles. At least

one of us will get what he wants." Honoria sighed and plumped the pillow. "I vow, but I did not expect the marquis to write the very day I made that horrid wager and offer to fulfill it so soon."

Cassandra's brow lowered. "What do you think it means?"

"I think it means that he is very confident in his archery skills."

"And how are your archery skills?"

"I shoot better with my eyes closed than I do open." Honoria tilted her head to one side and considered this. "Which pretty much says it all, I believe."

Cassandra managed a smile. "At least you can joke about it."

"Of course I can. And so can you." Honoria sat upright, setting the pillow to one side. "Cassandra, win or lose the archery contest, it is worth the opportunity to perhaps gain the marquis's support."

"To pretend to be my suitor." Cassandra's cheeks almost glowed, and she said with what was for her a strong dose of reproach, "I cannot believe you asked Treymount to do such a thing. I don't know how I will face him."

"I was rather surprised at my own nerve," Honoria confessed. "Although it was a good idea. If he can be moved to bestir himself just the littlest bit, every eye in London will be on you. And with your beauty . . . Cassandra, you would take the ton by storm."

"I don't wish to take the ton by storm. I just want —" She bent her head back over her stitchery, her golden brown lashes resting on the curves of her cheeks. "Never mind."

Honoria forced her own irritation aside. It was quite unlike Cassandra to complain, even when she had reason. "Cassandra, what is it? Don't you want a season?"

"Of course I do," her sister said swiftly, looking up, a stricken look in her wide violet eyes. "I know how important it is to the family and —"

"Forget the family. We shall come about without any sacrifices from you. I have been pressing so hard for a season because I thought it was what you wanted, what you always wished for."

Cassandra sighed. "It is. Ever since I was a little girl, I thought it would be wonderful to attend the balls and parties. I dreamed of it, as you know. Only now . . . only now I wonder if it is really worth it all." She managed a small smile. "I fear I am being poor spirited in the extreme."

"Nonsense. It has been a trying few weeks. We are all on edge." Honoria snuggled back against the cushions of the sofa. She reclaimed the loose cushion she'd held before and again wrapped her arms about it. The silken texture slid across her cheek and she smiled. "I wish you could have seen the marquis's face when I offered to wager for his ring." She looked down at her finger where the ring rested, a band of warmth about her finger. "He was astonished."

"I daresay he was. Honoria, I think you will win. You used to be quite good at archery when we were at the seminary."

"Lady Elpeth Dandridge's Seminary for Young Ladies of Fashion." Honoria grinned. "Archery was the most useful thing I learned during those entire three years."

Cassandra smiled. "I know you will do well tomorrow. In fact, I'm certain of it."

"I just wish I had more than a day to recoup my skills." Honoria had no doubt the bounder had requested the match be held so quickly merely because he'd realized she'd want more time to practice. It was just like Treymount to cause madness and mayhem in her life. He seemed to excel at doing just that.

The memory of his touch in the wild ride in the carriage came tumbling forward through her mind, landing hard in her thoughts and muddling them further. How had she allowed herself to so forget propriety as to sit in the man's lap and then kiss him? She'd done all of that and then, to make matters worse, she'd taunted him into a wager she wasn't certain she could win. She must be going mad.

She rubbed her temples hard. Perhaps that was it, some sort of temporary madness that made her lose her usual calm, logical way of thinking. Whatever it was, she wished it would stop.

Sighing, she placed the pillow back on the sofa and stood. "I suppose I had better practice some more. Treymount will be here in the morning and I want to be ready."

"Of course," Cassandra said, smiling. She hesitated, then said in a soft voice, "Honoria, I want to thank you. You do so much for all of us and —"

"Oh pother. I haven't done a thing yet." She stretched, reaching toward the ceiling and rising up on her toes, her skirts lifting up about her ankles as she did so. The tension flowed from her neck and shoulders.

Cassandra watched her, understanding deep in her violet eyes. "You are nervous."

"A little." Honoria dropped back to her heels and smiled. "But that is a good thing, I have been told. It will make me focus better."

"You will do fine. If you win, we are set. If

you lose, we are no different than we are right now."

Honoria nodded as she crossed to the terrace door. "Where we are now is intolerable." She paused, hand on the door knob. "I cannot fail, Cassandra. I cannot."

"You won't," her sister answered. "I know it."

Honoria wished she could be as certain, but all she did was nod and then leave, closing the door behind her.

Marcus lightly ran down the marble steps of Treymount House, the brisk morning air fresh and invigorating. He paused on the bottom stair and took a deep breath.

"Up early, ain't ye?" Herberts was standing beside the carriage, having once again shooed away the footman who normally stood there.

Marcus eyed his coachman's attire. "Your coat is buttoned unevenly."

"Aye, well, oiye don't have on me undergarments either, what with it bein' so early and all." Herberts gave a huffy sniff. " 'Tis not proper fer a man o' yer stature to be up and about so early in the morn. It's upset me day, it has."

"And how would you know what is proper for a man of my stature?"

"Oiye know more than ye realize, oiye do." Herberts held the carriage door open and stepped aside. "There's a hot brick in there, if yer toes are cold."

"Thank you, Herberts. I'm certain I won't need it, but the thought was quite —"

"Oh, oiye didn't do it fer ye. Oiye did it fer me. It gets a might cold up on the seat and oiye thought to nap into the carriage once't ye were gone."

Marcus paused in climbing into the carriage. "You get inside the carriage when I'm not here?"

Herberts blinked, his watery blue eyes wide with surprise. "O'course. Where else did ye think oiye might be?"

"I have no idea." Marcus started to say something else, but then changed his mind. He'd deal with this later. If he waited much longer, he'd be late, and he had no wish to leave his Honoria hanging anxiously by her windows, looking for him. The thought made him grin as he climbed into the carriage.

"Right as ye go!" Herberts peered inside the carriage. "There ye be, guv'nor."

"Herberts, it's not 'guv'nor.' "

Herberts nodded wisely. "Me lord, then."

"*My* lord," Marcus corrected absently.

Herberts chuckled, waving his hands.

" 'Ere now! There's no need fer ye to call me a lord! Not that oiye don't appreciate the gesture, fer oiye do. 'Tis just not necessary, is all."

Marcus eyed the coachman narrowly. Was the man joking? Or was he really that stupid? Marcus could not decide, though he was beginning to suspect that it was a combination of bravado and brains that made Herberts so particularly difficult to train. "If you were in my employ, I'd dismiss you."

"If oiye was in yer employ, ye'd be takin' far more drives through the park like yesterday." Herberts winked broadly. "Didn't oiye do ye proud t'other day when ye had the lady in yer carriage? Oiye drove fer nigh on half an hour, oiye did. And 'twas a hot day, as well. Oiye thought oiye might catch me death ·of the heat." The coachman's hand mysteriously appeared from the folds of his cuffs, cupped in a suggestive way.

Marcus lifted his brow. "Are you expecting a vale merely because you followed an order?"

Herberts appeared hurt. "Lord love ye, no! Who said anything about a vale?"

Marcus looked at Herberts's outstretched hand.

The coachman blinked at his own hand as if surprised to find it attached to the end of his arm. " 'Ere now, oiye didn't mean any-thing from thet, oiye didn't!" His hand dis-appeared. "Oiye suppose we'd best be on our way. Where to, guv— me lord?"

"The same address as yesterday."

"Ah! Off to see the lady, are we?" Herberts wagged his brows in a ridiculous manner. "Well now, that's a nafty idea, see if it isn't!"

"I would appreciate it if you would keep your opinions about my actions to yourself."

And with that, he slammed the door. Mo-ments later, the carriage rocked as Herberts scrambled into his seat.

Marcus had to chuckle a little as the car-riage began to move. The wretch was a cheeky bastard and filled to the gills with bravado. Marcus looked out the window as the scenery of London flew by. The carriage rocked and swayed, but Marcus had to admit they were making excellent time. And if one did not look too closely at how many times they almost ran over or into other con-veyances, the trip was actually rather pleasant.

Marcus smiled, leaning his head back against the squabs. Ever since yesterday when he'd sat in this very seat with the de-lectable Miss Baker-Sneed cozily tucked in his lap, he'd felt . . . not ebullient, exactly.

But close enough to make him wonder at his own good mood.

Perhaps it was just the thrill of a challenge. He had to admit that he'd never before faced a woman who met him so completely, jibe for jibe, sharp retort for sharp retort. And now . . . he glanced at the wooden box that lay on the seat opposite, placed there by one of the footmen long before Marcus had climbed into the carriage. Inside was his bow and arrows, relics from his school days, to be sure. But he'd always had a talent for archery and he rarely missed.

Last night, just to be certain of his abilities, he'd set up a target by the stables and shot six arrows. All of them had been within an inch of the center of the target. If Miss Baker-Sneed were going to win this wager, she wouldn't have to be good, she'd have to be excellent.

Which was why, of course, he'd immediately penned a note and suggested they meet first thing this morning. There was no sense in wasting time, and heaven forbid he give the wench time to practice, though he wouldn't be surprised to discover that she'd not slept a wink, but had stayed up the entire night, polishing what must be fairly good skills.

Marcus smiled, remembering the last

time he'd seen the usually unflappable Miss Baker-Sneed. She'd been fleeing as if for her life, dashing into her own home as if pursued by the hounds of hell. And all because of a somewhat innocent caress.

That was why he knew he would win today; he'd discovered her weakness. And it was him.

Laughing softly, he glanced out the window, glad to see that they were almost there. Soon, he would possess not only the talisman ring, but a win over his luscious and delectable Diana, which was a prize well worth the taking.

There were days when it paid to get out of bed early. Whistling softly, he watched London rumble past his carriage window.

"The marquis is here! The marquis is here!"

Honoria sighed. "Portia, please do not hop up and down so."

Portia obediently began to hop from side to side instead, from one foot to the next. "He's here! His carriage just whisked up to the door. Mrs. Kemble went to answer the bell. Shall I have her bring him here?"

Honoria took a steadying breath, aware that her chest ached, her stomach felt hollow and her heart thundered in her ears.

"Yes, of course. Pray bring him here. The quicker we get this done, the better."

Portia nodded and then quite literally bounced back inside to inform Mrs. Kemble that the guest was to be escorted to the garden.

Honoria watched her sister go, then turned her face to the sky. The day was cool, gray clouds hanging low, a strong east wind rippling her skirts. She frowned; the wind could be a problem. It hadn't been so bad just an hour earlier, but now it seemed to be growing.

A hand slipped into hers and she looked down to find George. He regarded her with a serious expression. "Remember to aim a little left. And keep your eyes shut."

She nodded and squeezed his hand, glad beyond words for the comfort he offered. Unknown to her sisters, she'd practiced for almost four hours early this morning, but this time she'd gone to the tiny stable house tucked behind the garden. She'd used a bale of moldy hay from the stables with a paper tied to it as a target and, with George as her coach, had garnered a touch of her old skills.

Again she squeezed his hand. "To the left. I shall remember."

"Good. And don't be nervous." He pursed

his lips thoughtfully. "If you don't win, we won't be any worse off than we are now."

She sighed. "I know. Cassandra said much the same thing. And you both are right, though that won't make losing any easier."

He nodded in understanding. "I don't like losing either." He cast a dark glance toward the spot most recently occupied by Portia. "Especially not to someone who always thinks they are right."

That was it, Honoria decided, clinging to George's words. She was determined to win this wager because she couldn't bear the thought of appearing less than capable in front of the marquis because she found him — What did she find him? Attractive? Certainly. She'd have to be dead not to notice his physical perfections. But the real culprit was his damnable pride. If she lost, she just knew the braggart would gloat. He was That Type.

The door opened and Mrs. Kemble said in a breathless voice she seemed to reserve for the marquis, "Oh miss! It's the Marquis of Treymount *again!*" Then, much in the manner of a magician producing a flower from a sleeve, she stepped back and gestured to the door.

Treymount stepped outside. He was

dressed in his usual somber black, a rather large, ornate box in one hand. The morning sun reflected off the shimmery marble slabs that outlined the terrace and traced a flicker of blue through his dark hair. Honoria was immediately pinned by the marquis's blue gaze. Ye gods, but the man's eyes were piercing. They made her feel hot and uncomfortable and inspired her with the rawest of desires to turn and run.

It was a most uncomfortable feeling. Steeling herself, she gave George's hand another squeeze and plastered a fake, but welcoming, smile across her face. "My lord."

He bowed, setting down the box and regarding her with eyes that seemed to twinkle with amusement. "How are you this fine morning?"

"Ready for our wager to be resolved. And you?"

His lips twitched up into a smile. "I am much the same as you. Shall we?"

Honoria wet lips that were suddenly very dry. "Of course. I was just —" She gestured lamely, her gaze settling on George.

Her brother didn't see her; he was far too busy glaring at the marquis.

Treymount's gaze followed Honoria's and he raised his brows at George's stubborn expression. "Well hello," the marquis said. "I see you've a man about the house after all."

George's face flushed red. "My brother Ned isn't here, or he'd be wagering you instead."

Treymount turned an amused gaze back to Honoria. "A whole family of gamblers, hm?"

She almost smiled at that. "Hardly." Placing her hand on George's shoulder, she led him to a small bench and pressed him into the seat. The wind rose for an instant and sent her skirts swirling madly about her ankles. "George, watch and tell me how I'm doing."

George nodded. "Just remember how we practiced."

"Of course." With a reassuring smile, she returned to the marquis.

"Practiced?" he said softly, his blue eyes laughing down at her.

"Merely an exhibition for my brother and sisters." Honoria's cheeks heated a little at the lie. "I didn't need to practice." She eyed him for a moment. "Did *you* practice?"

"For hours." He opened the box and drew out his own bow.

Honoria blinked. It was a gorgeous bow, made of the finest ash, the size of it almost twice hers.

In fact . . . she looked down at her own bow and wondered for a mad moment if she could perhaps change the wager. Surely there was something else she could have —

"Are you prepared to begin, Miss Baker-Sneed?"

The marquis's soft voice jerked her back into reality, not just by the richness of it, but by its proximity. Somehow, he'd moved until he was only a foot away, close enough that his knees brushed her skirts.

Honoria's heart raced and she found herself looking up into his face, her mind completely locked upon him. Ye gods, but the man was beyond gorgeous.

"Honoria?"

Cassandra's soft call made Honoria aware that she was staring at her opponent in a most distracted way.

"Oh. Uhm." Honoria forced her eyes away from the marquis, and the languorous heat simmered down to a gentle tickle. "Yes?"

Cassandra placed her hand on Honoria's arm. "I wanted to wish you luck."

"Me, too," Juliet said from where she'd just come out onto the terrace.

Honoria glanced around and frowned. "Where are Portia and Olivia?"

Cassandra's gaze followed hers. "I don't know. They were just here —"

"They went inside," Juliet said hastily, glancing at the doors. "They said they couldn't stand the excitement."

That was odd, Honoria thought. Portia especially had been ecstatic about the contest, while Olivia —

"Shall we begin?" the marquis asked.

Honoria gathered her thoughts. "Of course."

He bowed and stepped back. "After you, then. The better of two shots."

Heart thudding uncomfortably, Honoria faced the target and drew the arrow into place. Squinting, she pulled back, sited the target, then closed her eyes . . . and let the arrow fly.

Thunk.

George gave an excited yelp. Honoria opened her eyes and blinked. Then blinked again. The arrow had hit the bull's mark dead center. She turned to face the marquis, only to find him looking at her. At her astonished expression, his brows lowered a bit and he glanced toward the target.

His smile faded. He regarded the arrow for a long moment, then slanted a considering glance at Honoria. After a moment his expression relaxed. "You are surprised."

Surprised didn't begin to describe it. She

was astonished. Amazed. Incredulous. Flabbergasted. And completely befuddled. Not once in all the times she'd shot the arrow during practice had she come close to the center.

"Very good," Cassandra said, her voice light with amusement.

"Capital shot!" George cried. "You did just as I told you, closed your eyes and shot to the left!"

Honoria could scarcely believe her luck. It had to be fate at work. A smile began to tickle her cheeks. It spread from there to her heart, so that it was with real joy that she met Marcus's gaze. "I am a little surprised."

"Little?"

"Well . . . I did practice. And I was doing quite well, too. Only not *this* well."

Of course, it could just be beginner's luck. Or the fact that her blood was high from the whole idea of winning this wager.

Whatever it was, she could only be thankful. "I suppose I should take my second shot."

"By all means." There was a faintly sarcastic tone to his voice, but she ignored it.

Honoria put her second arrow into the bow. Her heart pounded in her ears. Her hands were shaking just the slightest bit and she drew in a breath to steady them. *Remember to close your eyes, and think a little to the left of center,* she reminded herself. Deep breath. Aim the arrow. Close her eyes. And . . . *Thunk.*

Honoria opened her eyes and then gave an excited hop. She'd done it! This one hit slightly to the left of the center, but close enough to the original arrow to make it quiver in place.

"Did you —" The marquis rubbed his temple.

"Did I what?"

He shook his head. "Nothing. It just looked as if — It's the wind. It appeared as if the target bobbled just a bit."

"The wind is very persuasive today."

"Yes."

Honoria smiled. It was all she could do not to give another excited hop. Ye gods, what excellent shots! It was a great deal too bad Portia and Olivia were not here, for Honoria was certain her sisters would be dancing up and down.

Feeling better by the minute, she smiled sweetly up at the marquis. "I believe it is your turn."

He undid the buttons on his coat, pausing when he caught her eyes upon him. He raised his brow. "If you don't mind?"

319

Heat touched her cheeks, but she forced herself to shrug as if she did not care. "As you wish."

Humor glinted in his eyes as if he knew her thoughts, and then he undid his coat and shrugged out of it. With a bow, he then laid it across the railing that lined the edges of the terrace. The wind immediately began rifling through his coat where it lay on the rail, making it dance a bit, as if it had a life of its own.

Honoria ignored the coat. She could not help but admire the marquis's athletic form as he lifted his bow and tested it a moment. The sunlight glinted off his hair and touched the fine lines of his face. It really was unfair for a man to have such thick lashes. She lifted a finger to her own lashes, which were of average length. Normally, she felt quite comfortable with them, but now, seeing Marcus's . . . She sighed.

But even more disturbing was the line of his well-muscled arm beneath the fine linen of his shirt. She'd not have believed him to be so well-defined. Most members of the peerage seemed to be rather soft and shapeless, or so she'd thought. Not all of them, of course. Just most. But Treymount was obviously one who was not.

Unaware of her regard, he pulled back the arrow and released it. *Thunk*. Honoria suddenly realized she'd been watching him and not the target. She spun on her heel and looked . . . His arrow was a good two inches from the center of the target.

"Well!" She said brightly, aware of a surge of exhilaration.

"Blast it, but —" He shook his head as if to clear his vision. "I thought — I thought that the —" He bit off the last word, his brows lowered, his mouth thinned. "Blasted wind."

"It is quite wretched, is it not?" Honoria felt she could be gracious if nothing else. She smiled broadly and waved a hand. "Are you ready for your next shot?"

He glowered. "Damn right I am." He lifted the bow, fitted it to his shoulder, and the let the arrow fly. Once again there was a solid thunk, only this time Honoria was facing the target. It was strange, but just as the marquis let his arrow fly, it seemed as if the entire target shifted ever so slightly to one side.

Heavens, the wind *was* horrid. As if in answer to her thoughts, a tiny whirlwind of leaves and debris swirled up onto the terrace and fell apart against the stone wall.

Honoria realized then that the marquis's

arrow was right where his first arrow was —
buried too far to the right.

She'd won.

She gave an excited screech and hopped
up and down. She'd won! The marquis
would have to help Cassandra now! All of
their worries were over! She could scarcely
believe her good luck.

She clapped her hands and turned to face
her competitor, then stopped when she
caught his dark glance. "Oh. Pardon me. I
was just — I didn't mean to be so —"

"You are enjoying the fruits of your win,"
he said, a reluctant smile touching his mouth.

"Only a little." She made a tiny space between her thumb and finger. "A very tiny
little."

A dry chuckle escaped him. "I don't suppose I blame you. I would be doing the same
thing, only . . . not quite so visibly."

He really did have a lovely smile. So
lovely, in fact, that she rather wished he
wouldn't use it. Not that she witnessed it
often — she didn't. But the damn thing was
nigh irresistible, and Honoria worried that
she might fall under its charm at a crucial
moment of some sort.

The thought was both fearful and intriguing, all at the same time.

Marcus's gaze flickered past her to the

target, the smile melting into a perplexed look. There was still a touch of chagrin on his face and for an instant Honoria felt badly for him. But then she remembered that all he stood to lose was a little of his oh-so-precious time and a thousand pounds, and that he would regain possession of his mother's ring as well.

Thus, when he finally managed to drag his gaze from the target and back to her, she was able to smile without feeling the slightest remorse. "I had forgotten how much fun archery could be. Would you like to shoot another round?"

"Oh no!" Juliet rushed forward from where she'd been standing to one side. She laughed awkwardly, her violet eyes bright, almost too bright. "I am quite certain you've both shot enough for one day! Why don't — I mean, perhaps we should all retire for some tea or some port or —"

Cassandra placed her hand on Juliet's arm. "It's too early for port. Perhaps the marquis would like some breakfast?"

Honoria looked at him. "Could we tempt you?"

"I am tempted, but I cannot." He picked up his box and replaced his bow, then started to walk toward the target to retrieve his arrows.

But Juliet was quicker. She ran before him, her skirts lifted as she dashed ahead. "I'll get them! You stay here with Cassandra and Honoria!" And with that she was gone, almost running to the target.

Honoria frowned. "I believe Juliet has had too much chocolate this morning."

"I was just thinking the same thing," Cassandra murmured, frowning as she watched their sister dash to the target and begin yanking arrows from it as if her life depended on it. What was worse, she was talking to herself, almost arguing about something.

The marquis said little, but finished replacing his bow, and then pulled on his coat. Juliet ran up then and handed him his arrows. He thanked her politely and then replaced them in their slots.

"Are you certain you won't stay for breakfast?" Honoria asked, suddenly feeling . . . lost.

He shut the box with a snap. "No, thank you. But I shall have my man of business contact you about how best to settle our wager."

Honoria dipped a curtsy. "Thank you, my lord. I shall look forward to it."

His eyes darkened at her prim manner. "You are a cheeky wench."

Cassandra gasped, but Honoria just grinned. "Only when I win."

He leaned forward, his blue eyes hard and unyielding. "Then I shall have to see to it that you do not win too often."

She opened her mouth to retort, but Cassandra chose that moment to say, "My lord, thank you for your assistance. I hope escorting me will not be too much effort."

The marquis turned to Cassandra, and it seemed to Honoria that his expression softened ever so slightly as he bowed. "It will be a pleasure."

Color suffused Cassandra's face. Honoria should have been pleased; certainly such gallantry was a step in the right direction. But for some reason she could not help feeling a flash of pure, raw envy.

Unaware that he was raising such unworthy emotions in her breast, the marquis smiled at Cassandra before sending Honoria one last fulminating look. Then turning on his heel, he left.

As soon as he was out of sight, Juliet threw her arms into the air and gave a huge whoop. "We won! We won!" She grabbed George and swung him around, much to his chagrin.

Cassandra smiled at Honoria. "What a lovely morning it has become."

"It is one of the best," Honoria agreed, linking her arm through her sister's. "But it will be even better once I've had my breakfast. For some reason, I'm famished."

"Winning will do that to you," Cassandra agreed. "Come, everyone. Let's have breakfast."

Chapter 13

So then I played the jack . . . or was it the queen? Either way, it was an error, for that harridan trumped me immediately. So then I played my ten. No, wait . . . it was an eight. But that was a poor choice, too. Over and over she won. She must have cheated, for you know how I am at cards. I do not like to brag, but I have a memory of steel and I never forget who is holding what.

Lord Edmond Valmont to
Miss Clarissa Ridgethorpe,
while strolling the hedgerows at Vauxhall
under the strict supervision of
Miss Ridgethorpe's mama

"You did *what?*"

Marcus took a drink of his port in an effort to cover his irritation. Why had he told Anthony about the wager? Why? "I am not repeating myself."

"Good, because I don't think I would believe it even if you did." Anthony shook his head, his tawny locks making him look like a disgruntled lion. "How on earth did Honoria Baker-Sneed get you to agree to such a thing?"

How? She'd sat there on the carriage seat, her rich chestnut hair tumbling about her shoulders, that intriguing streak of white at her temple, and then she'd fixed those large, hazel eyes on him with a look of utter disdain. He had to bite back a strange desire to smile at the memory.

That's all it had taken. He'd been so ripe for a taste of her, it was a good thing that all she *had* asked for was a simple wager. Marcus wasn't certain he'd have been able to say nay regardless of what she'd asked. Why, it was the thought of her that had made him soften toward Lord Melton, a fact Mr. Donaldson was still muttering about beneath his breath.

Marcus smiled, thinking of Honoria as she'd been this very morning, arrayed for battle, all pale and tense, the wind toying with the edges of her skirts. He'd wanted nothing more than to sweep her into his arms and kiss away the frown that rested on her brow. It was strange indeed that he was becoming so quixotic so late in his life. Why was that? he wondered. Did it have to do with the way Honoria tossed out challenges with her very breath? Or was it something far more simple? Like . . . chivalry?

The thought almost made him choke, and he had to clear his throat twice before he could even breathe again. Catching Anthony's inquiring glance, Marcus said hastily, "She offered the wager and I accepted. That's all there was to it."

"And then she beat you? At archery?"

"Yes." He frowned. He still wasn't quite certain how that had happened. Of course, the wind had been blowing quite hard, and that could have made his arrows fly to the side, but . . . he could have sworn he'd seen the target move. Perhaps that had been the work of the wind as well.

Whatever it was, he hadn't paid it as much attention as he should have — he'd been far too engrossed in watching Honoria shoot. She'd never looked lovelier, her hair touched by the morning sun, her eyes reflecting the green of the garden, her slender body as she drew the arrow —

"Perhaps she cheated."

Marcus frowned. "She would never cheat. She is not the type."

Anthony eyed him a moment, a slow smile touching his mouth. "I think you've gone mad. And I mean that in the best way possible."

"Mad? Why? If I'd won this morning, I would have mother's ring back. It was a perfectly sane wager."

"I think you're mad because in the grand scheme of life, seven thousand pounds isn't that much to you, and you'd have already had mother's ring if you'd just loosened up your purse strings a bit. No, there's another reason you didn't want to just pay the funds. And I think it has to do with that woman." Anthony's brown eyes sparkled. "I think you're intrigued with her."

Marcus wondered how he'd even allowed himself to have this conversation with Anthony. But . . . there was something in what his brother said. He couldn't remember ever being so fascinated by a woman. Never. Not to the point of agreeing to something as childish as an archery contest.

He caught Anthony's considering gaze and lied, "Perhaps I'd had a bit too much to drink."

Anthony grunted, leaning his large frame back in the chair and regarding Marcus through half closed eyes. Anthony always looked sleepy, especially when he was considering something.

Before his brother could come to any more incorrect conclusions, Marcus poured himself another spot of port, refilling Anthony's glass at the same time. "There," Marcus said, pushing the glass across the table. "Drink that and stop looking at me as if I've spouted two heads."

Anthony took the drink. "I wasn't thinking that at all. In fact, I was thinking that perhaps your head has finally moved to where it should have been all along."

"Oh? Where's that?"

"Connected to your heart."

Marcus frowned. "That is the second time in less than two weeks you have suggested I am coldhearted."

Anthony hesitated. "Coldhearted is too severe of a word. Actually, I rather think it is an instance of pride. You have been inordinately successful, and due to your standing in the family, weighted with a lot of responsibility. I think it has come to you so naturally that you forget other people have different capabilities, different interests."

Marcus clenched his jaw a moment. It was not pleasant to hear such things, especially from a brother. "I am not coldhearted, nor am I so eaten with pride that I no longer care for my fellow man."

"You wouldn't really notice it if you were, would you? That's rather the nature of such an affliction. You have a tendency to see things through a rather unemotional filter."

Marcus looked down at his glass, at the golden amber liquid that sparkled there. Damn it, there was something in what Anthony was saying. Not a lot, but . . . something. Marcus's mind wandered to the Baker-Sneed home. There had been plenty of evidence that the family was having financial difficulties, and yet the home felt . . . warm, somehow. Warm and comfortable. He'd been aware of a sense of familial support the very second his booted feet had crossed the threshold.

His own house, meanwhile . . . He glanced about the huge library. Two stories tall with shelves from ceiling to floor and a narrow balcony rimming the entire room, it was a thing of beauty. He'd paid a fortune to have a mural painted on the ceiling by an Italian with a penchant for plump angels and scantily clad graces. A long, narrow ladder was fixed to a metal track so that one could access the balcony from any part of the room, and thus the second level of books, with the greatest of ease. It was a beautiful room, impressive even. But it still lacked something. The truth was, it felt a little like a museum rather than a home.

The really irksome question was, he supposed, was it just his house that felt so barren of feeling? Or was it more? Was it possible that it was *he* who was so without warmth and compassion? Had he forgotten his own humanity in his quest to secure the family fortune?

He imagined Honoria this morning, pale and determined, her hands shaking ever so slightly. She'd wanted so badly to win. And not for herself, but for her sister. She'd put her honor and pride on the line. What had he put? Nothing, really. A few moments of his time and . . . that was it. And he'd complained about even that.

"Marcus?" Anthony's dark gaze rested on Marcus's face. "What is it?"

He sighed. "I was just thinking of what you said."

"And?"

Marcus shrugged. "Nothing. I am sure it's just a momentary flicker of humanity, one sure to pass if I will but allow it."

Anthony sighed. "I didn't mean to upset you."

"You didn't. But you have made me think. May we now speak of something else? Something more interesting?"

"Of course. Shall we discuss how you're going to woo the lovely Cassandra?" A tremor of laughter warmed Anthony's voice.

Marcus regarded his brother with a flat gaze. "I am not going to woo her. I am merely going to pay her some attention. Everyone will then begin to gossip and the chit's feet will be set on the path of social success. Or so Miss Honoria would have me believe."

"I really must spend some time with this Miss Honoria. She seems like quite a woman. A goddess, in fact."

"That's funny —" Marcus shook his head.

"What?" Anthony raised his brows.

"Nothing really. It's just that . . . I called her Diana because she looks so like the statue residing in the Elgin marble collection at the museum. But she objected so I suppose I really must cease."

"Diana the huntress? The one who carries a bow and arrows?" Anthony's lips quivered. "How appropriate."

That's exactly what he thought, as well. Only . . . as much as he hated to admit, it wasn't Honoria who was hunting. In all honesty, it had been him from the beginning. He was becoming more and more earnest in his desire to possess her. Not just in the carnal way, though that thought was precious indeed, but in other ways as well. He wanted to understand her, to know why she thought what she did, why she was the way she was.

And most of all, he wanted to know why just the sight of her made his life seem . . . brighter somehow. It was just possible that, while paying court to Honoria's sister, he would find the answers to his questions.

It was odd, but as of two weeks ago, he would have sworn that his life was perfect. Now, he wasn't so sure. Oh, he had some wonderful things in his life, he didn't doubt that. His family, his estates, even Treymount House, were all areas of great satisfaction for him. But how could he find that flicker of warmth that seemed to imbue all of the Baker-Sneeds? Was it Honoria who caused such a transformation of the plain to the wonderful? Perhaps she —

He sat up a little straighter, realizing how serious his thoughts were. Bloody hell, if he continued like this, he'd be marrying the chit, and what a fiasco that would be. What had gotten into him that he was losing sight of what was really important?

"Why are you scowling all of a sudden?"

Marcus collected himself, wishing Anthony wasn't quite so damned observant. "I was just thinking that perhaps I should avoid seeing any more of Miss Baker-Sneed."

Anthony's dark eyes fixed on Marcus. "Surely not! That would be a mistake indeed."

"No, it wouldn't. In fact, it would be the most prudent thing to do."

"Hm." Anthony regarded him for a long moment. "Perhaps you are afraid of her. She has forced you to break down that wall you were building —"

"While you have outstayed your welcome." Marcus stood. "It has been a lovely hour, but I have matters to attend to, none of them having anything to do with you."

Anthony grinned, but he placed his glass on the corner of the desk and stood. "Fine. Do as you will. Just realize this: you are playing against fate if you think to avoid the woman the talisman ring has led you to."

"For the love of — I do not believe that silly ring has any powers."

"Well I believe it," Anthony said quietly. "And before this is all over, you will, too."

With that cryptic comment, he winked, turned on his heel, and left.

Marcus refilled his glass, grumbling to himself as he did so. Why was he saddled with such a brother? One who took such delight in plaguing him to death about the most ridiculous things. The ring had power . . . ha! He wasn't so wet behind the ears as to believe that.

And yet . . . the ring *had* been in each of his brothers' possessions when they'd found their true loves, so perhaps — No. That was ludicrous. Still, just to be on the safe side, he'd avoid being with Miss Baker-Sneed. At least for a while. With that thought firmly in mind, he returned to the stack of waiting letters that graced his desk and tried to lose himself in his work.

Honoria blinked. "You did *what?*"

Olivia bit her lip. "We wanted to be sure you won so we tied a string to the target. We knew you shot a trifle leeward a bit so . . ." She glanced at Portia.

Just as red-faced as Olivia was pale, Portia promptly added, "We tugged the target just a bit in that direction when you closed your eyes. And then, when the marquis took his shot, we moved it back. But only after he'd released the arrow."

"It was horridly nerve-wracking for he kept looking at the target and frowning." Olivia shook her head. "I thought for certain we'd been capsized."

Honoria rose to her feet and took two steps forward. Then stopped. "You *cheated?* Or rather, you made *me* cheat? I can't — how could you do that to me?"

Cassandra shook her head, gentle reproach in her gaze as she eyed her two younger sisters. "Olivia, you and Portia should not have interfered. Honoria would have won the wager without your help."

"I don't know about that," Portia said a little defiantly. She looked at Honoria. "Did you know that the marquis is reputed to be excellent in all forms of marksmanship? *Including* archery?"

Honoria crossed her arms, too agitated to sit again. "It wouldn't have mattered if I did know it. I am no novice myself and I would have held my own."

"And if you'd lost?" Olivia asked. "What about poor Cassandra, then? Her dreams would have been floundered like a ship in a glassy sea!"

Cassandra frowned. "That doesn't make it worth Honoria's pride."

Olivia flounced a little. "We did nothing to Honoria's pride!"

"Besides," Portia added, "all we did was move the target just the tiniest bit. It's not as if we gave his lordship fouled arrows or anything of that sort."

"That's all," Honoria said bitterly. She'd been so proud of herself for winning. So proud that she'd managed to outwit Marcus. Only to find out that it wasn't a win at all, but a sham, was both disheartening and humiliating. She suddenly remembered how she'd teased him when he lost and her cheeks burned.

She sat down. "What do I do now?"

"I was just wondering the same thing," Cassandra said. She folded her hands in her lap. "I cannot accept the marquis's assistance based on an untrue wager."

"Neither can I," Honoria said grimly. She looked down at her hands, at the shimmer of the ring on her finger. "I must make this right."

"How?" Olivia said, her eyes wide.

"I must tell the marquis what has occurred and offer my sincerest apologies." Which would be as pleasant as swallowing a cup of bitters. "Treymount will positively crow over this and I will be left looking a fool." She eyed her sisters. "I hope you are pleased with the results of your foolishness."

Portia winced. "Honoria, surely you don't have to tell the marquis about this?"

"Of course I have to tell him! I am not such a paltry goosecap as to think I could stand by and collect on a debt that isn't owed me. I must tell him. Besides, what if someone else discovers your duplicity and it becomes gossip? Do you think I want the marquis to hear about our deception secondhand?"

Olivia sighed. "I don't know why you have to turn into a puritan about this, but . . ." Her shoulders slumped. "I suppose you are right. We thought it would be humorous if the marquis lost the wager. We didn't think of it as being dishonest."

"Besides," Portia added, "we wanted to help Cassandra."

Honoria swallowed a lump of irritation that threatened to overtake her. It was outside of enough that her sisters had interfered in her affairs. But what really hurt was that they thought her incapable of winning a wager — Honoria stood so abruptly her skirts swung forward. "If you ever interfere in my business in such a way again, I will —" What would she do? She clamped her lips together. "Just trust me on this: you will regret it."

Portia and Olivia both nodded, their

cheeks pink as they glanced at one another from beneath their lashes. "Yes, ma'am," Portia said quietly.

"As you wish," Olivia added. She hesitated, then said, "Perhaps Portia and I should visit the marquis and tell him what we've done. There is no reason you should be made to fix this problem since it was none of your doing."

Cassandra placed her hand on Olivia's arm. "That is a very noble offer, but I am certain Honoria would rather deal with it on her own."

What she'd rather do was not deal with it at all. But she knew from experience that ignoring something did not make it go away. In fact, inaction usually made the situation worse.

Honoria went to the mirror over the fireplace. She looked painfully pale, which made the streak in her hair look all the brighter. "It is only proper that I see the marquis and explain what has happened. Perhaps he will agree to another match."

Olivia brightened. "Oh, if he only would! That would be perfect for you'd certainly win and then he'd have to pay up!"

"When will you speak with the marquis?" Cassandra asked in her soft voice.

"I suppose I should do it as soon as I can. I

will send a note to his house and ask him to wait on me here."

"Perhaps we should invite him to dinner." Cassandra pursed her lips. "It would be only polite and we have a nice leg of lamb that Cook can fix."

Honoria considered this, then shook her head. "No, I want to tell him what has occurred, set up another wager, if he'll allow it, and then forget about it. I do not want him sitting across from me all during dinner if he decides to take the news badly. Glaring is so hard on the digestion."

Cassandra nodded. "You're right, of course. And if you wait until after dinner, someone might blurt out the truth and he'd never believe you were going to tell him anyway."

Portia immediately disagreed. She seemed to think they could all keep their mouths closed if it was important enough. She went on to suggest planning a large, lavish meal, one designed to put the marquis in the best possible mood. She also suggested saving the truth for the dessert, an idea that the drama loving Olivia found so much to her liking that the two immediately began to imagine all of the marquis's reactions.

Honoria listened with but half an ear. She would not have Treymount for dinner. No, the shorter the meeting, the better, as far as she was concerned. Furthermore, she had no desire to prolong the agony . . . she wanted to tell him now.

So, as soon as she could, she escaped her sisters' company and returned to the sitting room. Once there, she took pen in hand and wrote a short note.

My lord,

I must request the pleasure of your presence to discuss an issue that has arisen regarding our wager. Please come at your earliest convenience.

Sincerely,
Honoria Baker-Sneed

She reread it twice, then sanded it and sent it off before she could change her mind. An hour later she was sitting with Cassandra in the dining room, going through the linens and removing the ones that needed mending when the reply came. She immediately sat down and opened it.

Miss Baker-Sneed,

I received your missive requesting a visit

to discuss our recent wager. As I lost the wager and you won, you will forgive me if I tell you that I have no desire to discuss this issue now, or ever. I am sending the name of my solicitor. Through him, you can plan out the requirements of your sister's launch into society. I promise to appear at whatever appointed times you require.

Thank you and good day,
Treymount

Honoria set down the letter.

"What is it?" Cassandra asked, holding up a sheet to see if it needed repairing. Deciding it did not, she refolded it and replaced it on the stack. "What does the marquis say?"

"He won't come."

"Why not?"

"I believe he is sulking."

Cassandra frowned. "He didn't strike me as the sort to sulk."

Honoria folded the letter. "Well, he is certainly sulking now."

"What will you do?"

That was indeed the question. Ye gods, what *could* she do? She couldn't very well sit around and wait for Treymount to get over his tantrums. No, she needed to speak to him now. It would drive her mad waiting to tell him the horrid truth about Portia's and Olivia's little contretemps.

She handed a sheet that needed darning to Cassandra and then stood. "Father always said that one should meet fate well on the road."

Cassandra picked up her sewing basket and set it in her lap. "Which means?"

"Which means that if the marquis will not come to me, then I will go to the marquis."

Cassandra blinked. "But —"

"No. I must. It's either that or I'll be forced to admit what happened to the man's solicitor, and I cannot like that."

"Neither would I." Cassandra set the sheet and her basket aside. "I will come with you —"

"No. I'll take Mrs. Kemble. I don't wish you to risk your reputation."

"If you're taking Mrs. Kemble, I don't suppose anyone would say anything even if I did accompany you."

"Well, I don't wish to take any chances." Honoria straightened her shoulders and ran a hand over her hair. "How do I look?"

Cassandra blinked as if surprised, and then smiled. "Beautiful, as you always do." She stood and came to tuck a few stray locks away. "There. Shall I go and fetch your pelisse? It's getting cooler."

"Of course." Honoria pressed a hand to her knotted stomach, though she managed a fairly credible smile in the interim. "I'll find Mrs. Kemble while you are doing that."

"Very well." Cassandra took Honoria's hand and squeezed it. "And don't worry about the marquis. He may be angry with Olivia and Portia, but he will not blame you. He is a man of too much sense to believe you had anything to do with it, I just know it." With a reassuring smile, she released Honoria's hand and left.

"I wish I had your confidence," Honoria muttered as her sister's footsteps faded up the stairs. "What a tangle this is, thanks to Portia and Olivia! I could keelhaul the both of them."

But soon it would all be over. She'd have told her tale to the marquis and, hopefully, convinced him to take another wager. But what would they wager on this time? She didn't think he'd agree to archery once again. Perhaps pistols? She didn't know much about them, but how difficult could they be? Or perhaps she could think of something else, something more to her advantage.

She sighed. Whatever she did, she was not

going to enjoy this next half an hour. Hearing Cassandra's feet back on the stairs, Honoria pulled herself together and went in search of Mrs. Kemble.

Chapter 14

Men. I can't stand the way they flit from one topic of conversation to another. They have no ability to focus on more than one — Oh! Is that a new set of garnets? How lovely! Where did you get it? It is perfect with your hair color. Anyway, as I was saying, men have no ability to focus.

Miss Clarissa Ridgethorpe
to her best friend,
Miss Suzanne Welton,
as the two sipped warm orgeat,
while sitting out a waltz at Almack's

Head bent against the brisk wind as she stepped out of the hackney cab, hard on

Mrs. Kemble's heels, Honoria caught sight of the Treymount coach as it wheeled past, swerving wildly as it raced up the drive. The shining equipage flew to the front entryway, the matching bays prancing wildly. The sight of such high-spirited horses gave her pause.

"There he is, miss!" Mrs. Kemble breathed. She clutched her reticule tightly before her, her eyes as round as saucers. "And just look at those horses!"

"Uhm, yes. I was looking at them." Honoria's gaze traveled past the carriage to the house. What a mansion. What a mansion and what a man. It was a pity she was visiting under such distressing circumstances.

The coachman jumped down from his seat and, knocking aside a rather stalwart footman, ran to open the door. He opened it and stood to one side, beaming pleasantly.

Treymount appeared. He exchanged a few words with his coachman and then turned and climbed the front steps. He was bareheaded, the wind tousling his black hair and sending the edges of his multicaped great coat flying. Honoria took an impulsive step forward just as he disappeared inside.

"Here now, missus! Where's me fare?" demanded the driver of the hansom cab.

"Oh dear," Mrs. Kemble said. "Should I —"

"Of course not." Honoria unhooked her reticule from her wrist and paid the driver. "Please return in half an hour. We will be ready to depart by then." She didn't expect to be very long at all, but she didn't have the money to pay the man to wait.

"Half an hour?" The man eyed the huge, lavishly detailed house that lifted before them, then looked at the pittance Honoria had placed in his palm. "I might return. Then again, I might be on t'other side of town."

"You can go to the other side of town and hope someone hires you," she said, adjusting her gloves to a more snug fit. "Or you can return in thirty minutes and know for certain you will get a hire."

Her logic appeared to cause him some pain for he grimaced. "Well, just don't be expectin' me, is all I'm sayin'. Not fer a few pence."

"I shall try to hold my expectations to a minimum. In the meantime, I shall see you in half an hour." With that, she turned on her heel and made her way up the walk to Treymount House, hoping that no one could see how hard her heart was racing. She could hear Mrs. Kemble's labored breathing behind her as the older woman struggled to keep up while simultaneously craning her neck to stare up at the huge mansion looming before them.

The house was imposing in structure and stretching high into the sky and well to either side. Of white granite with Greek detailing, it was a masterpiece of architecture, a blinding example of what money and taste, when combined, could accomplish.

Honoria made her way to the huge mahogany doors, suddenly feeling very small indeed. She wasn't nervous, of course. After all, it was only Treymount, and over the years she'd brangled enough with the man to get over any kind of superficial awe his position might hold. Why yesterday she'd even cheated him at archery. How much more intimate did she need to become before she felt comfortable in the man's presence?

Still, though she might have gotten to the Trading Barbs Stage in their relationship, she had to admit that there was something about facing the man inside this huge, cavernous home that made her feel . . . less, somehow. *Which is nonsense,* she told herself. *I have never been intimidated by Treymount before and I refuse to be so now. This is a house. Just a plain, ordinary house. A large one, perhaps. But a house nonetheless.*

Gathering her nerve, she boldly swung the brass knocker and waited to be admitted. It took less than a minute for the door to open. A very proper individual dressed in the neat, black attire of a butler regarded her with a politely noncommittal expression. "Yes?"

The man's bland expression made Honoria wonder if perhaps she had a smudge on her chin. Swallowing a swell of uncertainty, she said, "I have come to see his lordship."

"Is he expecting you?"

Was that a note of disdain she detected in the butler's voice? She lifted her chin and said in her frostiest tone, "Please inform the marquis that Miss Baker-Sneed has arrived and wishes to speak to him."

The butler looked past her toward Mrs. Kemble, who was now standing on the top step, craning her neck back at an impossible angle in an effort to see the cornice work around the top of the portico.

"My chaperone," Honoria said in a lofty voice.

There was a moment's hesitation and then the butler moved back from the door and allowed her entrance. "Please come in. I cannot promise that his lordship is in, but I will see."

Having just seen his lordship striding up the front steps of his house, Honoria was fairly certain the butler would find Treymount at home. Still, one must observe the niceties whenever possible.

So all Honoria said was, "Thank you." And then she walked into the house, Mrs. Kemble scrambling to catch up.

The door closed behind them, and Honoria found herself facing a row of uniformed, rather stony-faced footmen. The very sight gave her pause — the sheer number of servants the man had just standing about made her shake her head.

"Sweet Mother Mary!" Mrs. Kemble said.

Honoria followed the housekeeper's gaze toward the ceiling. There, suspended from a heavy chain that was as thick as her wrist, was the largest chandelier she'd ever seen. It rivaled the one hanging at the Grand Pavilion, the Prince's summer residence. "Ye gods," Honoria breathed in awe. "That must be a horrid thing to have to clean."

The butler glanced up at the chandelier, his expression softening a bit. "Indeed, miss. It's not a thing we enjoy."

Honoria had to smile a bit at that. "I can only imagine." Slowly, she turned around, her gaze flitting over each and every item she found, her sure step slowly coming to a halt as each new piece of grandeur hit her. It was a palace. A genuine, marble encrusted palace. The entryway was as large as the entire first floor of the Baker-Sneed residence. Three stories of intricate plasterwork blended with the white marble floor until the room was ablaze with startling purity. The only color came from the swath of red carpet that lined the huge curved stairway that traversed up the center of the hall and the numerous tapestries that hung along the walls.

Once her gaze fell on the tapestries, Honoria forgot her nervousness for a few moments. They were magnificent. Some she recognized as Flemish, some Far Eastern in origin. All ancient and exquisitely preserved.

"Shall I take your pelisses and bonnets?" the butler asked, the epitome of politeness.

"No, thank you. We will not be staying that long."

The butler bowed and then led the way to a door off the entryway. "If you will please step in here, there is a fire blazing. I will see if his lordship is in."

Honoria blinked at the room. She was certain it must be one of the smallest rooms in the house — most sitting rooms were. But this one was enormous by any standard.

Mrs. Kemble looked about her and promptly dropped her reticule, her eyes seemingly glued to the huge crystal chandelier that hung in the center of the room.

Honoria's cheeks heated. She picked up the forgotten reticule and then managed a firm smile for the butler. "Yes well, please tell his lordship . . ." Honoria paused. Tell him what? That she'd come to confess to a somewhat slight misunderstanding? That she needed to renegotiate their wager? That her sisters had caused her to cheat?

She cleared her throat. "Please tell his lordship that I have come on a matter of utmost importance and I *must* see him."

There. That sounded quite interesting and very urgent. The butler bowed and then left. The second the door closed, Mrs. Kemble clasped her hands together. "Goodness, miss! Have you ever seen such a sight in all your born days?"

Honoria glanced around the room with grudging admiration, untying her bonnet as she did so. The walls were covered with red silk paper, the chairs covered in rich blue and red patterned damask. Long blue curtains hung from the windows, lined with deep green velvet. A huge bouquet of lilies sat on a rich mahogany table, while a thick Aubusson rug warmed the marble floor and displayed all the colors used in the room, bringing them all together somehow.

She sighed, slipped her bonnet from her head and then fluffed her curls. As she removed her gloves, she admitted to herself that it was the most beautiful room she'd ever seen. It was also the most imposing. Whoever had decorated it had done so with one purpose in mind: to remind all who entered who was really important in the world — the master of the house and no one else.

The thought did not sit well. Honoria refused to be cowed. It was a beautiful room, but surely there was something wrong with it, some sort of imperfection. She walked to the large fireplace and ran a finger over the mantel behind the ormolu clock. Feeling somewhat superior, she turned her glove over — and frowned. The glove was still pristine white.

Well. This called for a more thorough investigation. She glanced at Mrs. Kemble, but the housekeeper seemed too overcome to do more than stare up at the huge painting of a horse that hung over the fireplace.

Honoria glanced around, her gaze falling on a very large and leafy plant. There, surely, would be some dust or some potting soil, or something to prove that the house was just that, a house and nothing more.

She was just walking toward it, her gloved hand outstretched, when the door opened. "Miss Baker-Sneed?"

Face flushed, she whirled to face the butler, tucking her hand behind her back as she did so. "Ah, yes?"

"I am sorry to inform you that his lordship is not in. Would you like to leave a message?"

"No, I don't. And for your information, I saw him come in! He walked up the front steps no more than two minutes before I did."

The butler's expression went from politely blank to frozen.

Honoria glanced past him to the entryway where the broad stairs curved into the white recesses of the upper floors. That blackguard was shunning her. Of all the sneaky, horrid tricks to play on someone, and all because she'd bested the man at his own game. Or at least, he'd thought she had.

She flickered a glance back at the stiff-necked butler. "So the marquis is out, is he?"

"Yes, miss."

"And he is not in the house?"

"No, miss." The butler's gaze fastened on a place over Honoria's left shoulder.

"That is so strange. Perhaps it wasn't the marquis I saw coming in the house at all, but his twin brother."

The butler looked grateful for this suggestion. "While his lordship doesn't have a twin, he does indeed have quite a few brothers. I daresay it is possible you saw one of them when you arrived."

Honoria grit her teeth. "Perhaps you would be so good as to inform his lordship's *brother* that I wish to speak to *him* and that if I do not get the opportunity, then *he* will greatly regret it."

The butler's thin brows were raised so high on his forehead that he seemed to be in danger of losing them at his hairline. "I beg your pardon, but . . . is that a threat?"

"Oh no. It's a promise." Honoria went to the blue settee and plopped down on it, snatching up a pillow and holding it in her lap. "I will wait here while you go to see his lordship's *brother*. And tell him that I am not leaving until he sees me."

The butler hesitated, as if unsure what to do. But then he gave a small bow, turned on his heel and left.

Only a short minute passed before the sound of riding boots clicked on the marble floor from a distance down the hall, coming closer and closer.

Mrs. Kemble tottered to a chair and sank into it, fanning herself.

Honoria frowned. "Mrs. Kemble, are you well? You look quite white."

The housekeeper fanned harder. "I'm fine," she said, her voice warbling and faded.

The door opened and Treymount stood in the opening, large and imposing, making the huge room suddenly seem much smaller. His cool blue gaze flickered over her and then to Mrs. Kemble.

Honoria cleared her throat and rose to her feet. "My lord, I am sorry if we're intruding but —"

"Nonsense." He strode into the room and bowed a greeting, first to Honoria, and then to Mrs. Kemble. "Welcome to Treymount House."

Mrs. Kemble, who'd staggered to her feet when the marquis appeared, now flushed a deep red. "I — I — I —"

"Thank you," Honoria interrupted smoothly, a little irritated. "You have a lovely house."

The marquis flicked a glance her way, his eyes lingering on her mouth. Her lips began to tingle in the strangest way and she pressed her gloved fingertips to still the disruptive memories.

Almost immediately, he smiled. "Miss Baker-Sneed, is there something I can do for you?"

"Oh. Why, yes. As I indicated in the note I sent, I have something of great importance I must speak to you about."

His gaze flickered to the housekeeper.

Honoria shook her head. "Everything I have to say can be said in front of Mrs. Kemble."

The marquis nodded. "Of course." He paused a moment, as if weighing something, then said, "Perhaps we should repair to the library, where it's a bit warmer." He turned toward the door, holding it open and standing to one side.

Mrs. Kemble seemed unable to move, so Honoria gathered her thoughts, lifted her chin and made her own way out the door. When she reached the threshold, she glanced back at the housekeeper, who was still standing shock-still beside her chair. "Mrs. Kemble," Honoria said rather more sharply than she intended. "Lord Treymount has invited us into the library."

"What? Oh! Yes!" Mrs. Kemble fluttered a smile at the marquis. "I'm sorry, I'm just overcome. This house . . ." She gestured vaguely about her.

"It can be quite overpowering," Treymount said, a faint smile touching his mouth. "Perhaps a tour . . ."

Mrs. Kemble brightened. "Oh! What I wouldn't give for a tour. Miss Baker-Sneed, wouldn't that be the most wondrous thing?"

No, it would not. Honoria just wanted to tell the marquis what she had to tell him and then be on her way. So she said, "Perhaps another time."

"As you wish," Treymount replied with an easy shrug. "Mrs. Kemble? Shall we repair to the library?"

The housekeeper tittered. "Oh indeed!" Flush with pleasure at being directly addressed, she scurried forward and followed Honoria into the grand hall.

The marquis walked across the grand hall and to the wide double doors that stood directly across from the sitting room. As he neared the door, one of the somber footmen hurried to open it. The marquis stepped to one side. "Miss Baker-Sneed? After you."

Honoria glanced behind her to be certain Mrs. Kemble was following, and then marched into the library.

If the sitting room had been a glimpse into perfection, then the library was a look directly into heaven. Honoria could only stand and stare, her gaze roving over the towering shelves, the delicate iron-wrought railing that lined the second floor balcony, and last, the magnificent mural that hung overhead.

Honoria swallowed, walking farther into the room and coming to a halt dead center so she could look up at the painted ceiling. Good Lord, the house was beyond magnificent. It was —

"Mrs. Kemble, before you go inside . . ."

Honoria turned toward the open door. The marquis was speaking to the housekeeper, but what —

"If you'd like to see more of the house, perhaps I can assist you. In fact, my own housekeeper, Mrs. Bates, would be more than glad to take you on a tour and answer any questions you might have."

Why that sneaky cur! Honoria started toward the door, but Mrs. Kemble's voice stopped her.

"Your own housekeeper?" There was no disguising Mrs. Kemble's excitement. "I would love — I am honored that you've even thought of — I could think of nothing more — But . . ."

"But?" the marquis's deep voice followed.

"I cannot. I am chaperoning Miss Baker-Sneed and it would be highly improper for me to leave."

There! Honoria smiled to herself. Let that be a lesson to the marquis if he thought to bribe off her chaperone. What could he do now?

As if in answer to her question, she heard him say, "Mrs. Kemble, you need have no fear for Miss Baker-Sneed. I shall leave the door open whilst you tour the house. I'm certain you'll find our new cooking stove quite the thing. My chef dotes on it, and Mrs. Bates says it is the newest of its kind in the entire country."

Oh! The blackguard! To hold a new cooking stove out as enticement to a housekeeper! Honoria had to admit that the man was diabolically clever.

"A new cooking stove? Oh how —" There was a silence as if Mrs. Kemble was locked in a powerful internal struggle. "No. I really mustn't. I should —"

"As I said, I will leave the door open."

"That is not enough, my lord. What if someone comes and —"

"I shall have one of the footmen stand inside."

There was a long silence. Honoria frowned and turned toward the door.

Mrs. Kemble let out her breath in a whoosh. "Well! If you have a footman —"

"Two," Treymount said solemnly.

"Oh! Well! If there are two . . ." And with that, Honoria's chaperone deserted her.

That wretch! How could he? Honoria headed for the door, but she was too late. Already she could hear Jeffries's smooth voice and then Mrs. Kemble's reply fading as she followed him.

By the time Honoria reached the library door, no one at all was there but a row of frozen-faced footmen and Treymount, who was looking quite pleased with himself.

"Where is Mrs. Kemble?"

Marcus turned to find an outraged Honoria standing in the doorway of his library. He smiled and walked past her and into the room. "The stalwart Mrs. Kemble is on her way to visit Mrs. Bates, my housekeeper, a fact I'm certain you know, as the door was standing wide open the entire time."

He found his way to his desk. There, he paused and gestured to one of the chairs that sat facing it. "Won't you have a seat?"

She looked at the chair, chagrin darkening her eyes. He knew what she was thinking. If she sat in the chair, she'd barely be able to see over the huge edge of the desk. Her back ramrod straight, she shook her head. "No, thank you. I'll stand."

He shrugged. "As you wish." Hiding a

smile, he sat down, picking up the correspondence he'd left when he'd been informed that his house had been invaded.

He pretended to read the first of his letters, all the while keenly aware of the sound of slippered feet and rustling silk of the woman now approaching his desk. She planted herself to one side and stood staring down at him.

It was all Marcus could do not to grin, but he forced himself to remain somber, as if what he was reading was of the utmost importance and not just a report from one of his lesser holdings in the south of Scotland.

"My lord, I really must speak with you."

He glanced at her over the paper, pretending not to notice that her cheeks were becomingly flushed. Damn, how was it that he'd faced this woman over the auction floor so many times and had never truly noticed how attractive she was? He rustled the paper a bit. "So speak, Miss Baker-Sneed. I am listening."

A frown creased her brow. "I don't wish to talk to you while you are sitting at your desk. I feel as if I've been called into the headmistress's room for chastisement."

"So you were a bit of a romp at your seminary. Why does that not surprise me?"

She narrowed her eyes. "What I have to say is unpleasant enough. Please, can we just —" She frowned and glanced around. "Wait a moment. You told Mrs. Kemble that there would be two footmen in the room at all times."

"So I did. If you want them, feel free to ask them to come in. The door is open, after all, and with one loud voice they would arrive to see if something is needed."

"Oh. I suppose you are right." She fidgeted with her bonnet, but all the while her gaze flickered from him to the door, as if measuring the distance.

Marcus pretended to read. "I don't know what difference having a footman or two about would make. I have no intentions of attempting to make love to you while your housekeeper is in easy range. For all I know, she's already seen the new cook stove and is now on her way back here."

There was a moment's pause as Honoria absorbed this. Marcus watched her from under his lashes, noting every emotion that flickered over her face.

Finally, she sighed. "I wish you'd come to see me when I first asked, as it would have been much simpler. May I ask why you refused?"

Because he'd thought to protect himself

from the raging lust she seemed to cause just by breathing. A goal he was beginning to question. Why should he avoid her? The legend of the ring was just that — a legend. In reality, every time he saw her while she had the ring in her possession, it was further testament to the fact that the talisman had no powers, for he had not the slightest impulse to wed her — just to bed her. "Miss Baker-Sneed, you may ask me anything you desire, although that does not guarantee an answer."

She lifted one delicately winged brow. It was a peculiarity of hers, the ability to look so incredibly disbelieving without saying a word.

Marcus chuckled and stood, coming around the desk and making his way to the two chairs by the crackling fire. "Perhaps we should just have this conversation you've been wishing for." He gestured toward a chair. "My dear, sit."

The other brow joined the first, and with this simple movement, instead of looking disbelieving, she now looked supercilious, as if he'd insulted her parentage.

"What?" he asked.

" 'Sit' is what one orders one's hunting dogs to do. I, my lord, am not a hunting dog."

No, she wasn't. What she was, was an all too tantalizing package of brain and lace. She was a full-breasted, trim-waisted, long-legged, russet-haired wildfire that alternately fanned his desire and heated his ire. But Marcus was not about to admit anything to her. "Very well, then. Miss Baker-Sneed, please have a seat?" He placed his hands on the back of the chair and turned it ever so slightly in her direction.

"That is much better, thank you." She regally marched to the chair and took a seat.

He looked down at the top of her head, admiring the silky sheen of her chestnut braids and that unusual streak of white, aware of a deep desire to reach down and lift her into his arms. "So . . ." He forced himself to turn away and take his place in the seat opposite hers. "What do you wish to say?"

"I came to tell you that . . ." She bit her lip, then fisted her hands at her sides. "Treymount, you did not lose our wager."

It took a long moment for the words to sink in. Did not lose the wager? Then what — Marcus slowly leaned forward. "Pardon me?"

"You heard me. You didn't lose our wager."

"But . . . we both shot two arrows, and —"

"My sisters had a string tied to the target and they moved it when you shot." The words tumbled from her, almost running one into the other.

"*What* did you say?"

She took a quick breath. "My sisters thought that —"

"Which ones?"

Her cheeks flushed. "It doesn't matter."

"It does to me."

"Portia and Olivia. They are a bit romantic, you know, and never thought —"

"Bloody hell. If they did it a-purpose, then . . ." He sat back in his seat, a deep sense of pleasure rippling through him. No wonder the target had seemed to move at one time — it had. And had he not been so hot to stare at Honoria while she was shooting, perhaps he would have noticed the irregularities better on his own. "So I won after all."

She blinked. "You — What? No, you did not. No one won. Neither one of us."

She looked so outraged that he had to rub a hand over his mouth to stop from grinning. "I don't know," he said after he composed himself. "I rather think that if you cheated —"

"I did not cheat. My sisters cheated."

"On your behalf."

"Without my permission!"

"Hm. I rather think the rules of honor would be in my favor in this case."

She lifted her chin. "Nonsense. There is only one thing we can do. I propose a rematch."

"Well, I don't. In fact, Honoria, I believe we should —"

"I beg your pardon?"

He raised his brows, attempting an innocent look. He wasn't quite sure if he attained it or not, since it wasn't something he usually tried to do. But it seemed necessary and he was willing to spare no expense. "Yes?"

"You do not have permission to call me by my given name." Irritation darkened her eyes to deep hazel. "It is Miss Baker-Sneed to you."

"And it's Marcus to you. If we're to engage in a year long battle of wagers, we might as well skip the formalities."

"It will not take a year to settle this."

"I'm not so sure about that." He regarded her for a long moment, noting that the line of her leg showed very much to advantage through the simple gown she wore. "Very well," he said. "A rematch it will be. But this time I get to name the contest."

She brightened. "Excellent! But . . . what will you choose?"

Marcus considered this. He was good with pistols, but he'd thought himself an excellent archer as well. He rubbed his chin and eyed Honoria for a long moment. "Have you ever shot a pistol?"

Her gaze dropped to the floor. "Oh . . . once or twice."

"Somehow I get the impression that you know a pistol as well as you do a bow and arrow."

"What do you suggest, then?"

Marcus crossed his arms over his chest and smiled. "I believe that I'll choose . . ." An imp of madness tickled him. There was only one thing to say . . . just one. "I choose horses."

She blinked slowly, incredulously. "Horses?"

"Yes, horses." He waited a moment, then asked, "What is the matter? You seem somewhat pale."

"Nothing," she said, biting her lip. "I was just . . . no. Never mind."

Marcus looked at her for a long moment. "You don't ride."

Her cheeks colored. "No. It's just that . . . I don't have a horse, not one that I can ride. We just have a carriage horse and he pulled his fetlock the other day and cannot be ridden."

"That's not a problem. I have a stable full of horses. You can take your pick when you come tomorrow for the wager."

"I — I couldn't do that!"

"What? Have the wager tomorrow? Shall we make it Saturday, then?"

"No, it's not that. It's just that —" She took a deep breath, pressing her hands to her cheeks as if to cool them down.

Marcus continued, his gaze on her face. "I propose we take a ride through the park. And whoever handles his or her mount with most decorum, wins."

"B-But . . . I don't —" She pressed a hand to her temple, a dazed expression on her face. "Horses. I never thought you'd say horses."

He noted that her lashes were so long that they tangled at the corners. It was an unusual combination, those hazel eyes combined with dark, russet lashes. And he was quickly deciding that it was one of his favorites. "Are you comfortable with tomorrow, then? The quicker we end this, the better."

"Tomorrow? No. No, I couldn't possibly —" She caught his gaze and colored adorably.

He leaned over and traced the line of her cheek with his hand, lingering at the place where her dimple occasionally flashed. "What's wrong? Are you afraid?"

She jerked her head away, her cheeks flushed even more deeply. "Of course I'm not afraid. It is just a horse." Despite her bravado, her voice quavered the tiniest bit on the last word, an unconscious plea for assurance.

"Exactly," he agreed smoothly. "Horses are friendly creatures, as a whole."

She looked unconvinced.

"They rarely bite, you know."

Unconsciously, her hand went to her arm. Oh ho, Marcus thought. So Honoria had a story to tell, did she?

She swallowed, the elegant line of her throat moving as she did so. "I know they rarely bite, but when they do —"

He nodded. "Indeed. It can be most severe. You should ask Lord Estersham about that."

Her eyes narrowed the slightest bit. "Lord Estersham who has but one arm?"

Marcus nodded, struggling to keep his expression solemn. "Yes, that Lord Estersham."

She crossed her arms. "I'm many things, but an alarmist is not one of them. A horse did not bite off Lord Estersham's arm."

He pretended surprise. "I never said that, did I?"

"No, but you implied it."

"I apologize. Lord Estersham but lost a finger from a horse's bite, not his entire arm."

She blinked. "A finger?"

"From his good hand, too. He was most grieved when it happened, though it was years ago."

"Ye gods," she said softly, looking at her splayed hands for a long moment.

From beneath his lashes, Marcus watched her expression. Would she admit her fear and ask for another wager? He rather thought she would, but now . . . seeing her pale face, he began to wonder. She had more pride than any woman he knew.

She took a slow breath and then managed a cool nod. "Very well, then. Horses it is."

"That was very impressive."

She eyed him narrowly. "What was?"

"The way you said that. Almost as if you meant it."

"Oh. Well. I am grateful for the chance to redo our wager. It's just that —"

He waited. Would she admit her fear? Would she ask for the wager to be lessened? Changed?

Not her.

She stood, her bonnet in her hands. "I suppose there is nothing more to be said."

"No. I shall call on you tomorrow and we will see this wager to its end."

She nodded absently, her mind obviously moving forward to their meeting. He could almost smell her trepidation. Her hands trembled just a bit as she attempted to pull on her gloves.

After watching her struggle for a moment, he grasped her wrist and removed the mangled glove. "Permit me." With those simple words, he took the glove, shook it out, then began to work it over her fingers.

Honoria watched, almost mesmerized. His hands were firm and warm against her bare skin, his fingertips brushing her inner wrist. She started as the touch burned through her, sending tremors of fire and a deep ache through her.

She yanked her hand free and stepped back, her breath heavy in her throat. "I — I can put on my own gloves, thank you."

His eyes darkened, a smile touching his carved mouth. "What's wrong, Honoria? Do I frighten you?"

No, he didn't frighten her. But she frightened herself. There was something between them, something heated and raw that flared like a newly lit fire. It sped her heart, melted her insides, and clouded her thinking with images best left alone.

And now, looking up into his face, that heat linking them, tying them together with an invisible thread . . . she wanted to kiss him. Kiss him and kiss him and kiss him until they were both mad with desire.

The realization didn't shock her as she'd thought it would. But it did nothing to help her shaking hands. She pulled away and bent her head so she could focus on getting her blasted gloves fastened.

She fumbled with the pearl button at her wrist, relieved when it was finally buttoned. "There!" she said, breathing a sigh of relief.

"Are you cold? Your hands are trembling."

"No, I'm not cold. I'm —" Hot. That's what she was. She was hot. Her skin burned, her spirit yearned, and her mind stumbled with eagerness to follow where her body might lead. But she'd be damned if she would admit such a thing to Treymount. Let him laugh at someone else; she wasn't yet ready to be made sport of. "I am a little cold."

Some of the sparkle left his eyes, replaced by concern. He glanced at the roaring fire. "Perhaps you should stand nearer the fire."

"I'm leaving —"

He grasped her arms and pulled her toward the warmed hearth. "Not yet, you aren't."

"But I —"

"Stand here." He positioned her before the fire, his hands warm through the thin sleeves of her gown.

"Treymount, I really must leave, and I —"

"Bloody hell, must you talk so much? Just stand there and get warmed."

But she was already warm. Too warm. "I appreciate your kindness, but —"

Mrs. Kemble's voice could be heard in the foyer, raised in happy excitement. A tremor of relief flooded Honoria. She was mad to escape, but not from the marquis. Rather she wished to escape her own desires for they threatened her composure more and more.

The marquis took her hand and placed a kiss to the back of it. "One day, my lovely Honoria . . . one day there will not be a talkative housekeeper about to save your virtue."

She stiffened. "Was my virtue at stake?"

He leaned down until his eyes were at a level with hers. She could see the smoldering heat, feel it, even. "Oh yes. It was indeed."

"But — the door was open and the footmen —"

"Are well trained to come when *I* call them and no one else."

"Oh! And you said —"

"Never trust a man. I said that, too, at one time. And now perhaps you will remember it." He turned away then and faced the door. "Ah, Mrs. Kemble! There you are. What did you think of the cook stove?"

Honoria seethed as the lout charmed her housekeeper with a few choice words. Mrs. Kemble was so flattered, she didn't even realize that there were no footmen in the library as the marquis had promised.

Fuming, Honoria stole a look at him, wondering what it was about this man that set her heart to tumbling so. Whatever it was, she wished it would quit. It was difficult enough having a conversation with him in the midst of his palatial residence without succumbing to a maelstrom of heated feelings she had no business having.

Taking a calming breath, Honoria decided that now was the time for a retreat. She'd have to find a way to deal with this newest development. She might have been able to refurbish her rusty archery skills in one day, but overcome an aversion to horses? That would take more than one night.

Fighting the sinking feeling that she had

already lost the battle, she briskly cut off Mrs. Kemble's disjointed thanks for the tour she'd enjoyed, and bid a quick farewell to the marquis. It wasn't until later, as she and Mrs. Kemble entered the waiting hackney cab, that Honoria realized that Treymount had not set a time for their wager.

Sighing, she looked out the window of the cab and watched as the imposing line of Treymount House faded into the distance. She could only hope it was in the morning; the quicker it was over with, the better.

Chapter 15

Without consulting Mother, Father invited his aunt Beatrice to our ball. Mother is now forced to allow the old bat to attend, though everyone knows Aunt Beatrice hates Mother with a passion and will do whatever she can to embarrass her. So that is why Mother is not speaking to Father. Woe betide the man unwise enough to force a woman into actions not of her own choosing. She will make him pay for it every time.

Miss Suzanne Welton
to her younger sister,
Miss Charlotte Welton,
as that young lady
watched in awe as her
older sister dressed for a ball

"I would tie myself to the saddle when the marquis wasn't looking. Ned says that's what they do on ships, tie themselves off whenever there's a great storm."

Portia frowned at Olivia. "But how would you dismount when the time came? It wouldn't do if he discovered your duplicity."

"That's true," George said from where he sat trying to tie a makeshift saddle made of scraps of cloth from Portia's sewing to the poor, beleaguered Achilles. "If the marquis catches Honoria cheating again, he will certainly call off all wagers."

"Which is why we must do something to help her," Juliet said staunchly.

Cassandra looked up from where she sat by the fire, working on some delicate needlework. "I think you've all helped enough."

"More than enough," Honoria said, entering the room, her arms full of books. She made it to the table by the window without dropping a one.

"What are those?" Portia said, getting up and coming to the table. She picked up the first one and read, "*The Equestrian; Points to Remember for the Proficient Rider.*"

Juliet hopped up. "Oh, that is an excellent one! I read it twice." She made her way to the table and began reading the other titles. "You will not like this one." She set a rather small volume to one side. "It has the most outrageous suggestions for dealing with an aggressive horse. It's complete balderdash."

Olivia craned her neck from where she sat by the fire. "Honoria, where did you get all of those books?"

"From the lending library." Honoria took a book out of Juliet's hands and replaced it on the stack on the table, then seated herself. She adjusted the curtain to let in a bit more sunshine, then picked one up and began to flip through the pages.

"Honoria, you can't learn how to ride a horse from a book!" Olivia shook her head. "You're only at half sail with that daft idea."

"I know how to ride. I just need to learn how to ride *better*." Honoria turned the page, looking for . . . well, she wasn't exactly sure what she was looking for. Something about dealing with horses that might bite.

The thought sent a shiver up her spine, and she absently rubbed her arm where the scar lingered still. She'd never thought to ever have to ride a horse again — especially not now.

Juliet frowned. "You haven't ridden in years —"

"It has not been years. It has only been —" Honoria frowned.

"Years," Cassandra said softly.

"Oh. Well, years then. But still, I might find something in one of these books that could help make things more manageable."

Portia exchanged glances with Juliet, who shook her head, answering the unspoken question. "Highly unlikely. I mean, if she had the basics down, I could see her getting something from a book, but she was never any good at riding. Remember the time Honoria rode the parson's old mare and it got away from her and she —"

Honoria snapped her book closed. "Do you mind?"

Juliet flushed, then shrugged. "I was just —"

"I know, I know. You were trying to help. Just don't." Honoria leveled a gaze at the whole lot of them. "Whatever you do, do *not* help me again. Any of you."

And that was that. Honoria spent the better part of two hours learning all about horses; what they ate, which saddles fit best, and even some suggestions on how to take a low fence. But the parts she lingered over were the sections on dealing with difficult or nervy horses. Still, with every word she read, she became more certain that she'd lose the wager tomorrow. It was difficult to hide her low spirits from her sisters, though by focusing on other things whenever possible, she felt she'd done a fairly creditable job.

In fact, by the time dinner came, she was able to smile somewhat, and even joke with George about his plans to get more frogs and string them to his little wooden carriage and make them his mighty steeds. It wasn't until later, as she lay in bed staring at the ceiling as sleep eluded her, that all of her doubts and fears came rushing back. It didn't help to realize that the worst aspect of the entire thing was the fact that not only would she lose the bet and potentially make a fool of herself, but would do it in front of the marquis. For some reason, that sent her low spirits even lower.

Sighing, she thumped her pillows a few times and pulled the covers over her head. Why oh why did he have to pick horses?

"Where are you going?"
Marcus paused on the steps as he descended into the grand foyer and raised his

brows at his brother, Anthony. "When did you get here?"

Jeffries, who was halfway up the steps, said in an apologetic tone. "I was just on my way to inform you that your brother had called, my lord."

"I am informed now." Marcus came the rest of the way down the stairs, Jeffries falling in behind him. "Anthony, what are you doing up so early?"

"I came to see if you wished to go to Somerset with me for the auction. Langhome is selling off all of his horses."

Marcus led the way into the breakfast room and took his seat at the table. "Even his hunters?"

Anthony followed, waving off the hovering servant who tried to set a dish of eggs before him. "Especially his hunters."

"I didn't realize."

"Yes, well, he married a year ago, and I believe now that his wife is in the family way, he wishes to reenergize his estates."

"A wise move."

"A good one for me, anyway," Anthony said with a slow grin. "I've been looking for some likely mounts for the children."

Jeffries entered with a tray bearing the day's invitations. Marcus absently flipped through them as he ate. "I daresay the

Langhome sale will have exactly what you need. I wish I could go with you, but I've an appointment of my own."

"Oh?"

"Yes. Apparently I did not lose the archery tournament with Miss Baker-Sneed after all."

Anthony blinked. *"What?"*

"That was my reaction exactly. Apparently, Honoria's sisters played a trick with the target. And so, the entire contest was forfeit."

"How did you discover the deception?"

"From the lips of the vanquished. She apparently had no knowledge of the trick, and when she discovered it, she told me of it."

Anthony gave a silent whistle. "There's a strong proof of character for you. I'm not sure I would have told you if that had happened to me."

It had been a mark of character, Marcus realized. He was coming to realize that Honoria was a woman beyond the usual in many, many ways.

Anthony leaned back in his seat, his mouth curved in a wide smile.

Marcus caught the knowing look and frowned. "Don't say a word."

Anthony chuckled. "I don't need to."

"Good. As for the contest, never fear. I re-scheduled it, only this time we will be riding."

"That's good?"

"Unless I mistake her reaction, the lady is not comfortable with horses."

"Oh ho! Well, that should give you an advantage. Of course, the last time you thought to win —"

"As I said, not one more word." Marcus shoved the unopened stacks of invitations away. "I don't need your pleasant wit today. I shall have to spend at least an hour, perhaps two, in Miss Baker-Sneed's company. She will see to it that my character is ripped to shreds, my sense of self-worth destroyed, and my innate good breeding tested as far as propriety will allow."

"I really must spend some time with this woman. She sounds absolutely intriguing." Anthony idly picked up a pink envelope edged in white and sniffed it cautiously. "Good God!" He held it out with two fingers, blinking furiously, his eyes watering profusely.

Marcus grimaced. "Lady Percival. She writes no less than twice a day."

"Twice a — you must be joking." Anthony stared at the missive.

"No. I ignore them all, of course."

"Did she wear that scent when you were together?"

"No. I'd have left her much sooner if she had. I've noticed that the longer I go without answering her, the more fragrant her missives have become."

Anthony gingerly shook the letter, then eyed Marcus with a questioning gaze. "May I?"

Marcus shrugged and leaned back so the footman could remove his plate.

Careful not to touch too much of the scented envelope, Anthony opened the letter. He read it quickly, his brows climbing as he went. "She wants you back at any cost."

"How unfortunate for her."

Anthony finished reading it, then tossed it into the stack. As he wiped his hand on Marcus's napkin, he said, "I had no idea Lady Percival was still enamored of you."

"Of my bank accounts, perhaps. But not of me."

"I would tread cautiously. A woman scorned, you know."

"Yes, yes. I know. I shall deal with her the best way I know how, by ignoring her completely. That will do the trick eventually, see if it doesn't."

Anthony leaned back and stretched. "I

hope so. She isn't a woman to be taken lightly."

"None of them are." Marcus pushed himself from the table. "I'm glad to see you before you left. How long will you be gone?"

"Two days. Three at most."

"Very well. Let me walk you to your carriage. I need to visit the stable, anyway, and select the mounts for my wager."

They rose and made their way to the grand hall. "You get to select both mounts?"

"Oh yes. Miss Honoria does not possess a riding horse, though if she did, I do not think she would ever ride it."

Anthony frowned. "If she's actually frightened of horses, I wouldn't put her on a spirited mount."

Marcus sent a dark glance at Anthony. "I've no wish to kill her. I just want to win this wager and get that damned ring back in my possession."

"What horse will you give her?"

Marcus smiled. "The lovely Honoria will get the opportunity to test the paces of Lightning."

"Lightning!" Anthony appeared startled, coming to a halt at the front door. "Our sister's old mount?"

"None other." Marcus nodded to the

footman who held open the front door, and then preceded Anthony out of it.

"I can't believe that old lazy bag of bones is still alive."

"She is alive and well and in my stables, eating her head off. Sara lets that wild boy of hers ride him whenever they are in town. It is a severe trial for both of them, the horse and the child."

Anthony chuckled. "I daresay. I would give twenty quid to see Miss Baker-Sneed's face when she sees what a lunk you have chosen for her."

Marcus had to smile. "Indeed, I have been imagining much the same myself. She will not be pleased, though I can hardly put her on a more lively horse without endangering her."

Anthony made his way down the marble stairs to his waiting carriage. "I agree; you have no choice. Which horse will *you* ride?"

"Demon. I shall take one small hedgerow in the park, which Demon will clear without hesitation, while Lightning will do nothing but stand in place, mutinous at the thought of having to do anything other than walk."

Anthony grinned widely as he reached his carriage. "I can't see how you'll lose this one."

"I won't." Marcus's smile matched his brother's. "I'll let you know how I fare when you return."

"Indeed you will, even if I have to chase you down and pummel the facts out of you." Anthony climbed into the seat and allowed the footman to close the door. He leaned out the window. "Best of luck, although it doesn't sound as if you'll need it."

Marcus raised his hand and watched his brother's carriage as it lurched forward and then moved down the front drive and out into the welter of elegant conveyances that moved up and down the streets of Mayfair. Smiling a little to himself, he turned and went to the stables. The slowest horse in all Christendom waited there, soon to be ridden by the most outspoken woman in all of England.

Had there ever been a more perfect match?

Honoria climbed out of the coach, blinking woozily into the face of Treymount's unconventional coachman. "My!" she said weakly.

"Got ye here in nine and a half minutes flat, miss!" He helped her out of the carriage. "Oiye daresay ye've never made it faster, have ye?"

"No. No, I haven't." She shook her head slightly. She'd been somewhat shocked when the marquis had sent his carriage for her first thing this morning, along with a letter informing her that the two outriders were, in fact, going to accompany them on their ride so that she would not need to bring a chaperone. It was unconventionally high-handed, but very Treymountlike, and she had to admire his thoroughness.

To be honest, she hadn't thought about the proprieties. She'd been too busy fighting her fears. Even now, her palms felt damp, and her heart was ready to leap at any sudden sound. She just knew the man would pick a difficult horse. If she was smart, she'd admit her fear.

If she was smart, she'd never have made this bargain to begin with. She sighed heavily.

"There you are," came a deep, rich voice. Honoria turned to see the marquis standing on the top step of Treymount House. He walked toward her, pulling on his riding gloves. Dressed in a somber pair of black riding breeches and black coat, his white cravat the only bright touch, he appeared darkly handsome.

Despite her trepidation, Honoria couldn't help feeling a leap of attraction. She smoothed her riding habit. It was actually one of Cassandra's old ones, since Honoria had no need for one herself. Thanks to Portia's expert touches, no one would know that it hadn't been expressly made for Honoria. She just wished the hue was a bit more vibrant. Somehow, pale blue didn't seem to be her color. Perhaps a deep rich red, to embolden her a bit, would have been perfect.

He came to a halt beside her, glinting a smile that robbed her of the ability to breathe. "Well? Are you ready? I spent all morning choosing your mount."

"Oh?" She shrugged, feigning an indifference that she most definitely did not feel. She was certain the wretch had chosen the liveliest, most difficult horse in the stable. Ye gods, what if the thing actually bit people? What if —

A warm hand found her elbow. She glanced up to meet Treymount's concerned gaze. "Don't," he said.

Don't what? She pressed a hand to her nauseous stomach. "I — I'm sure I don't know what you're talking about —"

"There she is now."

"What?" She followed his gaze to the street. A beautiful black horse came prancing along, led by a footman wearing the Treymount livery. "Good God," she said weakly. "You can't mean . . . Wh-What's her name?"

"Lightning."

"Lightning?"

"My sister named her."

"Oh. She's —" The horse shied at a leaf that fluttered in the street, rearing back and yanking fiercely on the reins, hooves flashing dangerously near the man's head.

Honoria took a startled step back. "Treymount, I can't ride — you shouldn't have — there's no way I —"

He grasped her shoulders and gave her a shake. "What's wrong with you?"

"Th-That horse. I cannot —" Her voice locked itself away and all she could do was move her lips, tears springing to her eyes.

He frowned, glancing from her to the street. Suddenly, a dawning expression entered his face. "Oh no, Honoria. That is not your horse. Demon is my mount. Your horse is following Demon."

She turned and looked. And then looked again. Behind the frisky gelding came another horse. "That's Lightning? The fleetest horse in your stables?"

He released her shoulders, laughter lighting his blue eyes. "Who said anything about the fleetest horse in my stables? I would not have you injured, my sweet. Not for any wager."

For some reason, the words sent most of Honoria's fears flying away. He really was a nice man. A genuinely nice man. She'd spent a good portion of the night before thinking of his reaction to her sisters' duplicity, and she had to admit, he'd taken it quite well. Better, in fact, than she'd hoped. And now, instead of putting her on a steed guaranteed to win him the bet at first try, he'd given her a chance to keep her dignity.

She knew she wouldn't win — his horse was too sprightly, too capable, and her horse . . . She looked again and almost smiled. Honoria doubted it would win a single sprint or take even a little fence. But still, it would not be a humiliating, frightening experience.

"Well," he said, glinting a smile down at her. "What do you think of her?"

Honoria examined her mount from the safety of the steps. "She's fat."

"Nonsense. That's pure muscle."

The faintest quiver at the corners of the marquis's mouth made her hide her own smile. "And her back is swayed."

"Perhaps you aren't familiar with this particular breed."

Her brows lowered. "Old and sway-backed? I've seen farm carts pulled by horses with better form. Not that I'm complaining," she added hastily. "Does it . . . does it bite?"

"Only mush. One of Lightning's problems is that her teeth are . . . well, she has very few, and those are in the back. She only eats special feed."

Honoria couldn't believe her luck. "You must be joking."

"No. This was Sara's favorite horse, so . . ." He shrugged. "I haven't got the heart to retire it. She thinks of the stable here as her home. I think she'd waste away if we moved her." He lifted his brows. "Are we ready, then?"

She straightened her shoulders. "As ready as I can be."

"Then off we go." With a dashing smile, he followed her to the horse.

Honoria stood a moment, gathering her courage as Lightning cast a disinterested look her way. The horse's complete disregard was oddly comforting. If she wasn't interesting enough to merit more than a glance, surely she wasn't interesting enough to bite. Holding this thought to her, Honoria made her way to the horse's side and prepared to mount.

The marquis was beside her in an instant,

his hands warm about her waist as he assisted her into the saddle. Honoria's heart began to gallop with something far warmer than mere fear.

"There you are," Treymount murmured, his blue eyes meeting hers for a moment. "Are you comfortable?"

It felt very strange, sitting in a saddle after so long. Honoria had to remind herself to adjust her skirts. It was reassuring that the horse didn't move a bit as she tried to get comfortable on the sidesaddle. "So far, so good," she said to the marquis, flashing a smile she did not feel.

"We won't be long. I thought perhaps we'd just take a turn and then have the carriage meet us back at the gates. That should do it."

That should do it indeed. "What exactly are the terms of this little ride?"

"Whatever I do, you must do. And the first person to fall, or lose control of their mount, loses."

"Immediately?"

"Immediately."

Honoria gathered her thoughts and her still rather shaky heart. "Very well, then. Let's be off." The quicker they did this, the better.

With a smile, he left and went to his own

horse. The animal shied, but within moments the marquis was on its back, a commanding figure by any measure as he expertly stilled the horse and brought it under control.

Honoria gathered the reins and nudged Lightning to a walk, a command the horse reluctantly obeyed. Within moments they were on their way, the marquis and his prancing steed in the lead, Honoria on her faithful and almost toothless slug, followed by a groom on a placid gray mount.

"This isn't so bad, is it?"

Honoria glanced at the marquis. They'd arrived at the park to find it filled with people. In fact, they'd had trouble staying together at one point because so many carriages pulled up at the sight of the marquis on his black gelding. "No, it's not so bad." She tentatively patted her horse's neck. "Except Lightning keeps sighing."

"She hates the park. In fact, she hates everything but her stall."

"I can understand that. I'm not any more thrilled with this ride than she."

Treymount smiled, his teeth glinting whitely. "I can tell. Relax, my dear. You're holding the reins as if you think they're snakes. Just keep them between your fingers like so." He held up his own gloved hands as an example.

She changed her grip accordingly and decided it was much more comfortable.

As she was beginning to enjoy the ride once more, they rounded a sharp corner of the path and found themselves facing a small group of riders, three men and a strikingly beautiful blond woman whom Honoria didn't instantly recognize.

Immediately the marquis's horse took exception at the abrupt appearance of another black gelding, and it was some minutes before order was restored. To Honoria's immense relief, Lightning didn't even seem to notice the fray but stood contentedly to one side, chewing ruminatively on her bridle.

"I say!" said the man on the other black gelding. "Control your mount!"

"I am," Treymount snapped. "You'd do well to do the same, Buckram!"

Indeed, the other gelding was thrashing about, neighing and backing up, while the marquis's horse was quieting.

The woman waited until both horses were under control and then turned her attention to Honoria. "Well, well, well," she drawled. "What have we here?"

The marquis frowned at the sound of the woman's voice, but he nodded nonetheless, his manner noticeably cool. "Lady Percival."

Honoria looked from one to the other, aware of an unnamed tension.

The woman looked directly at Honoria and smiled, though it wasn't a nice smile at all. It was, in fact, somewhat catty. "Miss Baker-Sneed, isn't it?"

Honoria blinked. How had the woman known her name?

As if reading her thoughts, Lady Percival smiled even wider, tossing her head a bit so that the tall ostrich feather that adorned her hat bobbed gently. "I saw you at the Oxbridge Ball. Everyone noticed you with Treymount and was dying to discover who you were."

"Oh dear. I didn't think anyone would notice me."

Lady Percival's cold eyes flickered across her. "They probably wouldn't, under normal circumstances."

One of the men with Lady Percival gave an amused snort at that. "We were all agog to discover Treymount's latest flirt."

Flirt? Honoria's back stiffened. People thought she was Treymount's *flirt?* Of all the —

"Oh don't look like that, my dear," Lady Percival drawled. "Everyone knows you are not that type of woman. What you are, in fact, is the marrying kind of woman. Marcus, you should really have a care."

"Be careful what you say, Lady Percival," Marcus snapped, his eyes blazing.

Lady Percival flushed the tiniest bit at his tone but kept her expression serene.

"If anyone was curious as to Miss Baker-Sneed's identity at the Oxbridge Ball, it was because she was easily the most striking woman there."

Buckram grinned at that. "Touché, Treymount."

Lady Percival's eyes flashed irritation. "Really, Marc—" The woman placed a hand over her mouth in pretend consternation. "I mean, Lord Treymount. Forgive me, it's so hard to remember to call you that after — well, you know."

Honoria suddenly realized what was happening. It was painfully obvious what the woman was trying to do — somewhere along the way, she and Treymount had apparently had a connection of some sort that had turned sour. And now the woman was bent on revenge.

Honoria had not been born yesterday, and coming from a household full of women, she recognized rejection when she saw it. It wasn't a pretty emotion, but certainly it was a human one. "Lady Percival, it is very nice meeting you, but Mar— I mean, Lord Treymount — and I have a wager to settle regarding our horses." She then turned to Marcus and said coolly, "Shall we continue?"

A fleeting look of surprise crossed his face, followed by a genuine smile that crinkled his eyes in a most attractive manner. "Indeed we shall, my dear. Indeed we shall."

Honoria didn't bother to do more than nod politely before urging Lightning on down the path. Marcus was beside her in an instant.

"That," he said, "was masterful."

"That," she replied, "was nonsense. Who does that woman think she is?"

He sent her a sidelong glance, his expression intent. "She is the past. And nothing more."

For some reason, the answer sent a flood of color to her cheeks. They walked on a ways more, Lightning shuffling along while the marquis held his horse in check. It shied a bit here and there, causing Honoria some uneasiness, but the basic disregard of her own horse made her relax more and more. Eventually, she began to notice things — that the sun was shining warmly though the trees, brightening the morning into a gentle day, that the flowers were blooming all along the paths, and that the sound of birds singing in the trees was quite a pleasant change from the constant clop clop of carts that were usually found outside her own home.

Better yet, she couldn't help but enjoy her companion. He didn't try to monopolize the conversation, or even keep it going, but seemed content to ride beside her, soaking in the morning much as she herself was. Every once in a while his gaze would meet hers and something would flare between them, a flash of warmth and . . . something more.

Good heavens, she wasn't beginning to care for Treymount . . . was she? That would never do. She knew him far too well. He was about the chase, the excitement. She'd seen it in his eyes at the auctions, and knew it to be true from the way he lived his life, never settling with one woman long enough to be caught.

And that was what he would think of marriage — a trap to be avoided. Thank goodness she was not a marriage-minded miss. In fact, Honoria rather thought the state of marriage was grossly overrated. It was for other people, like gentle Cassandra, who enjoyed focusing her efforts on others. Honoria preferred to maintain her freedom, thank you very much. Which was a good thing, considering she seemed drawn to men of the same way of thinking.

They were just rounding the bend on the south side of the park where the traffic was lighter when Treymount finally pulled his impatient horse to a halt. "Here we are. I believe we can now conclude our wager."

A flicker of disappointment almost mussed her smile, but she managed to maintain it. That was why they were here, of course. Still, she could not help but regret that their ride would soon be at an end. For the first time since she could recall, she'd enjoyed riding a horse — and spending time with the marquis — and she was in no hurry to see either end. "Of course. What shall we do?"

He glanced around, nodding at a small hedgerow that was slightly off the path. "First Demon and I shall jump it . . . and then you and Lightning."

She nodded. "That looks promising." Which was an absolute lie. There was no way her tubby horse would take a hedgerow. Why, she suspected it wouldn't even leave the smooth pathway without some very strong encouragement. Still, it wouldn't do to look ill-natured to the marquis. So instead she turned her horse's head in the direction of the hedgerow and urged it forward.

The two horses started off the path; the marquis's almost bolting. The horse had been held back since they'd first gotten to the park and it had become increasingly energetic as time passed. Honoria watched as the marquis easily brought the horse under control. Meanwhile, her own mount had paused at the edge of the path and then, with great reluctance, left it behind, walking slower and slower toward the hedgerow, reluctance evident in every line of its rather rounded body.

The marquis and his horse arrived first and had to wait quite awhile for them to catch up. As she drew abreast, he flashed her a smile and said, "Ready?"

"Oh yes," she said, trying to match his smile, and failing miserably, a sudden thought catching her and making her stomach squeeze horribly. What if Lightning actually *did* take the hedgerow? Ye gods, what would she do then?

"What's the matter?"

She realized that her fear must have shown on her face, for the marquis was looking at her intently, his brows lowered. She swallowed the emotion and forced herself to say in a light voice, "Oh nothing! I was just —" Her gaze found the hedgerow and she had an instant picture of herself being tossed off Lightning's back and landing on her rump on the muddy ground below, the horse's hooves terrifyingly close —

"Honoria."

She blinked. Somehow the marquis had pulled his horse directly beside Lightning. He was leaning over, his face within inches of hers. "Don't worry. You don't even have to attempt it if you don't wish." Then, to Honoria's further astonishment, he bent forward and kissed her.

Marcus would never be sure what it was that set him on that path. But for an instant there was such a look of pure panic in her face . . . it had amazed and distressed him. She was not the sort of woman to face mindless fear. In fact, she possessed far more common sense than most men he knew. So to see her eyes clouded in such a way, her bottom lip caught between her teeth, her pulse beating wildly in her throat . . . he'd had no choice. He'd had to kiss her.

Unfortunately, Demon took advantage of his master's distraction. And just as Marcus's lips touched Honoria's, the horse bolted. Marcus, leaning far out of his saddle, fell forward heavily and knocked Honoria off her horse.

One moment they were upright, lips touching, hearts thudding wildly. And the next they were laying in the dirt, Marcus atop Honoria, his face pressed against her shoulder, his knees between hers. There was a flurry of dust as the groom went flying posthaste to capture the wild horse.

Marcus could not believe what had happened. He could feel the wild beating of Honoria's heart; smell the sweet scent of her hair. If he lay very, very still, he could feel her body growing softer beneath his, and feel his own reacting — He almost groaned. God, but she was lush. But this was not the time or place. So he raised up on one elbow — just as a sharp, feminine laugh rang out behind him.

Lady Percival. Marcus closed his eyes, and it was in that moment that he knew his fate; the blasted talisman ring had caught yet another St. John in its invisible net.

Bloody hell, what was he going to do now?

Chapter 16

And then Treymount rose from the mud and declared that Miss Baker-Sneed and he were merely celebrating their upcoming nuptials! Imagine that, celebrating your betrothal in the dirt on a Thursday morning in the park!

Miss Charlotte Welton to Lord Albertson, as they danced the cotillion at Almack's

"I cannot believe this!" Portia exclaimed, looking around the room. It was filled with flowers, cards, and boxes of various types. The entire room was transformed from ordinary into a fairyland of delightful, frothy items. She sighed happily and looked at

Honoria. "You and Treymount! Who would have ever thought?"

"I would have thought," Juliet said from where she was systematically opening a stack of well-wishes and invitations from various members of the ton. "After all, Honoria has been wearing the St. John talisman ring for weeks now. It was only a matter of time before it caught up with her."

Honoria, who had been staring miserably into the fire, looked up at that. "When did you find out about the history of the ring?"

"Oh, I've always known. Everyone knows."

Portia nodded wisely, peering into yet another gift box. "Indeed. We thought it was all a hum, but apparently not." She pulled out some paper and then brightened. "Oh! Look! Another teapot. You shall have hundreds by the time the wedding occurs."

"Not to mention," Juliet said, sorting yet another gilt-edged invitation into an acceptance pile, "that we are now invited *everywhere*. Honoria, you have made us! We will all get handsome, wealthy husbands now!"

Honoria didn't reply. Instead she glared down at the ring on her finger. Blast it, was the ring to blame for this mess? She didn't want teapots. She didn't want invitations. And while she did want her sisters to have every positive advantage in the world, she'd had no wish to sell her own freedom for such a thing.

Not that marrying Treymount would necessarily mean an end to her freedom. After all, it wasn't a love match. No, it was a matter of necessity, brought on by Treymount's inability to keep his tongue in his own mouth.

She seethed, thinking of all the things she had to say to Treymount, things as yet unsaid. After calmly announcing that they were engaged to the blackguards who had come upon them in the park, he had waited for their groom to return and then had escorted her home, maintaining a stony silence the entire while.

Honoria had been too stunned to say anything herself. Ye gods, this was not what she'd wanted at all, despite the delight her sisters were having at her expense. Cassandra finding a wealthy, handsome husband was one thing — she lived for that sort of thing. But Honoria found it horrid beyond belief. She didn't want to get married, especially not to someone who so obviously didn't wish to marry at all.

To be honest, that was the real heart of the matter — she was doing the one thing she'd never wanted to do, giving up her freedom, and for what? To be considered a burden? An "unfortunate occurrence"? God help her, but the relationship, which had been rather explosive to begin with, promised to become one of awkward tension and polite distance.

As if to reaffirm her worst fears, it had been four whole days since she'd heard from Treymount except for a series of impersonal notes asking her rather abrupt questions about their soon-to-be wedding. To still any further furor, he'd decided that they should marry as soon as possible and had gone about arranging matters with very little input from her.

The whole thing was maddening. And though she'd written repeatedly, asking to meet, he'd merely responded that as soon as he had everything arranged, he'd be with her forthwith. And so the days had passed . . .

The most frustrating thing was that she knew he was right — they *had* to marry. Thanks to the loose lips of that harpy, Lady Percival, everyone knew of her and Marcus's accidental embrace. If Honoria didn't marry the marquis, not only would her reputation be in tatters, but her sisters' as well. The ton was many things, but discriminating in spreading blame was not one of them. Any close relative of a shunned person would be shunned as well unless they had either money or social standing of their own. To her chagrin, her sisters had neither.

"Honoria, do you think it will be a grand wedding?" Portia asked for the thousandth time.

"No," Honoria answered for the thousandth time in return. "Not if I have anything to do with it." She only wished she could say there wouldn't *be* a wedding. The last thing she ever wanted was to marry a man who was only marrying her out of a sense of duty. And yet, because of their predicament, that was exactly what was going to happen.

She'd stayed away from Treymount as long as she could, truculently obeying his request for her to wait for an audience once he had things arranged. But then, yesterday, she'd broken. Accompanied once again by Mrs. Kemble, Honoria had gone to Treymount House, determined to regain some semblance of control of her own life. However, on arriving at the house, the butler had informed her that the master was out.

Honoria didn't believe it for a minute; it was barely nine and she was certain the marquis had not yet risen from bed, but beyond marching past the servants and searching the house, she had no other recourse than to leave a note and return home. Of course, the note she'd left had been pithy, abrasive, and rather impolite, but on the whole had expressed her emotions at being left out of the entire process.

Treymount had not answered her note. And now . . . Honoria shifted listlessly, staring down at the tips of her slippers. The sad truth was that she had never felt so low in her entire life. Which was why early this morning she'd penned Treymount yet another note. One demanding a meeting as soon as possible, or else she was once again going to descend on Treymount House and no amount of frigid butlers was going to keep her out. She was certain it would be ignored, too, but it had at least given some vent to her jumbled feelings.

The door opened and Mrs. Kemble entered, beaming from ear to ear. "Oh Miss Honoria! He's here!"

Finally. A wave of relief and irritation raced through Honoria. She stood and smoothed her gown. Oh pother! Why had she worn this old gown? She had at least a half dozen that were better and — She realized everyone was looking at her. Heat rose in her face and she said as calmly as she could, "Of course. Please show him to the sitting room."

Mrs. Kemble nodded and scurried off.

"But —" Portia frowned. "We want to see him, too!"

"Oh yes," Olivia said. "We want to welcome him into the family and —"

"Honoria and the marquis need some time alone," Cassandra reproached gently. "They have hardly had time to talk since —" She glanced at Honoria and flushed. "Since their engagement."

"Thank you," Honoria said. She glanced at the mirror over the mantel and wished her hair hadn't chosen today of all days to look so . . . frothy. It was horrid, and pin as she would, she could not keep it from wisping about.

Sighing, she tucked away one or two loose strands and, ignoring the considering stares of her sisters, she left. Moments later she faced the door to the sitting room, her heart pounding in her throat, her mouth almost painfully dry.

Gathering her courage, she opened the door.

Marcus turned, his hat in his hand, his greatcoat still on. His gaze raked her up and down before he bowed. "Good morning."

She curtsied politely, realizing with a sinking heart that because he had not relinquished his coat and hat, that he had no intention of staying long. "Good morning. I hope you are well?" Ye gods, what was she doing, trading pleasantries like a ninny? She had something to say and she was going to say it.

He must have felt the same way, for a smile tugged at his mouth, his blue eyes twinkling reluctantly. "The weather is nice, too. Shall we speak about that?"

"Please, no." She sighed and pressed her hand to her temple. "I'm sorry; it's just that this is painfully awkward for us both. I hate that it happened, for it is the last thing on earth that I wished."

He paused, his mirth disappearing before a considering look. His gaze searched hers thoroughly. "You hate that it happened?"

Her cheeks heated. "Of course I do. I have no more wish to marry than you."

A frown flickered across his face, followed by something else, an expression she couldn't decipher. "Well, since we are stuck with one another, I suppose we should make the best of it."

The words made her flinch inside, but she hid it. "I suppose so." She gestured toward the chairs by the fire. "Shall we sit?"

He glanced at the chairs, then at the sofa. "Yes, but here. I want to see your face."

That was an odd thing to say, she thought. But she did not demur and followed him to the sofa. They sat, slightly turned toward one another, the air about them heavy and awkward.

After a moment Marcus said, "You look tired. Is something wrong? Other than this mess, of course."

Her heart sank. It was a mess, wasn't it? A horrid, horrid mess. She wasn't sure, but hearing him say it, in that particular tone of voice, made tears rise to her eyes. She forced herself to swallow. She was sure she looked tired, but . . . Blast it, she hadn't seen the lout in four days and that was all he could say? "I daresay I do look tired. I've been here, all alone, trying to decide how to deal with things and —"

"I've written you every day."

"Oh yes! Two sentence notes saying, 'Do you wish orchids or lilies for the wedding?' and, 'Do you have a church preference?' It was so kind of you to think of me."

He frowned, eyeing her for a long moment. "I apologize if I've done something wrong, but I've had to get all of the details straightened out and —"

"Oh. Is that why you have not visited me

in four days? Not one time since that day have you spent so much as ten minutes in my presence." Honoria almost grimaced at her own waspish tone. Good heavens, they weren't even married yet and already she sounded like a fishwife. But she couldn't seem to help it; everything was so confusing, so . . . astounding, so . . . sad.

Suddenly, the strain of the last four days tumbled down on her. Her eyes grew moist and her lip began to quiver. Her chest ached and burned and it was all she could do not to sob aloud.

Ye gods, no. She did *not* want to cry. Not now. Not in front of Marcus.

But there was no stopping it. One moment she was sitting beside him, so angry that her toes curled, and the next, tears were welling and threatening to spill down her cheeks. She gasped out a sob, then another. And before she knew it, she'd dropped her face into her hands and gave in to a hearty bout of tears.

Marcus sighed and reached for her, pulling her into his arms and holding her tightly. Thank God he'd had a sister or he might have been cowed by such a reaction. Instead, he rubbed her shoulder and rested his cheek against her hair, letting the sobs pour out.

She was overwhelmed and perhaps a little frightened. So was he. He'd never thought to marry in such a fashion, under a potential cloud of scandal. And he'd certainly never thought his own behavior would be so risky as to cause such a thing to happen. But it had.

There was something about Honoria that sent his mind and body reeling to the detriment of his usual good, common sense. That was why he'd stayed away. Because he'd known that the moment he was with her again, he could very well lose what little control he had.

It had been that way from the start, though he hadn't realized it at the time. There was some sort of connection, some sort of physical pull that interfered with his usual orderly way of conducting his life. It had been pure madness to kiss Honoria in public in the middle of the park. But somehow, at the time, the gesture had made perfect sense. It was a staggering realization that, had he to do it over again, he would have. Even knowing the outcome, the taste of her lips at that precise moment was worth every bit of the nonsense and trouble he had to go through now.

It was confusing and damned irritating. How had he gotten so illogical? So bereft of common sense and calm thinking? What was it about her?

Blast it, he didn't want to marry anymore than she, not this way, forced by society and the snide laughter of Lady Percival.

Yet he sighed, releasing some of his anger as he rested his cheek against Honoria's silken hair, the soothing scent of lemon and roses rising to meet him. Her form was warm and pliant against his, and he bit off a curse as his own body reacted to her nearness. It had been this way since the first day he'd come here to demand his mother's ring, and he would be damned if he would succumb to it again.

And therein lay the greatest quandary of all . . . If he was tempted by Honoria when she lived far away, how would he resist her when she lived under his own roof? Could he? Was it possible that damned ring had something to do with this? That he was suffering from a curse of some sort?

Bloody hell, but he'd been right. It was a mess.

Slowly, her tears dried. And soon she pressed her hands against his chest and sat upright. The feel of her hands on his chest made his loins tighten even more, and he was glad he still had on the greatcoat to hide his reaction. He looked at her; she was blinking back tears, her long lashes spiked about her eyes, eyes that seemed the pure green of a new leaf after a rain.

She sniffed. "I'm so sorry."

"Nonsense." He found his handkerchief and put it into her hand, solemnly admonishing her to blow her nose or he'd blow it for her.

That made her give a watery giggle. "You cannot blow my nose for me."

"Oh?" He took the handkerchief and held it over her nose. "Now blow."

She yanked the scrap of linen from his hand and obediently blew her nose before managing a shaky smile. "My mother used to do that."

A faint smile touched his mouth. "So did mine." He leaned back against the sofa and watched as she dried her eyes and put herself to rights. She tilted forward to smooth her skirts, and his gaze found that streak of white at her temple. He lifted a hand and lazily traced it to her braid. She was overwrought, and it was no wonder. He was feeling a bit worn himself. He should have come to see her. He knew he should have. But he'd been afraid — He frowned. Afraid of what? Of this? Of an outpouring of emotion?

Or the realization that perhaps, just perhaps, it wasn't real emotion at all, but the effects of the talisman ring? He glanced at her hand, the silver band seeming to glint brighter. His jaw tightened. By God, he would not let a common ring make a mockery of him. If he was to marry, he'd make the best of it. To that end, he blurted out, "We have a lot in common, we two."

"Oh?" She folded the handkerchief and slipped it into a pocket hidden in her skirts. "Other than mothers who used to threaten to blow our noses for us?"

He chuckled. "Much more than that. Think about it, Honoria."

She pursed her lips, her eyes shimmery bright from her cry. "Well . . . we do share an interest in antiquities. Of course, that has frequently caused us to cross swords at various auctions and procurement houses."

"Ah, but if we were on the same side . . ." He raised a brow.

She smiled suddenly, her teeth a glimpse of white between her full, soft lips. "Imagine what we could do then."

Damn but her lips were lush. He pictured those lips touching his, moving over his skin, capturing his —

Bloody hell, he was rattled beyond thought. With difficulty he forced his attention back to her words. "Of course, a general appreciation for antiquities is hardly a basis for a solid marriage. What else do we have in common?"

She considered this a moment, regarding her slippered toes. "Well . . . we both like to win."

"That is, unfortunately, true." He had to grin a bit. "I fear that similarity would make us far more likely to murder one another than to have a peaceful marriage."

"Possibly." She tilted her head to one side, a faint quiver of a smile passing over her face. "What is worse is that we are both proud and unyielding."

"What?" he said, sitting a little straighter. "Surely not *both* of us."

"And arrogant and obstinate when it comes to things we believe in."

Bloody hell. The chit had the audacity of an invading army. She insulted with each breath, all the while looking at him with laughing eyes and a damnably sensual smile. He eyed her with a warning gaze, daring her to say more. Yet somehow, in the moment, he realized that he was fighting the oddest desire to smile. To grin back at her. To laugh at them both. "You may be proud and un-yielding, but I vow upon my dead mother's grave that I am neither."

She glanced at him, then at the ceiling as if addressing a spirit of some sort. "Don't listen to him. He's just angry we have to marry. And it's all because of this damned ring."

In all of Marcus's dealings, never had anyone offered to speak to the heavens in his name. Nor had anyone called him proud and unyielding, arrogant and obstinate. And never, ever, had anyone left him with such a ridiculous desire to laugh.

Damn the ring to hell and back.

He tried not to look directly at Honoria, who managed to appear very kissable even with her reddened nose and shining hazel eyes. He wondered why it was that in all the times he'd bid against her in various auctions in the years before, he'd never one time spoken directly to her. All he'd ever done was bow ironically whenever they happened to cross paths.

Was it possible . . . had it been pride? Or something else? Maybe even then he'd been aware of the attraction between them and had avoided her because of that. Surely that made more sense than a cursed ring.

To be honest, Honoria interested him. And he couldn't remember the last time he'd had a conversation with a woman who hadn't bored him to tears within the first fifteen minutes. Yet she presented such a lively turn of mind, such a warm and naturally friendly manner, that whenever he was with her, things seemed more . . . alive somehow.

He crossed his arms over his chest and leaned back against the pillowed softness of the sofa. "I must protest being called prideful and arrogant, especially since you claim those same faults yourself."

"Ah, well . . . I had a chef once who served the tenderest Beef Wellington. I had the audacity to compliment him on it, to which he replied that the secret was thoroughly tenderizing the meat using a very hard, wooden mallet."

His lips twitched. "And you would be the wooden mallet to tenderize my character?"

"Yes," she replied without hesitation. "With great pleasure. It's quite possible that together, the rougher aspects of our characters might well rub themselves smooth."

"Like stones in a grinding box."

"Exactly."

"I must say, that sounds very . . . unpleasant."

She frowned, a sad look entering her eyes. "Indeed. That is what I fear. I do not know that we suit."

"Balderdash. Of course we shall suit. We have similar interests, similar tastes, and we both love a good argument." He shrugged. "It's more than many couples have."

She tilted her head to one side as if considering this. "I suppose it could work, if we made an effort to compromise on things. Do you think you could change things if you needed to?"

He frowned. Change? Him? Why did she ask him that question? "What do you think I need to change?"

"Well . . . yourself, I suppose. Your manners and things. If it became necessary, of course."

"Honoria, I have no wish for either of us to change."

"You don't wish to improve." A faint curl of disapprobation lingered in her eyes.

That was the trouble with marriage. Women immediately felt they had a right to improve you, like a weedy garden or an unpolished doorknob. He scowled. "Improvement is a matter of opinion."

"Improvement is our duty to ourselves and those around us," she retorted loftily. "I always try to improve."

"Perhaps you have more to improve upon."

Her brows rose. "Apparently not."

That put him in his place. Despite his irritation, a faint smile itched to touch his mouth. "You are spirited, aren't you?"

"And you are impertinent."

"Sometimes," he agreed with alacrity, suddenly aware that he was hugely enjoying himself despite his doubts. "So tell me, for what other reasons shall we deal well together?"

"Well, in addition to sharing some common interests —"

"One."

"— one common interest *and* serving to smooth each other's character flaws, it's possible that this marriage could serve our respective positions well."

"Positions?"

"Yes. Mine as head of this household." She paused a moment, her brow creasing ever so slightly. "I will not hide from you that the greatest appeal from this union is the financial security and social benefits that it will provide my family, especially my sisters."

The words had stung his pride the tiniest bit. He was a man used to being feted and courted by his peers, and her comment made sense. He was, after all, head of the wealthiest family in England. But still, it was not pleasant to hear from one's prospective bride that one's fiscal strength was one's most endearing quality. Which was why he said in a rather rough voice, "It is plain to see the benefits gained by your family. But what of mine?"

That lit the fires. Her faint flush deepened and her violet eyes flashed. "I do not believe you need to be reminded of the Baker-Sneed lineage. We can trace our lineage from the time of William the Conqueror."

Marcus quirked a brow. "That would be important if I wished to improve the St. John claim to the throne, which is a ludicrous idea."

She blinked, a slow questioning blink that made her luxurious lashes tangle at the corners. "You don't care about lineage."

No, he didn't. But what he did care about was the woman at his side. The thought took him unawares and he almost stood.

He cared about Honoria. Oh, he wasn't in love, far from it. But he did respect her and he was coming to genuinely like her. There was not a line of artifice in her body, not a single false note. She was gentle and serenely beautiful with a sharp wit and a genuine appreciation for life. As wives went, he could do much, much worse.

If only he'd chosen her, and not fate. His earlier irritation surged and a slow heat rose in him. In fact . . . His gaze roamed across her, noting the fresh curve of her cheek, the lush turns of her body, the delicate line of her lips. The heat simmered beneath his skin, through his blood, and somehow he found himself moving slightly closer. And then closer still.

Her gaze widened, but she did not move an inch. Instead she sat, watching him approach, her hands nervously threaded in her skirts.

He moved again, this time slipping an arm about her waist. He lifted her and set her in his lap, his hands moving over her, caressing and touching. She gasped, and then suddenly her eyes flared and she reached up and twined her arms about his neck and pulled his mouth to hers.

He kissed her passionately, all of the energies and worries of the last few days disappearing in an onslaught of pure lust. She fit inside his arms and life all too well. Somewhere deep inside, he knew he was as afraid as she, as worried that this marriage might, at some point, cause them both pain. But at the moment, with his arms about her, her warm ass pressed against his lap, her arms linked about his neck as he plundered and ravaged her kissable lips . . . at the moment he didn't care about anything except making the delectable Miss Honoria Baker-Sneed his.

The kiss deepened and lengthened. Marcus ran his hands over her back, across her stomach, down her hips. She was firm and curved, filling his hands and then some. He stroked the outside of her thighs, never breaking the onslaught of his mouth over hers. God, but how he wanted her. How he craved to lift her skirts and lay between her velvet thighs. He wanted her like no other —

The door to the sitting room banged open. "Honoria, tell Portia that I —"

Honoria's eyes flew open, and for a startled moment she and Marcus just sat there, looking at one another, lips still locked, their arms still tightly in place.

"Heavens! I — We — I never knew you — Sorry!" With that, whoever it was slammed the door and left.

Honoria moaned and broke the kiss. "It was Juliet, my sister. She'll tell the others and — Ye gods, what must she think?" She pushed herself upright and stood, arranging her skirts into a semblance of order. Her cheeks were flushed, her eyes sparkling, and she appeared to be thoroughly embarrassed.

Despite the interruption, Marcus's blood was still boiling. But he knew that now was not the time to press his attentions. Besides, in a few days she would be his for the taking whenever and wherever he pleased. The thought lingered and then took hold. Yes, by God, once they were married, things would indeed change, and only for the better. He'd make certain of that.

"My lord — Treymount —"

"Marcus," he said smoothly, rising from the sofa as well and adjusting his cravat. "We might as well start with that."

"Of course. I just —" She bit her lip. "Is there *any* other way we could fix this? I'm not saying I don't wish to marry you, but . . . must we?"

Damn yes, she was going to marry him. One way or the other. "We have no choice; I've considered everything. There is no other solution, especially since Lady Percival made it her business to spread the word as quickly as she could. In fact, she had no compunction about exaggerating bits of it, although that has worked to our benefit since people have discovered discrepancies in her stories and wonder about the whole."

Honoria sighed, rubbing her neck as if tired. "Yes, well . . . I don't really care about my reputation except for how it affects my sisters. I cannot allow my mistakes to damage their good name."

"They would be outcasts before they even began the season, unless, of course, we marry." Marcus wasn't sure why he wanted to be certain Honoria knew this, but he did.

Perhaps he could sense a seed of doubt in her voice, a hint of sadness that for some reason tugged at him all the harder.

He picked up his hat and adjusted the brim. "I arranged to get a special license from the archbishop. We are to be married by week's end."

She nodded, then turned and walked with unseeing eyes to the front window. "I — I suppose there is nothing I can say." She rested her temple against the window trim and watched the tilburies and carts wobble by. "Saturday it will be, then."

Marcus wanted nothing more than to cross the room and take her in his arms, but he dared not. What flared between them was hot and unruly and had already overcome his good sense more times than he'd liked. He would not succumb again. Not until he had the right to make her fully his own, to possess her in the way he burned to. Perhaps that would return his usual strength of comportment.

Grinding his teeth, he bowed abruptly. "Good day, then. I will continue to keep you informed of events."

She didn't even look his way, her gaze fixed on the street outside, her expression far away. "I know you will."

The words were soft, drenched in loneliness. Marcus fisted his hand as some emotion he didn't recognize broke free in his chest. The pain of seeing her there, standing by the window, looking so forlorn, was somehow more than he could stand. "Honoria?"

That woke her some, for she looked at him, her hazel gaze clear and direct. "Yes?"

"I —" Whatever he'd been about to say, the words locked in his throat and he was left with none. Floundering, he managed to blurt out in a rather abrupt voice, "I will see you soon."

Then, feeling like the most awkward individual to walk the earth, he bowed, turned on his heel and left.

Chapter 17

Women always seem to have the most damnable ways of changing things just as you get comfortable. Take my own wife. Sweet woman, salt of the earth really. Lately what's she do but go on a reducing diet and expect me to join in with her. I've nothing against her losing a stone or two — she ain't as trim as she once was. But as for me, why I've never been in better shape. So I'll be demmed if I go the rest of my life eating nothing but boiled potatoes in vinegar!

Lord Albertson to
his friend Sir Harry Brooks,
while the two enjoyed a cigar
late one evening at White's

The day of Honoria's marriage proceeded as if in a dream. She felt nothing — neither excitement nor dread nor concern. Nothing but a strange sense of detachment. It was as if her life was careening out of control and somewhere along the way she'd lost all sense of direction. She sat at the dressing table in her bedroom and looked at herself in the mirror, noting her empty eyes.

How had this happened? This sort of thing occurred to women who had no control over their emotions, to women who were willing to forego the trappings of respectability to gain a bridegroom at any price. This sort of thing was not supposed to happen to *her*.

All night long she'd asked herself the same questions over and over, going from a state of near panic to a strangely dead calm. How had she allowed this to happen? How could she marry a man who'd never wanted to marry? A man who freely admitted this was not the route he'd have chosen?

She met her gaze in the mirror. She had no choice. None at all. It was her freedom or her sisters' ruin. Surely it wouldn't be so bad. After all, Marcus had admitted that there were reasons they'd make a good match; why, she herself had thought of several yesterday. That didn't make the marriage more palatable, but it did give her some hope that perhaps, with time, they could come to care for one another.

And that was what she wanted. She didn't want to marry at all, but if she must, it would have been nice to have married for love. She sighed disconsolately. There was a very strong physical bond between them that was impossible to deny. Perhaps that was something, for it was certainly powerful, so powerful that it had led to their demise.

And this was a demise of a sort . . . the demise of her life as she knew it. In a scant thirty minutes she would no longer be a Baker-Sneed. No longer be unwed. No longer be free to decide what she wanted to do with her life.

No longer anything that she was familiar with.

What she would be was the wife of one of the most powerful, wealthy men in the country. A man who was so distraught with the circumstances of their union that he had not spent more than twenty minutes in her company since they'd announced their engagement.

The thought should have depressed her.

And in some abstract way, it did. But overall she felt nothing. Nothing at all. She met her gaze in the mirror and pressed a hand to her cheek. She could feel her fingers against her skin, so she wasn't completely numb. Just her heart.

The door opened and Cassandra appeared carrying a small bouquet of flowers. Her gaze met Honoria's in the mirror, and for a second Cassandra hesitated.

Honoria forced a smile to her lips. "There you are. Is everyone here?"

By "everyone" she meant the marquis, and Cassandra knew it. "He arrived ten minutes ago."

"Why didn't you come for me?"

Cassandra lifted her chin. "Because he was not to arrive until ten. He has already won you by foul means, and I refuse to let you go one second earlier than I must."

Honoria had to smile a little at Cassandra's uncharacteristically stubborn tone. "There is no reason to look so dour. I am certain the marquis did not plan these horrid circumstances. He had no wish to marry any more than I."

Cassandra eyed her with an anxious air. "No? Are you certain of that?"

"I am positive; he told me so."

"Oh Honoria!"

"No, no. It's not a horrid thing. It's actually a little reassuring."

Tears filled Cassandra's eyes. She impulsively grasped one of Honoria's hands. "There are times I cannot like the marquis. He seems so coldhearted, so thoughtless. He only came to see you once this week, and when he left you'd have thought the hounds of hell were on his heels. His carriage practically ran up on the curb as he —" Cassandra shook her head. "I wish you'd reconsider this."

"And ruin your chances of ever contracting an eligible marriage? I could not do that. Not for a thousand pounds."

"This is all the marquis's fault! Why he must try and kiss you while riding a spirited horse —"

"Cassandra, it was an accident."

"Hardly. He is a man, and far more experienced in the ways of the world than you. He took advantage of your innocence and —"

"No." Honoria turned to her sister. "I cannot allow you to put the blame for all of this on the marquis's head. It's true that he did try to kiss me, but . . . to be honest, I rather wanted him to."

Cassandra paused. "You wanted him to?"

Honoria's gaze fell on the flowers. They were beautiful, a collection of pinks and purples. She reached out and ran a finger over the velvet surface of a petal. "I am not a green girl, to be taken in by a rakehell. I knew what I was doing, but I could not seem to stay away from him. Every time he kissed me, I felt so —" Heat touched her cheeks and she dropped her hand from the bouquet. "I don't suppose you need to know that."

Cassandra sank into the chair beside Honoria's, concern darkening her violet eyes. "Honoria, is it possible that you care about the marquis?"

Care about him? It was possible — after all, she'd certainly spent a good amount of time in his company in her efforts to come to an agreement on the ring. She absently rubbed the talisman ring, fingering the warm metal band. "I care for him, of course I do. And I certainly hold him in esteem. He's stubborn beyond reason, but his heart is good."

"How can you be so certain?"

"Because of what he does for his family and his brothers. His face, when he talks of them . . ." A smile touched her lips. "He is proud of them, though I'm not certain he realizes how much."

Cassandra looked as if she might say something more, but a rapid knock sounded on the door. It opened and Portia rushed in. "The vicar is here and we're ready to go — Oh Honoria! You look lovely!"

Honoria picked up the bouquet and stood. She was wearing her best gown. Of soft white with a pink underskirt trimmed with rosettes, it hung in graceful folds to the floor. "Thank you, Portia. I believe I'm ready now."

Cassandra reached over and took her hand. "Honoria . . . are you certain?"

No. But what else could she do? If she took a stand against society, she would be ousted, which was fine with her. But to sacrifice the potential future of her sisters . . . she simply could not do it. She'd made the mistake of forgetting the propriety society demanded, and she alone would pay the price. She and Marcus.

It was difficult to accept that this was it — that there was no turning back. But there wasn't.

Still, it would have been nice if, during this week of preparations and plans, the marquis had come to and told her — What? What was it she wanted to hear? Perhaps it would have been enough just to know that he was thinking of her as much as she was thinking of him, which was ludicrous of course because he didn't love her the way she loved him.

Ye gods. She didn't just care for Marcus, she *loved* him. The truth hit her with such clarity that she had to reach out and hold onto the back of a chair to keep her knees from failing her.

Cassandra gripped her elbow. "Honoria! Are you well?"

"Yes," she said, using all of her strength to collect herself. "Yes, of course. I just . . ." She'd just realized she was in love with the man who was marrying her simply to fulfill his duty. What a horrid coil. No matter what, he would see her as a duty he'd fulfilled, while she saw him as . . . She closed her eyes.

How could she face him, knowing that she'd already allowed herself to care far, far more than she should? Whatever she did, she would not give up her pride. Lifting her chin, she gathered herself and turned to the door, pasting a smile on her face. "Shall we go? I don't want to keep the marquis waiting."

Cassandra and Portia exchanged a look.

Portia shook her head. "Honoria, if you don't wish —"

"Don't be silly," she said somewhat desperately. "The marquis is wealthy and titled. Why wouldn't I want to marry him?" Her head held high, her heart frozen in fear, she swept past Cassandra and Portia and stepped into the corridor, almost running into Marcus.

He glared down at her, the light from the doorway slanting over his face, highlighting the hard slash of his mouth, the unsmiling look in his eye.

Heat flooded her cheeks. Good God, had he heard her sounding so trite and foolish? She'd only meant to allay her sisters's concerns and no more. "M-Marcus, I —"

"Are you ready?" His voice, cold and impersonal, flickered across her like a whip.

Honoria nodded.

"Good. I will wait for you at the vestibule." With that, he turned on his heel and left.

There were only a few guests at the wedding — two of Marcus's brothers and their wives and families. Anthony and Anna, Chase and Harriet, were in attendance, as well as Anthony's five wards and Harriet's two sisters and two brothers, all of whom had come to town for the express purpose of visiting Astley's Amphitheatre and seeing the famed caged lions, only to find themselves the guests of a rushed wedding.

Marcus was irritated to have even these few members of his family present. He'd have much rather had the ceremony in private, and had planned to do it with the minimum of fuss. But to his chagrin, as he was coming out of the cathedral, the special license in his pocket, he'd run into his brother Chase. Though Marcus had wanted privacy, he refused to ask Chase to keep a secret, with the result that there were almost as many St. Johns and proxy St. Johns as there were Baker-Sneeds.

The ceremony went without flaw, though the blushing bride was neither blushing nor very bridelike. Oh, she looked lovely enough — very lovely, in fact. The pearl-colored gown made the exotic streak in her hair glow whiter, her skin seem creamy and warm. By all accounts he should have been a happy man . . . but he wasn't. If he closed his eyes, he could still hear her words in the hallway. He scowled. Damn it, what did it matter that the main reason she was marrying him, besides saving her family's good name, was because of his wealth and title? People married for just such reasons all of the time. In fact, he, himself, had expected to marry for just such a reason.

Only . . . it did bother him. He slanted a look at his bride, but her expression was frozen, her gaze distant, the same exact expression she'd assumed when he'd seen her in the hallway.

The distant look began to worry him. At first he attributed it to nervousness. But when she remained coolly aloof throughout the celebration luncheon following the ceremony, his concern grew.

The sad truth was, despite her words to the contrary, she hadn't wished to marry him any more than he'd wished to marry her. But hell, *he* had managed to reconcile himself to the situation. In fact, he'd even found himself humming as he dressed this morning, which had completely surprised him. It wasn't as if he was marrying an ogre or an unattractive woman or one lacking in sense or interest — he could think of a dozen women who'd have bored him before the end of the ceremony. But not Honoria.

There, he thought. He'd admitted the positive aspects of such a union and warmed to them all, in more ways than one. Why the hell hadn't she, dammit?

The worst part of it all was that his blood burned for her, and this last week had only made things worse. Every day, every night, he thought of her, dreamed of her with an intensity that left him restless and yearning. The realization that soon she'd be gracing his bed dulled any irritation being married could cause.

The truth was, he was primed and ready and impatient for the ceremony to be over. Just sitting beside her at the luncheon and having to watch her lips closing over the bowl of her spoon, feeling the occasional pressure of her knee whenever he bent over to whisper something in her ear, smelling the lemon and sunshine of her hair . . . it drove him to distraction.

As soon as he could — and actually a little sooner than he should have — he took matters into his own hands. He called for the carriage and bid an abrupt farewell to the wedding party. Ignoring the knowing looks from his own brothers, he rushed her through the teary embraces of her family and outside to the waiting carriage.

Herberts was holding the door wide, his nearly toothless grin stretched from ear to ear. " 'Ere ye are, guv'nor! 'Tis a good day to get wracked by the parson, ain't it?" He pulled down the steps as Honoria came forward. "Coo 'ee, me lady! 'Tis a nice gown ye have. And look at the sparkles on yer toes! Ain't often oiye see feet so well shod."

He might have continued on in this vein if Marcus hadn't slapped a healthy vale in his hand and said tersely, "Waste no time."

Herberts's grin widened even more and he gave a broad wink. "Impatient, aren't ye? Well now, havin' seen her la'yship, oiye can't say as oiye blame ye."

Marcus had the uncomfortable impression that had Herberts dared, the man would have nudged him in the ribs right along with that impudent wink. Really, he had to do something about that damned coachman, but now was not the time.

Marcus climbed into the carriage, achingly aware of Honoria sitting across from him, pale as a wraith. "Herberts, do you know where we are going?"

"Aye, guv'nor! To the huntin' box. Lord Brandon was mighty fond of that place hisself, why once't —"

Marcus slammed the door closed, and within moments the coach rocked slightly as Herberts climbed aboard. Soon they were off and Marcus was blessedly alone with his new bride.

Finally they were underway. Now, short of throwing herself from the moving conveyance, Honoria could not suddenly bolt. Marcus felt immensely better, realizing that had been one of his chief fears. But now . . . she was all his.

He clenched his hands into fists and stilled his heated impulses. For all her strength of character, Honoria was an innocent, and he was determined to make this, her first time, the best.

Teeth set against his own traitorous body, Marcus crossed his arms and prayed Herberts would make excellent speed to the hunting box. The small lodge was perfect for a seduction, and that was exactly what Marcus had in mind — he was going to slowly, deliberately, and with all due care and passion, seduce his own wife.

Across the seat from him, Honoria tried to find something to say, something to remove the confusion and angst of the day. But she couldn't seem to find the words to get over the awkwardness of the last few hours. All she could think of was that this was it — she was married, now and forever. And to a man she barely knew.

Well, that wasn't exactly true. After all their competitions on the auction floor, she did know something about his character. She knew, for instance, that he rarely allowed his emotions to overcome his good sense — when he made a purchase, it was because he liked an item and knew its value. She also knew that when he'd made up his mind to possess something, God help those in his way. He was ruthless when occasion demanded it, bidding with a cold heat that bespoke great control and even greater determination.

She also had grown to know more about him these last few weeks as they'd brangled over the talisman ring, too. She now knew that he had a sharp sense of humor, that he was innately fair, and that though he seemed rather cold and aloof, he was actually a very passionate, giving man.

Honoria felt the ring through her glove. They'd used the simple band as a wedding ring, something that had surprised her. Surely Marcus had had time to get another ring this week? But perhaps with all of the arrangements to be made, he hadn't. Or perhaps it just hadn't been important enough.

Her shoulders sagged at the thought. Heavens, this wouldn't do at all. She collected herself and stole a glance at him through her lashes. To her surprise, she found him watching her with an intensity that made her suck in her breath. His eyes, they were so serious; his face, so set.

She unconsciously began smoothing and resmoothing her silk skirt over her knee, the material sliding effortlessly beneath her fingertips. What did she say now? That she was sorry they'd had to marry? She'd never wanted to be someone's duty? Especially not in this manner.

"Are you cold?"

Honoria's gaze flew to the marquis. No, not the marquis. Her husband. Her incredibly handsome, very passionate, incredibly virile husband. The man that she should love above all others. Heat stained her cheeks and she caught herself looking down at his thighs. In a manner of speaking, those were *her* thighs now. Her spirits lifted slightly at the thought as she remembered the feel of them against her skirts, the firmness of his body, the —

"Bloody hell, don't look at me like that."

Her gaze flew to meet his. "Look at you how?"

"You know damn well," he said grimly.

Her cheeks heated anew. "I'm sorry. I was just —" Her gaze flickered back to his thighs, and she noted the rippled muscles were now clenched. Her mouth went dry and she flicked the tip of her tongue to her lips.

A sound almost like a groan escaped him.

Honoria pressed a hand to her throat, aware of the tension surrounding them. Her body felt flushed and heated, and her heart thumped against the base of her throat. Her gaze met his and locked. All she said was "Marcus," but the word was fraught with meaning, almost a pleading.

"That's it." With that, he reached across the carriage, plucked her from her seat, and put her in his lap, his hands warm through the thin silk at her waist. He settled her there and then buried his face in her neck, his breath hot on her skin.

Honoria just sat, stunned. She was now sitting on those very thighs she'd been studying so astutely. They were just as firm as she remembered, rock hard and finely muscled. And it felt . . . good. Very good, if she was honest.

He stirred, lifting his face and smiling at her. He touched her cheek in a careless caress. "I have wanted to hold you for a week."

Her heart leapt. "Yes? Then why . . . why did you stay away?"

"Because I had already put you in one untenable situation, and my control —" A faint, lopsided smile touched his lips, self-derision on his face. "You affect me strongly."

And he affected her. Of course, physical attraction wasn't love. But perhaps . . . perhaps it was something.

"Honoria, I don't pretend that this is the best way to begin a marriage. But it's what we have, and considering everything, there is a very real possibility we can make this work."

The carriage swayed wildly and he caught her tight against his broad chest. Honoria let him hold her, closing her eyes and savoring the feeling of . . . what was it? Simple comfort in having someone to lean against? Or was it more?

They swerved again, only this time so wildly that she was almost thrown off Marcus's lap. He had to catch her firmly to keep her from flying through the air.

"Blast Herberts!" Marcus said, glaring at the roof as if to send a heated message to the coachman.

"He's quite unusual."

"He's horrid. I had thought to train him to a higher level and then return him to my brother, but I am beginning to believe it an impossibility. The man remembers nothing of what you tell him and — But that is neither here nor there. We were talking about our marriage."

"Yes," she said, taking a deep breath. "We should discuss our expectations."

His thumb began a slow, circular movement on her waist, the gesture most likely unconscious and meant to sooth. But instead of soothing, it sent a lightning strike of sensation all the way through her, heating her skin and making her breasts swell as if in anticipation.

Honoria had to swallow twice just to breathe. Her whole body was focused on the feel of him, on his thighs beneath her rump, his hand on her waist, his chest against her arm. Heat began to simmer in her stomach and move lower. She hurried to blurt out what few thoughts she could still reach through the haze of sensuality he was weaving with his touch. "I — I told my brother and sisters that we would be living with you."

"Of course."

She regarded him through her lashes, enjoying the splay of his strong hand over her hip. "It might be difficult at first, since you aren't used to having a large family about."

"I grew up in a large family."

"Yes, but that was some time ago. I daresay you have gotten used to being alone."

He shrugged. "Treymount House is large enough that I daresay I won't even know your brother and sisters are there."

"If you think so," she said, doubt thick in her voice. "What do you expect from me, as your wife?"

For an instant it seemed as if his expression froze. But then he said slowly, "Well . . . I suppose I expect this."

With that, his hand closed gently over her

breast. Honoria gasped, a flash of sensation scorching through her, sending her thoughts flying in a thousand different directions. "I — I see."

"Do you like that?" He rubbed his hand slowly over her breast, gently kneading it.

Heat built and her nipple hardened. "I — Yes. That is quite nice." It was better than nice; it was divine. "Marcus, I — is there anything else you think we should discuss?"

"Other than how good this feels?" he murmured, lowering his lips to her cheek and tracing a line across the crest.

She swallowed. "I just wanted to know what you expect."

He paused, lifting his head so he could meet her gaze. "I suppose I expect decorum and honesty and . . . the usual sort of things."

"What else?"

A frown darkened his face. "I don't know. For you to oversee the household staff, which shouldn't be too taxing. I've an excellent chef, Antoine. And Jeffries is quite competent to —" He frowned. "That's not what you meant, is it?"

"Not quite. I just didn't know . . . what do you expect from me as . . . as a wife?" She held her breath.

Realization crossed his face. "I see. Very

well, then. Until you have done your duty in the way of an heir, I will also expect your fidelity to none but me."

Her heart sank. What did he mean "until" she had done her duty? Did that mean that after that he didn't care what she did?

He took her silence to mean something else. "I will, of course, provide you with a generous allowance and enough pin money that you should be able to enjoy life to the fullest." He paused, then added, "And I will sponsor all of your sisters." An ironic smile touched his lips. "As you've always wished."

Honoria tried to find the words . . . some words, any words. By all accounts, she should be quite happy. After all, he was offering what every woman of the ton wanted, what every woman of the ton dreamed of. But somehow . . . she had to know.

She cleared her throat. "And when I've given you your heir? What did you mean by 'until'?"

"Well —"

The carriage hit a wild bump and seemed to fly a moment before landing with a hard jounce. Marcus was tossed against the ceiling; he cursed under his breath. "Damn it, Herberts!"

Honoria held onto Marcus a bit tighter,

wondering if they would make it to their destination or land in a ditch.

"Don't worry about him," Marcus said. "He's actually rather competent. He has never once gotten lost, never overturned. Added to that, he makes the most damnable time."

She relaxed a little, leaning against him, enjoying the feel of his hands as they splayed over her back, her waist, moving constantly. If he could touch her, she supposed that now she could touch him. She began with the top button of his waistcoat, unfastening it, then fastening it back.

His gaze darkened, so she said hurriedly, "You haven't answered my question."

"No, I haven't." His hand closed over hers. "Honoria, how do you want me to answer?"

Ye gods, what a question. "I — I suppose I just want to know . . ." She gulped, then took her emotions firmly in hand. This was not the time to become faint of heart. Collecting herself, she met his gaze steadily. "Marcus, what happens after I've given you an heir? Am I free then? To do as I please?"

His brows lowered and he growled, "When you have presented me with an heir, you and I will go our separate ways. Is that what you want?" His voice was almost savage in her ear, his hands no longer gentle, but harsh in the way they held her.

Honoria closed her eyes, fighting back tears. She would never be able to simply walk away. She couldn't do it now; she'd already given him her heart.

The thought made her throat tighten. Loving Marcus wasn't an act she had control of . . . it was just something that had happened, and all she could do was watch, dismayed and flinching at the inevitable pain. But now there was nothing she could do about it. They were married and she would see him day in and day out, and as the days passed what she felt for him would only deepen. Slowly, by degrees, her heart would continue to slip away.

But in the meantime, before the time of pain and suffering, she might as well enjoy what she did have of him. Enjoy life as his one and only wife, if not his one and only love. At least until she'd presented him with an heir.

It wasn't much, but it was all she had. Honoria reached up, twined her arms about his neck and pulled his mouth to hers as the carriage lurched madly to one side.

He was still but a moment as the carriage swung back the other direction, and then he was kissing her as passionately as he had a week ago. Kissing her and holding her and touching her, his hands roving over the delicate silk, ruching it as he pressed closer, closer.

His hands moved fervently now, finding the sensitive skin on the inside of her knee, sliding up, higher and higher, touching her through the softness of her undergarments, rubbing her as she moved restlessly against him, her body on fire, her mind twined around every sensation he produced.

Suddenly, he stopped. "Take off your clothes."

"Off? But . . . we're in a carriage."

"I don't care." His gaze locked with hers. "Do you?"

She didn't. She didn't care at all. All she knew was that she wanted him, had wanted this, for far longer than she'd admitted to herself. She reached up for the tie behind her shoulders . . .

Within seconds all of her carefully pressed skirts were laying on the opposite seat and all she had on was her chemise. She reached for the neck, but his warm hands forestalled her. "Please," he said, his voice deep and husky. "Allow me."

Cool air abraded her bare skin as he removed the silky garment and tossed it away. Her breasts peaked and tightened, a sight that seemed to affect him strongly, for he groaned and immediately lowered his mouth to the crest. Sucking gently, his hot mouth sent a volley of lightning through her. Honoria moaned, clutching his broad shoulders, holding him tightly. "Marcus," she managed to breathe.

One arm wrapped about her shoulders, his mouth moving from one breast to the other, he slid his free hand to her knee, then higher. Up the line of her thigh, where it stopped. She could see his mouth fastened on her breast, feel his breath on her bare skin, and see his hand resting so close . . . She opened her thighs and pulled his wrist up, so his fingers were against her tight curls.

He lifted his head at that, his eyes almost black with passion. And then he touched her. Deliberately, smoothly, parting her innermost secrets and finding the center of her heat.

She moaned, arching back, aware of his heat, of the mad, crazed passion that was rising inside her, of him, everywhere at the same time. Suddenly, she clamped her thighs closed over his hand. "Wait," she panted. "Please. You must undress, too."

"Are you certain? I can —"

"No. I want you. Please."

That was all it took. He set her to his side and kissed her, his tongue stroking, suggesting. Keeping her mad with lust. She never knew how he did it, but he was soon as naked as she, breaking the kiss only to rip off his cravat and pull his shirt over his head.

The second he was free of his clothing, they tumbled together, the wild throb of the carriage urging them on.

He held her thus, pinned against the thick cushion, the coach rocking madly from side to side, his engorged manhood against her slick flesh. "Honoria —"

It was a question, a last gasp of control. And she answered in the only way she could. She locked her legs about his waist and pulled herself against him, impaling herself on him, filling herself. Her entire body stretched, hot and ready, a flicker of pain causing her to halt.

His breathing was harsh in her hair, his body deliciously warm. "Hold me," he gasped against her ear, his breath stirring her hair and sending a new wave of heat through her.

She did as he said, wrapping her arms about his shoulders, pressing against him even as the pain increased.

He pressed harder and all of time held still. For the space of a moment there was nothing but the two of them, straining together, their skin damp where it touched, their bodies rocking with the rhythm of the coach. Then there was a sharp pain and he was inside her, deep and pressing. The pain swelled and she cried out, but he captured her cry with a kiss so heated, so passionate, that she found herself kissing him back, clinging to him as she gave herself to movement that was growing between them. Every thrust was exquisite, every stroke agonizingly delectable.

She was awash in feelings she'd never experienced and never thought to feel. He moved faster now, as did the coach. There seemed to be a connection. The faster Marcus moved inside her, the more wildly the coach swayed, every bump and jounce sending waves of pleasure though her.

Honoria's heated response was exquisite torture for Marcus. One especially wild turn sent them shifting to one side. He moaned as he buried himself ever deeper into her, the warmth of her sheath clenching about him almost too much to handle. He grit his teeth and continued on, determined to make this time — her first — memorable. He didn't have to wait long, for she was as wildly passionate as she was innocent and burst in wild cries as she came, her juices hot and creamy over him. Marcus was unable to hold on another moment and he came with her, emptying himself into her delectable warmth.

How long they remained thus, locked together, breathing hard, their bodies clasped about one another as the carriage drove ever onward, he would never know. But the slowing of the coach made him raise his head. They must be nearing the smaller road that led to the hunting lodge. They only had a short time longer.

Marcus lifted onto his elbows and looked down at his bride. Her eyes were closed, the thick lashes resting on the crescents of her cheeks, a rich color warming her skin.

She'd been a virgin, as he'd expected. The thought pleased him. Not that he had any right to demand such a thing — after all, he was scarcely in a position to demand anything. Nor had he been a saintly man in his life. But the thought that she was all his and had never had the touch of another man made him wish to shout out his possession from the rooftops.

He ran his thumb over her cheek and she instantly turned her face toward him, as if savoring the warmth. His heart softened a little at the unconscious gesture, as trusting as a child's.

He'd expected her to be passionate after

he'd taught her the arts of lovemaking. But she'd been a natural, moving against him, moaning so richly, her hands automatically clutching, pulling, and urging him on.

Good God, if she was this tempting as a virgin, how would she be once she'd learned a thing or two? The idea sent a shiver of pleasure through his replete body. This was going to be a marriage of fate, indeed. He reached down and touched the talisman ring, where it rested on her finger, surprised at how warm the metal felt, as if it was a living thing . . .

Honoria sighed, her lips parting sweetly, a smile touching her cheeks.

He'd made that smile happen. A heated tremor raced through him, and he realized with surprise that he was ready for another round. Good God, but she had an effect on him.

Smiling to himself, he kissed her cheek. "Are you well, madame?"

Her eyes fluttered open, a smile in the hazel depths. "I think so. Is that . . . is that normal?"

Marcus chuckled. "Indeed it is."

An amazed expression crossed her features. "And it will be thus *every* time?"

"If I have anything to say about it, yes."

She sighed, smiling sleepily. "I hope so."

461

"As do I." He sighed and rested his head against her shoulder. "I hate to mention this, but we need to dress. We're almost there. I wish we could stay longer than one night at the lodge, but we must return to London and be seen. It will stop the gossipmongers faster than anything else."

She sighed, some of her smile disappearing. "I had forgotten about the scandal. There will be talk, won't there?"

"Not if we go back and pretend nothing untoward happened. All we have to do is convince everyone that it was a love match and the tongues will have nothing to tattle about." Marcus caught her glance. She appeared quizzical, almost as if she was about to ask a question. "Yes?" he prompted.

"I'm sorry all of this happened."

He wasn't.

The carriage swung around a tight curve, and Honoria glanced at the curtain that covered the window. "I wish — I hate having to go back and face all of that. But it must be done, I suppose."

He placed his fingers over her lips. "One thing at a time. First, we have at least one night together. Then, we go home and face whatever fate has in store."

She hesitated, and he could see she was tempted to argue. But after a moment she nodded. "You are right, of course. There's nothing we can do about it today. I can worry about all of this tomorrow."

"Indeed you can," he said, watching as she collected her clothing and dressed. At least she was no longer the polite stranger she'd been at the wedding. With time . . . yes, he thought suddenly. With time, he was certain she'd not only become reconciled to their fate, but would see the benefits as well as he.

Feeling immensely better, Marcus dressed, finishing just as Herberts pulled the carriage to the front door of the hunting box.

Chapter 18

It wouldn't surprise me if the old bat left her entire fortune to that horrid bossy parrot she loved so much. I'd rather have a house full of monkeys than a pet like that.

Sir Harry Brooks to his sister,
the rather opulent and
bejeweled Lady Thistlewaite,
as they sat at the funeral of
their wealthy great-aunt,
Lady Wilhelmina Frotherston,
who did not, it turns out,
leave either of them a single pence

Two weeks later the Treymount carriage swayed and bumped through town. Marcus stretched out, relaxing against the squabs. He'd discovered that if he didn't fight the swaying, he didn't feel so ill afterward.

It was odd to think about it, but here he was, a married man of two whole weeks. Two whole weeks of passion-filled nights and days of . . . he rubbed his chin thoughtfully. Chaos wasn't quite the right word. Disorganization was closer.

He and Honoria had enjoyed their brief moment of respite at the hunting lodge, but the efforts to staunch the scandal that had arisen around their marriage meant they had to return and immediately begin a dizzying round of visits, balls, musicales, soirees, and more. It worked like a charm. Now everyone was talking, not about the circumstances surrounding the engagement, but about how lovely the new marchioness was, and how beautiful her sister. Cassandra was guaranteed to be the belle of the season, so widespread were reports of her beauty and fortune.

Marcus smiled to himself. He'd told one person and one person only that he intended to put a solid twenty thousand pounds into Cassandra's dowry fund, but it had been enough. Lady Carlisle was not known as the ton's most gossipy gossip for nothing. She'd been so consumed with the need to spread his secret that she'd cut him short in saying good-bye and had practically run across the room to unburden herself. Marcus had been hard pressed not to laugh aloud.

Sometimes, things were amazingly simple. But then other times . . . he thought of Honoria and all desire to laugh faded. That was the problem, the one rub in his otherwise well-run life. Oh, the difficulties of having her sisters and brother in his household had caused most of the chaos that surrounded his life now; he admitted that. But strangely, he rather enjoyed the constant hum of activity that seemed to pervade Treymount House. Whether it was Portia's raptures over a play she'd attended on Drury Lane, or Olivia's recounting one of Ned's colorful letters, or Juliet's enthused appreciation for Demon, who was quite falling under her spell; Treymount House was no longer the austere, rather somber place it had become. Even little George, in his nankeen breeches, his pockets stuffed with string and bits of rocks and God knew what else, had made Marcus laugh on more than one occasion.

All in all, it had proven to be a very satisfactory arrangement. Except for one thing. His marriage. Marcus's smile faded. Honoria was a conundrum of no small order. As passionate as any woman he'd ever been with, she met him willingly between the sheets — and anywhere else he cared to meet her. The truth was, other than when they were intimately involved, Marcus felt that Honoria was holding back in some way.

He stirred restlessly on the seat, absently holding onto the roof strap when the carriage rocked over a large bump of some sort. Had anyone asked him before his marriage what he thought the perfect comportment for a wife should be, he might well have used Honoria's current demeanor. She was always pleasant, always composed, and always smiled when he came into the room, even if that smile was a trifle perfunctory.

However, with her brothers and sisters, he saw Honoria laughing at their jokes and teasing them mercilessly. He watched as she ruffled George's hair and impulsively hugged Cassandra. And suddenly the words "composed" and "pleasant" weren't enough. He didn't want a pleasant companion. He wanted Honoria, as she really was. The one who argued and made cutting remarks. The one who gave an excited hop every time she outbid him at an auction.

The thought irked him more and more. It wasn't that he wanted hollow protestations of affection, he thought crossly. He just wanted genuine . . . what? Emotion? Yes. That was it. He wanted genuine emotion.

He sighed, leaning his head back against the squabs. He'd thought at first that perhaps her demeanor was due to normal nervousness. But now, two weeks from the day of their marriage, she still seemed reserved, except when he had her in the throes of passion.

For that reason he took her there as often as he could. And each time, he was left feeling that for a moment, at least, she was with him body, soul, and heart. But as soon as their passion was sated, she'd look at him with eyes so distant . . .

Marcus looked out the window at the houses marching by and absently rubbed his chest. Perhaps she felt the changes in her circumstances as much as he. Though he enjoyed the new liveliness her sisters and brother had brought to Treymount House, it sometimes made getting Honoria alone a bit difficult. And added to that, their overly full social schedule left them both more weary than usual.

Perhaps the ball they were having a week from Thursday would ease things. Anthony had suggested it, and Marcus had decided it would be a good way to formally introduce his wife to society. Plus, it had been years since he'd had a ball at Treymount House, so he was well overdue.

The carriage rolled to a stop and Herberts opened the door.

Marcus climbed out, consulted his pocket watch, then grinned. "Excellent time! Better than last, even."

"Oiye do me best, guv— me lord." Herberts offered a winning smile, showing all of his broken and brown teeth.

Marcus fished in his pocket for a guinea. "By the way, I've bad news for you. My brother wrote to say he was detained in Italy yet again. It may well be another month."

" 'Ere now, that's a horrid thing, it is. Oiye knew he don't like his wife's father, but then —"

"Wait. Did you say that Brandon doesn't like his wife's father?"

"Not at all. And oiye don't blame him one bit, oiye don't. The man is a nafter. Why, he'd steal the coins off the eyes of a dead man!"

"So would you."

"Aye, but only if oiye needed the funds. He'd do it fer nothin' more than a laugh or two."

"I wonder why, then, Brandon went to Italy at all."

Herberts blinked his surprise. "Why fer

the missus, of course! She couldn't do it alone, not without him. And he loikes it that way, he does. So off he goes, fixin' things so she won't be worryin'. Thet way she can put all of her attentions on him, if ye get me meaning." Herberts gave Marcus a broad wink.

Good Lord, but the man was incorrigible. Humorous, but incorrigible. "Did you know that I was going to turn you into a proper coachman before I gave you back to Brandon?"

"But . . . oiye am a proper coachman!"

"A better one, then. Now, however —" Marcus slipped his watch back into his the pocket of his waistcoat. "Now I find that I rather like getting where I want to go with speed."

Herberts's thin chest puffed like an adder's. "It's a right nafty thing, travelin' loike a bat outta hell, ain't it, guv'nor? In fact, oiye'd say —" His gaze, which had wandered past Marcus, faltered, then came to a halt. "Oh ho! Looks as if ye've come home to a spider's nest, ye have."

Marcus turned and looked. The front door stood wide open and not a face was to be seen. Normally when the carriage pulled up to the porch, there was a rush of footmen to see to it that doors were opened, parcels fetched, the good port brought out to the library. This time, nothing but silence and the wide open door.

Marcus's heart stumbled, lurched, then thudded to a faster beat. "Bloody hell." He took the steps two at a time, and reaching the entryway, he yelled, "Hello!"

Almost immediately Honoria appeared in the doorway of the white sitting room. A flood of relief washed over him, and without a thought, he walked up to her, grabbed her to him and kissed her full on the lips.

She felt so good, so right, here in his arms. He tightened his hold and deepened the kiss.

The sound of amused laughter from behind her reminded him that in all likelihood, his wife was not alone. As usual. He reluctantly released her, noting that her face was as pink as her gown. "I'm sorry. I didn't realize we had an audience."

She gestured rather blindly toward the room.

He glanced around. Portia, Olivia, Juliet and Cassandra were all there, sitting in various chairs, as pink-cheeked as Honoria. Meanwhile, George stood alone in the center of the room, looking as if he was facing a firing squad. Which he was, in a way. For standing before him, their faces folded in disapproval, was both Jeffries and the chef, Antoine.

Marcus walked forward. "What's happened? The front door is wide open, the footmen all gone."

"Mon dieu!" Antoine said in a loud voice, his black eyes flashing. "It is a madhouse, this place. I cannot work here!"

"My lord, it is my fault the door is open," Jeffries said, a harassed look on his face. "I asked the footmen to assist with something and did not take the time to check the latch."

"Where are the footmen?"

Honoria answered this. "They are searching for Achilles."

"The footmen?"

"Especially the footmen. Several of them had frogs of their own as children and so they have been a great help in assisting George in the past week. But this time, Achilles seems rather determined to remain hidden. We think he may be outside." She cast a glance at Jeffries, as if looking for help.

The butler swiftly stepped in. "My lord, the true crisis is not the footmen. They are in the herb garden now, attempting to find the lad's frog. The problem is Antoine." He bowed to the chef, managing to convey both respect and disapprobation. "Perhaps you should tell his lordship of your problem."

"Bah!" Antoine threw up his hands. "What good will it do? I will not stay another moment in this house. I have decided and that is that!"

Portia looked at Marcus. "You can't let him leave; we have the ball in two days."

Olivia nodded. "We won't have time to find anyone else."

"At least no one with Antoine's way with pastries," Cassandra added, giving the chef a winsome smile.

At her violet gaze, the Frenchman seemed to relent. But then George hopped from one foot to the next and drew the chef's gaze. "You!" the chef cried, pointing his finger at the boy. "You have caused all this! And there you stand, refusing to admit your duplicity!"

Honoria crossed the room to stand beside her little brother. "George, you must see that you were in the wrong."

The boy clamped his mouth together, a stubborn line forming where a grin was usually lodged.

Antoine's eyes narrowed and he rounded on Marcus. "When I took this position, I was led to understand that there were no children on the premises."

"There weren't. Then."

"Well, there shouldn't be now. I cannot perform in the kitchen when the house is in an uproar! I cannot!"

"What happened?" Marcus asked.

Jeffries looked at the chef. "I believe you should explain why you are so upset."

The chef nodded. "But of course. First I am making the pastry bread, thinking to do something special for my lady —"

"Which I appreciate so much," Honoria hurried to intercede.

Antoine bowed, but then glared at George. "And then *this* one comes running into the kitchen saying I have cooked his fat toad into my dough and he begins to tear up my lovely loafs! All of them!"

George sent a guilty glance at Marcus. "Achilles likes to hide in the flour bin. He'd just been in there a few moments before and I thought —"

"*Mon dieu!* To think of that dirty toad —"

"He's a *frog*," George said hotly.

The chef pointed a bony finger. "You *knew* that fat toad was in my flour bin and yet you did nothing to stop him!"

George rubbed his ear, glaring defiantly. "He likes it in there. And he's not a fat toad, but a frog, and a damned fine one, too."

"George!" Honoria said.

474

"A little hellion, isn't he?" Marcus said under his breath, so that only she could hear him.

Her gaze narrowed on him. "If you have nothing beneficial to add, please save your breath for ordering your servants about."

"What if I saved it for kissing you?"

Her color deepened even more and she turned a shoulder his direction and faced the outraged chef. "Monsieur Antoine, George owes you an apology."

"More than an apology!" the man snapped. "I demand satisfaction."

George's brow lowered. "Satisfaction?"

"Aye," Portia said from where she sat, watching the proceedings with interest. "Georgie, it's like this — Achilles is your pet, right?"

"Right."

"And he did something wrong, didn't he?"

George sent a sly look at the chef. "Maybe."

That was enough for Portia. "Then you, as his owner, have to fix things."

Marcus quirked a brow at the chef.

"It cannot be done! That fat frog not only hid in my flour bin, but he jumped into a dish of almond paste and then *ate* some of it! Then, while I was trying to catch him, he knocked three glass dishes to the floor and broke them all."

George's hands fisted at his sides. "If you had not chased him about with a carving knife, he would not now be lost outside!"

"If I had my way, I would see him in a pot!"

George's face whitened. "With hot water?"

Antoine snapped his fingers. "And thyme!"

"No!" George's eyes brightened in a suspicious manner, his lips quivering.

The chef began to nod, but then caught George's fixed gaze. For an instant the two stood staring at one another. A fat tear grew in George's wide violet gaze. It quivered, then rolled down his cheek.

Another soon followed.

"Oh, make him stop," the chef cried, covering his eyes. "He looks like a cherub!"

Honoria choked slightly. "George is many things, but a cherub is not one of them."

"No," Antoine conceded. He looked at George again, and sighed. "I was but teasing. Your frog, he is too big to eat. He would be far too tough, even for someone with Antoine's way of preparing things."

George dashed a hand across his eyes. "I don't believe you."

"Ah!" The chef threw up his hands. "That

is it! I am leaving this house! I will not be called a frog killer and a liar all in the same day!"

Marcus rubbed his neck. What a coil. "Antoine, is there a way George can work off the damage done by his pet? Floors to sweep? Pots to scrub?" He glanced at George. "You're willing, aren't you, George?"

The boy sent a cautious gaze at the chef. Then, slowly, he nodded, his hair flopping across his brow. "I will do whatever needs to be done. But you have to promise you will never, ever put my frog into a pot, with or without thyme."

The chef found himself the object of three identical pair of hazel eyes, three identical pair of violet eyes, and one rather amused pair of blue ones. "What an impossible situation! Here am I, Antoine du Fraer, master of the kitchens! Yet how can I work my magic in this hodgepodge household?" He looked around, but no one answered him.

Finally, Antoine said, "Bah! I will never understand the English. It is beyond me." Sighing dramatically, the chef turned to the boy. "Oh very well. The little one can come to the kitchen and make reparations. But only if he will keep that frog out of my kitchen and out of my flour barrel."

"Excellent!" Honoria said. "That is very kind of you. We all appreciate your efforts."

"*And* your roast chicken," added Miss Cassandra, who beamed at him from across the room. "I believe it is the best I've ever eaten."

Under her lovely gaze, some of Antoine's irritation melted. "Antoine must be a great chef if even an innocent miss can appreciate his capabilities."

A footman entered the room, a very muddy Achilles clutched in his hands. The man's uniform was a mess, mud streaked from knee to shoulder. But the sight of the frog brought a joyous screech from George.

As George clutched his frog, Portia eyed the chef with a hungry look. "Antoine, what's for dinner tonight?"

"Duck l'orange and roasted brisket and —"

"Brisket!" George finally smiled.

The chef nodded. "You like the brisket, eh?"

"Oh yes!"

"Well. I might make a little extra." Drawing himself up, Antoine bowed. "Now, my lords and ladies, if you will excuse Antoine, he would return to the kitchen to finish his preparations."

"Of course," the marquis said. "Shall I

have dinner held back a half hour to give you time to recoup?"

Antoine appeared offended. "Move dinner? Never!"

"Sir?" It was George. He stepped forward, a determined look on his face.

The chef turned to the child. *"Oui?"*

"Shall I come with you now? To sweep the floor?"

"No child! Not now. You have to get ready for dinner. Come to me tomorrow. In the morning. We'll see what we can find for you to do."

"Yes, sir! I will do what I can to keep Achilles out of the kitchen."

"I'm certain you will." Something almost like a smile flitted across the Frenchman's face, then left as he turned back to the door and then left.

"Well!" Portia said, flinging herself back on the settee. "That was certainly amazing. Treymount, I believe your chef was experiencing a change of heart."

Marcus's brows rose. "Oh, I believe you'll see Monsieur Antoine change his mind about both the child and the frog before the day is up." He looked around the room. If everyone was in here, then there was a possibility he might be able to get Honoria alone in another part of the house. And if he got her alone . . . well, there was no telling what might occur.

He walked to her side and drew her hand through his arm. "Since I'm home and there's a whole hour before dinner, perhaps you can assist me in the library?"

Portia jumped up. "I'll go with you. There's a book I've been dying to get, but it's on the second floor and I do not trust that ladder. It seems so unstable putting a ladder on wheels. Do you think —"

"Portia," Cassandra said hurriedly. "I do believe I need your help in examining the ballroom. Jeffries had it cleaned, but I want to make certain it's as it should be."

"But I —"

Marcus made good his escape, pulling Honoria out into the hallway, where the footmen were once again reassembling. He ignored them all, pulling her into the library and shutting the door firmly behind them. Marcus kept her hand in his. "Since I didn't get to say it before, good evening."

She smiled. "Good evening. Thank you for assisting with George. He's really a good boy."

There was a bit more warmth in her smile than her usual perfunctory manner. Leaning against the door, he reached up and stole a pin from her hair. "George is fine."

He threw the pin on the floor and freed another.

A fat curl dropped to her shoulder.

"Beautiful," he breathed, taking out yet another pin and watching another strand of hair fall.

Honoria's cheeks heated. "Marcus, what are you doing?"

"Seducing you."

A flash of passion crossed her face, melting some of the reserve. He released her hand and took a step forward. To his surprise, she stepped back. But then she continued to back away, although more slowly now. He followed, matching her step for step. It was a seductive dance, he moving forward, she moving backward, their gazes locked, both knowing what was going to happen the second he caught her.

Finally, she bumped into the desk and could move no more.

"There!" Marcus said, stretching his arms to either side. "I have you now." He said it in his best comedic villain voice, rather like the farces that played at Drury Lane before the main play.

She gurgled with laughter, even more of her reserve dropping. Ah, Marcus thought. She cannot stay removed if she's laughing. Passion and laughter would be his weapons, then. And with them both, he would woo his wife. He wasn't sure why he wanted to do it — perhaps it was the thrill of the chase. Whatever it was, it was heady stuff indeed.

Before the laughter could die from her eyes, Marcus swept her into his arms and kissed her, bending her back, his hands never still, his mouth hot and possessive. He pressed her against the desk, placing his hands about her waist and lifting her slightly so she could slide onto the smooth surface. He was careful not to break the kiss, but he needn't have worried; Honoria not only allowed him to lift her to the desk, but she helped, sliding back until a loud thump caused her to break the kiss and look around. "Something fell off your desk —"

With a sweep of his arm, he cleaned the surface, sending papers and pens flying. Not that he cared. All he wanted, all he could think about, was the delectable, passionate woman who was even now moaning softly against his mouth, her hands clutching his lapels. Marcus broke the kiss long enough to trace the line of her jaw. She writhed beneath him, sending a demanding ache straight to his manhood. God, but she was a hot piece. And passionate. He loved the stubborn sweep of her chin, and placed a kiss on the end of it before trailing his mouth down her neck to nuzzle the sensitive point behind her ear.

Honoria moaned and tilted up her chin, letting the heat of his mouth capture the sensitive skin of her throat more completely. Shivers raged through her, her breasts tightening, her nipples rigid against her chemise. The firm surface of the desk pressed against her bottom, and the pressure of Marcus's body as he leaned forward to torment her with his hot mouth made her legs spread slightly of their own accord. His rigid manhood pressed against her, sending a deep ripple of longing that began between her thighs and traveled outward. Ye gods, but she was in heaven. Or close enough to taste it — she wasn't sure which. All she knew was that her body ached and yearned with a passion that drowned all thought. She was held prisoner in a maelstrom of red passion.

It was swiftly becoming evident that the man knew what he was about. His mouth teased and tormented until her skin heated as if burned. His hands never ceased moving, caressing, holding. He reached down and cupped her bottom, lifting her hips from the desk and parting her thighs as he rubbed against her suggestively.

Honoria gasped. Her thighs quivered and grew damp at his onslaught, at the wants of her own body, at the thought of going further . . . doing more.

She loved this man and wanted him passionately. It was the only complete, coherent thought she could hold in her mind; all others fled before the raging rush of feelings and wants. Somehow, someway, her arms twined about him and she held him closer, opening her mouth beneath his, her knees weakening when he gently thrust his tongue inside.

The raw sensuality of the act made Honoria clutch more feverishly at Marcus's lapels. Her skirts were ruched up about her hips, and her legs now clamped about his hips. It was the most natural thing in the world, the most right feeling thing she had ever done.

He moaned now, his breathing as harsh as her own. A part of her reveled in her mastery, in the knowledge that she — Honoria Baker-Sneed St. John — was able to win a deep, heartfelt moan from the throat of such an incredibly virile and seductive man.

Marcus stilled. Honoria's eyes slid back open. When had she closed them? She wasn't sure. All she knew was that Marcus was strangely still . . . too still. A horrid thought arose. "Marcus? What —"

Then she heard it . . . a soft knock at the door, followed by a discreet cough.

"Bloody hell," Marcus growled, turning his head to glare at the door. "It is Jeffries." He sighed and looked down at her, the smile returning to his face when his gaze met hers. "I will kill him. There are other butlers."

She had to laugh, some of the passion leaving her. "Yes, but you'd have to train another."

Marcus refused to move, remaining between her legs, resting on his elbows so she could breathe easily. He trailed a kiss over her forehead. "I'd train a thousand Jeffries for one moment with you."

Her breath tightened painfully. What was she supposed to do when he said such things to her? She knew he was fond of her, she could sense it in his gaze, in his touch. But . . . did he feel anything more? She'd waited for the past two weeks for a sign. Though he seemed to enjoy being with her, she had yet to hear him admit to anything more than lust and like.

Her chest tightened miserably. "I — I think perhaps you should let me up."

He sighed, but didn't move. "I suppose I should."

The knock sounded again. "My lord —"

"Just a bloody moment!" Marcus said to the door.

A muffled "Yes, my lord!" was the answer.

Marcus's dark blue gaze flickered to her, his brows raised in a silent question.

"I — I'm glad he didn't walk in on us."

Marcus raised a brow.

Honoria flushed. "You think he came in?"

"And then saw us and decided to take a different approach to entering the room."

"Oh no! Ye gods, how embarrassing! I hope he didn't see us."

"Seeing as how he has exceptionally good eyesight and how we were sprawled across my desk, which is the center of the room . . . yes, I think he saw us." A faint smile touched Marcus's mouth. "I daresay he is as red as you are now."

She pressed her hands to her cheeks. "How embarrassing to be caught —"

"I believe the term is 'in flagrante delicto.' "

"I beg your pardon, but we hadn't gone that far!" At his amused glance, she said, "I really should get up and straighten my gown."

He rested his forehead upon hers, his dark blue eyes gazing into hers. "I suppose you should."

It should have been awkward, lying on her

back, her legs wrapped about his hips, but it wasn't. The room was quiet as they stayed where they were, looking solemnly into each other's eyes. She tried to see what he was feeling, what he was thinking, but she simply could not tell.

After a long moment he said, "Honoria?"

She wet her dry lips. "Yes?"

"Why do you hold back from me? Sometimes I feel as if you're hiding a part of yourself away."

The clock seemed to tick very loudly in the silence. Honoria's heart ached, it was beating so hard. Should she tell him? Could she? "Marcus, I don't think I should say —"

"I want to know what is wrong."

"I love you." She gasped when she heard the words. Good God, but she hadn't meant to say them aloud! Not like that.

She waited, her heart in her throat. Marcus didn't move, didn't react. He merely looked at her, stunned realization in his own eyes.

Then, suddenly, he stood. "I see. I had no idea —"

Another knock sounded on the door. "My lord, I'm so sorry to bother you, but your brother is here and he —"

"*Marcus!*" Anthony's voice rose in greeting.

"Damnation," Marcus growled, raking a hand through his hair. "Honoria, I don't know what —"

Honoria slid off the desk, automatically righting her clothing and checking her hair for pins. The moment had taken on an unreal quality, like a very bad dream. She heard herself saying in a calm, unemotional voice, "Marcus, don't worry — it's nothing. Really. I just —" She stopped, a surge of hurt flooding her throat. "I must go. Anthony is here because he escorted Anna. She is to take me shopping for the ball."

Marcus tried to settle his mind, but he couldn't. She loved him. The words had taken him so completely by surprise that he couldn't seem to settle on a single coherent thought. All he could do was nod briskly and then move to open the door, wondering as he did so what he was going to do. His own wife loved him, while he . . . what did he feel? Good God, he wasn't ready for this, for any of this.

She must have read his expression, for her face hardened back into that distant expression he'd grown to hate. He reached for her, but she stepped away. *Don't.*

"Honoria, I can't just —"

"Not another word," she responded, her voice clipped. "I didn't mean to make you

488

so uncomfortable. Rest assured, my lord, that I will not allow my excess feelings to get in the way of our relationship. As you said, until I've produced an heir, our way is set. But after that —" Her gaze narrowed, her chin lifting. "After that you will be free of me and my family. Now, if you will excuse me, your brother awaits."

Without meeting his gaze, she opened the door and walked out. Marcus was left alone, his tongue still frozen in place, his mind reeling. He could not answer her, not until he knew for certain. They had passion, certainly. And he respected her as well, more than any woman he knew. But . . . love?

Bloody hell, what was he to do now?

Chapter 19

There are three things all men should practice: how to make money, how to make love, and how to grovel. The last is especially important.

Lady Thistlewaite to the
Duke of Devonshire,
while attending the launching of a balloon
decorated in the Whig colors
of blue and gold

Honoria pressed her forehead against the cool glass, her gaze fixed unseeingly out the window. Had she been focusing on the view before her, she might have admired the perfectly laid out gardens, the bubbling fountain, or the charming terrace steps that cut a white ribbon through the green expanse. Today, she didn't really see anything. All she could do was feel.

She'd ruined everything. She closed her eyes and sighed. Why oh why hadn't she kept her mouth closed? He wasn't ready for a declaration. Ye gods, he might never be; love was the furthest thing from his mind. That much was obvious from his reaction. She could still see his stern face, still feel the sinking in the pit of her stomach as he tried to find something — anything — to say in answer to her declaration.

She wished with all her might she could unsay the words, take them back and bury them deeply, but she couldn't.

"Honoria?"

She started and turned to find Cassandra not two feet away, a concerned look in her violet eyes. "Goodness," Honoria said, dredging up a smile. "You startled me."

"I'm sorry. I said your name twice, but you didn't hear me, so I said it a bit louder." Cassandra came to sit on the window seat beside her. "Honoria, is there anything I can do? Since last week, there seems to be some sort of tension between you and Treymount."

That was an understatement. Since that horrid day in the library, the air between her

491

and Marcus had thickened into icy walls and he'd taken to spending more and more time away from the house. She wasn't comfortable around him, and he seemed awkward around her . . . except when they exploded in passion. Somehow at those moments, they seemed able to put aside their differences, although afterward, in the silence that followed, her declaration seemed to linger over them, unspoken now, but there nonetheless. It was horrid, and many times she'd found herself turning away from him after their lovemaking so he would not see her tears. Why oh why had she told him?

Forcing the unpleasant thoughts aside, Honoria put her hand over her sister's. "I am fine. It's just that . . . all relationships have their ups and downs."

"Yes, but lately I seem to sense more down than up." Cassandra gave her hand a gentle squeeze. "It's a pity, for I thought the marquis was adjusting rather well to having a family all of the sudden. George certainly seems to look up to him. Honoria, what happened to turn things so suddenly? Did you argue?"

"No." Deathly silence could not be called an argument. She absently patted Cassandra's hand. "We'll be fine. We just need some time." Time to stop feeling. That's exactly what she needed to do, stop feeling so much. But she couldn't help it; she loved Marcus though he didn't return her sentiments. Oh, she was certain that he cared for her in some way, but it was not enough. Every day that fact was becoming painfully obvious. Soon, there would come a time when she'd have to act, to preserve her own peace if nothing else.

She caught Cassandra's worried gaze. "Never mind about me! How have you enjoyed your season? I don't believe I've ever seen so many cards or invitations."

Cassandra's cheeks pinkened. "It has been quite amusing, although . . ." A shadow passed over Cassandra's face.

"Yes?"

"I don't know. I rather thought I'd enjoy it more. I've certainly met some nice people, but —" She sighed.

"Have you met any nice *men?*"

Cassandra's flush deepened. "Some. There was one —" She shook her head. "But he's not — It's not important."

Honoria blinked at her sister's rather shuttered expression. This was something indeed. "Cassandra, who —"

A masculine voice sounded in the hallway, raised in seeing disagreement. "Ye gods," Honoria said, frowning in the direction of the voice. "That doesn't sound like Trey-mount. He's more apt to growl than yell."

The voice sounded again, closer to the door this time. Cassandra surged to her feet, her gaze locked on the door. "That *isn't* Treymount!"

"Then who is it?"

As if in answer to her question, the door burst open and a well-dressed young man strode into the room. Honoria recognized him. She'd seen him at several events. Once, he'd even danced with Cassandra. At the time, Honoria had thought they made a beautiful couple, both so fair and accomplished looking. Of course, Cassandra danced with everyone. She was much in demand. Still . . . Honoria glanced at her sister and then froze. Cassandra was looking at the gentleman with an expression of almost extreme rapture.

Jeffries rushed in, pausing when he realized the room was not empty. "My lady! Miss Cassandra! I apologize, but this gentleman has come uninvited —"

The man rounded on Jeffries. "I have been here three times to see his lordship, and each time you tell me he is not here! I must see him!"

"His lordship is not receiving anyone," Jeffries said rather coldly.

Honoria winced. It seemed to her that Marcus spent more and more time locked away in his study. And it was all her fault.

"But he told me to come to him when —" The young man fisted his hands at his side. "I must see him."

Jeffries frowned. "Lady Treymount, Miss Cassandra, I apologize that you were so rudely interrupted." He glanced over his shoulder at the footmen who were now assembled at the door. "Remove him."

The gentleman raised his hands into fists. "I'll not go without a fight! Not this time!"

Cassandra stepped forward, her color high. "Jeffries, Lord Melton has come by invitation."

The butler stiffened. "He is not on his lordship's preferred list."

"He is on mine."

Honoria blinked at her sister. There was steel in Cassandra's words; it was not a tone she usually used.

Jeffries seemed conflicted. He looked from the young man to Cassandra and then back.

Cassandra inclined her head at Lord Melton. "How kind of you to accept my invitation. Won't you have a seat?"

Surprise flickered over the man's face,

and it dawned on Honoria that he was as astounded by Cassandra's intervention as she was.

Melton quickly regained his balance. He inclined his head, a faint smile touching his handsome face. "Thank you, Miss Baker-Sneed. I would be delighted." With that simple utterance, in the space of a mere moment Lord Melton went from being an uninvited intruder to being Miss Cassandra's guest. He approached the small grouping of chairs by the fire and then waited for Cassandra.

Her head held high, she crossed to where he was and took a chair. Honoria, feeling bemused, did the same. Immediately, Melton claimed his own chair.

"Jeffries," Cassandra said softly.

The butler drew himself up. "Yes, miss?"

"Some tea for my guest, please."

That did not sit well with the butler, but years of good training overcame his irritation. He took only a few seconds to gather himself before bowing. "Of course, miss. I shall bring some tea immediately."

While they waited for Jeffries to leave, Honoria looked more closely at the young man. Lord Melton was decidedly young, but he was as handsome as the day was long. Which was unfortunate, for in addition to a very pleasing visage and form, he also possessed a sense of rather reckless ardor.

Honoria glanced at her sister and found that Cassandra seemed to have lost her earlier starch, for she sat with her hands tightly clasped in her lap, her gaze locked on the tips of her slippers. It was left to Honoria to make the requisite small talk.

She cleared her throat. "Lord Melton, I'm sorry for the misunderstanding. Is there some way I may assist you?"

He pulled his gaze from Cassandra with obvious effort. "Assist? I don't —" He paused, his dark gaze regarding her seriously. "Perhaps you can."

"And so I will, if you will tell me what you need."

"I must see Lord Treymount, but he has not been available."

Honoria's chest ached anew. "I'm afraid his lordship is a very busy man."

"Yes, but he told me to come to him when —" Melton broke off, glancing uneasily ay Cassandra. His color rose slightly. "I cannot tell you why I need to see him, only that I must."

Honoria shook her head. "If you cannot tell me why you need to see Treymount, then I am afraid I am powerless to assist you."

His gaze flickered once more to Cassandra, a deep flush staining his cheeks. "I can't tell you! It's personal and —"

"Thank you for visiting," Honoria said, standing swiftly.

Cassandra finally looked up from her slippers. "Honoria, please . . . give Lord Melton some time. I'm sure he will explain himself well once he's had time to consider it." She gifted the young lord with a look brimming with gentle light. "You will, won't you? Explain everything to us?"

No man could have withstood such a gentle plea. Honoria sank back into her chair, waiting as Melton went from red to pale.

"Miss Baker-Sneed, I —" He swallowed, the sound painful in the silence.

Cassandra leaned forward. "We will not betray your confidences."

"I didn't think you would," he replied just as seriously. "I never thought you would." Melton glanced at Honoria and gave a surprisingly bitter laugh. "I'm a fool, Lady Treymount. A horrid fool. I had a fortune — not a large one, but enough, and . . ." He spread his hands wide. "I lost it."

"All of it?"

"More than likely."

"I don't understand."

He sighed. "I inherited my title at a rather young age, both of my parents succumbing to smallpox while I was on the continent with my tutor, doing the Grand Tour. I'm afraid, what with the shock of my parents' death and the fact that I was so young — I did not handle things well at all. In fact, I was a fool of the worst sort. I didn't stay at the family seat, but came to London and found myself consorting with the wrong kind of people. With no thought but pleasure, I began to work my way through my funds at an alarming rate."

"Did you have no one to guide you?"

"A distant relative had been named trustee, and he did what he could. But I was young and foolish and I didn't understand how things were. Frankly, I didn't want to. I just wanted to enjoy myself, to forget that my parents were gone. I — I'm afraid my behavior was far from what it should have been. Eventually, I had markers all over town."

Cassandra paled slightly. "You gamble?"

"Not anymore," he said quickly. "That is all in the past."

"Good," Cassandra said, smiling encouragingly.

Honoria frowned. "I'm sorry, but how does Treymount play into all of this?"

"He purchased a goodly number of my

markers and offered to settle them all if I would but sign over the family seat and lands."

"Heavens!" Cassandra gasped. "That doesn't seem fair."

Melton grimaced. "To be honest, it is more than fair. The lands and house are not in good repair, and the amount I owed — it was a generous offer, though at the time, it seemed horrid. I didn't want to take it. So I asked Treymount if he would give me some time to think of another way out of this mess, another way to find the funds to purchase the markers myself."

Honoria leaned forward. "What did Treymount say?"

"He said no at first. But something made him change his mind, and so he offered to let me find a venture where I could *make* the funds back providing I will no longer gamble."

"Have you stopped?" Cassandra asked.

"Yes. Completely." A rueful grimace accompanied Melton's words. "I have to say, it was something of a release. I would tell myself that I was not going to gamble, but I knew I owed so much — there seemed no other way to regain my fortune. So I gambled and hated every moment of it."

Cassandra beamed. "Good for you."

"Thank you," Melton said. For a long moment he and Cassandra just looked at one another.

A flicker of alarm traced through Honoria. Did Cassandra harbor a tendre for this man? She cleared her throat. "Lord Melton, you still have not told us why you must see Lord Treymount."

"Because he offered to let me find my way out of this mess, if I could think of a way to earn it. And I have."

A smile touched Cassandra's face. "Which is why you are here, arguing with Jeffries."

His gaze softened as he looked back at Cassandra. "Yes."

"Lord Melton," Honoria said with some firmness, "what is your idea?"

He tore his gaze from Cassandra. "There is only one thing I do know — horses."

"Ah," Cassandra said. "How exciting!"

"Yes. There are some excellent stables at my property, and I already own two likely mares. All I'd need to get is a stud and —" He suddenly seemed to recall who he was talking to, for he flushed and shook his head. "This is not an appropriate conversation. I'm sorry."

"Oh it's no problem," Honoria said smoothly. "I can see why you are anxious to

501

speak to Lord Treymount." She stood. "If you will wait here, I will fetch him."

He stood as well. "Thank you so much! I cannot express how much this means to me."

She looked at Cassandra. "Perhaps you should find Portia and then take Lord Melton to see the fountain. I will send in one of the footmen to accompany you."

Cassandra's color rose, but she stood. "That would be lovely. Lord Melton, I think you will enjoy our garden."

"I am certain I shall."

Cassandra sent him a pleased smile and then left to find Portia.

The second Cassandra was gone, Melton turned to Honoria, a troubled look in his dark eyes. "I must admit something."

"Yes?"

"I was planning on regaining my fortune ever since the marquis offered me this chance. But then I met your sister —" He flushed. "I don't wish you to think ill of me, but it has made me think. I — I know I don't have a chance, but if I can straighten out the mess I've made —"

"Lord Melton, Cassandra is her own person, and she will decide who she wishes to be with. I can only say that she is very mature and responsible. I cannot see her being with someone who is not the same in that aspect."

A determined light entered Melton's eyes. "Lady Treymount, you will see that I am a changed man. I will do what I must to be worthy to call on her."

Honoria smiled, though her heart ached at the determination she saw in the young lord's eyes. Why hadn't Marcus been so quick to answer her when she'd needed him to?

Cassandra returned, Olivia in tow, since Portia was engaged in placing a pattern for a small silk suit for George's frog for their new play, *The Frog Prince*. Honoria saw them off into the gardens, Olivia chatting away while Lord Melton gazed in admiration at a blushing Cassandra.

Honoria sent a footman to escort them all and then made her way to Treymount's study.

Marcus was sitting at his desk, half listening to Donaldson wax on and on about some obscure aspect of his holdings in Yorkshire. It was annoying, but for the last week he could not seem to concentrate. Thoughts flitted in and out of his mind and made him shift restlessly in his chair.

Honoria loved him. It was odd, but he

wasn't quite sure why the admission bothered him so. Surely it was normal for a wife to love her husband . . . and surely it was normal for that to be discussed. If only he could figure out why the thought of holding her affections made him feel so conflicted.

What *did* he feel for her? Was it love, this warm gentle glow that made him smile at odd moments? Surely he'd never felt this way before, but . . . he'd never been married before either. What if, instead of love, it was merely an appreciation for companionship, for the delight of her company?

Until he was certain, he would not utter the words aloud. He could not.

A soft knock came at the door.

"Come in," he said quickly, interrupting Donaldson with something like relief.

The door opened and Honoria entered. Marcus's heart quickened and he stood, Donaldson following suit.

"My lord. Mr. Donaldson." She came to stand in front of the desk, giving them each a friendly nod. The sun glinted across her hair, warming the chestnut curls and brightening her lock of white. "I hope I'm not disturbing anything."

"Oh no," Mr. Donaldson said, replacing some papers into his leather satchel and sending Marcus a rather dry look. "I was merely informing his lordship of a border problem and he was politely dreaming about other things."

Marcus winced. "I apologize if I did not appear to be listening —"

"Nonsense." Mr. Donaldson collected his papers and satchel, a smile on his round face. "You have other matters to attend to, which is as it should be. I shall return in the morning when you have more time."

Blast it, Marcus thought, he had time now. He was just . . . He slanted a glance at Honoria and then wished he hadn't. She was dressed in green today, a pale mint color that made her hazel eyes seem all the more vivid. The silk gown was perfect for her softly rounded form, flowing over the curve of her hip and the long, smooth expanse of her thighs —

Good God, in a moment he'd be writing a sonnet to her toes. He was distracted, that's what he was. Completely distracted.

He waited until the door closed behind Donaldson before he asked, "To what do I owe the pleasure?"

A faint color touched her cheeks. "I am sorry for intruding. I didn't mean for Mr. Donaldson to leave."

"He didn't leave because you arrived; he left because I was busy thinking of something other than what he was saying. I'm afraid I haven't been very attentive today." He returned to his chair, his gaze flickering over her. She looked fresh and delectable in her gown, but he knew that she would look even more delectable out of it. His body stirred instantly and he frowned. Damn, but he hated this odd state of affairs. A surge of irritation sliced through him and he flashed a disgruntled glance at the cause of his discomfort. "Did you want something?"

She lifted her brows at his tone. "Yes, I do."

"Then say what it is. I've work to do." He didn't mean to sound so harsh, but whenever they were together, he felt as if he was missing something.

"Marcus, I was just speaking to Lord Melton."

"Melton?" Marcus hadn't thought of Melton in over a week, though the young cub had tried to corner him on any number of instances. "When did you talk to him?"

"Just now. He came to see you, but Jeffries told him you were out, so I spoke to him instead."

"I didn't ask you to do that."

"No, but he seemed so upset, and Cassandra —" Honoria closed her lips. "I thought someone should talk to him."

"That should have been me."

"Yes, but he . . ." She paused and a faint smile touched her lips. "You should hear what he has to say. I think it might surprise you."

Unknowingly, Marcus's hand clenched about the pen. What the hell was that look? She appeared amused, almost tender. A flash of feeling he'd never before experienced exploded hotly in his chest. Before he even knew what he was about, he snapped, "To hell with Melton. Honoria, you have no authority where my business is concerned. You are to limit yourself to the house and nothing more."

"You — You —" Fury, mingled with hurt, flashed in her eyes.

Bloody hell, he sounded like the biggest ass on earth. What the hell was wrong with him? "No, no!" He threw down the pen and rubbed his temples. "Honoria, I didn't mean that. I'm sorry. I just —"

"There is no need, my lord. I understand you perfectly." Shards of ice could not have been colder or more pointed. "I shall endeavor to keep my onerous presence to a minimum."

"Honoria, I just — for a moment, I thought you and Melton —"

She stiffened, her eyes widening. "Melton

and I what? We what? We spoke, Marcus. That is all. About his obligation to you."

Marcus stood. "I didn't mean to imply —"

"Lord Melton is in the garden with Portia and Cassandra. If you have nothing more to do than mull such empty thoughts, perhaps you will find the time to meet with Lord Melton." With that, Honoria turned on her heel and swept toward the door.

Marcus was around the desk in a flash. He caught her just as she reached for the door. "Honoria!" He held her by both arms and turned her to face him. "I'm sorry, I —"

She broke free, her eyes flashing angrily, tears welling even as she stood before him. "I don't want you to be sorry. I'm already sorry enough for both of us. Sorry I married you. That was the biggest mistake I've ever made."

He released her. He never meant to make her cry. Never meant to make her sad or angry. Feeling like the world's largest heel, he watched her turn and leave.

Marcus left the house almost immediately. He made his way to White's and sat in a corner, drinking port and trying to dull the strange emptiness that filled his chest. After an hour, slightly tipsy, but still feeling uncertain and pained, he left and made his way to Anthony's house.

He was greeted by the butler and then escorted into the red salon. There, he waited.

After several minutes the door opened.

Marcus turned to speak, but stopped. It was not Anthony standing in the door, but his wife, Anna. Almost as tall as Marcus, red-haired and elegant with a Roman nose, she looked at him through gray eyes that usually sparkled with humor. Usually. Today, they sparkled with indignation. Marcus swallowed a sigh. "You've talked to Honoria."

"Yes I have. I stopped by to see if the dressmaker had brought the gown we ordered and I found her crying."

Marcus rubbed his temples. She was crying. Good God, what had he done?

Anna's mouth thinned. "Well, Treymount? What have you to say to your hateful behavior?"

"I apologized."

"Yes, but you did nothing to correct things. An apology without true remorse is not worth a farthing."

"Damn it, Anna! I said I was sorry, and I am. What else am I to do?"

"I don't know. All I do know is that your little spat is the reason your wife was crying." Anna's gaze grew even more accusing. "What have you said to that woman that she could be so heartbroken?"

"Anna, is Anthony here? I came to speak to —"

"He's at White's."

"But I was there and —"

"He just left, looking for you. I daresay he's just arrived."

Marcus bowed. "Thank you. I am sorry to be abrupt but —"

Anna grasped his sleeve, her clear gray eyes meeting his. "Marcus, whatever you've done, set it to rights. She is worth too much to be hurt."

He paused, placing his hand over Anna's. "I know. I just need — I have to figure out a few things first. As soon as I do, I will speak with her and solve this problem."

"You promise?"

"I promise."

Anna looked steadfastly into his eyes. Suddenly, her usual smile lit her eyes to silver. "Why Marcus, you — I never thought I'd see the day."

"What?"

She laughed and released his arm. "Nothing. Nothing at all. Go and find my husband and see if he can't knock some sense into you."

"I shall do just that." He turned toward the door. Just as he reached it, Anna called after him.

"Marcus? In case you are wondering, the gown Honoria has chosen for the ball is red."

He frowned. "And?"

Anna shrugged. "Nothing. Just in case you were wondering. That's all."

Marcus shook his head. Women and their mysterious warnings. His sister, Sara, used to do the same thing. Sighing, he nodded once to Anna and then left.

Marcus found Anthony sitting in one of a pair of chairs before a neat fireplace, his feet crossed at the ankles and resting on a stool, a cigar in one hand, a glass of port in the other. "There you are."

Anthony raised his brows. "Obviously."

Marcus scowled and took the chair. "I have been looking for you. Anna said you'd be here."

"And now you have found me." Anthony took a slow puff of the cigar, eyeing Marcus all the while. "Well?"

Marcus rammed his hands in his pockets and stretched his legs out before him. "What?"

"I was sent here on a mission, and if

you've already seen my rather opinionated wife, you know what it is." Anthony set down the glass of port. "Marcus, what happened between you and Honoria?"

"Nothing," he growled.

"Whatever happened, you're as grouchy an old bear. It's a pity, because Chase and I were both talking just yesterday about how much more pleasant you were now that you had Honoria in your life."

That was probably true. Before she'd burdened him with an admission of her feelings — he could still see her now, could still feel the weight of her crestfallen expression when he hadn't answered her. Good God, why did he feel so *bad?*

"Damn it, Marcus. If you aren't going to talk, at least stop sighing all over the place."

"Was I sighing? I didn't mean to. I'm just —" He shook his head.

Real concern flickered over Anthony's face. "Marcus, marriage is not an easy thing."

"No, it's not." Although . . . he'd rather enjoyed being married to Honoria at one time. They had passion — and an astounding amount at that. More than he'd ever had with anyone else. And his life was certainly pleasanter with her and her family about.

He thought of the little scene between George and Chef Antoine. There was never a boring day with the Baker-Sneeds, a fact he was just now beginning to appreciate.

Honoria had also moved almost effortlessly into Treymount House and things had never been better run. He'd already noticed some improvements to his comfort that had left him feeling almost cosseted. But . . . she loved him. His own wife loved him. He couldn't seem to get his mind around that fact. He caught Anthony's gaze and shifted in his chair. "I am a bit overwhelmed."

"I see," Anthony said, pouring a generous amount of port into his own glass. "The siblings?"

"No, no. They are fine. A pleasure, actually."

Anthony grinned. "I take it then that none of them are as opinionated as your Honoria."

"More so, except perhaps Cassandra." Marcus leaned his head back against the chair back. "They are a lively group. Juliet is horse-mad and will not leave Demon be. What's odd is that the blasted horse actually likes her and is as docile as a flower around her. Then there's Olivia, who has an amazing propensity to just blurt out what she thinks, will you nil you. And Portia who is, I think, destined for the stage."

"They sound delightful."

"They are. Except yesterday when Olivia said my wonderful Flemish tapestry had less to offer than — oh, what did she say?" His frown cleared. "Ah, yes! She said it had less to offer than 'a square-masted rig in flat waters.' Whatever that means, though I'm fairly certain it was an insult."

Anthony shook his head. "She is just as bad as Chase and Brandon. Neither of them concerns themselves with the arts. By the way, how is the boy doing?"

"George, the terror of Treymount? He and that damned frog find more things to get into. Just this morning I went to put on my favorite riding boots and they were gone. Seems he'd decided they'd make a good house for his frog and so he just took them. And when I taxed him on it, he pointed out that he'd left a shilling to pay for them."

"And had he?"

"Well . . . yes. I just hadn't seen it because I was looking for my boots and not a coin."

"How old is this little fellow?"

"About seven."

"That's pretty decent of him then, to pay so much."

Marcus dropped his chin to his neck

cloth. "Anthony, Honoria and I had a conversation . . ."

"So? I hope you have many."

"No, no. We were talking, and to my surprise, she told me that —" His tongue tangled about the words and he fell silent.

"She told you what?"

"That she loved me."

Anthony's eyes widened and then he broke into laughter, so loud and long that eyes began turning in their direction.

"Enough," Marcus growled, feeling like the biggest fool to walk the earth. Dammit, what was wrong with Anthony?

"Good God, Marcus. She tells you that she loves you and you look at me as if you've just been stabbed with a knife. Why is that? I don't see —" Anthony's smile faded. "Bloody hell, Marcus. What did you tell her when she admitted she loved you?"

Marcus didn't move.

"Marcus?" Concern darkened Anthony's his brown eyes. He leaned forward. "What did you tell her?"

"Nothing."

Anthony's eyes widened. "*What?* Marcus, you had to say something!"

Marcus shook his head. "I couldn't."

"Why not?"

"Because I don't know how I feel. I just —"

Marcus frowned. "Love is not a word I ever thought to say."

"You are the one who used the talisman ring as a wedding ring. I'd say that of all of us, you are the one most assured of finding love."

Marcus wondered why he had done that. He'd had plenty of time to get another ring and even looked at some, but none of them seemed like Honoria. None of them had seemed as right as the talisman ring. "It doesn't matter about the blasted ring. I just — Anthony, what am I going to do? She says she loves me, and I'm not sure —"

"Aren't you?"

"I don't know! I care about her, of course. But . . . love?"

"Bloody hell. When did this happen?"

"A few days ago."

"But . . . what happened today? Anna went to your house to see Honoria and found her crying her eyes out."

Marcus shook his head. "Melton came to the house. I've been meaning to speak to him, but . . . things have been hectic. Anyway, Honoria took an interest in him, and for some reason it made me furious and — Damn it, Anthony, why are you laughing?"

"Because you are the biggest fool to walk the earth." Anthony flicked his cigar into the fire and then set his empty glass on the table. "Marcus, I am going to do you a great favor. I want you to think of your life *with* Honoria. And then I want you to think of what life would be *without* her. Then, when you've done that, I want you to take a long look into that overly controlled heart of yours and figure out just who you are and what you want."

He stood, looking down at Marcus with a frown. "And when you do all of that, you had better pray that your wife didn't take your silence to mean that you do not love her, for if she did, she will leave you and nothing you can say will make a difference from that point on."

Marcus stiffened. "She'll leave?"

"She's not the type of woman to stay where she thinks she is not wanted, Marcus. Even I can see that, and I've only spoken to her a half dozen times. That, and Anna said —" Anthony stopped.

"What?"

"When Anna went to your house, she found Honoria piling trunks into a carriage and —"

Marcus didn't hear a word. He was already on his way to the door.

Chapter 20

I said, "Do you like the lobsters in butter" not "You look like a Labrador to the butler!" I vow, but I am moving down to your end of the table. This distance is putting a strain on our marriage.

The Duke of Devonshire to the
Duchess of Devonshire,
while collecting his silver and plate and
moving to her ladyship's end of their new
twenty-four-foot-long mahogany dining table

Marcus promised Herberts twenty quid if the coachman could make it back to Treymount House in less than ten minutes. They had to get there before she left. They just *had* to. Sitting in the wildly swaying coach as it charged down narrow streets, jumped curbs, and clattered madly through one corner of Hyde Park, Marcus's mind raced ahead as he planned just what he'd say to Honoria. Surely he could say something — do something to change her mind.

Perhaps he should kiss her first and then talk to her. That seemed a more likely approach. If he could soften her heart and get her to drop her shields, then perhaps she would listen to his request to stay with more heart. If only he could —

The carriage pulled up to the house. Marcus didn't even wait for Herberts to open the door, but threw it open himself and jumped down.

"Me lord!" Herberts called, affronted at having his duties supplanted.

But Marcus had no time. He raced up the steps, taking off his greatcoat the second he walked through the front door. "Ah, Jeffries! There you are!" He handed his coat and hat to a footman. "Where is her ladyship? I must speak to her —"

Jeffries held out a silver salver. In the center sat a single note.

Marcus looked at it, realizing for the first time how the house had grown icily silent, the feeling of warmth he'd come to love absent. She was gone. They all were. He could feel the emptiness of Treymount surrounding him, pressing in, weighing him down.

Swallowing hard, he took the note. Somewhere in the back of his mind he realized that his hand was trembling ever so slightly. The paper was cool and smooth beneath his fingers, but he could not seem to gather the thoughts necessary to open it.

Someone took his arm and he heard Jeffries's voice in his ear. "A bottle of brandy, sir. In the library."

The letter seemed to crumple in his hand. Marcus realized that he was crushing the note, his fingers tightly curled about it. Somehow, he was sitting at his desk, Jeffries saying something that he could not really hear. As soon as Jeffries left, Marcus uncurled his fingers from the note and read.

My lord,

After much thought, I have decided that I cannot continue in this marriage. I apologize for my error in admitting my feelings; you will never hear those words from me again. I know you will feel it incumbent to profess these same sentiments, but it has become painfully obvious that you do not return them.

To spare ourselves any more embarrassment, I suggest that after Cassandra is successfully launched, that you and I quietly seek an annulment. I am willing to do as you feel is best.

I will, of course, return on the morrow for the ball, and I can assure you that you will have nothing to fear in my comportment.

All best,
Honoria

His first impulse was to go to her, to take her in his arms and declare — What? That his life was empty without her? That his house and his heart were empty without her? That . . . he leaned back in his chair, his gaze fixed on the ceiling. A slow seed of truth began to sprout. He respected Honoria. He admired her.

He loved her.

He had loved her since the time he'd gone to visit her and she'd overpoured her teacup.

He sat forward suddenly, almost gasping at the heaviness that pressed in on his chest. *He loved her.* Happiness flooded him and he leapt to his feet. He must tell her! He crossed to the door — then stopped, his hand on the knob. As she said in the note, any attempt to profess his love now would be seen as appeasement.

She wouldn't believe him. And he supposed he couldn't blame her. He thought of his own impetuous words this afternoon, of his unreasonable jealousy over Melton — good God, what a fool he'd been. She loved him, not Melton. Why had he been so crazed with jealousy?

Because he'd been fighting his own feelings instead of admitting them. He was a bloody fool. But now was the time to fix things.

He'd have to think of something. Some way to prove to her that he loved her with all of his heart.

The door opened and Jeffries appeared with a decanter and a glass. "There you are, my lord." He placed the tray on a small table by the fire. "I'm sorry it took me so long, but I had to turn away that young man, Lord Melton. He was most distraught to discover that —"

"Melton is here?"

Jeffries looked up from where he was pouring port into a glass. "He was. But he left and —"

Marcus was out the door, yelling for one of the footmen to catch up to Lord Melton and bring him back. Perhaps, just perhaps, that was a way to show Honoria that he had changed. It wouldn't be enough to prove his love, but it was a start.

Marcus returned to the library to await Lord Melton. What *could* he do to really prove his love to Honoria? He needed something large, significant. Something far definitive. Something . . . Marcus sat silent at his desk, staring with unseeing eyes at the fire. His thought flashed and flared, making him frown and shiver. After a few minutes he began to straighten.

Then he began to smile.

The door opened and Jeffries reappeared, escorting a wide-eyed Lord Melton.

Marcus stood and stepped around his desk to shake hands. "Melton! I'm glad we caught you."

Melton flushed. "Yes. Well. I didn't —"

"Come, sit! Have some port. And then, I want you to tell me your plan to recoup your fortune."

"I'm not sure you will approve. It will take some investment capital, but —"

Marcus held up a hand. "Wait. Before you begin, do you mind accompanying me on some errands?"

"Errands?" The young man blinked. "Why, ah . . . no. I suppose that would be fine —"

"Excellent." Marcus started to the door, then stopped and smiled at Melton. "I need to go to Rundell's."

"The jewelers?"

"The one and the same." Marcus turned back to the door, opening it and stepping into the hallway, certain Melton followed close behind. "I only know one thing. Tomorrow night, at the ball I'm giving? The most beautiful woman in the world will be the lady in red."

Melton's brow shot up, concern flickering in his gray eyes. "Miss Baker-Sneed will be wearing red? Isn't that unusual for a woman just presented?"

Oh ho! So that was the way that went, was it? Suddenly, Melton's new demeanor made sense to Marcus. He slapped the man on the shoulder. "No, not Cassandra. My wife, Honoria."

Lord Melton blushed to the roots of his hair. "Oh! I see. I'm sorry. I didn't think you —"

But Marcus was already walking down the hallway, yelling for Jeffries to call Herberts to the front entrance. There was no time to waste.

It was a solemn group that watched Honoria and Cassandra prepare for the ball.

"I never before realized how small our sitting room is," Portia said, looking about her with dissatisfaction from where she sat perched on the edge of Honoria's bed.

Olivia shook her head. "And the hallways, so dark and cramped. I can almost think I'm on a paltry fist-weighted schooner and not a house."

Juliet sighed, leaning against the bed railing. "I shall miss the food most of all. Antoine was a genius."

Cassandra was already ready, attired in a white gown with a blue sash, blue and green flowers nestled in her hair. She glanced uncertainly at Honoria. "Well I, for one, am glad we're back here. As beautiful as Treymount House was, it wasn't a home."

No, Honoria thought disconsolately, it hadn't been a home. Not really. Oh, she'd thought that perhaps — Her throat closed and she could once again see Marcus, his face shuttered as she told him of her feelings. What a fool she'd been. What an incredibly stupid, utter fool.

Well, she could not dwell on that. Not if she wanted to keep her wits about her and not ruin the ball for Cassandra. This was important for it was as much Cassandra's launch as it was her own induction into polite society. An induction that was to be temporary, at best.

She caught Cassandra's sympathetic gaze and forced a smile. "I think I am ready to dress." She turned to the bed and pulled back the layers of tissue that hid the gown.

"Oh my!" Portia said, her eyes widening. "Honoria! It's lovely!"

"That's the perfect color for you, too," Cassandra said approvingly. "You have such lovely hair, and the red silk will make it seem darker."

Honoria held up the red gown and allowed Cassandra to help her put it on.

"Oh Honoria!" breathed Olivia, her eyes shining. "You look lovely!"

Honoria turned and looked at herself in the mirror. It was a far more daring gown than she'd ever worn, but the second Anna had seen it, she'd been determined that Honoria should have it.

And now Honoria could not be sorry. The gown was made of deep red silk and was beaded from top to bottom so it clung and shimmered with every move. The neckline was lower than she usually wore, and it framed her shoulders and the gentle swell of her breasts.

There was a knock on the door and Juliet went to answer it. Mrs. Kemble bustled in, coming to a halt when she saw Honoria. "Oh miss! I mean, my lady! You look lovely, you do."

"Thank you," Honoria said, wishing she felt better in some way.

Mrs. Kemble held out a large box. "This just came from his lordship. I didn't know if I should — Well, I'll just lay it on the bed for you."

Honoria didn't even look at the box. But the second Mrs. Kemble left the room, Portia pounced on it. She opened it up and gasped. "Rubies! Honoria, look! Real rubies! A necklet and a bracelet!"

Despite her desire to do otherwise, Honoria couldn't help but look. The jewelry winked and blinked, beautiful beyond description.

"And there's a note!" Olivia said, holding it up. "Should I . . . ?" She looked expectantly at Honoria.

"I don't care. Treymount can say nothing I wish to hear."

Olivia ripped it open. She read it silently, her lips moving, her eyes widening.

"Oh for the love of —" Portia snatched the note. "Let me see!" She read it. "Oh!"

"Well?" Juliet demanded. "Read it aloud!"

"Oh. Right. It says, 'My lady, I will not importune you with words you are not yet ready to hear, but know this, I will take it as an act of nothing but kindness if you would wear this small tribute to what is, I now know, the most beautiful woman in the world.' "

"My goodness," Cassandra said, her gaze softening. "That is very prettily worded."

Honoria turned away. "I am not going to wear his jewelry. I'll send it back."

"Of course," Juliet said staunchly. "You will give it all back." She removed the necklace from the box and held it to her throat. "Or you could save it for one of us. You know, that would be the thrifty thing to do."

Olivia held her wrist to the light, the bracelet shimmering brightly. "Or you could just keep it as a sort of consolation gift. I've heard that men often give those to their mistresses when they tire of them."

Portia turned at that. "Where *did* you hear that?"

"Oh leave Olivia alone." Juliet suddenly frowned. "Where's George?"

"He's supposed to be in bed," Olivia offered.

Honoria said, "Could one of you go and make certain of that? He's being very quiet."

Portia handed the necklet to Cassandra. "I'll go and see. But you cannot leave until I see Honoria wearing this."

"Of course," Cassandra agreed as Portia left.

Honoria eyed Cassandra for a long moment. "I will not wear that. Nothing could convince me otherwise."

"I know, but you need something with that gown, and we own nothing that is nearly grand enough. Just wear it this evening. You can return it tomorrow."

Honoria supposed she could at that. Besides, it was just one night. Her chest felt weighted, her legs heavy, as she realized that this was the last time she would be standing next to Marcus. The last time she'd feel his hand in the small of her back as he guided her into a room. The last time she'd see his smile or hear him laugh.

Tears threatened and she had to blink rapidly to fight them off.

All she had to do was get through this one evening. Just one. Surely she could do that.

Sighing, she held out her wrist and let Cassandra gird her for battle, for that was what it was — battle. All she had to do was force her pride to battle the inclinations of her traitorous heart.

The ball was a huge success. Carriages lined up for blocks, the huge ballroom was packed from wall to wall, the orchestra and refreshments were declared above the ordinary, and the host and hostess a shockingly handsome couple.

Honoria had arrived just before the first guest. Marcus had been waiting, his dark gaze fastened on her with an intensity she hated. It was awkward and painful and a dozen other horrid things.

But to her surprise, disappointment, and relief, he didn't try to talk to her. Instead, his gaze lingered appreciatively over her and he said in a deep, quiet voice that she'd never looked lovelier.

Honoria had fought her tears and won. Still, it was with a heavy heart and faltering step that she took her place at Marcus's side and began the laborious duty of welcoming their guests.

Marcus, meanwhile, could hardly keep his eyes off Honoria. She looked beautiful — beyond beautiful. She was wearing such a gown — the red rich against her dark hair, the streak of white glowing like the rubies that sparkled against her white skin.

She was lush, breathtaking, and his. All his, dammit. And he'd do whatever it took to make her realize that. He was a man used to getting what he wanted, and this time, above all others, he was determined not to fail.

Honoria belonged to him, every glorious

inch, and he'd be damned if he'd sit by and let her slip away. If his plan tonight failed, there would be another night. And if that did not work, he would try again and again. However many times it took.

In fact, if it took tonight and every night until he was old and gray, he'd make her face the truth — he did love her. More than he could say.

Still, it was torment being beside her and yet unable to hold her. He wished he could sweep her away to his bedchamber. Perhaps, soon enough, that's where they'd be.

Until then, he tried to keep his thoughts on greeting their guests. But as they stood in the receiving line and welcomed guest after guest, each brush of her arm against his sleeve became a delicious agony.

Finally, he could stand it no more. He nodded to Jeffries, who fetched Anthony and Anna to come and take their place. Then Marcus took Honoria's arm.

She stiffened. "Marcus —"

"Come. One dance."

"No."

"It's expected, Honoria. People will talk if we don't."

She sighed. "Oh, very well! I suppose that since we are the hosts, we have to start the dancing."

She allowed him to lead her through the throng. Marcus strode forward impatiently, ignoring the called greetings and other attempts to catch his gaze. Though he didn't realize it, that caused even more attention to focus on their progress. He was a man with a purpose, his entire being focused on the woman at his side.

He led her to the center of the room and gestured to the orchestra. The talking quieted as everyone waited.

But no music came. The orchestra merely silenced, then sat waiting. Marcus took a steadying breath, his heart thudding hard in his chest. Now was the time.

"Why isn't the orchestra playing?" Honoria whispered, plainly concerned.

"Because I asked them not to."

Her hazel eyes widened. "Why?"

Marcus took her hand in his. "Honoria, I wish to speak to you." He spoke clearly, his voice ringing across the ballroom.

Even more people looked their way.

Honoria began to tug on her hand, trying to free it from his grasp. "Please, Marcus, do not —"

He refused to loosen her. "No. I have something to say."

"Marcus," she said quietly, suddenly pale. "There is nothing left to say."

"That is not true. And I believe, once you have heard me out, you will have a great deal to say in response."

Her lashes trembled on her cheek. Marcus, aware that every person within hearing distance was openly listening to their exchange, was encouraged that she did not refuse to listen to him. Had she done so, he could not have blamed her.

He looked at Honoria standing before him, a vision in red silk and rubies, proud, defiant, her own woman in her own right . . . things that had once irritated him and now fascinated him to no end. "Honoria, I came to tell you that I have thought of what you said to me."

Color touched her cheeks. "Marcus, I —"

"No. Just listen. Please. I didn't answer you because I couldn't. Because I wasn't certain — but I am now."

There was a moment of surprised silence, not just from Honoria, but from every person surrounding them. Marcus knew that word of this conversation would be all over town tomorrow. His and Honoria's name would be spoken by every gossipmonger there was. At one time he would have decried such a public display. But not now. Now all he cared about was that Honoria should come home. That she would be his wife, but in more than name. In heart, as well.

He took her hand, unresisting and cold, and held it between his. "This is not easy for me to say. I have been a man alone for many years. And in that time, I made some decisions which I now realize were incorrect. I didn't think I needed anyone in my life. I thought happiness came from success in business and that caring for another over and beyond a genteel, distant sort of love would make me less successful somehow. In a word, I was the worst kind of fool because I was wrong. Wrong, and I didn't know it."

Her gaze lifted to his, her eyes wide. "Marcus?"

He pulled her close and looked into her eyes, his heart curiously thick in his chest, as if aching for air. But he was breathing, the sound loud against the growing silence from around them. This was it; the moment of truth. The moment for him to make himself heard — make her understand — all the things he'd only just discovered.

Marcus opened his mouth, praying that the words might find their way out. "Honoria, you have to —"

"She doesn't have to do anything," came a soft but determined voice. Cassandra, dressed in the innocent white of a debutante, planted herself in front of her sister. "Honoria does not wish to speak to you."

Honoria murmured something to Cassandra, who turned and whispered loudly over her shoulder, "No, you don't have to speak to him if you don't wish!" Cassandra turned back to Marcus, a surprisingly pugnacious tilt to her chin. "She doesn't need you. We will get along just fine without you."

Marcus raked a hand through his hair, struggling to find the words, the meaning of his feelings. It was like swimming through Yorkshire pudding, his mind and soul both fighting for expression. His gaze found Honoria's from where she stood just behind her sister. "I was wrong, Cassandra. I love your sister. She is the other half of me and I will not rest until she knows it."

Cassandra shook her head. "You shall not have the opportunity to hurt Honoria again. Honoria, come —"

"Miss Baker-Sneed?" Lord Melton, handsome and blond, cast an apologetic glance at Marcus, then bowed to Cassandra. "I beg your pardon, but I believe this is our dance."

"There is no music."

Melton held out his arm and she automatically rested her fingers on it. "Until the music begins, we can talk about my new project. The marquis has agreed to sponsor my horse breeding scheme."

Honoria's gaze flew to Marcus. "You did?"

Marcus smiled at her. "Melton and I agreed to the terms last night. If things go well, he will have his debt settled in less than three years." Marcus eyed Cassandra's hand where it rested on Melton's arm. "Perhaps then he will be able to take on other, more important responsibilities."

Melton bowed, a smile flickering over his face. "Yes, my lord." He glanced down at Cassandra, a glow of emotion in his eyes. "I look forward to fulfilling all of my responsibilities, whatever they may be."

Cassandra blushed, though she did not move from Melton's side. She cast a hesitant glance at her sister. "Honoria, do you want me to stay and —"

"Lady Treymount is well able to take care of herself." Lord Melton tucked her hand more firmly in the crook of his arm, attaching Cassandra to his side. "Leave your sister and her husband to their own affairs." He glanced over Cassandra's head to meet Marcus's gaze. "And perhaps they'll leave others to theirs."

Marcus had to smile a little at that. The lad had bottom, he did, and enough grit to win back his fortune. "Lord Melton, we will speak about this later this evening. Over port, I hope."

Melton flushed, a sparkle lighting his gaze. "I shall look forward to it. Cassandra, let us visit the refreshment table while the orchestra rests."

"But Honoria —"

"Is fine," Marcus said.

Cassandra reached out with her free hand and laced her fingers with Honoria's. "Are you certain?"

Honoria squeezed her sister's hand. "Yes."

"Very well." With that, Cassandra released Honoria's hand and allowed Melton to lead her away.

Marcus turned back to his wife. "I have a gift for you."

"A gift?"

"Yes." He nodded to Jeffries, who stood hovering behind Honoria. The butler stepped forward and lifted a silver salver. There, in the center, sat a ruby tiara, a match to the jewelry Honoria was already wearing.

Her lips parted. "Oh my!"

He took the tiara and gently placed it on her head, where it gleamed warmly in her rich brown hair. "You once told me you weren't the type of woman to wear tiaras. I beg to differ. You deserve tiaras and rubies and everything else life has to offer."

"Marcus, I don't know what to say. I can't just —" She bit her lip, her gaze suddenly searching his. "Marcus, why are you doing this? Why?"

"Because I want you and the whole world to hear what I have to say. You said you would not believe any protestations of affection because it would only be spoken out of duty. I am not speaking out of duty."

"Marcus, please. I — I understand. You cannot help the way you feel."

"But I do feel," Marcus said shortly. "And strongly, too. When you said that you loved me, I wasn't ready to hear it. But now I know. Now I'm ready."

The room around them faded, and all Marcus saw or heard was his wife, his beloved Honoria, who infuriated him, tortured him with her busy schemes and grand plans, who upturned his life with her busy brother and sisters, and in general made life worth living. She stood before him, resplendent in red silk, adorable in shoes that must pinch, and so beautiful that his heart ached as if pierced by an arrow.

He loved her. He loved her with his body and soul and he could not imagine life without her. The memory of his own house, cold and silent and waiting for him like a great empty shell, sent a frozen shiver through him and finally — finally — unlocked his lips.

He reached down, took his wife's hand in his and pulled her to him. She came, unresisting, a question in her eyes — and a hint of such sadness that tears blurred his own vision for an instant. "Honoria, I was wrong about so many things. I now know how much you mean to me. How much life and laughter your sisters and brother brought to Treymount House. I want you back. I want all of you back."

Tears filled her eyes even more. "Why?"

"Because I cannot live without you. I was just too blind to realize it." He was using every thought he possessed to try and make her understand. But he could see from the hurt that still lingered in her eyes that he hadn't yet convinced her. He held her tighter. "Honoria, I want to be married to no one but you."

"No," she said with a gulp. "I don't believe that. And I never will." She shook her head and stepped out of his arms. "Marcus, it is too late."

Distressed by her tears, he let her go. "Honoria, please listen —"

"No. I can't — no more, Marcus. Just let it be. You don't love me." With that, she turned and walked away.

Marcus's heart sank. He almost staggered to the floor with the weight of his disappointment. She didn't believe him. Perhaps she never would.

A hand touched his sleeve. He looked down to see Cassandra. "Treymount," she said with some spirit. "What are you doing? Go and get her!"

"She doesn't want me." Marcus's voice seemed removed, as if it belonged to another person. He hurt so badly that he could feel nothing — not his booted feet firmly set on the floor, not the scratch of his cravat at his chin, not the beating of his own heart. "I love her but it is not enough. I . . . I have killed her feelings for me."

"Oh for the love of — Are *all* men so sapheaded? She didn't say she didn't love you. She said *you* don't love *her*. Don't just stand there. Prove her wrong!"

The words tumbled over Marcus. Was it possible . . . He could just make out her proud head, crowned with the ruby tiara and that damnably erotic streak of white, as she swept toward the door. Cassandra was right. He could not allow Honoria to just walk away.

★ ★ ★

Honoria was clenching her teeth to keep from crying. All around her, curious eyes followed her as she pushed toward the door. At one point a robust lady tried to stop her flight, but Honoria merely brushed on past, fighting to keep the tears at bay. She'd thought he would say it, the words she'd been longing to hear — but he hadn't. He'd spoken of missing her family, of missing the laughter and the companionship, but he'd never said he loved her.

Honoria wondered if a heart could literally break, for the pain in her chest was so acute. She managed to make her way clear of the crowd and back into the foyer. To her chagrin, Anna and Anthony were still there, greeting the latecomers. Honoria hurriedly asked one of the footmen to send for Herberts and the carriage.

Anna broke free from the line of guests and came to Honoria's side. Elegant in blue silk, she smiled questioningly at her. "Honoria! Are you leaving already?"

"Yes. I — I must." Or she would melt into a puddle of regret.

Anna's gray eyes darkened. "It's Marcus, isn't it? He's making a mull of it. He's the most stubborn man I've ever met and — Well, you know what he is."

"He's the most stubborn, foolish, idiotic man *I've* ever met."

Anna's worried expression vanished behind a grin. "Exactly. He's also a very intelligent, very capable man, who cares far more than he shows. He's always been that way."

Honoria blinked back tears. "Thank you. But . . . I have to leave."

Anna's gaze flickered over Honoria's head to the ballroom and then back. "Very well." To Honoria's relief, Anna stepped quietly out of the way. Honoria gave her a grateful smile and then made her way outside.

Some people were still entering, but they paid her no heed, standing to one side. She was relieved to see Herberts pulling up.

He hopped down and opened the door. "Here ye are, missus. Where to?"

She opened her mouth to say "Home" but could not make the words. This was home. And then, just as she lost the battle with her tears and one slipped over her lashes and onto her cheek, Marcus was there.

He caught her arms and turned her to face him. "You didn't give me time to finish. You must listen to me. You must!"

"Cooee!" Herberts said, his brows shooting up his forehead. "Ye'd best hear him out, m'lady! Oiye've never seen him in such a lather."

"Yes, you should listen to me," Marcus said, his voice deep with meaning. "I love you, Honoria Baker-Sneed St. John. And like a fool, I did not realize it until you had left me."

"You love me." She tasted the words, afraid to believe them.

He nodded once. "You are the most honest, the most genuine woman I have ever met. But I didn't wish to be in love and so I tried to convince myself that it was simply lust."

"Some of it is."

"As it should be. But what I feel for you is much stronger than lust. Once you left me, I missed you so badly that I could not breathe. It was as if Treymount House had shrunken in size and there was no room in it for anything or anyone, especially me."

"There is enough room in Treymount for a thousand marquises."

He captured her hand and placed a fervent kiss on it, right where the talisman ring rested. "Not without love. Not without you. Honoria, know this: if you do not believe me now, I will understand. But I am not giving up and I will not go away. I will woo you back, prove to you that I love you with every ounce of my being."

"Woo me?" A faint hint of a smile touched her mouth. "With flowers and gifts?"

"I will shower you with rubies and diamonds. I will flood your house with flowers and fans. I will be on your doorstep day and night, and I do not care what anyone says or thinks of it."

"Lor' love ye, miss!" Herberts added, looking impressed. "If ye won't have him, oiye will."

"Herberts, please," Marcus said. "Go to the front of the carriage."

The groom sniffed. "Oiye was jus' helpin'."

"I don't need your help. Now go."

"Very well, though ye're makin' a mistake. Oiye could help ye, oiye could."

"*Go.*"

"Very well! No need to get naffy on me." Herberts turned his back on the two and slowly walked to the front of the carriage.

Honoria had to stifle a laugh as Marcus looked down at her. His arms tightened about her and he said in a deep voice, "I love you, Honoria. And I will not rest until you are back where you belong; here, with me, at Treymount House."

Happiness so bright that it sent a shiver all

the way to her toes rippled through her. "You don't need to go to such lengths as showering me with rubies, although . . . they are nice."

"Honoria, I must have you back. I know I have made a mull of things. I wouldn't blame you if you didn't feel for me as you once did —"

She placed her fingers over his lips. "I love you, Marcus. I always have. And right now, I just want to be with you."

His eyes blazed. And then, with a shout of triumph, he grabbed her to him and held her tight. Honoria threw her arms about his neck and held tight as well, her feet off the ground, Marcus's strong arms holding her aloft. She loved him. And he loved her. Happiness surrounded her.

A loud, wet sniff interrupted the moment.

Honoria opened her eyes to find Herberts standing on the walk, wiping his face with a none too clean handkerchief. "That was beeooteeful, guv'nor. Blimee if it wasn't."

Marcus didn't lift his cheek from where it was comfortably resting against Honoria's. "Herberts, didn't I ask you to wait at the front of the carriage?"

"Indeed ye did, guv'nor. And oiye was goin' to go, but then oiye thought that per'aps ye moight need me to back up yer version o' how miserable ye've been without her ladyship about." The coachman leaned an arm against the carriage and said in an undertone to Honoria, "He's been a bear, mistress. Ugly to everyone and actin' as if he thought the world was comin' to an end. There was no pleasin' him."

Marcus sighed, his breath warm on Honoria's cheek. "He will not quit."

She chuckled. "Not until he's had his say."

Marcus slowly lowered her feet back to the ground, savoring the feel of her body rubbing down the length of his. Hmm. Perhaps in addition to admitting his love, he should show her his love as well. "Herberts, since you are here —"

"Wait, guv'nor. Oiye haven't finished tellin' her la'ship how horrid it's been without her at Treymount. Ye would not believe how 'tis been. Oiye thought about leavin' the guv'nor's employ and takin' a position with the Duke of Rutland, as he said he'd like to have me and he offered me twice the wage —"

"Rutland said no such thing," Marcus said inexorably. "He said he'd have you in his employ *if* he ever needed a competent pickpocket. I was there, remember? When I made you return his watch?"

"Weeel, now. A competent pickpocket is not such a bad thing to have. In fact, me mother used to say —"

Marcus reached into his pocket and pulled out his purse. Without looking to see how much was in the heavy bag, he pressed it into Herberts's hand. "This is for you if you'll shut up and drive us around the park."

"The park?" Honoria exclaimed. "But . . . the ball."

"To hell with the ball. Anthony is there to make certain all goes well, and if I'm not mistaken, Cassandra is in good hands."

The coachman closed his eyes, his fingers clutching the purse. "Cooee, but 'tis heavy! Thank ye, guv'nor! The park, 'tis!"

Marcus opened the door and assisted Honoria into her seat. Then he followed. The second the door closed and the carriage jerked into motion, Honoria reached across the seat and began to undo her husband's cravat.

He laughed, his fingers closing over hers, delighted at her eagerness. "In a hurry, my love?"

"It has been two days, m'lord. So yes, I am in a hurry." Her gaze met his, soft and luminous, shining with love and excitement. "Aren't you?"

His feelings swelled with his flesh. She was his best friend, his equal, his partner now and forever. And she was his, this beguiling lady in red. And he loved her more than life itself.

He undid his own cravat. And his own breeches and shirt. And then, with the greatest tenderness and even greater haste, he undressed his adorable wife, divesting her of everything but the red tiara. She looked so beautiful, reclining on the velvet seats, naked but for the thick fall of hair about her shoulders and the tiara perched upon her head, that his excitement had trebled in but a moment. He'd caught her to him, murmuring words of endearment and passion.

And it was with the greatest presence of mind that he then showed his beautiful lady wife exactly how much he loved the park . . . and her.

Epilogue

Well! The last St. John has finally fallen. I wonder what will become of that cursed ring now ...

The Duchess of Devonshire to her friend, the unwed and unhappy Miss Castlehope during a rather boring sermon at St. Paul's

"Well . . . here we are." Anthony looked around the table at his brothers. They were at White's, comfortably ensconced about his favorite table. The room rang with masculine laughter and talk, the fragrant scent of cigar smoke and old leather wafting through the air.

It was the pleasantest of places, and yet Marcus glanced at his watch. Honoria was out with Anna and Cassandra and Portia, purchasing new silk to use as draperies for the ballroom.

He smiled. When he'd left Treymount House this morning, the footmen had been engaged in taking down the old curtains. Portia and Juliet had confiscated the blue salon to practice a play they wished to present, while George and Chef Antoine were busy in the kitchen making cookies cut into the shape of a frog. The house was noisy and bright and once again filled with love, and he was, for the first time in his life, genuinely happy. Funny how he'd never realized what his life was missing until he'd almost lost it.

"Well, the St. John talisman ring has finished its work," Chase said.

Brandon nodded. "Leg-shackled the lot of us. I never thought to see that happen."

"Marcus, what will you do with the ring now?" Chase asked, stretching his leg before him.

"Do? Why . . . nothing. It is Honoria's wedding ring. I hope she may never remove it from her finger."

Devon chuckled. "B'Gad, that's the perfect thing! So long as it's on Honoria's finger, it cannot bedevil anyone else."

"Bedevil?" Anthony raised his brows

"You should be glad your wife, the lovely Kat, is not present to hear such nonsense."

"She knows I love her," Devon said complacently. "And yes, she does bedevil me. In all the best ways a woman can."

Anthony grinned around his glass. "*Is* there a bad way for a woman to bedevil you?"

"Not that I know," Devon replied. "And lord knows, Kat has tried." He leaned over to the table and poured a splash of port into five waiting glasses. "Let's have a toast."

Chase passed the glasses around. "Indeed, let's do. And I shall begin." He held his glass aloft. "To us, the happiest men in England. And to our wives, who taught us the joy of true love."

Marcus drank his toast, his gaze meeting each of his brother's in turn. As soon as they'd all drank their toast, he held his glass aloft. "One more. To the St. John talisman ring. Would that all men were so cursed."

Marcus grinned as they laughed, then one by one they drank the toast. At one time he'd pitied them their lives of domestic upheaval. But that had been because he hadn't understood the transforming power of love, and because somewhere along the way he'd forgotten this part of his life, the genuine pleasure of just being with those he loved the most. With Honoria's help, he'd never forget it again.

About the Author

Karen Hawkins was raised in Tennessee, a member of a huge extended family that included her brother and sister, an adopted sister, numerous foster siblings and various exchange students. In order to escape the chaos (and whilst hiding when it was her turn to do the dishes), she would huddle under the comforter on her bed with a flashlight and a book, a habit she still embraces to this day. For more information about Karen, or pictures of her chasing a box of donuts while training for a road race, visit her at www.karenhawkins.com or write to her at Karen Hawkins, P.O. Box 5292, Kingsport, TN 37663-5292.

ML   10/0